THE LEGEND OF LILITH

BOOK I

HILLARY OLIVER

PHOENIX
RISING

First published in Canada, January 2020 by PHOENIX RISING PRESS

For updates on new releases, join the online newsletter at hillaryeoliver.com

Cover illustration by Salome Totladze

Edited by Iveta Cvrkal

Map of Augusta by Hillary Oliver

Library and Archives Canada Cataloguing in Publication

The Legend of Lilith | The Legend of Lilith, Book I | Hillary Oliver | ISBN 978-1-9992318-0-4 (Paperback) | ISBN 978-1-9992318-1-1 (Hardcover) | ISBN 978-1-9992318-2-8 (EPUB)

First Edition: January 2020

For my grandparents,
Don & Mary Oliver
Keith & Isabel Mark

You taught me selflessness, the meaning of true love, what it means to persevere against the bleakest odds, and that the morning is the best part of each day.

Without your wisdom and guidance, I would not be where I am today. Your love will always whisper to me on the darkest of days and enlighten me under the sun's rays.

May you always know what you mean to me.

AUGUSTA
NORTHERN GALATËA SEA
ISLES OF NYSÍA
PORT OF KAWARTHA
JOURNIA
PHEBOS
THE MEGALOS FOREST
FROURIO
IOYNOS
SONÖS
OBSYDIAN MARSH
ELIATH
KENORA
WESTERN GALATÊA SEA
DUNES
ASPÉNDOS
UTICA
THASSÓS
DODÖNA
THE AOÖS
CHIOS
TANTALÓS
TO DALEGONË
CALYDON
PAROS
HÉLORUS
DION
RIFT OF DODONA
ARGOLIS
GULF OF HÉLORUS
PETRAS
THE GÄEA VALLEY
N
W
E
S

Lilith stirred to the twang of steel on steel. Nestled under the heavy quilts of her bed, she listened to that familiar *zing*, wishing that the melody would lull her back to sleep. But instead, her heart thumped, a cadent chant to rise. Obeying the rhythm of her pulse, Lilith sloughed her covers and padded discreetly to her bedroom door. The comforting *shush* of woollen socks sliding along the oaken floor was the only sound.

The door creaked as she pried it open and crept into the tenebrous hallway, hissing her ire at the boisterous mice that held communion beneath the floorboards. If they were any louder, they'd wake up all of Utica.

Papa wasn't in the smithy, and Mah wasn't in the kitchen. Lilith eyed her brother's bedroom door warily, his form visible through the crack in the wood. His lanky limbs spread out across the mattress, face obscured by his dark mane. Larkin's slow, heavy breathing met her ears, confirming that he'd yet to wake. Sighing heavily, she moved on.

She padded into the living room on silent feet, unsurprised to find it empty. There were burning embers in the hearth, indicative that no one had tended to it for at least an hour.

The clangor grew louder. Insistent. A beckoning cacophony.

Curious, Lilith donned her cloak before marching outside into the gelid winter air. She skipped down the porch steps, wincing at their creaky protest. The sun was rising in the east, casting the narrow streets of Utica in a golden glow.

Making her way around the house and past the entrance to her father's smithy, Lilith surveyed the empty field behind her house. Two figures, one large and one slight, were visible within the thick golden air, the smog parting for them as they twirled around one another in a dance of stealth.

Assuring herself that she was undetected, Lilith inspected her parents from the side of the forge. They twisted, they turned; the hilts of their blades clasped between their palms. Her father wielded Gladius, his notorious makhaira, he'd fought and survived several battles with that sword. Her mother wielded a shortsword of Obsidian Steel: Constance. Colors of the rainbow danced along the blade, reflecting the growing sunlight. Her mother gasped every time she deflected her husband's attacks, but she moved gracefully, unhindered by his domineering size.

They came to an abrupt halt. Lilith ducked down behind the barrel that collected water from the eavestrough.

Gods, please don't see me!

After a substantial period of silence, she peeked around the corner. Her parents hadn't suspected her espionage. Lilith exhaled a pent breath as she continued to survey the scene. She thought her mother was panting as she fell into Papa's muscular arms, dropping the sword as she did. But Lilith knew her mother well, and those were not sounds of exasperation, but of despair. Mama was weeping, and judging by the mood that was so clearly radiating off her father, he'd nearly succumbed to tears as well.

Lilith's heart slowed drastically as Papa stroked Mah's long dark mane, offering words of comfort. Lilith strained to hear the reason for their lament. It was unusual, that sombre mood that settled over them like a pall.

"You'll be fine, Lynne. I will be home in a few weeks, and everything will return to normal."

"You wouldn't be teaching me this," her mother said on a sob, "if you believed your own words!" She pulled away from him to pound her fists against his broad chest. Her father took the assault without deflection, no anger or pain distorting his features.

Mah sunk to her knees and wept. Papa knelt before her, still attempting to comfort his wife. "Shh, my love," he cooed. "You'll wake the children." Her mother glanced up at her husband and nodded, sense composing her emotions.

London Oak pulled his wife into a tight embrace, allowing for a moment of recovery together. Lilith's heart pounded, her mind reeling as she gazed upon them. Her parents were *Pràgma*. Everlasting love. Nothing could tear them apart. Not even war.

They stood and resumed their sparring dance as if nothing had ever happened. But this was not nothing. Lilith wanted to scream it. This was not *nothing*!

Papa had been summoned to war again. And as skilled as

he was, there was always a chance he wouldn't return. Turning back toward the house, Lilith sprinted to the porch steps, her blood humming in her veins, a death song to her ears.

War is coming.

FIVE YEARS LATER

A mighty gale brewed in the distance as Lilith sprinted through the trees, weaving her way around the thick trunks. The oaks groaned in protest as the wind assailed their branches. She didn't falter or lose her footing. The oaks' soughing propelled her feet, a melody fit for the huntress she was at heart. Lilith had long since mastered agility, acquired litheness. She belonged to the forest, but tonight she wasn't hunting the usual buck or doe.

"Rally, come back!" she called to her dog.

The collie had been spooked out of the house by the impending storm. He was one of the few things that kept her tethered to her parents. One of the few things she loved, that she would follow into the most stygian crevices of Augusta—and in the height of the Dark Age, there were many such places.

Rally was part of the Oak family. He'd mourned with her and Larkin when their parents passed away. Even after all these years, grief's insufferable hands were still clenched around her neck. She'd be damned if Rally's death compounded it, coercing it to further constrict its viselike grip.

Halting, Lilith observed the oncoming storm, worry furrowing her brow. It didn't seem any graver than the average gale that so often tumbled through the land. It was rather odd of Rally to act in such a frantic manner. The static electricity in the air sent Lilith's long mahogany hair rising, each strand separating from the rest, creating a nebulous around her head. She cursed herself for neglecting to braid it.

Prancing through the brush on trained, nimble feet, Lilith's emerald eyes flashed, scanning and assessing. There was little light to go by this time of night. There were no distinct footprints. Not in the fall months, not with so many leaves blanketing the earth. The forest was usually her safe place, the oaks' boughs normally evoking equilibrium. But tonight, they elicited antipathy.

Running at breakneck speed, she called for Rally. Her feet ached from the chase, her sandals unsuited for this terrain. But nothing else mattered more to her at this moment than getting her dog back to safety. Hades, she would have sold her soul to Spiro in order to bring that mutt home alive.

Lilith had never anticipated that she would enter Elysium today, the eternal sanctuary of the Gods. She beseeched Them to bring Rally back to her. To return them both home unscathed—but her prayers couldn't be heard over the din of the tempest.

A flash of lightning tore through the trunk of the oak before her. Lilith dodged the shards as they became airborne, threatening to tear through her mortal skin. If that wasn't a sign that the Gods wanted her to return to town, then she didn't know what was.

Reaching the eye of the mighty gale, Lilith entered a small meadow. No one dared venture this far from the walls that surrounded and protected Utica. She was reluctant to be clear of the trees, for without their cover, the rain assaulted her, making it difficult to see. She was also exposed to any beasts hunting for prey. Too many of Spiro's monsters ran rampant in Augusta, killing any and every living thing they set their beady black eyes upon.

Shadows moved in the distance and Lilith's heart pounded inside her chest. Despite the frenetic beat of her heart, awe shrouded the fear. *Find your testicles, Lilith. Run!* But she couldn't. The soles of her boots were rooted to the earth.

Rally barked, calling her back to the trees, toward safety. She turned to him, elated and relieved that he was still alive and unharmed. But that sense of relief swiftly disintegrated into dread. To Lilith's detriment, she'd been betrayed by her own dog.

The monsters!

Lilith reared around to face the shadows. They were indeed beasts, and they'd heard Rally's bark. A tremor rippled through her body. She blanched as they charged. There was no time to debate what course of action to take. It was either navigate the tempest's mighty maw toward freedom and safety or succumb to the wretched beasts that dwelled beneath it.

Naturally, there was only one option.

Sense composing her, Lilith retreated. If she could reach the forest before the monsters were a mile out, she'd be able to evade them. The branches were thick and dense enough, the beasts would be slowed considerably. But not Lilith. She'd become an arboreal creature, weaving through the oaks' masts with ease.

Lilith dared a furtive glance over her shoulder. The monsters had gained on her, but they were not yet close enough to attack. She was within arm's length of the trees as lightning struck the ground in a blinding flash. The world lit up.

Silver.

White.

And then there was only black.

◎ ⓽ ⤳ ⋔ ⬧

LILITH AWOKE, VISION CLOUDY, MIND FOGGY. SLOWLY, SHE SAT UP and checked herself over. Her clothes were now dry, her long hair a mess of matted waves. The tunic she wore was torn at the elbows and along the neckline, the garment no more useful than a kitchen rag. She'd been lying on the grass just outside of the forest… sleeping?

The rising sun's rays pierced the gaps in the trees, spearing the glade with lucent beams. The storm had cleared finally. The firmament now a magnificent indigo, the horizon an enigmatic pink.

Rally sat beside her, whining ruthlessly, his tail wagging with vigor. Lilith focused on him. His snout in her face. His tongue eager to taste her skin. She laughed hoarsely and pushed him away. Everything was louder; his gusting breath, his tail rustling the long grass. When she inspected him for any sign of injury, every detail of his fur stuck out to her. Every strand of his black hair, dirt, and burs that clung to him were sharp and defined.

Had she been lying in the field unconscious all night? Lilith cast Rally a bemused glance before she looked herself over a second pass, deeming that she'd indeed survived the attack unscathed.

The monsters!

Lilith whirled, frantically scanning the horizon for any signs of the rutting beasts. There was no movement beyond the breeze caressing the golden leaves above. Lilith took a moment to gather her bearings, allowing Rally to lick her face clean. Stretching her limbs, she sighed deeply to calm herself. Breathe in. Breathe out. Her brother must be worried sick about her!

Long spears of grass rose to her knees, drenching her bare feet in dew. She'd lost her sandals at some point, but that mattered little now. Rally pranced beside her. He was as calm as he ever was, snorting occasionally as if to spur her onward faster. Exploring was his favorite activity, although they rarely got to do much of it. Lands beyond the forest were considered too dangerous for any human to traverse. Because of these vile beasts, trade was a luxury of the past. The people of Augusta made do with what they had.

Lilith had never seen another town other than Utica. Did other towns possess the same austere square buildings? The same bland walls of stone? How far away were these other civilizations? Were there roads leading to these other towns? Questions like these often kept Lilith up at night, assailing her mind when she worked the forge.

The map of Augusta indicated that there were many other towns and cities, and roads indeed existed to tether them, but Lilith doubted they would be distinguishable. Too many years had passed without the wearing of feet and hooves. Even long before she was born, the roads had become deserted. Anyone who dared attempt to travel never returned.

To the west, forest ranged for miles. Oaks would guide her home and continue beyond until they cleared and the Western Galatëa Sea dominated the horizon. On the other side of the country were mountains, or so her father had told her. He'd painted a map of Augusta on their harvest table before he left for battle for the final time. It was so old and faded now—too many years had passed since—she could hardly make sense of it.

That was the last time she'd seen her father. London Oak's rendering of the Empire was like a final caveat to his children: never stray too far from home.

2

MY ENTIRE UNIVERSE

When Lilith glimpsed Utica on the horizon, her legs had transformed into logs beneath her, leaden from the previous evening's foray. Her muscles beseeched her to rest, protesting her every step. How she'd survived such an attack, she had no idea. She had already lost too much to those beasts, yet she had survived. Why?

As she approached the gates, the guards looked at her askance but poised no inquisition. Their polished helms glinted in the morning light, the plumes of Augustan blue horsehair swaying with the autumn breeze. Lilith hoped they would keep their mouths shut. It wasn't the time of month for her to be hunting. If they talked, there was no way she could explain her absence to her brother, or to her fiancé, Jude.

Lilith strode through the streets with her head downcast. Succeeding in returning home undetected, her mind sifted through her responsibilities. Only ten days remained in the month, and if she wanted a few days off to hunt, she needed to finish her quota for Utica's armory.

Larkin met her on the porch of their family home. Her brother's amber eyes settled on her fiercely. His dark hair, matching hers, hung to his muscled shoulders where he had her trim it blunt every month. He rose to his feet as soon as she reached the base of the steps. He was at least a foot taller than her, and three years her elder, but he regarded her with such deep respect, she never felt minimized by his dominating stature.

The wooden planks of the porch groaned loudly as she approached, drawing more attention to her delayed arrival. To her surprise, Larkin didn't inquire, nor did he seem suspicious.

"How's Jude?" he asked, forgoing a greeting. "He's been working like a warhorse as of late," he said, not granting her enough pause to answer his question. "It's been a tough harvest this year. I haven't seen him around much. I hope that's not taxing on the two of you?" His gaze swept over her expectantly. His question wasn't meant to be prying. Larkin was rather fond of Jude and he was always pestering her to finalize the wedding arrangements.

Since it was just the two of them, her brother had become increasingly interested in the coming generations, in building their family up again. Though he showed little desire to pursue a wife of his own, he was exceptionally eager for Lilith to wed Jude.

"We are managing, Larkin," she said on a sigh. "There's nothing to be concerned about."

Leaving the conversation at that, she pushed her way inside and grabbed a slice of bread and buttered it hastily.

Rarely was there time to cook a proper meal, let alone enjoy one. Thankfully her best friend, Kathleen, often baked for them. Lilith was forever beholden to her friend's munificence.

"Larkin!" she called, and not a second later, her brother materialized beside her. He stood keen, broad shoulders squared and prepared for duty. Between gulps of fresh milk, she instructed him on her plans for the day.

"Well, if you hope to get all of that accomplished by night-fall, we need to get started now… or an hour ago!" He chuckled, offering a cavalier shrug of his shoulders.

They made their way into the workshop with haste, donning the leather smocks their mother made years ago. Neither was in a mood to work. It was a beautiful sunny day —they hadn't been blessed with many this year—and here they were, sweating away at the bellows before the forge.

Lilith and Larkin worked together to fend for themselves. As a young girl, Lilith loved to observe her father working the forge. Now that he was gone, it was she who held the knowledge to keep their business afloat. She preferred to work in solitude, Rally's companionship the only exception to her sequestration. But Larkin was adamant that he be of assistance during the final quarter of the month.

The majority of what Lilith produced was sold in shops about town. She made nails and axes for the building hardware shop. She had a quota of weapons to maintain monthly for the armory. The quota was taxed, so they were spared collections in the spring when the Emperor's men visited.

The family workshop was an organized mess. The plaster walls were adorned with the most beautiful metal workings, art and weapon alike. Her father had enjoyed instructing her while working on abstract artistic pieces. On thick wooden beams hung a mass assortment of tools: files, tongs, pliers, different sized hammers, angles, and chisels.

The weapons on display were those that her father had created and some that he'd wielded himself. She loved the detail he put into crafting them. They weren't just swords, axes, and glaives, but beautiful and deadly works of art. Eloquent, with intricate details along the handles and cross guards. Her father was respected by blacksmiths across Augusta. Even smiths in the capital knew their family emblem and vaunted of her father's craftsmanship.

Lilith and Larkin began by pulling out the nearly finished makhairas. The scims were next. She was running low on ore, which she would have to worry about later. Trading wasn't possible, so in order to gather materials, they had to accept donations to recycle.

"We might have to make a trip to the mine tomorrow." Larkin released a defeated sigh.

Lilith could only manage to make one monthly trip to the mine where she collected as much ore as she deemed necessary to meet the month's quota. She travelled home on horseback and carriage to transport it, the horse graciously lent by Kathleen's fiancé, Tavisk.

"There's no time, and we don't have the drachmae. We will have to make use of what we have." Lilith didn't mind a trip to the mine. She knew how to distinguish rare pieces that contained fragments of stronger metals. Her father had taught her when she'd travelled with him as a girl. He once found a piece of ore so rare, it was multicolored and glittered under the light, yet at a distance, it resembled a black rock, easily dismissed by the untrained eye. He smelted it and with the steel extracted, he created the most beautiful sword for her mother. Obsidian Steel, he'd called it. It was the last weapon he'd ever forged. That sword was now Lilith's most prized possession.

Working in haste, the two siblings moved in tandem. Larkin opened the large wooden door that exposed the eastern wall of the smithy to the field behind their house. Lilith inhaled the fresh air as it drifted inside the sweltering shop. She cast her worries into the forge as she so often did, letting their songs of old carry her away. They sang and worked, laughing when their voices cracked and their harmonies clashed. Larkin assumed the female lead with a lilting soprano that set Lilith's abdomen on fire with mirth. "You lackwit!" she said on a breathless laugh.

It wasn't long before they were covered with sweat and soot. Together they worked the bellows, the glistening coal betraying its worth within the confines of the forge.

Lilith drove down the hammer with recurring fervor. Sweat dripped down her temple, snaking along her jawbone. The muscles of her arms moved with calculated ardor. Only a few more days of pushing herself to her extremities and then she would be reunited with the wilderness, even if only for a day. In the wild, Lilith could pretend there were no bounds, no fetters, no beasts. The spectre of her mother would lope along beside her, trilling melodies that somehow lured the animals to her. And Lilith could pretend she wasn't angry with her. That she didn't wake every morning cursing her mother's name. *Lynne Oak. Deserter. Dissenter.*

By nightfall they were able to complete the sword, though not to Lilith's satisfaction, but she waved it off. It would suffice. Larkin muttered his good night and took his leave.

Instead of following suit, Lilith began to clean the shop, preparing the smithy for another honest day's work.

Once the forge was doused, she made her way back to the house, yawning as she shut the large door. It took all of her strength not to drag her feet across the ground and ruin the soles of her boots. As she pulled herself onto the steps leading to the front door, a slight shift of motion startled her.

Jude's face entered the dim light of the moon. His expression was sombre, doe eyes heavy. His long blond hair was braided back messily.

Her marriage to Jude had been arranged by her parents five years prior, just before they passed. Lilith didn't deny them their wish of betrothal, and she wouldn't rescind on her promise now that they were gone. She was fond of Jude, and very comfortable with him. They grew up together, and he supported her desire to be a blacksmith, regardless of public censure. The town had long since turned a blind eye to her errant ways. If taking to smithing meant being near to her father's spirit, a dissenter she would be, and anyone who disapproved could go to Hades.

"I just spoke with Larkin," Jude said gravely. "He mentioned that you stayed with me last night... but oddly enough, I don't remember seeing you at all yesterday." His tone held an air of accusation and it warranted an explanation.

A spark of shame spindled down her spine. "I went hunting," Lilith lied quickly. "I just needed to get out in nature and clear my head. I was worried that I wouldn't get the chance this month." She spared him a glance, unsure whether he would believe her lie. Of what she could perceive of his expression, she'd succeeded in placating him. If she was honest with herself, she didn't know why she felt the need to deceive.

Lilith lowered herself down onto the bench beside him. Jude placed a comforting arm around her shoulders and pulled her into his warmth. Letting out a deep sigh, he said, "I can understand that. I only worry about you when you go out of town. It's not safe. My life would be ruined if anything were to happen to you." He planted a tender kiss on her brow.

Lilith fought off the guilt pressing down on her chest. His words should have provided her with an unmatchable level of comfort, yet it achieved the opposite. Unnerved, she leaned her head against his shoulder so that he couldn't read her face.

"It's the most beautiful night," he said with a wistful air. "I can see all of the Guiding Stars. We should go for a walk." He got to his feet and proffered his hand. She placed her soot-blackened palm in his and the two headed down off the porch and into the street.

Together they gazed up at the night sky, the stars cascading around them. If she positioned her head just right, she could see nothing but the black sky and the glowing lights. Standing like this, it was as if she had disappeared. Lilith was only faintly aware of Jude's arm around her protectively, like he was the only thing securing her to the earth. As if he were a fetter attached to a ball and chain. If he let go, she'd float away to join the stars.

Jude led her to a wagon filled with hay. He helped her up before climbing up in pursuit. Side by side they lay on their backs, staring up at the twinkling expanse. He grasped her hand and placed it on his chest, her fingers splayed against his warm skin.

"I don't know what I would do without you," he said, voice thick with emotion.

Lilith didn't respond. She couldn't. Hearing those words tumble from his lips should have been more… *stimulating*. But his charm summoned not so much as a shiver. Instead, with every tender word he said, she felt a dull ache blossom inside her chest. A moment later, her throat had formed a lump that no words could slip past.

Jude was nineteen, one year her elder. They were past the ripe age for marriage, but he didn't care. He'd wait to marry her until they had one foot in their graves.

It hurt Lilith to hesitate when Jude was so persistent. He wanted nothing more than to share a home with her, to start a family, but that would require her to forsake the forge and take to him. The thought of marriage turned her insides as if she'd downed sour milk.

"My *kyría*," he said as he pulled her closer to him. *My lady*. And then he said so softly, it shouldn't have ripped at her heart the way it did, "You are my entire universe."

⊙ ⚙ ⇒ ⋔ ⚙

Four days passed and Lilith still hadn't made a significant dent in her quota. Any hope that she'd escape into the woods for a few days of freedom had been dashed. With every strike of the hammer, Jude's words echoed in her mind, and her chest ached under the weight of them.

You are my entire universe.

Tonight, she tossed and turned in her bed, unable to sleep. Lilith dressed herself into a casual blouse and leather breeches. She'd decided to make use of her excess energy.

When she couldn't sleep, Lilith worked late hours in the smithy, if only to quell the worries that troubled her mind. Her only wish was to be cradled in the arms of a great oak, bow in hand, arrow nocked. But that didn't seem likely to happen now. Not for another bloody month!

Ever so quietly, she made her way down to the forge. Within minutes the shop was a hive of fireflies. At last, she was finally alone with her work.

Lilith released a sigh of contentment and took out Kathleen's wedding ring. It was a month earlier when her best friend's fiancé, Tavisk, came to her and asked her to design Kathleen a wedding band. Lilith couldn't deny that Kathleen and Tavisk were made for each other. In a crowd of people, they were alone, swimming in the warm depths of each other's gaze.

Of course Lilith couldn't refuse. She'd drawn sketches of the perfect ring and presented them to Tavisk with an eagerness she didn't quite understand. She couldn't fathom how she could be so excited for Kathleen's wedding, yet she cared so little for her own.

Lilith had spent countless restive nights attempting to comprehend her trepidation where Jude was concerned, but to no avail. It made little sense why she was so hesitant to marry him. He was handsome, and though he was awkward in his own way, many found his quirks endearing. Yet she held back where so many others gave in.

Already the air was thick with creosote. So much so, she barely noticed the shadowed form of a man standing in the doorway. Startled, Lilith jumped, wiping her dirty palms on her smock. "Uh… hello," she said, failing to mask the unease in her tone. No one visited this late.

"Good evening, Miss Oak." The stranger's voice was a smooth velvet rumble. "I was wondering if I could place an order with you?"

Doubt sprouted like a flaming weed from Hades. Lilith stood still as marble. Half in shock, half dissecting this stranger's motives. He'd likely come for a sword, but her glare was already flinging daggers at him. The man had a blade at his hip, why did he need another?

When he entered the dim light of the forge, Lilith nearly choked on her breath. He was striking, beautiful in a way that she couldn't comprehend. He was tall, broad shouldered, muscular yet lean. His beard was cropped short and well groomed. His shoulder-length, blond hair fell to his collarbone in gentle waves, more bronze than gold. Whoever he was, he must be extremely dextrous to have traversed these lands and survived. Rarely did strangers pass through town.

Never did they come alone.

At the unusual sight of the stranger, unease crept up her spine. But she wouldn't balk. Lilith would not cow in her father's smithy.

The man waited patiently for an answer. He tore his eyes of steel from her and surveyed the many works of art that decorated the walls. He wore a black tunic, breeches, and knee-high boots. A sword hung at his hip, the scabbard well embellished.

Lilith tracked him as he moved, like prey in the forest. His confident carriage stoked her unease, but she gulped down the jitters in her stomach, taking the opportunity to fill her pockets. She gathered any small objects of value—including the wedding ring—in case his intentions were to rob her.

Schooling her features into indifference, Lilith said, "I may have some spare time. What is it that you wish to order?"

"I need a sword," he said briskly, his soft-spoken timbre belied his warrior's physique. "It doesn't have to be beautiful or spectacular, just sharp and made of strong metal." His fingers tapped a rhythm on his outer thigh, the only indication of his impatience.

She shook her head. "I do not make weapons for strangers. As uncertain and dangerous as these times are, I'm sure you can understand that. I will, however, guide you to the armory. They have most of my weapons stocked there and they would gladly sell you one. Though they will not serve you until morn."

The man didn't seem angered by her refusal. Instead, he bowed his head and politely bade her farewell. Upon his leave, Lilith held her breath as she waited for the opportunity to close and lock the door to the smithy. With her heart still pounding, she removed the artifacts from her pockets. She brought out the gladius she'd been working on, grabbed her hammer, and began to pound it against the anvil, determined to perfect it.

Rarely had Lilith ever spoken to or even glimpsed a stranger pass through town. Though she didn't know every inhabitant in Utica by name, she knew their faces. It was odd for someone to travel alone, yet to be searching for a weapon, searching for her… How on earth did he make it here? Where did he come from? Did he know her father?

Lilith persisted with the hammer until her shoulders ached and trembled with exertion. Of their own volition, her traitorous thoughts returned to Jude.

Memories flashed through her mind: Jude's long blond

hair hung far below his broad shoulders. He almost always braided it back. On several occasions she'd plaited it for him. She began to feel an intimacy she had never experienced with anyone else. Lilith should marvel at the line she'd crossed, a line that any other girl would be elated to trespass before her wedding night. But she was overwhelmed, as if she'd committed the most unforgiving of crimes.

You are my entire universe.

For she *had* committed a crime. Never had she loved Jude the way she knew she should. Never had she been elevated by his touch. Never felt warmth rush through her body when he tore his coat from his limbs, when he shared parts of himself only a lover should know. This wasn't even lust. It was a friendship that had been stretched into something more.

You are my entire universe.

Yet the guilt would evidently overwhelm her. Jude loved her more than anything. He worshipped her every move, respected her every word. There was no doubt in her mind that leaving him would devastate him.

You are my entire universe.

Lilith's chest contracted. It ached as if her muscles were spasming. Her throat swelled, dried out. The muscles of her face contorted as she fought back sobs, sweat dripping from her brow onto the anvil below.

You are my entire universe.

Her body was heating up, and the sweat began to drip down her arms, her back. Her hair was plastered to her head and chest. She panted but she struggled to inhale oxygen.

Terror spiked through her—an invisible dagger—its pointed tip to alert her senses, not to kill.

And alert her it did.

The forge was ablaze! The smithy was alive with flames, her only exit blocked.

Lilith ran from the anvil toward her mother's blade. She secured it to her belt and faced the flames. She needed to run through the fire, lest the roof collapse in on her. The heat was almost unbearable on her skin and the thought of running through the inferno locked her in place, petrified.

Readying herself to run, she balled her hands into fists and clenched her jaw, steeling herself for whatever pain she would inevitably endure.

You are my entire universe.

She counted down to herself. "Three... Two... One...."

CRACK!

3

THEIR VASSAL

Lilith came to beside a small campfire, her body aching abominably. Iron coated her pasty tongue. She rubbed at her eyes; they burned, refusing to focus. The sound of crackling wood woke her senses, her vision far too bleary to distinguish anything beyond the oaks that surrounded her.

Was this Elysium? Or was this Hades, the afterlife for the evil and corrupt? The crepitating could very well be the Five Rivers: Styx, Lethe, Acheron, Phlegethon, and Cocytus. The Five Rivers were rumored to be flowing with the boiling blood of the inhabitants of the underworld. The overwhelming scent of burning—

FIRE!

Lilith sprang to her feet with renewed alarm, her mind flooded with visions of the burning smithy. The door to the shop had been blocked by flames. She vaguely recalled preparing herself to run through them. How did she get here? She needed to warn—

LARKIN!

Was her brother all right? Did the house start on fire too? She searched the camp but found it vacant, save for the sore excuse of a pair of boots. Her boots—or what remained of her boots. But Lilith didn't remember removing them. She didn't start this campfire. She wouldn't have thought to after narrowly escaping death by inferno. And how did she even get out of town? The guards wouldn't have let her outside of the gates after hours. Maybe they thought she was hunting…

And horses can fly.

The snapping of twigs broke her torpor. Lilith twisted toward the sound. A man approached, two limp turkeys dangling from his hands.

Larkin?

But it wasn't her brother. It was the stranger who visited her shop.

"Who are you?" Lilith demanded. "Where is my brother?" Her heartbeat raced, her face flushed, burning as hot as it had felt surrounded by the flames in the shop. It was only when she reached for Constance's hilt that she realized the blade was gone. "Where is my sword?" she snapped.

"I am Arduen," he said calmly, ignoring her questions. "I rescued you from the fire last night. You should never have left the forge lit and shut the door. That was nonsensical and irresponsible."

Lilith ground her molars at the accusation coating his tone, but she counselled her irritation, smoothed out her erected hackles. "You…" She took a moment to gather her thoughts. It made perfect sense how the fire had begun. She was careless and put off by this strange man's presence in her smithy, so she shut the door without dousing the forge. "You saved me… but… but where is my brother? Did you get him out? Answer this at least!"

Arduen remained unflappable. "The house was untouched by the fire. Only the smithy was destroyed."

"You…" Lilith couldn't find the right words through her building rage. "It's your fault!" she bellowed, her voice faltering. "My brother could be injured! How am I supposed to know that you didn't start the fire? You could have been angry with me for refusing to sell you a sword." She scowled at him, but he remained unaware of her impertinence—or at least he pretended not to notice—which only fueled her ire.

"Actually," Arduen said cautiously, hands raised in supplication, "I visited because I needed to meet you. My apologies if my presence caused you alarm. As for your brother, the fire was not large enough to kill anyone who wasn't inside the smithy."

"You needed to meet me? Why?" She retreated a step. The man's only reaction was a vaguely amused expression.

"Because you are the newest member of our race." He stepped toward her. Too close. "Lilith, you were Anointed Divine five nights ago when you were attacked by Spiro's beasts." He spoke slowly, like a teacher would a bemused student, slow enough to digest every syllable.

The situation beggared belief. The Gods hadn't Anointed a new Divine in decades. Though Lilith couldn't bring herself to believe it, she couldn't deny that it made sense. The lightning. The beasts' disappearance. Had the Gods taken her life before the beasts? How else could she have survived such an attack except for Divine intervention?

The Gods claimed humans who faced death early in life, remolding them, creating them anew for Their Divine purpose. Warriors of the deities. But Lilith was not a warrior.

She conceded a step. Two. Three. Her mind reeling with futile plans of action. But she couldn't outrun him. Not if he truly was Divine. No matter what she did, the consequences were equally woeful.

"It can't be..." she whispered to herself.

"But it is," Arduen said. "You must come with me to the Frourío where you will train. It is imperative that you receive instruction on how to control your gifts before you gain strength, lest you cause yourself or others harm." He spoke with an air of such authority, Lilith felt compelled to answer to him despite her indignation.

Though she didn't trust the man, no one could fabricate this story. No one would dare test the Gods in such a way. Nonetheless, a beast would never knock out its prey without consuming it, and they would never disappear without a trace. For how else could she have survived the beasts' predations?

"The Frourío?" Lilith arched a brow and crossed her arms, weighing her options. She needed to know if Larkin was safe. She needed to assure him that she was safe, too. And apologize for the destruction she wrought upon Papa's smithy. The reality of her situation was almost impossible to conceive—yet this was too lucid to be a vision of her dreamscape.

"It is where all Divine noviciates are instructed," Arduen said. "It is located deep in the Megálos Forest, on the shore of the Northern Galatëa. Newly Anointed Divines reside there while they are under tutelage. Once they are deemed worthy to graduate, they are free to return to the world, wherever they please."

The parables spoke of Divines past, of the majesty of the Gods' disciples, yet Lilith had always dismissed them as yore.

"So, what if I believe you?" she asked. "I don't want to go with you. I belong here with what remains of my family. Especially now that I have to rebuild my father's shop." She paced the camp.

"There was no one else in the house when I arrived," Arduen reassured her. "Wherever your brother is, he is safe from the fire." He watched her from across the camp, completely composed. He seemed almost amused by her discomfort, which only empowered Lilith's bitterness.

"Why are you smiling?" she yelled. "My life has been ruined. Can't you see that?"

"You do not know much about Divination, do you?" He cocked his head, eyes narrowing in scrutiny.

Lilith halted her pacing, her arms crossed not out of defiance, but an ill attempt to hold herself together. "No... I always thought it was legend. Just a mythical backstory to explain the evils of this world. To be honest, I didn't think Spiro existed either."

"You have much to learn," Arduen said on a laugh. "I suggest you settle down and make yourself comfortable. I'm going to prepare these turkeys for us. As I do that, I will teach you all that you need to know to understand the purpose of the Divine. To understand *your* new purpose." She expected to be met by a façade of pretence, but the stranger feigned nothing.

Overtly so, Arduen lowered himself to the ground and signalled with a wave of his hand for her to follow suit. Reluctantly, Lilith acquiesced, settling down across from him. She was too tired to fight him off. Too tired to attempt to flee. Arduen tossed a turkey at her feet. She accepted it. The prospect of doing something so familiar was oddly soothing.

As he rolled up the sleeves of his tunic and began to pluck feathers, he lapsed into silent contemplation. Lilith sieged the moment to observe him, keeping her head downcast. The stern set of his face yielded no insight. He was different from the other men she knew. She couldn't discern what qualities set him apart, but without a doubt, he was exceptional.

Divine. He is Divine.

As he worked, veins rippled over the tendons in his hands, a latticework that stretched up his exposed forearms. There was no denying it would be impossible to best him. Not to mention, he'd confiscated her only weapon.

"We were created many centuries ago," he began. "Our purpose was to exact the Gods' wills upon the earth. We were more powerful then because we were trusted, not as vain and arrogant as we have become. Our freedom was limitless. We protected the people and led them through tragedies and disasters. We had only ever been granted with the gifts of one God each, but when Spiro was blessed doubly, many of us were tainted with jealousy.

"We didn't understand why he'd been favored over the rest and it sowed disunion. We were once like a family, now ruined by covetousness.

"When Spiro was granted his fourth blessing, many of us were outraged, including myself. None of us had been Anointed more than once. We felt inadequate, insubstantial.

"Our gifts are the wielding of the elements. As you know, each of the Gods represent an element: Xander, God of Fire;

Thëo, God of Earth; Kyril, God of Water; Isidore, God of Wind; and Constantine, God of Aether."

Arduen lifted his head and regarded her with a stern gaze, his pale-blue eyes illuminated by the flames. "Constantine is your God. You are the next Divine He has chosen, and I was the last..." He raised his hand, snapped his fingers, and instantly the trees surrounding the camp were obscured, swathed in a mass array of darkness. Within the darkness were flashes of violet light so lurid, Lilith couldn't stop her eyes from flinching. Just as quickly as it occurred, it vanished with another snap of his fingers.

Lilith gawked, unable to translate the incoherent thoughts that plagued her mind. "Unbelievable," she whispered to herself. Before her was a man with ageless eyes set deep in a young man's face, an abyss blossoming from his palms. There was no denying it, and yet all she wanted was to run home to her brother. To tell him the truth. To apologize. For this to be over.

"In time," Arduen said with hubris, "you will learn how to control the abyss that is Aether."

Over the past five years, Lilith had lost faith in the divinities. When They had stopped staunching her tears. When They ignored her ululating pleas for her parents. Faith wasn't a weapon, only a false assurance that there was more beyond this world; that mortals shan't quake when death beckons. Truth told, she'd been convinced there were no Gods. No Elysium. No eternal sanctuary. That Hades was a place on earth, not beneath its surface. Yet standing here before a man touched by Their hands, she knew that wasn't true. The Gods were there, answering at Their wills.

Lilith rose to her feet. "I c-cannot do this. I'm n-not made for this," she stammered. "I'm a blacksmith and a s-soon-to-be-wife. I have my duties… Becoming a warrior for the Gods is not one of them!"

Arduen gave an arid chuckle. "Are you implying that Constantine has made a mistake?"

Lilith shook her head with vehemence. The Gods didn't make mistakes, even she knew that. "I'm just so ill-equipped for the task," she conceded, slumping her shoulders.

Arduen abandoned his turkey and approached her on cautious feet, as one would a skittish, wild animal. "That is why I must train you," he said with a gentleness she didn't think a man like him could possess. "It will take time, but it will be done traditionally; the exact way that I was instructed by my Master."

"I'm expected to call you Master?"

"Yes, you are. All noviciates have expectations, and that is but one of them. We will travel to the Frourío and begin your instruction immediately. We can save the rest of this discussion for the road."

"I'm not going with you!" Lilith shouted fiercely, turning to face the trees. She didn't know which direction Utica was; the Guiding Stars were concealed by clouds and golden leaves.

Arduen stepped in front of her, a spectre of a frown curving his lips as if he'd been just as inconvenienced by her Anointment as she had. "You cannot return home. If I failed to make that clear, my apologies." He placed a firm hold on her arm for emphasis. He didn't need to restrain her, his countenance was enough to pinion her in place.

Lilith wanted to tell him to piss off, but accosting him would do little good, especially when she was likely to spend the next several days—or years—with him. No matter what she did, the outcome would be the same. She'd never been pious. Never truly believed the Gods still had Their hands in this world. But now that she'd seen the truth, a fatalist she'd become.

"I'm not meant for this life," she said. "And I cannot go with you until I know my brother is safe." Tears stung the backs of her eyes. If Larkin was dead because of her imprudence, she would never forgive herself. Better to run off and take her chances against Arduen.

"Lilith, you cannot go home," he said. "If you refuse your purpose, the Gods will smite you down."

How dare he use the fear of death to foment her into abandoning her home! If he wanted to abscond with her, then he'd have to bind her wrists and drag her in his wake.

"Your life is no longer your own," Arduen continued. "You belong to Them. You are Their vassal. Four days ago, you died, Lilith. Four days ago, the Gods put the blood in your veins. They healed your wounds and returned the breath to your lungs. You have many choices, but whether you are or are not Divine, that is not one of them."

Lilith's blood ran cold. Becoming Divine was more daunting than entering Elysium. Death was not loathsome enough to deter her. But yet, the Gods were unlikely to grant her entry into Elysium after denying Constantine's will.

Tears threatened to stream down her cheeks. She needed, in her own way, to mourn herself; to mourn the life she always thought she'd have.

Arduen had to understand her lamentation. He let loose his hold on her arm and instead, placed his hand on her back, attempting to provide her the slightest amount of comfort. Lilith didn't reject the gesture, though she kept her body faced away from him. She didn't know the man at all, yet she'd become acutely aware of a sense of intimacy, a closeness the likes of which she had with no one else.

After a moment of silence, Arduen returned to the campfire. He continued to prep the turkeys, then placed the pieces of meat into an iron pan he retrieved from his pack. He kept to himself, allowing Lilith space to digest it all. It was dawn. Once the food was prepared for the journey, they would be off.

As the turkey simmered, Arduen broke the silence. "There are many wonders of this world. It is time to face them."

Lilith closed her eyes, the way many do when they spare a moment to mourn the loss of someone or something. All of it would be in her past in only a short moment. There would be no assuring Larkin that she was safe. She would be leaving him with nothing but the disaster of the shop to sort out on his own.

"How do I know Larkin is safe as you say?"

"I wouldn't lie to you about that, Lilith," Arduen said. "Never regarding family."

Opening her teary eyes, she stole a glance toward Utica, barely visible in the distance. She was suddenly aware of where it stood, as if it was calling to her, bidding her farewell. For now.

"You may write him when we reach the Frourío," he added. "I won't deny you correspondence. It will help you adjust to your new life."

Lilith bristled. "That's weeks away! He will be worried sick. We're here now. Why can't I say goodbye?"

"Because it's too dangerous. If you hadn't caused that fire, I would have politely knocked on your door, sat you and your brother down and explained all of this." He waved his hands about. "But since that is not the case, there will be a horde of people around your house. They will want to know what happened, and I cannot risk being blamed for this. And I cannot trust you," he admitted. "If we return to Utica, you could scream for help, scream to the skies that I am kidnapping you."

"Aren't you?" she questioned haughtily.

"No!" he shouted. "You must be trained, Lilith. You are a weapon now. You are a danger to yourself and all those around you."

Lilith covered her face with her hands.

"You must trust me when I say that your brother is safe," he pleaded. "We will send a message as soon as we are able."

"Why didn't you sit me down and talk to me last night? Why bother pretending to request a commission?"

Arduen sighed through his nose. "I shouldn't have come into the shop. I wanted to ensure that I had the right location, the right girl. My apologies. My plan was to return in the morn to speak with you and your brother. But when I saw the fire..."

Her conscience warred with her heart. At this point, running away and dying were tantamount, but it would be the denying of a God's will that would damn her and whatever family Larkin went on to establish—if he could even convince a woman to marry into the family. The Oak name would be forever tainted.

Once Arduen packed up the food and wares, he donned his pack and kicked dirt over the dying embers. Then he reached up into the oak behind him and procured a sheathed Constance.

"Can I have my sword back?" Lilith asked, only to be

impaled by a withering stare. "No?" she prodded. "You think I could best you?"

A chuckle rumbled inside his chest. "No, I don't. But I am not willing to risk it. You can have your sword back when I deem it necessary to arm you." He gestured to the camp with splayed arms. "Since we are not in any immediate danger, I don't see a reason you need it in your hands."

Lilith grit her teeth but withheld her retort. She would have to display her fidelity if she wanted Constance back. But that would prove to be the toughest challenge yet.

4

ROAD TO THE FROURÍO

"Three weeks?!" Lilith stared wide-eyed at Arduen as he nodded in confirmation. The journey to the Frourío would take little over three weeks. From what she could recall of the map of Augusta, there was only one town between Utica and the location Arduen described of the Frourío. To make matters worse, he planned to avoid the town altogether. There would be no sleeping in a real bed for many nights.

That was also three weeks Larkin would spend worrying sick over her disappearance. Lilith's abdomen knitted at the thought. It was cruel to leave him in the dark, especially after all they'd suffered together. Even if she understood why Arduen was so adamant not to return to Utica, guilt still plagued her.

Isidore's Wind daemons swirled on the horizon. Lilith licked at chapped lips, the cool breeze tousled her hair, obscuring her face from Arduen's view. She was strangely thankful for the privacy it granted.

Arduen insisted that they travel along the tree line. Their route through the fallow land would be unobstructed, and they would have the shelter of the trees in the evenings and in the event of predators.

Lilith kept a regular eye on Constance. It was strapped across Arduen's back, snuggled beneath his pack. It was safe there, she was sure, but without it clasped at her hip, she felt oddly vulnerable. Out in the open, there were no city walls to protect them, and she couldn't shake the sinking intuition that they were being followed.

The chill autumn gusts burned her eyes, her fingers froze stiff, and her bones ached. Her Master halted to analyze the sun and eat before they continued. As he retrieved the turkey from his pack, he pulled out two cloaks and handed the smaller one to Lilith. "It is cold and will only get more frigid from here on out." Thankful that he'd considered her well-being alongside his own, she gladly accepted the heavy woollen garment.

"Since we were unable to return to collect any of your belongings, I've brought with me some clothing. They will likely be too large, but your belt will help with that." He sifted through the items inside his pack, pulling out a honey-dyed cotton blouse to replace her own, which had been destroyed in the fire. Her breeches had survived, thankfully.

Lilith took the shirt, mumbled a quiet, "Thank you," and sauntered into the trees for privacy. Shrugging on the blouse, she tucked it into her breeches and secured her belt. It was a few sizes too big, but in this weather, she didn't mind. When she returned to Arduen, he had two vambraces of boiled leather, which he insisted he secure to her forearms himself.

"Why do I need these if I'm not granted access to my sword?" Lilith asked, resentment soaking her tone.

"Because you must be prepared for battle at any moment," he said. "If danger is near, I will know long before it finds us. In the event of an attack, you can have your sword back."

She shelved any further inquisitions. Arduen didn't seem the type who deigned to answer curious questions, and now that her incredulity had settled, there was much to mull over in the confines of her mind.

As they trod in silence, she observed her new Master. Under the light of the sun, she could see that there were no lines etched into the smooth skin of his face. He looked young but she didn't dare ask him how old he truly was.

When Arduen finally spoke, after spending so many hours in utter silence, his words pierced the air like a shout. Lilith started, too exhausted to bother attempting to conceal her irritation.

"There is much that you need to learn about your new life," he said. "It is imperative that you understand the changes you will be undergoing in the near future."

"What changes?"

He regarded her with what she perceived as caution. "Your entire genetic makeup will be altered throughout the course of your training. You will become harder, stronger, stealthier. Impacts that may have once killed you, will now only cause you to bruise. There is now no one quite your equal, lest it be another Divine."

Lilith listened intently. If she were being honest with herself, she had always dreamed of power—not of ruling over others, but of power over herself. "I can accept that," she said with forced certainty. "I want to know what is expected of me and what my day-to-day schedule will be like."

Arduen slowed, then paced through the long grass. "We will begin training immediately. You will be given a strict routine. It is important that you learn the bones of this country, and of our religion. You will also learn how to honor and spend time with Constantine; that will become most important to you. You will be schooled in ways of thinking, logically, open-minded to the world around you and the many races that we serve."

Lilith released a blunt cackle before clamping her mouth shut promptly. "You say I am to battle any man with ease, then will I not be training physically as well?"

"I will be training you in bearing arms. You must take up a weapon of your choice and learn to wield it with skill. Not every Divine becomes master of their element within the first decade of Divination. It is of the utmost priority to send you into the world equipped for duty, especially in times of hostility." Arduen lowered his voice. "With an enemy as great as Spiro, we do not take lightly to sending noviciates into battle. Right now, there are only two Divines in development, one that we have great confidence in, and… *you*."

Lilith didn't take umbrage to his statement; it would take time to grasp the knowledge she needed to fulfil her expectations. It was difficult to imagine becoming a warrior. Difficult to envision herself killing others. The thought was repulsive. It wasn't her place to determine who was worthy to live and who wasn't. It was not in her nature to kill innocents at the behest of a covetous ruler.

"What is Aether?" she asked. "You've never really explained it."

Arduen made a chuffing sound. Maybe he was impressed by her curiosity, her will to learn, or maybe he was annoyed. Either way, Lilith cared not.

"Aether is an abyss that sucks the life from our enemies," he said. "It cleaves the soul from the body and renders the physical nothing more than a charred mass of matter. It can be shaped and formed in many ways, but that will take some time to learn. First you must succeed in summoning the void."

Lilith contemplated his words, her entrails coiling painfully.

"It is also important that you know just how indefinitely your life has changed..."

"What do you mean?"

"You will endure," he said, "while others of our race will not."

Lilith arched a brow. "Your riddles have only succeeded to confound me." One thing was clear, the man was attempting to beguile her. Callow she may be, but she was not witless.

"We are immortal," Arduen explained. "Much like the Gods, except that we can be thrust into Elysium through mortal injury." He stopped and turned to face her, seizing her hands—though not unkindly—he squeezed them gently. "We are your family now, Lilith. Everyone else will perish in time. Your Divine family will be the only constant in your long life."

Lilith glanced up at him through dark lashes. No longer could she return to Utica to take up the life she'd once aspired. She had family and friends that she would have to watch die. Did those relationships bring her enough joy that they were worth every moment of mourning? They were, and she resolved to return to Utica when she was first free from training. Least of all, she owed them an explanation. It would be the first thing she did when she arrived at the Frourío.

Arduen gave her a moment to digest what she'd learned and set his pack down against the large stump of a tree. He chose to set up camp at the base of a small knoll, granting them slight coverage from the south, where the open plains welcomed predators.

Obscured by the trees, Lilith lay out the bedroll Arduen provided. Resting her back against the trunk of an oak, she drew her cloak tight around her body. Setting her chin on her knees, she watched as Arduen made a quick fire and removed the turkey from his pack.

They ate in silence as the sky changed color. For the first day or two, all Lilith could manage was to chew a few morsels of each meal. Everything tasted of ashes. She ignored Arduen's shrewd gaze as she picked at her meal. He didn't have to speak, she felt chagrined for wasting precious food.

"Your cheeks are hollowing out," he said with a pointed look. "Eat." That was an order.

Lilith scowled. "Maybe if you'd allowed me the chance to say farewell to my brother, I'd feel a lot more at ease."

Arduen's expression was genuinely rueful. "I am sorry, Lilith. But I am sure you are sensible enough to understand the predicament." *It was, after all, your fault.*

She slumped back against the tree, defeated.

Following dinner, Lilith removed her boots and warmed her feet by the campfire. They were mottled with bruises and sores, and she winced at the sting of exposing them to the brisk air. As a distraction, she pondered the many questions she had for Arduen. If they were indeed to be spending every day together for the next few years, she wanted to know all that she could about him.

In her opinion, it was her right to know him, yet she was intimidated and anxious. So she settled on a harmless question: "Do you have any living family members?"

"Yes, I do," he replied vaguely. "As promised, when we arrive at the Frourío, we will send a message to your family immediately."

"I only need to write my brother," she said.

"Oh?"

Avoiding his inquisitive look, Lilith locked her eyes on the flames. "My parents passed away five years ago. I was just coming of age."

"I'm sorry," he said softly. "Be careful who you love. Life is short for most, but for us it is long, and pain does not diminish. It has deeper effects on the mind and soul. Deeper than one's desire for power and control. Beware of that."

At his words, a deep-seeded fear that had been brewing for too long suddenly flared to life. Perhaps returning to Utica wasn't a good idea.

Lilith sat in silence, considering her predicament for a moment, long enough to notice Arduen studying her beneath lowered brows. When their eyes met, his expression was doleful.

She didn't want his pity.

Anything but pity.

⊚ ⑮ ⇒ ⋔ ♭

ARDUEN WOKE HER EVERY MORNING BEFORE DAWN, NOT THAT SHE needed much more than a gentle prod to rouse her.

Lilith was distracted from her harrowing thoughts when the sunrise stole her breath. As the flaming orb's rays penetrated the grassy field, she was suddenly standing in her kitchen. The dust particles floating in those same rays as they shot through the crystalline windows. Mah was kneading dough at the counter. Larkin was devouring a bowl of oats at the kitchen table. Papa kissed her mother's cheek before he began a long day's work in the shop.

The shop she burnt down.

Lilith shook her head clear of the vision. With a weight forming in the pit of her stomach, she lowered her gaze and willed her mind to nothingness.

Her Master assumed the rear as they strode through the grass. When Lilith dared to glance back at him, Arduen was using a long stick to ruffle their tracks through the plain's hairs. They'd spent the entire morning travelling in silence. She tried to think of questions she could ask him pertaining to his accomplishments as a Divine—questions that wouldn't require intimate answers.

"Have you fought many battles?"

After a tense moment of silence, Arduen answered, "Many. I fought alongside my brothers and sisters in Divination. We fought together, celebrated together, adventured together, and we mourned together. It has only been this past century that we separated."

Lilith hesitantly inquired further as to why they decided to abandon such a bond.

"Ah. It is not so simple, Lilith. When you undergo such devastating experiences with a group of individuals, those people start to embody the horrid memories. It becomes almost difficult to heal and move on when you are surrounded by those you've suffered with. Those whose faces encourage your mind to relive the tragedies." He sighed heavily. "I myself am not innocent of this. I have also distanced myself from those I care most deeply for. That is why it is important to value your mental health as much as the physical. It is, in my opinion, much more important."

Lilith nearly choked on the lump forming in her throat. Maybe that was why her mother abandoned her and Larkin for the afterlife. "I'm sorry…"

"Don't be," he said. "It's part of our life and, unfortunately, an area upon which every Divine must learn to accept and improve. There will be healing, and there will be rejoicing, once we are strong enough to thwart Spiro. Therefore, it is imperative that you understand the devastation that the Great Divine has wrought upon this land. He has even caused the Gods a great deal of pain, for even They are susceptible to mundane emotions. That is why there are only two noviciates. We are praying avidly for more of us every day.

"There was a great deal of rejoicing when we received news of you. I was close to Utica when I received word. I am very fortunate to have found you when I did, or you may not be with us."

For that, Lilith was thankful, but she couldn't bring herself to voice it.

✶ ✶ ✶ ✶ ✶

They travelled for weeks, stopping only in the evenings to rest or when they spotted game. Lilith had never felt more awkward relieving herself. Arduen provided distance, whistling as he pretended not to hear her.

During this time, Lilith so conveniently received her moon cycle. And since she hadn't been allowed to return home to gather her belongings, she was without supplies. In the evenings, when Arduen's eyes finally closed and the rise and fall of his chest steadied, Lilith sliced off strips of fabric from the hem of her cloak and stuffed the scraps into her undergarments.

With every passing day, she traipsed onward, her steps listless, somnolent. She pulled her hood over her face, fighting for a semblance of confidence—if only for dignity's sake.

Several evenings they were forced to forgo a fire and eat their dinner cold. Lilith didn't ask Arduen why they did, she only assumed it was because he sensed danger nearby. Someone who travelled the land as often as he did would know when not to light a fire. She barely slept on those nights.

One dark evening, Arduen constructed a small campfire whilst Lilith prepared the turkey. She picked some Augustan mushrooms and placed them on the rocks beside the fire to roast. Settling herself across from him, she pulled her cloak around herself. Shivering, she watched her breath materialize in the air like smoke. Autumn was in full force.

A soft glow of white light emanated through the trees to the northeast. Lilith jumped into a low crouch, made eye contact with Arduen, nodding toward the strange spectacle. Her Master showed no indication of alarm. But Lilith remained poised on her haunches, reaching for Constance's hilt, grasping thin air. An angry flush singed her cheeks. How was she supposed to defend herself if he harbored her only weapon?

As the light drew nearer, Lilith could make out movements and shapes. Figures. They appeared like floating maidens.

Twenty of them, possibly more. Diaphanous skirts swayed on the breeze. All of them lit as if the moon shone through them, illuminating their lithe bodies, painting them silver and gold. They danced through the oaks with utmost elegance.

Transfixed, Lilith couldn't remove her gaze. They were the most beautiful sight. Though they'd caused her alarm at first, they now inspired in her the deepest sense of wonder and... sorrow.

Lilith and Arduen sat in silence and observed, listening to the eerily beautiful requiem that emanated from their lips. Though their bodies and gowns were evident, the dancing ladies' faces remained elusive. They floated through the trees, the view often obstructed by the trunks. The songs wavered from notes of lament to ebullience, toying with her emotional state. Did they affect Arduen as well?

"They are spirits, Lilith," he whispered. "They shall not harm you. Their lyrics are of a primeval dialect, ancient rhymes that our people can no longer understand." The spirits didn't react to his voice, but she dared not respond to him, lest she break their routine.

Once the spirits had dissipated into the darkness and Lilith could glean no more of their glow, she released a pent breath. "They are beautiful," she said. Arduen nodded agreeably.

Once their hunger had been sated, she attempted to make herself comfortable enough to get some rest before another day of travel. The moss that coated the roots of the tree only supplemented as a slight cushion beneath her bedroll. Arduen, propped against an oak across from her, retrieved her blade.

"I named it Constance," Lilith said, watching intently as he pulled the sword from its sheath. "My father said it was a good omen to name your blade. That the metal was an element, it was alive as we are. And if a sword is to save your life, you best give it a name, for it will be your most faithful servant."

"If one knows how to wield it," Arduen added.

Lilith ignored the sear rising beneath her skin.

Arduen held the blade in the air. The sword was two feet in length, the blade thin. The steel was a dark iridescent collection of colors that changed in the light. It was one piece, the handle being of the same material as the blade itself. Chiselled vines decorated the base of the blade, the cross guard two large leaves with their stems attached at the middle. It was a piece of art and her father's finest weapon.

Lowering Constance onto his lap, Arduen rifled through his pack. When he acquired what he needed, he set to work.

Lilith started. "What are you doing?"

Without answering, Arduen proceeded to wrap a thin strip of leather around Constance's hilt. "Your sword was in need of a grip," he said.

Settling back down, Lilith watched as he worked. He continued to mutter about how painful it was to see swords created for aesthetic purposes.

"My father forged that blade for my mother specifically," Lilith said in defence.

Arduen responded with a terse grunt. "I will teach you how to properly care for a sword. Your father was smart enough to put a hole at the tip of Constance's scabbard, but you have not lined the inside with oil as you should. Any water that doesn't drain will cause your blade to rust, especially when travelling."

"It's Obsidian Steel," Lilith countered. "It cannot rust."

Arduen sighed smoke. "Everything rusts with time."

She digressed, too exhausted to argue. Perhaps he was right, he was ageless—ancient, even. But she couldn't help but feel rankled by the fact that this man was lecturing her about how to care for the very weapons she created.

When Arduen finished he proffered the blade to her, hilt first. "How does that feel?"

Lilith wrapped her fingers around the grip, and—however grudgingly—admitted that it did feel better. Pleased, Arduen retrieved Constance and sheathed it, returning it to his belongings.

SEVERAL HOURS LATER, LILITH AWOKE WITH A START, ARDUEN'S hand clamped firmly over her mouth. It took her eyes some time to adjust to the darkness, but her ears were sharp. Twigs and branches snapped in the distance.

Something large was approaching their camp.

5

FRIEND OR FOE

Arduen positioned himself above her, one hand clasped firmly over her mouth, the other clutching his sword, primed to defend. Whatever was the cause for alarm, it was cloaked in darkness.

It wasn't yet morning, the sky was a deep, dark cyan, with tiny shimmering dots scattered across the firmament. Lilith could make out the soft crunching of brush in the distance. Arduen had doused the fire with dirt and water, rendering their camp one with the darkness, guarding them from detection. But she'd heard the stories, Spiro's beasts were smarter than that, for they hunted by scent.

Lilith hadn't deigned to notify her Master of the arrival of her moon cycle. Perhaps it was her scent that had lured the beasts. But even if she and Arduen were meant to become close, they weren't yet, and she doubted he meant *that* close.

Arduen stole a warning glance at her, half her face still concealed under his large hand. He spoke in a hushed whisper, "You now possess senses greater than ever before. You will know if another being is present, human or other, and you will know whether or not you are in danger." His hand slackened. "Friend or foe. You will know."

When he released his hold on her, he pressed the hilt of Constance against her palm.

Pushing herself up into a crouch, she ignored the protest from her cramped limbs. Grasping the hilt of Constance, she assumed her best defensive stance. It wasn't until she wrapped her hand around the grip that she noticed her palms were slick with sweat.

Keeping her eyes peeled in the direction of the beasts—or what she assumed were beasts—Lilith grappled for her bearings. She waited for Arduen to move first, trusting in his mature intuit over that of her own. It was only when he rose to his full height that a beast burst from the trees, landing on him with a thud.

The impact would have rendered any mortal man lifeless, but Arduen wrestled with the beast, fully conscious. Once he was able to draw his sword, he began to slash at the monster with a fury Lilith had never beheld. She blanched, standing well out of the way. Her mouth hung open, her body trembled, and her heart pounded in her ears, drowning out the creature's roars.

Arduen yelled at her from under the beast, "Your sword, Lilith!"

Her heart fell like an anvil. Over and over and over. Her gut turned frigid, cooled by the breath of fear. If she fought, Arduen would see her ineptitude with a blade. If she didn't fight... she would die.

For the final time.

Instinct bellowed at her to run, but her feet wouldn't rise. She silently cursed her impotence, then she brushed off her concern of Arduen's censure. *Survival, Lilith. That's all that matters right now.*

Breaking free of her trance, she bound forward, ignoring her fear of the beast. Now was the best time to attack, while it was preoccupied with Arduen. Stabbing at the beast, Lilith provoked it just enough to provide the distraction Arduen needed to embed his sword through its trunk-like neck. Its skin was tough as bark, and she watched in awe and disgust as her Master grit his teeth and pushed, the muscles of his arms bulging through his tunic. Black blood sprayed over him as he pulled his blade free. Rolling to the side as the beast fell lifeless where he'd been lying seconds before.

Arduen panted and Lilith helped him to his feet, satisfied when he gave her a nod of approval. At her Master's behest, Lilith inspected the creature. The beast was large and black like that of a giant bear, except that its face and hands were scaled like a reptile. Its claws—or talons—were several inches long, and she could discern every muscle corded beneath its hide.

Vibrations rattled the earth, drawing her attention away from their fallen foe. Another two beasts broke free of the trees and entered the camp. One beast set itself upon Arduen, this one much larger than the last. But he wasn't overcome so easily.

"Pay attention, Lilith!" he called to her.

Lilith receded several paces, attempting to buy herself time and space to fight. She had hoped that Arduen would slay his beast fast enough to aid her in her own battle, but the longer his bout lasted, the more unlikely that became.

The beast stalked in her direction.

During her few sparring lessons with her father, he'd instructed her to always watch her opponent's weapon, never the opponent. "But when you strike," he'd said, "don't aim for the weapon, aim for your adversary." *Steel cannot deceive.* But this was a monster wielding his own body as a weapon. Where was she supposed to look?

Muttering a curse under her breath, the beast slashed at her, close enough to stir the air. With every advance, the ground shuddered beneath her feet and her knees threatened to buckle. She widened her stance to stabilize herself before she slashed at the beast, the movements her father taught her roaring in her mind. Finally, she caught the monster by its nose, and it loosed a deafening cry as dark ichor sprayed into the air.

The beast kicked Lilith to the ground, and she rolled away from it, her stomach clenching from the pain. She lost her grip on Constance, and the sword skittered away from her. She watched in horror as the beast stood upon it, rendering her defenceless.

Her blood chilled.

Lilith let loose a desperate cry as the beast lifted its massive paws into the air and brought them down in a fatal blow. Her veins surged. Her skin prickled. Senses piqued, her palms burning. There was a charge of energy so great, everything went white.

And then there was nothing.

Cool rain splattered against Lilith's skin. Blessed Xander, she was thirsty. Why was she so famished?

THE MONSTERS!

Lilith rose with a start. It was still dark, and the sky was clear. She relaxed slightly at the sight of Arduen seated behind her. It was clear she'd been lying with her head in his lap, and what she'd perceived as rain was just a wet cloth in his hand. He cast her a concerned glance and brushed her tangled hair away from her face. The gesture was so tender, she deigned to ignore it.

"How are you feeling?" he asked warily, hand on her shoulder to steady her.

Lilith observed her surroundings, trying to formulate an appropriate response, but words were elusive. The three beasts lay slain in the remnants of their camp. Trees had been blown to shards, and what remained of the carcasses was nothing more than black soot. She reoriented herself by focusing on the water that trickled down her neck.

"What happened?" she asked dryly.

"You've discovered Aether. Fortunately for me, I had slain my opponent and was on my way to you when you released the blast. I was able to shield myself."

"I don't know how I did it..." She shook her head frantically. *Gods, it hurts!* "I don't think I could recreate it even if I tried."

Arduen tipped his head back, eyes tapering. The way he looked at her now, a glint of wonder and awe evident in his pale-blue eyes, almost as if he recognized her outburst as some form of manifestation—as a promise of what was to come.

But Lilith knew better.

This was just a fluke. A vast display of her incompetence.

The magnanimity of the power she now possessed within could kill her before she ever learned to harness it.

"It's part of who you are now," he said. "And I will help you control it. We will not be training in such stressful environments. You'll likely not experience adrenaline such as this for a long while." He placed a firm hand between her shoulder blades and pressed the cold cloth to her forehead.

It was clear by the way he spoke that her outburst was a mere testament to the fact that she had absolutely no governance over Constantine's element.

As if reading her mind, he said, "A callow Divine faces the risk of explosion or implosion. Just be thankful it was the former."

Feeling properly chagrined, Lilith pushed herself to her feet. Her exposure to the uncanny birthed an incessant itch beneath her skin. But like the good noviciate she was becoming, she did nothing to negate it. Not that she could, but griping about her situation seemed like a sure way to distance herself from her Master.

As if noting her mood, Arduen continued his lecture. "Constantine's element is part of your nature now. Like breathing air and the beating of your heart. Your body will now summon Aether of its own will, when it believes it is in its most dire need. It is your responsibility to harness and command that power."

Lilith listened as intently as her ringing ears would allow, letting Arduen feed her what food they had left. Then they retrieved their belongings and took to the road, leaving behind them the blackened camp. It would be impossible to erase their footprint there.

LILITH HAD WATCHED THE LANDSCAPE TRANSFORM YET AGAIN. From lush golden fields, to towering pines of the deepest emerald. Long gone were the familiar oaks.

According to Arduen, this was the final day of travel, and she was thankful for it. She'd developed an ill temper birthed from fatigue. Her body was overexerted, and if she had to eat any more dried turkey, she would vomit. Arduen seemed to be of a much more patient mien, and she couldn't help but resent him for it.

Together they ambled through the dense pines in silence. When a shadow moved in their direction, Lilith froze abruptly, drawing Constance from the scabbard at her hip. Arduen didn't elicit much of a reaction. Her Master simply halted, waiting for the creature to approach.

A foreign voice emanated from the shadows, "Master was expecting you later tonight."

A young man emerged, stepping into the light. He was clad in a one-piece leather suit. Besides a sword at his hip, he bore no other accoutrements. The young man held out his hand to greet Arduen with a smile, and to Lilith's surprise, her Master returned the genial expression in kind. The men clasped each other's wrists and Arduen patted the young man on the shoulder approvingly. "Good to see you, Julius," he said kindly. He turned to Lilith with an expression of expectancy.

The young man—Julius—took a tentative step in her direction, his hand extended. "My name is Julius, and yours?" He spoke with an air of confidence similar to Arduen, his foreign accent rich in her ears. He had a full head of thick, sable curls resembling a midnight halo. His dark-hazel eyes sparkled with undeniable energy as he gazed down upon her. His charm was exotic, handsome in a way she had never before seen.

Without relinquishing her hold on Constance's hilt, she extended her arm and grasped his wrist, just as Arduen had. His fingers curled around her own, his grip redolent of iron, steady as stone.

Lilith spoke amiably, but she couldn't mask the lethargy that crept into her voice. "I am Lilith."

A slight smile parted his lips. Releasing his grip, he raised his arms and spread them wide. "Welcome to the Megálos Forest."

Lilith took the opportunity to smooth her knotted hair, suddenly conscious of her ragged appearance.

Despite his disheveled image, Julius was perfection incarnate. His bronze skin gleamed in the blazing afternoon sun, delicate beads of perspiration decorated his brow. His hands—marked with swirls of scars, traceries of iridescent pink and silver disrupting his gloriously tan skin—fidgeted with his belt. He could have been southern, half-Vunosoï, or not Augustan at all. Lilith's lack of travel deprived her of the wisdom to discern his heritage.

"Your journey has been long and you've completed all those miles on foot… I'm impressed," Julius flashed her a grin. "Then again, no one unimpressive becomes Divine."

Lilith struggled to conceal her flattery. Yet she still tensed at the mere mention of the word *Divine*. How could she be a chosen one? What did she know about epic battles and protecting people? *Nothing*. Yet the Divine feared no enemy. Except Spiro.

Arduen continued on ahead toward a large stone tower that rose hundreds of feet into the air, fifty feet wide at its base. An assortment of varying stones composed the structure, dotted frequently by stained-crystalline windows. Lilith squinted, craning her neck to take it all in. This must be the Frourío. At first glance, she thought the structure appeared to be leaning, as if it could topple under the force of a determined breeze. Could Aether bring the looming fortress crumbling down into the sea?

Julius glanced at her sidelong and beckoned for her to follow. Lilith obliged, forcing her expression cavalier as she marched in his wake, weaving expertly through the masts of pines.

"You and I have different Masters," said Julius. "But we will acknowledge them both with the title. Each Divine has a Master who trains them. Who we are placed under is determined by what element we wield." He laughed almost nervously. "I'm sure Arduen has already informed you of this."

"What is your element?"

Julius shot her a wry smile. "Fire!" He snapped his fingers and a small flame appeared suspended above his hand.

Lilith couldn't help the smile that split her lips.

"Where are you from?" Julius asked.

"Utica."

"Interesting," he said, then turned away from her, humming a tune as they meandered through the trees.

Though the pines were dense, their masts were barren of branches halfway down, and they rose a hundred feet above them, creating an emerald canopy. As their feet strode along the carpet of pine needles, Lilith studied Julius. He was almost a foot taller than she, with a lean body, though he was quite muscular. He wore black leather boots that rose to mid-calf. Lilith noted the stubble that lined his jaw, indicative that he was well into his manhood. With his sleeves rolled up to his elbows, she could see that his forearms were corded with defined cuts of sinew. Formidable as her Master.

They edged into a clearing, and in the centre stood the Frourío. Behind it was what appeared to be a small field, and beyond that, waters of the deepest azure Lilith had ever seen. The Galatëa Sea.

Julius walked toward the tower with his arms outstretched. "This is our magnificent home, the Frourío. It was built by the first Divines. Every noviciate travels here to train."

Lilith was transfixed by the sight of it all. Could this really be home? "It's beautiful," she breathed.

Julius beamed down at her, revealing near-perfect teeth. "I'm glad you like it. You will be here for a few years yet. It takes time to become a Master Divine."

Frowning, Lilith stared off at the glistening expanse of water. She didn't need to be reminded. Nothing churned her stomach more than not having a choice. Forcing a smile, she answered, "It will have to do, won't it?"

Julius let out a choked laugh. "That it will."

He walked to the shore, letting Lilith wander and explore her new surroundings. Aware that he was watching her as she stepped onto the sand, her heart nearly stopped as she sank into it.

The beach was firm, given the time of year, though it still engulfed her tattered boots. Her pace was slowed significantly as she approached the water, causing her cramped calves to burn, drawing her attention to just how drained she was. Her eyes settled on the horizon. The sea looked like a giant bath of molten silver meant for a God. It was a fantastical metal-smith's dream… but she wasn't a smith anymore.

"It is beautiful here, isn't it?" said a voice like grating stones.

Lilith twisted in surprise. Two men stood on the grass before the beach. One of them was Arduen, standing proudly with his arms crossed over his chest. The other man—the one she assumed had just spoken—wore similar attire to what Arduen had gifted her. He was armed with a scim at his hip. He had dark hair cut blunt at his shoulders, a short-cropped beard concealed the bottom half of his face.

"I am Quintus," he said with his gravelly voice. "But you can call me Quin. I helped rebuild the Frourío a few centuries ago. It stands strong still, despite its age. We don't have too many rules here, Lilith. We want you to feel as though this is your home."

She bowed her head in polite deference.

"Well," Arduen said, clasping his hands and grinding his palms together, "let us indulge in a hot meal!"

6

ON BENDED KNEES

Promptly following her first hearty meal in weeks, Lilith was escorted to her quarters. It was a single austere bedchamber, utterly bare, unadorned; a modest accommodation. The outer wall was curved and set with two stained-crystalline windows facing the sea. Nothing but a four-poster bed, a wooden dresser, and a nightstand inhabited the grim space.

Arranged at the end of her bed were two black leather suits, the same style that Julius had worn earlier. Beside them were several ivory blouses, a few undershirts, two strophiums to support her chest when she trained, two new pairs of leather breeches, a nightgown, and a set of new leather boots. Lilith changed into the nightgown immediately.

Seating herself on the mattress, she ignored the protest it made at the shock of her weight. How long had it been since someone occupied this room? In solitude for the first time since leaving home, she lay back and sighed as her body sank into the soft mattress.

"You would do well to listen to your Master, dear."

Lilith sat up at the sound of the voice. A tall woman stood in the doorway. Her ashy hair bundled atop her head in a heap, with misplaced tendrils hanging down past her shoulders. She glanced at Lilith with gentle eyes. "He will explain everything you need to know about your new life in great detail. Do not think you can leave this place without permission. You will see your brother again sooner than you think."

Lilith didn't know what to say.

"I am Olga," the woman said. "I am the Divine Oracle, the chosen mouthpiece of the Gods. Please consider me an adviser." She smiled empathetically and lowered herself onto the windowsill.

Larkin… how could she have forgotten?

"I need to write my brother," Lilith said. "Can you help me with that?"

Olga set her dark eyes on Lilith. "You cannot write?"

Offended, Lilith bit back a retort. "I can write, I'm just unfamiliar with the Frourío." Her eyes darted around the room. "Can you direct me to a study or someplace I can write a message?"

Ignoring Lilith's question, Olga gazed out of the window at the glittering waters. "The Gods are all-knowing. They can hear your thoughts and see your every action. Right now, They can see your brother talking with some fellow townspeople. They are concerned for your well-being, and your disappearance has alerted the Emperor's Frourà." *The Guard.*

Lilith gaped, glancing hopelessly up at the ceiling, her eyes welled with fresh tears. Would she never return home again?

It was unfair. Larkin was forced to face the consequences of her mistakes.

"Please tell me he's okay!" she blurted. "Is he going to rebuild the shop? Did our dog survive? The Emperor's men won't hurt him, will they?" A million endless queries assailed her brain until her head throbbed. Of course the Emperor's Guard would get involved, she was a blacksmith. Augusta had been at war for nearly a century, the Emperor would be notified directly of the incident.

"Larkin and Rally are both safe and in good health, although they are off-put by the circumstance, as is to be expected." Olga joined Lilith on the bed. "Larkin will be fine without you. He is a grown man."

"I would like to send him a message," Lilith said. "Explaining everything. I don't want him to worry. He must be frantic."

"Constantine selected you because you bear a mind and soul worthy of possessing great power," Olga cut in, "to become a mortal instrument for His will."

It was as if the woman hadn't heard her. Lilith looked up into a face of gentle maternity, her attention piqued. Gods, the Oracle must be Elder Tongue for 'mad woman.'

"Your element has been far outnumbered in our history as it is extremely difficult to wield," Olga proceeded. "And the Gods haven't deemed many among our kind worthy of such power. Not even Spiro was blessed with it."

Lilith was flattered, but equally frightened. Hearing those words from the Oracle applied more pressure than she could ever imagine. She'd already begun to dread Arduen's training, and the more she pondered what could lie ahead of her, the more anxious she became.

Olga peered out the window again, a soft smile spreading on her lips, the fine lines on her taught skin deepened. Lilith wondered how old she was. She appeared to be in her fourth decade, but she couldn't be certain.

"Rest tonight, Lilith." Olga patted her shoulder. "Write a letter to Larkin first thing in the morning."

Lilith yielded. Curling up on her bed in fetal position, she tried to force all the worries from her mind, her body begging for sleep. If she was going to survive, she needed to focus on a single task at a time.

With her back to Olga, the Oracle began to hum a melody. On the verge of sleep, she brought the quilt over Lilith's limp frame and quietly took her leave. Lilith was enveloped by fatigue. The sound of crashing waves lulled her into the dreamscape of her mind.

AT DAWN, LILITH JOINED THE OTHERS FOR BREAKFAST. THE kitchen was a large, round stone chamber and the first one entered when they graced the Frourío. In the centre of the room was a large oblong harvest table, enough chairs to sit five families surrounded it. Despite its grand size, the room was cozy, the scent of garlic and cardamom permeating the air.

No one turned to greet her. Lilith waited for everyone to take their seats before she followed suit, wary that there might be assigned seating. Olga sat at the head of the table with Arduen and Quin on either side of her. Julius sat beside Quin, and Lilith, only assuming, lowered herself into the vacant chair beside her Master.

There was a young man serving their breakfast. His name

was Ambrose. Lilith had met him when she first stepped foot inside the Frourío. He was ordained as the designated knight of the Divine, but he also assumed the role of caretaker. His skin was dark-ebony, like the mountain people were rumored to be. He wore a sword on his left hip, the faded leather scabbard matching that of his boots. His attire was covered in the remnants of their breakfast, bits of eggs clung to his dark curly hair, and flour dusted his apron.

The group ate in silence, Lilith devouring her meal far faster than the others, too ravenous to notice the looks of amusement directed her way. Only a moment passed before she slid her empty plate away from her, sated.

Arduen addressed her then. "Your first lesson will commence in the study," he said. "If you will follow me."

"Can I write my brother now?" she asked, a deluge of relief flooding through her when Arduen nodded.

Lilith stood and muttered a quick polite thanks to Ambrose before following her Master up the stairs. With every step, she took note of the carvings on the doors, finer details she'd missed the night before when she was too weary from travel to notice such things. Her door had etchings of what appeared to be an intricate swirl, a symbol of the abyss that now roiled within her.

Arduen came to an abrupt halt in front of double oaken doors. He pulled the latch and they swung inward, revealing a large circular room. The walls were covered entirely with spines of uncountable books. Lilith had never seen anything like it. Her family possessed storybooks passed down through generations, but there were so few of them.

Near the window was a large desk and set neatly upon it were journals and ink pots, feathered quills sitting at the ready beside them. It had been a few years since Lilith had written, long enough that she feared she no longer possessed the skill. She sat down and inspected the artifacts on the table before her.

"It's important—"

The door burst open and Ambrose entered the study. He shot Arduen a regrettable look. Perched upon his arm was a large eagle, its wings flared to stabilize itself. For the first time in days, Lilith truly smiled.

"Dear Lilith would like to send a message," Ambrose announced.

With a sweep of his arm, Arduen gestured for the knight to approach. Lilith perked up as Ambrose lowered his arm and the eagle settled onto the desk.

"This is Evös," said Ambrose. "She is the Divine eagle. Responsible for our correspondence."

Lilith regarded the bird with interest. "There was once an eagle that lived in our backyard," she said. "He used to swoop down and peck at my brother and I as we played with our wooden swords."

Arduen sighed, evidently relieved that his noviciate was talking. He sifted through drawers, then set an ink pot, quill and parchment before her. "Write away," he said.

Lilith eyed the parchment. What would she say to her brother? *Hi Larkin, I'm alive and well. I died a few weeks ago, but now I'm a warrior for the Gods. Don't wait up. See you in a year or two. Have fun surviving on your own.*

Her brother's absence was palpable, as if she'd forgotten how to breathe or walk. She'd never realized he was a crutch until he was no longer by her side. Larkin was the pillar that kept her aloft. The temple that housed her soul. And without him, she was forced to face the gaping, tooth-infested maw that was her grief. It was a beast that had taken residence inside the marrow of her bones. A beast she could never escape.

Dear Larkin, she wrote. Bloody Hades, would he understand? Would he ever forgive her for what she'd done? Gods, she'd damned them both.

Tears pooled in her eyes unbidden, but she wouldn't let them fall. Wouldn't let them snake down her cheeks like the vile serpents they were. At least not until she was alone, or as alone as she ever would be on this perpetual journey.

This is transient, Lilith. You will train, you will learn, and then you will leave.

Evös nudged her hand, the one wrapped around the quill, as if to say, "Write something. I long to be reunited with the sky as you do your brother!"

So Lilith wrote.

It was bland, unfeeling, unlike the turbulent emotions that writhed inside her. If she wrote them, she would break. And she couldn't let Arduen see her weakness.

When she finished, she folded the parchment and Arduen sealed it with wax.

"You can pet her, you know?" Ambrose said. "She won't bite."

Lilith stroked Evös's feathers gently and the eagle preened under her touch.

"Don't touch her chest, though," Ambrose warned. "She only ever allowed my husband to."

Beaming, Lilith inquired, "Does your husband stay with us, too?"

His smile faltered. "My husband departed for Elysium many years ago."

"I-I'm sorry…" Lilith bit her lip. What was she supposed to say to him? *We can relate?*

The knight waved her off. "Don't be. Such is the way of life, but there is still joy to be found in it."

Arduen cleared his throat and opened one of the large windows behind the desk, and Ambrose guided Evös to it. The eagle took off with Lilith's note tied to her leg.

"Thank you, Ambrose," Arduen said, a dismissal of sorts. Then he faced the desk.

"Now, where were we?" he pondered. "Ah, yes! It's important as a young Divine that you are well acquainted with the history of Augusta and the world beyond. It is vital that we thoroughly study our heritage and learn from past misgivings, if only so that we can ensure that our future is greater."

Arduen scanned the shelves, searching for a specific spine. Once he spotted the book, he raised a finger and made to retrieve it. He placed the massive tome in front of Lilith with a thud. *The Complete History of Augusta.*

"You are to read this in the evenings, one chapter a day," he said. "We will discuss what you learned the following morning in this study. I cannot stress the importance of this book, especially in regard to Spiro. Not only is it the Empire's history, but much of it has to do with the Divine interference and how we came to be."

Arduen seated himself across from her and cleared his throat. "We need to discuss what lies ahead of you, Lilith. This life is not easy and, as I am responsible for you to an extent, I need to be certain that you understand what is expected of you as a Divine. There are many unwritten laws that the Gods use to govern us from above." He leaned back in his seat, his eyes settling on her gravely.

Lilith remained silent, her eyes pinned to the tome in front of her.

Arduen continued, "I am rusty when it comes to teaching, so bear with me. Ask all the questions on your mind because you must have an in-depth understanding of the content."

Lilith nodded her understanding. When Arduen didn't continue, she croaked submissively, "Yes, Master."

Pleased, he continued, "The Gods bestow Their element upon one novice at a time, although They can grant existing Divines—that are not Their own—Their element to wield in addition to their originators. Though it is highly unlikely that this will happen again. The Gods have you and Julius bound very tightly—"

"What do you mean?" Lilith asked.

"I mean that it is unlikely that the Gods will heighten your power without your earning it," he elaborated. "That's why I stress to you, Lilith, pray as often as you can. Earn the affection and trust of Constantine, for He is the only one who can grant you the strength you need to fight and survive."

A soul-chilling dread drifted over her like a shroud. Arduen had explained that any Divine who refused to follow the Gods' wills is returned to the soil. It almost seemed like the better option. Life as a Divine was going to be harrowing, with subtle cruelties disguised as rewards.

"I have told you before," Arduen said, "when we become Divine, time is forced to relinquish its hold on us. We refrain from aging as mortals do. Once we reach the peak of our maturity, we halt. Frozen. Yet we function as all other humans and we can be killed just as they can. We grow old over millennia, but we endure."

"How was Spiro able to defy the Gods and remain powerful?" Lilith inquired. "How have They not claimed his life?"

Arduen sighed, steepled his fingers on the desk before him. His pinky twitched rhythmically. Lilith pretended not to notice.

"That is a question that none of us can answer," he said. "We have been researching for decades. We hoped that the Gods would reveal the answer to the Oracle, but They have not."

The atmosphere grew somber and stifling. Lilith was grateful when Arduen announced that it was time for prayer.

◎ ⎈ ⇒ ⋀ ⎔

ARDUEN LED LILITH BACK TO HER BEDCHAMBER WHERE HE instructed her how to formally pray to the Gods. Then he left her in solitude to begin building her relationship with Constantine.

Lilith sat on the floor beside her bed as she pondered her Master's instructions. He'd informed her that the Gods expected them to be undressed when they sought an audience. They must reduce themselves to their most vulnerable state, signifying their obedience, fealty, and trust.

The silence felt eerie and the thought of talking into the air was disconcerting. Checking twice to ensure that the door was locked securely, Lilith reluctantly removed her clothing and knelt beside her bed. Tiny bumps spread across her bare skin as she assumed position. Laying her hands palm-up on the floor, she bowed her head until her brow rested on the wooden boards.

For a long moment she didn't speak. She lay in silence, releasing the tension from her limbs, relishing in the feel of her stiff muscles stretching. She was utterly exhausted despite her long night's rest. However, feeling nothingness wash over her was strangely comforting. Though she didn't speak, she didn't feel alone either. A presence washed over her, neither friend nor foe, but entirely foreign.

A knock at her door sounded through the room. Lilith jumped, hitting the back of her head against the wall.

Ambrose's soft voice echoed into the chamber, "Excuse me, Lilith. Lunch is about to be served. Please join us in the kitchen."

7

A GOOD OMEN

The monotony of her schedule, and the toil of training, helped Lilith to slough the dismal pall that had settled over her since departing Utica. She found Ambrose's cooking to be exceptional, the company at the kitchen table wasn't so bad, either. Julius often engaged in conversation. He asked about her training, and if she had any questions regarding her readings, she was welcome to ask him.

Arduen cleared his throat, sliding his lunch plate toward the centre of the table. He stood and signalled for Lilith to do the same. She acquiesced, offering the others a curt wave before following her Master.

Arduen paused by the base of the staircase. "You will begin the afternoon's lesson in the armory," he said. "Ambrose will fit you with a suitable sword. We will then meet in the training field."

"Master, I already have a suitable sword," she began to

protest. Lilith was reluctant to relinquish Constance. The blade was more than adequate and constructed of Obsidian Steel. It would be a shame not to wield it.

The look Arduen flashed her was regrettable. "I'm sorry, Lilith. It was not forged by our blacksmith and I cannot guarantee that it will hold up as you grow stronger." He turned away, brooking no argument.

Reluctantly, Lilith followed Ambrose downstairs. The spiralling staircase was illuminated by the candle in his hand. When the stairs came to an end, they opened into a dark chamber. The air was musky, damp. Her new boots scuffed against the stone floor, the sound echoed by skittering mice.

"This is the armory," Ambrose proclaimed as he lit the sconces on the walls. "We keep our weapons in the cleanliest condition possible. We don't take kindly to rust. If our blade is to save our life, we must treat it like it possesses life itself."

With the armory illuminated, Ambrose strode forth with arms outstretched, gesturing to the bevy of weapons. The wall he approached bore swords and blades alike, the array ranging from daggers to swords longer than Lilith's outstretched body. She couldn't imagine the audacious size of someone who could wield such weapons. The adjacent wall contained bows and arrows, and the far-reaching wall held weapons that Lilith had never before laid eyes upon.

There were workbenches aligned in rows throughout the space, and behind them, more weapons. She squinted in the dim lighting to get a detailed view; bows, the sight of them pierced her heart. She glanced away instinctively.

Lilith was thankful when Ambrose placed the pommel of a blade in her hand. Curious, she raised it and examined the metal in the glow of the candlelight. It shone as though it had never been used before, as if Ambrose had polished it moments before.

"You must tell me exactly how each blade feels in your hand," he instructed. "It is crucial that you are exact with me, as your survival depends upon the weapon you choose." He studied her as she raised the blade.

"But you wouldn't let me walk out of here with an ill-fitted sword," she countered.

"You can count on me to ensure that you are well equipped. I only ask that you are entirely honest. Not all issues can be seen with the naked eye."

Confused, Lilith replied, "I'm not entirely certain how it's supposed to feel." She flushed with embarrassment. She loathed her ignorance. Her father was gone before he was able to instruct her thoroughly in swordplay; a crucial element in a blacksmith's training.

"It should feel like a deadly extension of your arm itself." Ambrose stood back and studied her as she held the sword and moved it about the air. The weight of the blade tugged at her shoulder uncomfortably.

Ambrose picked up on that. "Maybe that's not the blade for you." He retrieved the sword from her and hung it back on the wall, then proceeded to scan the vast collection of blades nestled in their sheaths.

Lilith spotted another shortsword with a thinner blade. She pointed to it and Ambrose brought it down. He unsheathed the blade and handed it to her. It fit her palm almost perfectly, light enough that she wouldn't tire if she found herself confronted with a lengthy fight.

"I like this one," she said, pleasantly surprised. It wasn't Constance, but it felt fairly similar in her grip, its weight nearly identical.

Ambrose, with his hand clamped thoughtfully on his chin, studied her. He began to circle, his gaze sharp and critical. After a tense moment of silence, Lilith moved the sword around, twisting her arm as she imagined herself in battle with an invisible foe, careful not to slice Ambrose as he rotated around her.

Finally, he nodded his approval. "That shall be your sword, dear Lilith. Treat it well and it shall serve you."

Content, she studied the sword in her hand. The blade shone bright in the dim candlelight, and the smooth metal possessed an emerald sheen that would no doubt intensify in the sunlight. Lilith marvelled at the accuracy of the smith's work. The blade bore no crest as to indicate who had forged it.

"Who's your smith?" she asked.

"We have a designated blacksmith who knows our abilities and strengths and what grade of ore required to compose our weapons. That is a lesson for Arduen to give you, I'm sure."

Lilith continued to study her new blade.

"Now, one last thing," Ambrose interrupted, "what shall you name it?" He looked at her with expectance.

This was always Lilith's favorite part of selling someone a blade: granting the weapon an identity. She contemplated many names. She considered naming the blade after her parents, but it felt wrong deciding between the two. If she called it Larkin… well that just didn't feel right.

"I think I shall name it Oak," she said finally. "For my family."

A delighted smile flared upon Ambrose's face. "Oak it is!"

ARDUEN LED LILITH TO THE TRAINING GROUNDS, A LARGE clearing in the trees to the east of the Frourío. She admired the impressive view of the tower rising up from the peaked pine tops. From the field, she could spot the study and what she thought was the outer wall of her bedchamber. If there was one thing worth rejoicing, it was the majestic view she'd acquired.

The grass was lush and mossy for the time of year, a dark green with the odd gouge in the dirt from boots. Quin and Julius duelled near the trees on the eastern side of the clearing. Arduen and Lilith observed them from afar.

Julius matched his Master's speed and accuracy, their swords clashing and clanging all the while. Their feet shuffled with trained celerity as they parried each other's blows. Sparks flew through the air when their blades met, grunts audible even at a distance.

Arduen signalled to the sword strapped at Lilith's hip. She drew the emerald blade from its scabbard and handed the weapon to him. He studied it for a short moment, his brow slightly furrowed in concentration.

"I had a hunch that you would select this one with it's likeness to Constance. I will teach you how to clean and sharpen your blade after your lesson." He returned the sword to her. "What name did you happen to grant this blade?"

Lilith smiled down at the pommel. "Oak."

"A decent name that is," he said. "And a good omen it is to name your blade after loved ones."

Removing his sword from its scabbard, Arduen pointed it away from his body, demonstrating to her how one must hold the weapon. Lilith tried her best to mimic his pose, frequently glancing over to observe his posture.

"I am first going to focus on your grip," Arduen said. "Then I will critique your stance. Place your hand around the pommel like this." He showed her how his hand was positioned and waited patiently while she made the alterations to her own grip. "You must align your thumb with the blade. Do not grip your sword as you would a hammer, that will restrict your mobility and strength." He repositioned her fingers properly.

Stepping in front of her, Arduen positioned himself as if to duel. "Now watch carefully. Observe first, then attempt to become a mirror reflection of me."

Lilith scanned his body, noting the distance that separated his feet and the angle at which they were offset. She then positioned herself like so.

Arduen murmured his approval, then said, "You must keep your body weight centred on the balls of your feet. Never lean back on your heels, you'll be less stable, and it will be easier for your opponent to throw you off balance." He gripped her shoulder and pushed her backward, and she collapsed with a thud.

"What was that for?" Lilith groused.

Arduen barked a laugh. "Testing to see whether you listened. You didn't. Shift your weight."

Lilith stood and resumed position, shifting her weight several times before he tested her again. She moved, as he was strong, but she did not fall.

"Very good," Arduen commended. "Now I want you to bend more at the knees. This will make it even more difficult for your enemies to knock you down." He waited for her to apply the knowledge before moving on. "Perfect, Lilith!"

She blushed, satisfied with herself.

"It seems," said Arduen, "that you have instinctively chosen to lead with your right leg, but you must be strong enough to lead with both and exchange your blade between hands as well. You must become competent with both arms in the event that your right side is injured. Becoming ambidextrous is not easy, but in the heat of battle, you'll be grateful for it."

Lilith maintained her stance as she waited for further instruction. The clanging of metal and grunts met her ears. Her nerves piqued with every huff that travelled across the field. Would she be strong enough to keep up with Arduen? Maybe this wasn't the best form of battle for her.

Maintaining her pre-approved position, Arduen shifted her arms, allowing her to feel the movements of cutting and striking. His chest was pressed against her backside, and heat singed her cheeks at the closeness of their bodies, foolish as it was. Her nerves abated slightly when he praised the strength of her arms. Forging had paid off, one way or another.

"Now, when I move, you must mirror my movements," Arduen said. "When I cut down, you must cut up. A descending cut is easy to parry, but you must be able to read my body language and react quickly, else you won't have the strength to block me. If your arms are too low when our blades meet, I will overpower you."

Arduen picked up two wooden swords. Keeping one for himself, he handed the other to Lilith. She sheathed Oak and gripped the wooden sword as he had instructed. The mock sword was significantly lighter, easing her consternation.

They assumed starting positions and began to duel. At first, Lilith thought he was moving painfully slow, but within a few minutes, Arduen doubled his speed. She did her best to focus and stay with him, matching his movements with near-perfection. He raised his sword above his head and she lowered hers a moment too late. When their swords met, she was overwhelmed by his strength. A searing sensation lanced up her arm and she let go of her sword immediately. She winced and gasped at the shock.

"That is exactly what I mean by reading my body movements," Arduen scolded. "You must be able to anticipate what I will do next and act instinctively to stop me." He waited patiently for Lilith to retrieve her sword.

Slightly out of breath, she muttered a litany of curses between clenched teeth. Her frustration causing her muscles to tense even more. Her back was already a mess of painful knots, and they'd only just begun.

Arduen spoke softly, "You are doing well for your first time. This takes years of practice, yet you are trying to become the greatest in the smallest amount of time. Expect less and be patient with yourself. Results will come."

Lilith took a deep breath. Arduen had given her a moment to cool down before he attacked. She managed to block several of his blows. Gaining confidence, she took the offensive and began to cut down on him. He reacted faster than she could've imagined, and she lost her sword every time.

Her attacks intensified as Quin and Julius approached. Lilith, determined to impress her audience, spun around in the hopes to take Arduen by surprise. But while she spun, he'd already prepared to block her, and she lost her sword again.

Arduen grinned with blatant amusement. "I admire your creativity and ambition, Lilith, but you must focus on the basics today. I will show you different moves that you can use to throw your foe off guard, but let's keep it simple for now. I want you to duel Julius. Now that there's two of you, it'll be easier for us to critique you."

Dread pooled in Lilith's gut as she watched Julius take the wooden blade from Arduen. She'd seen how fast he and Quin duelled. How dexterous they were with real blades. There was no possibility of her emerging triumphant. She resolved to take the bout motion by motion, cut by cut.

They assumed positions. Julius's brow was beaded with sweat, his chest visibly rising and falling. He was tired. Good.

Several moments passed and neither noviciate shifted even a twitch. Even the slightest flick of the wrist would cause the opponent to jump. Lilith's anxiety calmed as she fixated her eyes on her colleague. He was much too gentle to cause her harm.

Julius moved first, darting forward with impressive speed, jabbing his sword at her ribs. With a slight step backward, she was able to deflect his advance with a swat of her sword. His grip was firm, and his veins bulged on the back of his hand, rising up through his forearm. The sight was enough to restore Lilith's unease, and it was also enough to distract her while Julius slashed upward, catching her in the side. She stumbled and fell to her knees, gasping from the pain.

It took a moment to catch her breath, to gather her bearings. She flashed Julius an angry glare as he extended his hand. A peace offering.

Lilith scoffed. "Why would you do that?" she shouted at him, her voice hoarse, as he lifted her to her feet.

Guilt flashed behind his eyes. "Lilith, I'm..."

Quin's voice rose to answer first, "We fight each other as if we are truly opponents," he lectured. "We must rely on each other every day for the sake of our lives and the lives of everyone in the Empire. Do not forget that. We cannot train lacking in intensity."

Lilith shook her hands clean of dirt and stepped away from Julius with a sneer.

"If it helps," Arduen added, "don't imagine your comrade in front of you. Try picturing a monster or a beast. Try imagining your loved ones in dire need of your aid." His low, gentle timbre eased her anger, but it did nothing to soothe the searing pain in her side. Julius would grant her no mercy.

Taking up position again, Julius waited for her to move first. She did. Lilith slashed at him, holding back nothing now that she understood what was expected of her. He blocked and parried every blow and strike. She did her best to block his cuts, but she managed only to block one for every three he dealt, leaving her covered in aches that would be discolored by morn.

Julius managed to knock her off her feet again, though this time he refrained from landing the final blow. Rather, he let her stumble backward on her own until she finally fell to the mossy ground. She pounded her fists on the earth and jumped to her feet, ready to return to battle.

Arduen cleared his throat before they could resume. "That is enough for today," he said. "Well done, Julius! Well done, Lilith! It's time to bathe and prepare for supper. The three of us will bathe in the sea. As for you, Lilith; Olga will show you to the bathing chamber."

The three men exited the field in the direction of the shore. Julius called back to her, "Don't berate yourself, you did extremely well today. You left not one of us unimpressed."

"I didn't berate myself!" Determined not to accept defeat,

Lilith flashed him a grin that he reflected. He wasn't thrown off, amusement shone in his hazel eyes.

THE BATHING CHAMBER WAS LOCATED TWO FLOORS ABOVE LILITH'S bedchamber. It contained a sink with a polished mirror suspended above, and in the centre of the room, a sunken marble tub. Lilith exchanged her dirty garments for clean ones as the tub slowly filled. Olga placed a towel on the counter and showed her how to drain the dirty water.

Alone, Lilith began to scrub herself clean. The heat helped relax the muscles that seemed perpetually tense. Colorful bruises adorned her limbs. She winced as her fingers brushed over the massive welt on her rib cage, only the beginning of the results from Julius's blow.

When she was finished bathing, she dressed herself in clean clothes and lay on her bed, staring up at the ceiling above. She longed to rest but she refrained, for the scent of roast meat and spices wafted up to her from the kitchen below.

A knock at the door pulled Lilith from her slumber. "Come in," she called.

Expecting Arduen had come to upbraid her for her overt display of frustration on the training field, she was pleasantly surprised to see Olga standing in the doorway instead. The Oracle pushed the door open timidly and slid into the room. She flashed a saccharine smile at Lilith before sitting down on the edge of the bed, her ashy hair a glimmering bird's nest atop her head.

"You did very well today, Lilith," Olga praised. "Don't beat yourself up. You are only learning, and Julius has had years of experience."

"I didn't do as well as I'd hoped," Lilith admitted. "I'm a blacksmith, I should be a decent swordsman."

"*Swordswoman*," Olga corrected.

Lilith chuckled dryly. "Yes, you're right." She sighed and sat up beside her new friend. "I am still so disappointed in myself. I know what's at stake, and my future terrifies me. I just want to be strong and confident enough that I don't have to fear anything." Her throat constricted. She didn't understand how Olga could pull the truth out of her so easily, but it provided relief nonetheless.

"I admire your determination, Lilith. You remind me of myself when I was first Anointed. I understand what it is like to train with only men to challenge you."

Lilith's interest piqued, she asked, "How long ago were you in my position?"

Olga flashed her a mysterious grin. "It was but several centuries in the past, my dear. Not long at all when you consider how long we are meant to live. I have outlived the love of my life and my entire family, yet I am still so young and full of purpose."

Lilith smiled; the Oracle's optimism was contagious. "I bet you have many stories to tell."

Olga released a hoarse cackle, her eyes crinkling at the corners, the only testament to her age. "I do have many, yet not enough time to tell them all. I promise I will share with you all the tales worth reciting."

Lilith laughed, then winced as sparks of pain pierced her side.

Olga frowned, her eyebrows meeting in a fine line. "Let me see that wound, darling."

Doing as she was told, Lilith lifted her blouse for Olga to examine her rib cage. The point of contact was already dark-blue. Around the edges, the blue faded into purple and then a yellowish orange color. Spots of red were scattered throughout where blood vessels had broken. Olga ran her fingers over the wound, feeling for swelling. Lilith bit her lip at the discomfort of it.

"Forgive Julius," she said finally. "He does not realize how strong he has grown over the years. I think this is a worthy wound for healing, considering it could very well impede upon your training, don't you think?"

Olga didn't wait for Lilith to oblige, but instead she closed her eyes, and appeared to be praying. Olga murmured words under her breath, words that Lilith couldn't decipher. Then the Oracle began to rock back and forth, her murmurs growing louder until she was nearly shouting.

As the words faded into echoes, Lilith's skin began to tingle. All the hairs on her body stood on end and her skin turned to gooseflesh. The welt began to bubble like boiling water, the color slowly receding. After a few moments, her skin returned to normal, all signs of bruising and swelling completely diminished.

Olga removed her hand and studied her work. She patted Lilith on the side and proclaimed, "Much better, hmm?"

Lilith stared down at her rib cage in awe. How was this possible? She cast Olga a bemused glance, unsure whether she had thought out loud or not.

Olga responded as if she had, "A gift from the Gods

granted to the eldest living Divine. I couldn't allow you to carry on with a wound that could staunch your training."

Bewildered, Lilith continued to observe her side, pinching her skin. The flesh was numb, unfeeling. It was as if all the nerves that once inhabited that part of her body had died.

"Sensation will return in a few days, dear. Do not fret!" Olga's eyes wandered through the room as Lilith studied her face, fascination clouding her mind. How this woman had endured so much and still held the desire to serve and protect the world gave Lilith inspiration to persevere where she fell short.

Olga's intense gaze fell on her once again. "If you wish, I can spar with you every morning before you meet with Arduen in the study. This will help build your confidence and I promise not to cause you any more pain than the boys will. Those wooden swords are almost worse than the real ones."

Lilith grinned. "I would greatly appreciate that, Olga."

The Oracle clapped her hands together and exclaimed, "Great! There is no better sense of purpose than helping someone in need." She rose to her feet and motioned for Lilith to accompany her. "Now let's get down to the kitchen. I don't know about you, but my stomach is *ravaging*. I could use a good meal and I bet you could, too!" And with that, the two women made their way down the spiral staircase arm in arm.

◎ ⵀ ⵛ ⋏ ◊

AND SO IT WAS, THE NEXT MORNING, WHEN THE SUN HAD NOT YET risen over the treetops, Lilith and Olga made their way to the training grounds. Olga shared little bits of experience with

Lilith every day, helping her to better understand what she was doing and why she was doing it.

At first, Lilith was hesitant to put forth all of her strength, afraid she might hurt Olga. But the old woman proved to be extremely difficult to touch, if not stronger than her. Casting her trepidations aside, Lilith summoned as much strength as she could. She began to read her opponent's movements and anticipate several forms of attack. When next she sparred with Julius, he was beyond impressed with her progress.

"It has been but a week and you're already proving yourself a worthy swordsman!" Julius beamed at her, his teeth sparkling in the sunlight like pearls.

"*Swordswoman,*" Lilith corrected him coyly.

He clapped her on the shoulder. "Keep it up and you'll give me a good run for my drachmae."

8

LARKIN

arkin Oak was frantically trying to survive harvest without his sister. He'd acquired the assistance of her fiancé, Jude, who was splitting his time between his own farm and their field. Worry of Lilith's well-being plagued his consciousness, yet he still had to reap what they'd toiled all year to sow. It wouldn't help his sister's cause if he starved to death over the winter.

Every morning before he began another day of chores, Larkin would tell himself that Lilith would return. *She's just in shock from the incident. She'll be back soon.* But no matter how many times he repeated the words, they never penetrated deep enough to convince.

Larkin had spent his days cleaning up the remnants of their father's smithy. He was able to salvage most of the metal, and the stone forge was still intact. Once harvest was over, he would begin to rebuild. He hoped this would bring Lilith home.

Sweat dampened his brow as he labored, filling each wagon with goods and pushing them to their tiny shack of a barn. He switched back and forth between picking vegetables and cutting wood, working tirelessly until the sun was a faint russet glow on the horizon.

Larkin didn't have much time before the frost would hit, and not long after that, the snow would suffocate Utica, bringing an end to another season. This was dismaying. There was so much work to be done and he only had enough harvested for a couple of weeks. Though he was alone now, he planned to secure enough provisions for two.

The townspeople were on edge since Lilith's disappearance and the destruction of the smithy. Several young men had volunteered as extra guards and were set up along the inner walls of town, ready for the possibility of an attack from the foul beasts. An ominous shroud lay over the town as the weight of terror crashed down upon them. An abiding fear of the beasts and their cultivator, Spiro.

A month had passed since the incident. Larkin found himself avoiding others, he couldn't stand their voices tainted with pity and sympathy. It was shameful for someone to forsake their family, especially one that was already broken.

Working diligently offered him the distraction he needed to keep his thoughts from wandering into darkness. He'd spent most of his nights awake, going over all the possible scenarios in his head. He couldn't believe that he was the last remaining Oak in Augusta, possibly the world. The morbidity of the thought made him ill on several occasions. Lilith couldn't be dead.

Seating himself at the dinner table, Larkin set his bowl of *fassolatha* down on his mother's lace tablecloth. Mah used to scorn him for dropping bits of his meal on it. A faint smile spread across his lips at the memory.

As he so often did, Larkin pondered all the possible places Lilith could have gone. He didn't believe her to be foolish enough to fall prey to the monsters that stalked the lands day and night. No. Lilith was a huntress and she survived dozens of trips out in the wilderness unscathed. She was not preyed upon. She was the predator.

Larkin swirled the last dregs of tea in his mug, lost in contemplation. Rally, having been lying on his sheepskin bed, rose to his paws at Larkin's side and nudged his elbow, spilling tea across the table.

"Shit!" he gasped. The dark liquid spread across the cloth, rendering it transparent, revealing the painting beneath: the map of Augusta.

Larkin retrieved the empty bowl and mug, placing the dishes on the kitchen counter. Then he pulled the cloth from the table in one swift movement, revealing the faded, yet intricately painted map beneath.

At first sight, his mind was overwhelmed with memories of Pa familiarizing his children with the Empire. The lands that they would likely never set their eyes upon. Larkin vividly recalled his father pinpointing where the most significant battles were waged. Larkin hadn't been the highest scoring student, but he was genuinely interested in history and geography.

Larkin gazed down upon the five realms, quickly glancing over each one before settling his stare on his home, Elïath. He dragged his fingers along the shore of the Western Galatëa Sea, until he came to rest upon his hometown and his current location—his *only* location—Utica.

A single tear dripped from his chin onto the scarred wood below. "Where are you, Lilith?" he moaned.

He resolved to turn in for the night when a knock at the door disturbed him. He grumbled. He'd waited what seemed like years for the comfort of his own bed. The knock sounded again, and Rally began whimpering, pawing at Larkin's calves.

"You get the door then," he said caustically. When the canine didn't move but continued to stare at him with imploring eyes and a cocked head, Larkin finally rose to his feet and shuffled to the door.

The knock sounded again.

"I'm coming!" Larkin shouted. It wasn't uncommon for Jude to come over in the middle of the night with some absurd theory justifying Lilith's disappearance.

Unnerved, Larkin grabbed his father's sword, Gladius, before opening the door. Should it turn out to be a beast, he would slay it without a moment's delay.

Larkin opened the door to be faced with two men clad in the Emperor's uniforms. The Emperor's Frourà: The Guard. Both men were middle aged with soft features, probably nervous being outside so late. No one dared venture into the darkness except for the Emperor's Frourà or Milítia. They were the only humans who could match Spiro's beasts in battle. The soldiers spent nearly a decade in brutal training before they were considered fully capable of serving the Empire.

Larkin waited a moment, uneasy, and then returned Gladius to its sheath when he was certain that the soldiers meant him no physical harm.

"We are here to speak with Larkin Oak, elder brother of

Lilith Oak." They spoke in unison, their formality at odds with their disheveled appearance.

Larkin bit into his lip. Should he cover for himself? He could claim that he was a friend watching over the house while the real Larkin was out searching for his missing sister. He decided better of it. The truth would always come to light, and if he were caught lying to the Emperor's Frourà, he would face the gallows.

"I am Larkin," he said.

The two soldiers continued to speak in unison, their tones dissonant. "You have been summoned by Emperor Obadïa in regard to your sister's disappearance and the devastation of London Oak's smithy."

Larkin hadn't expected interference from the Empire. People went missing often enough that it didn't arouse suspicion. Many of Spiro's beasts could eat a human whole, leaving no trace. Why had Lilith's disappearance disturbed the Emperor? In most cases, it was the family who went knocking on the Emperor's doors, pleading for help. And that was only if they could survive the trip to Kenora.

Without hesitating, Larkin asked, "When will this meeting take place?"

The soldiers exchanged glances and chuckled. "You are to accompany us to the capital," one replied curtly.

Larkin couldn't leave, not for a few weeks. When he asked the soldiers if the Emperor could hold off until harvest's cessation, they broke into a fit of hysterical mirth. "Emperor Obadïa waits for no one, not even his concubines!" They continued to laugh, tears welling in their eyes.

Larkin didn't understand what was so hilarious. Surely they understood his predicament. Travelling to the capital would take over a week on horseback, excluding inclement weather. Even if he met with the Emperor upon his arrival and was dismissed minutes later, he would still return home after first frost. He was doomed to starve. But to deny the Emperor's orders meant public humiliation—or execution.

"Will you come willingly or not? You do realize that your options are limited to one." Only one soldier spoke this time. He was the taller of the two, his silver-gauntleted hands larger than Larkin's head.

"I will go with you."

9

NO EASY LIFE

The days began to meld together. Every morning Lilith stepped onto the training field to spar with Olga. When the Oracle had other business to attend to, Lilith deviated to long runs through the pines. The activity gave her a sense of freedom that only hunting ever could before. Her thoughts gave way to a sense of independence and liberation as she navigated through the masts at top speed.

Following her morning exercise, she'd return to the Frourío where she bathed quickly before joining Arduen in the study. This shortly became her favorite part of the day as she loved discussing what she'd read the previous evening. The Empire's history was intriguing, and much of Augusta's past was woven like a fairy tale.

In the study, Arduen seated himself across from her. "What did you read last night?" he asked. "Give me a full summary and analysis, please."

"Yes, Master." Lilith, excited that this had been the first chapter where the Divine were mentioned, summarized what she'd learnt. She emphasized that the Gods rarely interfered with political matters on earth, but the two rulers of East and West Augusta were at war with one another. After an atrocious amount of bloodshed, the Gods felt a great responsibility to restore the world to its former glory by introducing the Divine. And the Gods created Elïath. He was a noble knight of West Augusta. He'd died in battle from an arrow to the throat. Elïath was able to halt the Great War and negotiate terms of a treaty between the two monarchies.

"Very good, Lilith," Arduen commended. "Do you have any questions regarding what you read? I want to proceed with today's lesson."

"What is an Athánatos Star?"

Arduen spoke almost wistfully. "It's the gift to us from the Gods. A Star in the sky, crafted from the ashes of our earthly body. It smolders for as long as we reside in Elysium."

"How?"

Arduen flashed her a patient smile as he explained, "Another Divine must sing the Hymn of Divination over the body. As the song comes to an end, the body dissipates and creates the new Star."

"How is that possible?"

"The Gods. Anything is possible when we open ourselves to Them."

Lilith regarded her Master with a furrowed brow, not totally convinced. "Will you be teaching me the Hymn?"

"Eventually." Arduen, having sensed the mood change, studied her face. His tone softened as he said to her, "Do not fret about the things we cannot change. This is no easy life, Lilith, but I promise you that there is joy to be found in it."

She could only whisper in response, "Yes, Master." She had a few questions about Elïath but kept them to herself. Instead she asked, "Why is it that Augusta has only one ruler now?"

Her Master seemed pleased with her question. "The King of the Western monarchy failed to produce an heir, so when the last king passed, he submitted his kingdom to the eastern monarchy. That is how we have the united Empire we do today. The nation was split into five realms in honor of the first Divines: Elïath, Sonös, Aspéndos, Dodöna, and Hélorus."

Arduen sat back in his chair, clearing his throat, he stated firmly, "Enough of this talk! Tell me, child, what do you know of magic?"

Lilith shook her head. "I didn't think such a thing really existed. Utica has a fortune teller, but I always thought the prospect a silly one, illegitimate. At least that is what my mother always taught me. No one can know the future for certain."

Arduen smiled smugly. "Ah, but there is such a thing. It's considered dark, obverse of Divine, therefore we may never wield it. It is strictly forbidden and failure to oblige by this rule will result in death by the Gods."

Disappointed, Lilith allowed her bottom lip to protrude slightly. She'd always dreamed of summoning and willing the world to change about her without lifting more than a finger.

"Only Enchantresses may wield magic. Though we have had to ally ourselves with them on many occasions, we have never taken it upon ourselves to attempt their craft: to legislate magic. It would mean sudden death for us. Only those who bear the Mark possess the ability to command magic through the use of ancient words."

"Ancient words… Elder Tongue?" Lilith asked.

"Elder Tongue," Arduen confirmed, a spark of sprite igniting in his eyes. "The ancient language breathes life into magic. The same spell could be uttered by a powerful Enchantress or Magí in Modern Tongue and it will result in nothing. Elder Tongue is the tool to unlocking greater power. All those who can wield magic are extremely well versed."

"What is a Magí?" she asked.

"A male who bears the Mark of magic."

"Can you speak Elder Tongue?"

"Most Master Divine are fluent," he said. "Julius has become exceedingly well versed over the past year. He's had many years of instruction in Dalegonè, as well."

Lilith gazed up at her Master, perplexed. "Will you be teaching me?"

Arduen released a breathy laugh. "Yes, we will get to it eventually. But as war may well be approaching us, it does not take precedence. Bearing knowledge of the language will not save your head in battle."

"Where do the Enchantresses live?"

"They are located in the Obsydían Marsh, far to the southeast of the Forest. Their community is split into four covens, each worship one of the Guiding Stars. They acknowledge the Gods' existence and they fear Their wrath, despite their own power.

"They are governed by the High Enchantress, Ophelía. She was appointed many centuries ago by Astoría Glades, the Enchantress who founded the Obsydían Marsh and freed the Enchantresses from the Empire's oppressive thrall."

"They live together, but do they marry? Do their husbands live in the Marsh, too?"

Arduen shook us head, expression dismal. "No men are permitted to live in the Marsh. Not even a Magí. An Enchantress must seek out mates throughout the Empire and when she returns with child, she will give birth among her sisters. The child must be female and bear the Mark, otherwise the babe is discarded."

Lilith let her voice falter slightly. "What do they do with the babies who don't bear the Mark?" There was another level of cruelty for those who could harm or *let* harm come to a child.

"Most of them are delivered to the capital to become orphans or slaves. If the males do possess the ability to summon and dictate magic, then they are usually claimed by the Emperor and trained as Magí for the Milítia—the army."

Arduen clapped his hands and said, "I think that's enough for today. It is essential that you know what is expected of you by Constantine, so let us pray."

◎᛬ ᛏ ᛝ ᛘ ᛦ

THE KITCHEN TABLE WAS LITTERED WITH FOOD; BOWLS OF steaming vegetables, meat, potatoes, and sauces. Lilith had to restrain herself from scooping too much onto her plate. Hunger pains had been eating at her insides since she left the training field that afternoon.

Arduen was the first to break the silence. Clearing his throat, he said, "Quintus and I have discovered another camp due west of here, only two miles from the Frourío. I think it wise that we send you, Julius, and you, Ambrose, to take care of it. We cannot have beasts this close to us."

Ambrose sat erect, squaring his shoulders with renewed purpose. "I will get my things in order straight away."

Julius placed his utensils down on his plate with a clank. "When do you wish us to leave?" he asked, voice rippling with zeal.

"We think it would be best for you to leave tonight. It shouldn't take you long to break them and take their supplies," said Quin.

"Make sure you investigate their camp thoroughly," Arduen added sternly, holding eye contact with both Julius and Ambrose. "It is vital that we discover anything indicative of Spiro's plans. The lands have been unusually peaceful these past few months."

Julius gave a reverent dip of his chin and resumed consuming his meal at an accelerated pace. Ambrose sat with his arms crossed, lost in deep contemplation, creases appearing on his forehead.

"Is it just the two of us?" the knight asked.

"Yes, the two of you will manage," said Arduen. "When I was last there, it seemed that there were only six beasts. If you see more than you can handle, retreat immediately. Do not tarry. We cannot afford to lose you." He fixed a stiff gaze on Julius.

"Can I accompany them?" Lilith inquired. She longed to escape the Frourío. An adventure would be ideal, yet she doubted Arduen would allow her to join.

"I am afraid you are not ready, Lilith. When you have more experience handling a blade, I'll be more confident sending you on a raid. For now, I feel as though you will only be an added responsibility for Julius and Ambrose. They cannot be distracted worrying about your safety." Arduen was kind when he spoke, not as stern as Lilith had expected, yet his words stung like a backhanded blow.

"I understand, Master." Lilith couldn't mask the disappointment in her voice.

"Your time will come, Fledgling," he assured.

⚬

LILITH RETURNED TO HER BEDCHAMBER, SLUMPING DOWN ONTO her windowsill with a sigh. From her window, she watched as Julius and Ambrose prepared for their mission. Sharpening their swords, extra daggers set in their belts, bows on their backs. She longed to join them. It was the strongest sense of aspiration she'd experienced since she'd arrived.

An idea crept into her mind as the men bowed their heads in prayer. They'd only remain like that for a short period of time—she didn't have long. Grabbing her pillows, she placed them under the quilt, making a slightly too-bulky façade of her body fast asleep beneath the covers. Hastily, she donned her leather sparring suit, the same one the men wore. The vital areas were reinforced with boiled leather, suitable for action. Fastening Constance to her hip, Lilith checked her handiwork. She only needed a few more items before she deemed herself fit for battle.

Lithe as a feline, she crept down the spiral staircase, listening for anyone that may be in the kitchen. The Gods were on her side. The kitchen was vacant, the room rendered dark by the setting sun.

She continued down to the armory. Once she'd equipped

herself with well-fitted and essential gear—a bow and a full quiver—she crept out of the Frourío and disappeared into the Forest, exactly where Julius and Ambrose had entered just moments before.

Once she was certain that she was concealed by the colorful leaves, Lilith bowed her head and recited a quick prayer to Constantine.

THE ENCHANTRESS

Rhéa nestled herself comfortably into the sofa that lined the southern wall of her mother's home. The walls were made of dragon bone, as all cottages in the Marsh were required to be. Her mother often recited the tale of how she'd acquired them; how she had convinced one of the Emperor's battalions to trudge through the Orösía Mountains to the Obsydían Marsh, carrying the bones upon their metal-plated shoulders. It took nearly ten men to carry each rib of the gargantuan beast. Her mother had bewitched them, a manipulative gift that every Enchantress possessed, though very few could wield it effectively.

Rhéa relinquished a strained sigh. Which hour would she lose her mind? How it was possible for the others to remain in this reclusive domain while there was so much astir within the Empire, it never ceased to amaze her. Yet here she was.

For several years since Rhéa's return, she had done nothing but sit and confer with the other Enchantresses. She trained often with others of the Ilíos coven, yet Rhéa found their antics meddlesome and insignificant.

Tatiana DaSylvà, her mother, was the First in command of the Thirteen of the Ilíos. The Thirteen eldest of every coven answered to the High Enchantress. They held sway in any vote or trial, as the voice of their coven.

After hours of tending to Ophelía's needs, her mother stormed into the cottage, door slamming shut behind her, rattling the entire structure. Rhéa shot out of her seat and stood at attention, awaiting her mother's approval to speak, but it was Tatiana who broke the painstaking silence first.

"The Thirteen have been summoned to meet with Ophelía. The others are on their way over."

Rhéa perked up. "For what reason?" Only the most severe quandaries required a meeting with the Council of Thirteens.

Tatiana rolled her eyes, irritated. Council meetings were time consuming and tedious. "We are to send an Enchantress to serve Emperor Obadïa as healer."

"Ophelía is sending an Enchantress to the capital?"

"Yes... I don't see why she'd refuse the Emperor. At least only for a duration of time. It's just a matter of *who* we send and from which coven." Tatiana thrust her spider-silk scarf onto the table.

Rhéa raised her arms into the air, a grand and dramatic gesture. "It must be someone from the Ilíos! We are the most skilled in the practice of healing. You are the First of the Thirteen, can't you persuade Ophelía to send me?"

Her mother's annoyance was redirected at her daughter. "I have no doubt that you can manage, and I do believe the other leaders would agree with me, but it is not us who need convincing." Tatiana paused and cast Rhéa a dour, knowing glance. "Ophelía would never allow it. She has not favored you since your return."

Rhéa scowled. "It's been years since I graced the Marsh with my presence, and Ophelía slackened that leash several Solstices ago. There is no practical reason to send anyone else if I am graciously volunteering my service."

Tatiana only chortled and said, "I will do what I can, but something tells me that the High Enchantress won't be effusive when she hears your name."

⟡ ⟡ ⟡

Common Enchantresses were exempted entrance into the Council, so Rhéa could only wait. She spent the time scouring through her mother's salves and vials of potions meant for healing broken flesh. Knowing her mother would never deny her, she stuffed what supplies she could into her pack before seating herself at the kitchen table, tapping her fingers restlessly as she waited.

Several hours passed before her mother finally returned.

"And?" Rhéa asked, instantly rising to her feet, her pack hanging from her shoulder.

Tatiana eyed the bulging bag. "Sit down," she ordered, though not unkindly. Rhéa did no such thing, only prodded her mother to elaborate on the meeting. "Do as you're told," her mother admonished, warning coating her tone.

Rhéa obeyed.

"An Enchantress from Ápeiro Astéri has been chosen," Tatiana stated. The Infinity Star coven was renowned and celebrated for their expertise in wisdom and guidance—*not* healing.

"Who?" Rhéa demanded.

"Selene Anastas."

She tore her eyes from her mother and pouted.

"Rhéa, I'm only going to ask you once, why do you insist that you travel to the capital?" Maternal concern transformed her mother's demeanor instantly.

"Miles resides in the capital. I must find my way to him. If that means that I must do so under Ophelía's nose, then so be it." Her husband was mortal, Rhéa was not. Their years together were limited. "I don't want to waste the remainder of our years."

"Remember what happened the last time you crossed the High Enchantress…"

"Yes," Rhéa acknowledged, "and I have given you two beautiful grandchildren because of that. Are they not worth the sacrifice?"

Tatiana released a gust of air as if her daughter had struck her. "You are all worth the price! I just wish you would go about this properly. What of them? What of your childrens' mortal years?"

Rhéa only waved off her mother's questions, but Tatiana continued, "And when the Frourà turns Selene down at the castle gates? What will you do then? Do not assume Ophelía wouldn't stoop so low as to harm your beloved. Your children won't be safe. Miles won't be safe." She never mentioned that she wouldn't be safe, either.

"If I fail to intercept Selene," Rhéa explained. "Then I will deal with the consequences."

"Rhéa…"

"I won't be gone for too long. If I can intercept Selene, I can make an arrangement with her. I just need to be with Miles for a few weeks, no more. I will ensure that Selene lays low. No harm will come to my family, lest Ophelía wishes to endure a long, slow death at the mighty hands of Rhéa DaSylvà!"

Tatiana cackled at the crude gesture her daughter made. "You know that I will cover for you. I always have, as is expected of any mother. But how do you know this Enchantress will take kindly to you stealing her quest?"

Rhéa gave a shrug of nonchalance. "I don't know, but like I said, I will deal with the consequences. You just claim ignorance. Ophelía can't scry me in the capital. I will only get caught if she finds Selene here, and then she will punish me and no one else."

"How do you know that?" Tatiana arched a manicured brow.

"Because Ophelía delights in my torment," Rhéa said darkly.

"She will punish every one of us who deceived for your sake. And then she will go for your children to get even."

"Am I a bad mother?" Rhéa asked vulnerably.

Tatiana took her daughter's hand. "No, you were just born into an incredibly trying situation. Perhaps someday, under other leaderships, our lives can be much less beleaguered and much more… *lively*."

Rhéa agreed before she began sifting through her belongings, ensuring that she hadn't forgotten anything important.

"If you're going to do this, you best get a move on before dawn, while the dusk cloaks your leave."

Rhéa turned her back to her mother and thrust her long hair over her shoulders. All the women in her family had been born with dark waves. Even Tatiana's hadn't grayed in the many centuries she'd trod the earth. On many occasions, Rhéa braided her own daughter's hair. She missed her so much sometimes, her body ached because of it. Missing out on the limited years of her family's mortal existence was a grand mistake, and one she knew she would come to regret. Unless she could convince her daughter to accept the Mark, to make the oath… *Stars be damned*, that would be foolish!

Clasping her mother around the waist in a gentle embrace, Rhéa kissed her cheek and thanked her. "I will scry you," she said.

Tatiana's reply was dripping with sarcasm, "Oh, I'm sure you will."

◎ ⓑ ⟿ ᶆ ◊

WITH HER FAMILIAR, EZÍO, SOARING OVERHEAD, SURVEYING THE road for possible dangers, Rhéa rode forth into the darkness. She didn't dare look back, not even to check for pursuers. She was an Enchantress of the sun, an Enchantress of the Ilíos coven.

The winds were changing, they had been for months. This was a gift from the Guiding Stars, bestowed upon the Enchantresses only: reading and assessing the air.

The coming and going of another era was upon them, and having already survived one, Rhéa deigned it impossible to avoid entangling herself in the whims of transition. Indeed, like a spider's web, she was caught whether she liked it or not, and she would will the outcome to be of her own devise. The Dark Age was coming to an end, and Rhéa would stand among the vanguard that brought about the new age.

The shadows swallowed her whole as she galloped into the night, spurring her steed into a full sprint. The Obsydían

Marsh had become a pinprick in the distance, far behind her now. She'd packed only a few personal belongings when she readied herself for the trip ahead. Time was of the utmost concern as she needed to arrive at the capital before Selene, otherwise she would never succeed in convincing the Emperor's Frourà that she was the official healer sent by the High Enchantress.

"I am coming for you, my love," Rhéa breathed into the air, willing the wind to carry the message to her beloved.

11

GÏSTROOT AND MÓLYEYE

Maybe this was a harebrained idea. Maybe it wasn't. Regardless, Lilith sprinted, determined to catch the men before they advanced too far ahead. She remained a safe distance behind. She would need to break her espionage soon, before Julius or Ambrose picked up on her and attacked. It would be difficult to recognize her, veiled as she was by the night and the trees, and something about their dexterity told her that neither man would miss a shot in the dark.

Within the coverage of the branches sat Julius and Ambrose. They appeared to be devising a plan of attack. Lilith didn't know how, but she'd sensed their presence long before they entered her line of sight.

She sat patiently, careful not to move before they did. She couldn't see the camp, though she could hear the beasts' caterwauls, their voices ranging from screeches to thunderous grunts. Images of the beast she'd killed flashed through her mind. Lilith didn't know if she could face them again, but she wanted to try, she wanted to be capable.

The steady beat of a drum reverberated through the ground, and she wasn't entirely convinced that the beat wasn't her own traitorous heart. The leaves around her shook with every bone-jarring beat, droplets of water spraying off of them with every vibration. The lush foliage was so full of life, ignorant to the evil that sojourned within its territory. The rhythm compelled her feet to dance, but she ground her heels into the Forest floor in rebellion.

A flicker of movement tore Lilith from her reverie. Her attention fixated on Julius, she waited patiently, her fingers tapping her knee to the rhythm of the monsters' music.

The shadow caught her attention yet again. A beast. It was aware of Julius and Ambrose, but they weren't aware of it.

Before the brute could attack her comrades from behind, Lilith nocked an arrow, strung her bow, took aim, and fired. The arrow pierced the beast's giant head, embedded halfway through its thick skull. It fell to the ground with a thud, lifeless.

Julius and Ambrose whipped around instantly. They stared at the beast in shock, bafflement. Lilith rose to her feet, taking advantage of their temporary perplexity. They relaxed slightly when they saw her. Although Julius was more interested in ensuring that the other beasts hadn't heard anything. To their luck, they remained boisterous and ignorant of their company.

Ambrose approached her on silent feet. "Thank you for that," he whispered. "We'd both be gone had you not followed us."

"You're welcome." She flashed him a modest grin. "Does this mean I've earned my right to stay?"

Ambrose sighed. Though his face was mostly obscured by the darkness, she could make out an expression of defeat. "Yes, you can stay," he relented, "but you must obey our orders. Every one of them."

Lilith nodded excitedly and followed Ambrose. She listened to the men as they conversed, but she couldn't take her eyes off the beast's corpse behind them, paranoid that it wasn't truly dead. Did they possess enough of a brain for that sort of trickery?

"So that's the plan then. Listen up, Lilith!" Julius whisper-shouted. "You," he pointed to her, "will shoot the beast in the lookout. Get rid of him first so that he can't sound the horn and warn the others of our presence."

Julius's eyes darted around the camp as he machinated. "Then, Ambrose, you sneak up and take their weapons. They don't look worthy of our own hands, so destroy them. When they do see us, I want them unarmed. Most of these beasts will be formidable opponents without a weapon, and there are too many to take on at once if they're armed."

Julius regarded Lilith again. "Shoot the watchman on my command. I'll approach from the west side of camp. Ambrose, do not enter until I'm situated on the other side. Lilith, you are not to enter the camp at all, understand?" His hazel eyes narrowed in warning, as if to say, *Cross me, I dare you.* "You will pick off the beasts one by one with your bow. I trust your aim to be accurate enough not to hit us."

Lilith didn't like the idea of remaining on the sidelines of battle, but she had to admit, she had no real fighting experience. The one thing she did have: exceptional skill shooting at a moving target.

Not a moment later and Julius set off for the other side of

camp, crouching and observing, camouflaged by the foliage. Ambrose waited patiently, his demeanor revealing no sign of anxiety or excitement.

After receiving the signal from Julius, Ambrose nodded a sign of approval in Lilith's direction. It was time. Her bow already strung, she took aim and waited for Ambrose's second signal. Once he gave her another nod, she released the arrow. A second later, the watchman was no longer visible atop the lookout. The only telltale sign that he was dead was the lack of alarm.

They were clear to enter camp.

Ambrose gave Lilith a clap of approval on the shoulder. "May the Gods watch your back." Then he disappeared through the brush. He moved fast into the camp, crouching so as not to be seen. The monsters continued to bellow their songs, cavorting around the fire, oblivious of their Divine presence.

The weapons—mostly clubs and long glaives—were situated at the base of the lookout. Ambrose hid behind the scaffold, his eyes fixed on the beasts that were only a stone's throw away.

Perturbed, Lilith wanted to scream at him to remove the weapons quickly, but Ambrose didn't. Instead, he crouched, clasped his palms together, and... *prayed*? She rolled her eyes and muttered a curse under her breath.

When Ambrose finally lifted his head, the weapons caught fire. He remained where he was. The monsters didn't take notice of the fire immediately; they continued to dance and sing, wrestling each other by the campfire.

Lilith blinked once, twice, thrice. *Ambrose is a Magi?*

Anticipation getting the best of her, Lilith strung her bow

and took aim at the dancing figures. Ambrose lifted his finger, signalling that he wasn't ready. She waited, keeping an eye on the beasts, searching for any trace of Julius among the trees beyond.

Another long moment passed, and they went unnoticed. Lilith's legs had begun to tingle. She'd been crouching for far too long. She wanted nothing more than to run into the camp screaming, with Constance brandished above her head. Instead she vowed to be on her best behavior and follow the orders she'd been given. She'd already broken too many rules tonight.

At the far side of camp, branches shook, then Julius emerged, swift as a wolf. He grabbed a beast from behind and slit its throat. He was merciless in his animalistic rage, yet elegant with his movements, his halo of raven curls a tenebrous cloud. A vitriolic grin lit his features. He was a true warrior, fearless and lethal, and at the same time, regal. Every move graceful, calculated.

The monsters around the fire bellowed and pounded their giant fists upon their hairy chests. Corded muscle rippled beneath their rough, oily hides. At the sound of their anguished cries, Lilith's heart palpitated. A vision of the beast that had once trounced her played unbidden in her mind. "Keep it together, Lilith," she breathed.

Without delay, the beasts angled for their weapons, then let out another cry of outrage. Nothing remained of their weapons but a pile of burning embers. Ambrose chose the moment to emerge from behind the lookout. He charged toward them, gladius drawn, an angry bellow sounding from his mouth.

Heady, Lilith watched as Julius and Ambrose fought.

They slew each adversary within seconds. Their bodies moving so fast between each monster, she was reluctant to fire any arrows into the cluster of bodies lest she hit one of them.

Several of the beasts tore away from the battle and disappeared into the Forest. Were they worth pursuing? Lilith resolved to let them flee. It was safer to remain where she was and watch over Julius and Ambrose, should one of them get into trouble.

A large beast with three ram horns curling from its brow knocked the sword from Ambrose's hand. Astonished, Ambrose looked up at the beast, giving no indication that he intended to retrieve his weapon. Lilith took aim at the monster and fired. The arrow pierced the back of its shoulder. The beast lifted its head and roared to the stars as blood ran down its back in a thick rivulet. It tore the arrow from its flesh and broke it over one knee.

The brute roared at Julius and Ambrose, baring several layers of colossal teeth, each tapered as if filed to points. Bloody streams ran down the beast's olive hide from several punctures, suffusing in pulses.

Ambrose hastily retrieved his sword and assumed a defensive stance beside Julius. Any sign of dread that once painted the knight's features had completely diminished, replaced with an admirable determination.

Nocking another arrow, Lilith waited for the opportunity to fire. Behind her, a stick cracked.

She spun on her heels. A small beast stood over her, grinning mockingly, its face contorted. She let out a shriek of terror as the beast bore its long talons into her thigh, leaving several deep gashes. She lashed out but to no avail. Before she could strike, the beast had turned tail and fled. Lilith wasted no time. She gathered her wits, took aim and fired.

The little beast fell a yard away. Lilith rose to her feet, wincing as blood spilled down her leg. To be sure she'd killed it, she fired a second arrow at the corpse, embedding it into the centre of its back. It was lifeless.

Lilith turned back to camp, wincing as pain spread through her thigh. The men were still fighting. Julius was mounted on the herculean beast's shoulders, slashing into its chest with his dagger. Ambrose remained on the ground, slicing from below. They stabbed until the beast finally toppled.

As it tottered, Julius dismounted and landed gracefully beside Ambrose. They nodded to each other in approval. Then Ambrose began to search the camp while Julius made his way over to her.

"I heard you scream," he said worriedly. "Are you all right?" His eyes were rounded with concern, and Lilith struggled to find the words to ease his anxiety.

"There was a s-stray," she stuttered, "and it caught me off guard. I heard it approach, though it still managed to slash me… I'm bleeding." She indicated her leg, the tears in her leather suit stark in the light of the moon.

Julius muttered a curse. "We can't leave Ambrose here alone. But we must get you back to the Frourío immediately. We have to tend to this." His eyes flicked to her thigh warily. "We should tell Olga. I know you broke rules tonight and you probably don't want Arduen to find out, but you don't want to lose your leg, do you?"

Lilith shook her head, avoiding his gaze. This whole evening had been a mistake. She was a fool! She'd fought well, but she wasn't quite fast enough. Arduen had been right.

Julius rushed to Ambrose to notify him of her condition. The Magí pinched the bridge of his nose between two fingers, frustration evident upon his face. Lilith couldn't discern much beyond that, but it was clear that whatever they found in the camp was worthless. The men set fire to whatever structures and belongings remained and retreated into the Forest.

Faint, Lilith could no longer stand on her own two feet. Julius caught her as she swayed, and he lowered her to the ground gently. As she lay between her comrades, Ambrose cut the leather around her gash to expose the wound. He inspected it, lips pursed in concentration. This close, Lilith could see the splatters of ichor staining his ebony skin.

Ambrose poked at the wound, eliciting a sharp wheeze from Lilith. The gashes wept blackened blood, and the surrounding skin had begun to turn a greenish hue. Already, it emitted a pungent scent, and a yellowish fluid blended with her blood. There were three lacerations in total, the two outer incisions were shallow, but the middle one was a few inches deep.

Lilith released a hoarse gasp. Never had she been so severely injured. Surely blacksmithing offered many instances where one could be gravelly wounded, but Papa had always preached of precautions.

"It's okay," Julius said, unsuccessful at masking the worry in his voice. "We're going to get you home."

Ambrose frowned. "We'll have to take turns carrying her."

Julius placed an arm under Lilith's shoulders and his other under her knees. Sparks of pain lanced up her thigh, through her hip and into the pit of her stomach. Crying out, she leaned over and retched bile.

"I'm sorry," he said. "This isn't going to be a comfortable trip home."

Lilith closed her eyes, resting her head on Julius's chest, her throat burning. At first, his footsteps caused her a great deal of pain, but after a few moments she began to fade in and out of consciousness, taking no notice of whose arms were wrapped around her.

LILITH CAME TO ON HER BED, TWO LONG LEGS BRACKETING HER own. She glanced up. Julius's sunset eyes peered down at her, wide with worry.

"How are you feeling now?" he asked, voice raw. "You've been out longer than we'd like." His eyes were rimmed by dark circles; a testament to his own exhaustion.

"I'm not sure. My entire leg is numb, and my head is pounding. I feel nauseous…" She scanned the room for a place to be sick.

"Ambrose is in the kitchen preparing a concoction to kill the infection. Beast talons are toxic. You'll start hallucinating soon if you haven't already. We are trying to administer the antidote as quickly as possible. Once we've done that and your wound is clean, we will stitch you up." Julius rested his head against the wall behind him, and Lilith relaxed her shoulders into the rise and fall of his chest.

"Ambrose can't heal me?"

If Julius was confused by her question, he didn't show it. "No, he isn't strong enough."

Ambrose rushed into the room then, the scent of something astringent drifting in his wake. Cradled in his arms was a large bowl and various vials were packed haphazardly into his palms. He dropped into a crouch beside Lilith, his eyes limned with rue.

"This will hurt," he warned. "That's why I put Julius behind you. Most people think the stitches cause the most pain but that's not true. This antidote will kill the venom and it will cause your leg to burn. By instinct, you'll want to flee, but please *do not* move. Dig deep. Try to remain still and it'll be over soon."

Arduen pushed through the door, Olga shadowing him. Lilith's chest seized as their eyes met from across the room. But her Master said nothing as he approached and inspected her injury.

Ambrose addressed her Master, "I have gïstroot and mólyeye."

Arduen nodded once in response, jaw set firm, eyes panning Lilith's mangled skin. Why wasn't he chastising her for being so rash?

"The gïstroot will leave your skin insensate," Ambrose said, returning his attention to Lilith. "The mólyeye will help with the pain. I've added an extra fluidrachm, ensuring that you won't become infected from within." With pursed lips, he began to work, using a lancer to carve away the flesh that had been rendered unsalvageable from the poison.

To distract herself, Lilith turned to Olga. "Can you heal me?"

The Oracle stroked Lilith's hair and tutted. "I cannot," she demurred. "The Gods will not allow it. It is Their power that enables me to heal. If They will not grant it, I cannot be of much more assistance than moral support."

"Why won't They—"

"Ready, Lilith?" Ambrose cut in, regarding her with raised brows.

Julius offered her a cloth. "For you to bite down on," he said. "You can squeeze my hands too, if it helps."

Lilith placed the cloth between her teeth and gripped Julius's hands. He folded his over hers, his thumbs stroking a soothing rhythm along the sensitive skin of her palms. She focused on the swirling scars that decorated his forearms, her eyes grappling for anything to distract her from the pain. Anything other than her Master's glare.

Ambrose scooped a ladle-full of the steaming antidote and let the clear liquid drip over her wound. At first, Lilith felt nothing, but in a matter of seconds, her entire leg began to burn.

Arduen held her down by the ankles as Ambrose continued to administer the antidote. The coagulated blood began to bubble. It took all of Lilith's remaining strength not to writhe. Julius held her against him with both his arms wrapped around her chest. She bit down hard on the cloth, her hands squeezing Julius's forearms with all her strength, which was—fortunately for him—feeble at the moment.

Ambrose poured the last of the antidote onto her gashes and waited. He then began to stroke the wound with a damp towel.

Tears rushed from her eyes as he probed the wound, distributing the antidote throughout the incisions. She ground a litany of colorful curses between her teeth, whilst Julius whispered prayers in her ear. She focused on the words he said as he prayed to each God for shielding and healing. His words offered a slight distraction from the agony. She tried to focus on each syllable in an attempt to block out the sensations, but it was in vain.

When Ambrose finished, he sat back on his heels and examined her wound. Layers of flesh could be seen inside the swollen gash, but her blood ran red. Pure.

"It's time to stitch this up," Ambrose announced, glancing up at Olga.

Lilith sank back into Julius. She wanted nothing more than for this to be over. She wanted to sleep, even if the monsters chased her through her dreamscape.

The Oracle took only a few minutes to sew her up. Once she'd studied her handiwork, once she deemed it would suffice, Julius released Lilith and sat back against the wall with a sigh. Beneath her, she could feel his muscles relax.

"You must be monitored throughout the night," Olga said, casting a knowing look at Arduen. Her Master stood at the end of her bed, silent and watchful. "I am certain that we've killed all of the infection, but we can't afford to lose you in your sleep because we were too lazy to keep watch. Julius will stay with you, and I'll check in every two hours. Dawn isn't too far away."

Olga and Ambrose tidied up the mess and disposed of the blood-stained rags, but at the foot of her bed, her Master remained.

"I cannot fathom just how good sense has deserted you..." Arduen trailed off, jaw clamping shut.

Lilith couldn't summon the words to defend her actions. There were no excuses. She'd been rash. Foolish. And she doubted admitting as much would gain any recognition from her Master.

Heaving a final sigh of exasperation, Arduen gave a dismissive wave of his hand, promptly taking his leave.

Julius shuffled his legs free, careful not to cause Lilith further discomfort. "I'll sleep here." He took up position on the floor beside her bed. "When I call for you, just mumble."

Lilith stared up at the ceiling. The pain had abated slightly, though her wound was taut where the sutures tugged at swollen skin. Her mind wandered back to the raid.

"Why were the monsters celebrating?" she asked. "And why did some of them flee? Are they not so feared by the entirety of Augusta, yet they took off like cowards at the sight of you two?"

Julius folded his arms beneath his head and chuckled quietly. "Spiro's beasts are complicated to say the least. Understanding their nature is nigh impossible. I've spent countless hours studying them, for they will remain in this land even after we thwart Spiro. Though they are creations, they possess the ability to procreate like any other species."

Lilith bit her lip, tasting blood from several wounds on the inside of her cheeks. "I still don't understand why so many fled. They seem like strong enough opponents without even bearing a weapon, so why run?"

He hesitated.

"What is it?" she prodded.

Julius's voice was colder now, his accent clipped. "Lilith, the monsters that fled were female."

"So?"

His cheeks flushed with color. "The music and the chanting, it was a mating ceremony. The females fled to save their potential offspring."

12

A BORED MONARCH

arkin was travel worn and exhausted. His stomach grumbled a dialect of its own devise, a protest of the absence of food. It had been too many days since he last ate a meal that consisted of more than stale bread and dried meat. The soldiers fed him only enough to survive while they gluttonously filled their bellies, forcing him to watch as they swallowed every bite. Sadistic bastards.

They entered Kenora through the northern gate. It was the closest to the castle, so they managed to avoid a crowd. The soldiers led Larkin inside through a small door near the stables, through rows upon rows of stacked cots. The barracks.

The soldiers escorted him down a dark, steep staircase. His buttocks spasmed with each step, a result of too many days sequestered in a saddle. The soldiers ignored his queries as they thrust him into a prisoner's cell. Larkin's blood seethed at their callous treatment. Why was he here? He'd come willingly. He was not arrested. He trembled as realization dawned.

Not one of the soldiers answered his desperate queries, and he was granted no more than a grunt in response.

He burst, "Will someone tell me why I'm fucking here?!"

"At least you have the manners to say 'please,'" a guard quipped from the shadows, but he didn't answer Larkin's question.

Terror gripped his chest with invisible talons. He was not a guest of the Emperor but had somehow been mistaken for a criminal. Larkin tugged at his hair anxiously, fingernails digging into scalp, drawing blood. His breaths came in labored rasps. His eyes darted around the cell at a dizzying speed. Nausea overwhelmed him, and he bent double, coughing bile.

Demoralized, Larkin lowered his aching body onto the empty cot. The cell was cold, damp. There was nothing inside save for his cot and a small steel bucket to relieve himself.

As night fell, he was cast into darkness, his mind exhausted from travel. He'd spent every moment awake and aware of his surroundings, always on the lookout for Spiro's menaces. He groaned audibly, hoping someone would notice the mistake that had been made. No one acknowledged his unease. No one came to rectify the mistake.

With his back to the cell door, it wasn't long before he lost his mind to the mercy of his dreams, filled with violence and despair, and the succor of his deceased mother.

◎ ⑤ ⤳ ⋔ ◊

For days, Larkin remained prisoner. He'd spent the time lazing on his cot, attempting to train his mind not to linger on thoughts that caused him grief. He stirred only when servants brought him food, once every day around the time his strength began to wane. When he first glimpsed the scraps, he cared not if they'd poisoned it, he cared not for the lack of utensils. He'd swallowed the gruel with eagerness. He didn't mind eating like a ravaging canine, so long as the churning in his gut ceased its torment.

The air was putrid, moist, so thick that it clung to his skin like an emollient. He couldn't imagine standing before the Emperor smelling like this, not having bathed in nearly two weeks. He stank like offal and sweat. His hair was matted to his head, greasy and lank. His face was coated in oil and dirt that could only be removed by a scrubbing, and his lips were cracked and bloodied as a result of dehydration.

A loud knock sounded through the cell. Larkin jumped to his feet. He rushed to the door, eager to be free of this prison.

"Yes. I'm here!" His voice shook with uncertainty. He was trying desperately to comport himself as a guest, though he was being treated like an invalid.

A baritone thundered in response, "You have been summoned by Emperor Obadïa. You are to follow us."

The cell door swung inward and two men entered. Not the same legionnaires that had brought him to the capital. These men were broader, fiercer, warrior types; strong as oxen. Larkin focused on the cadence of their heavy breathing as they pinioned his hands behind his back. He tried not to gasp when they fixed the knot too tight.

They led him out of his cell toward the staircase leading up to the castle proper. They traversed the wide stone hallways with great urgency. Larkin was escorted with respect, save for the binding of his wrists. No soldiers restrained him, but rather surrounded him as though he was a person of great importance. Anyone who neared wouldn't be fooled, his stench betrayed his status.

Two large redwood doors swung open as if of their own volition. The soldiers walked Larkin to the base of a dais, where upon a large golden throne, sat Emperor Obadïa.

The Emperor was a broad man, and although he was sitting down, it was obvious that he was tall and distinguished. He held his chin high as his dark, deep-set eyes followed Larkin's path down the carpet toward the base of the dais. He possessed a full head of thick silver-blond hair and a carefully groomed beard to match. His complexion was flushed as if sunburnt, his skin glistening with excess oil. He was clad in crimson robes that complimented his muscular physique; they pooled at his feet like the blood of his enemies.

When Larkin and his escorts reached the base of the dais, two soldiers stationed on either side of the Emperor raised their voices together, signalling the group to halt. Vigilantly, they gripped the hilts of their swords as their eyes bore into Larkin.

The Emperor cleared his throat, his teeth flashing gold as he spoke. "Larkin Oak," he greeted. "I have waited so long to meet with you. Welcome to Kenora. I am disheartened to hear that it is your first time visiting our beautiful capital, although I understand why you have not, given the conditions that we live in. These times are tough on us all, rich and poor, we are united. We both lack the most valuable asset to life on this earth: freedom." Obadïa spoke with vehemence, but his eyes remained flat, lifeless. Bored.

A bored monarch was never a kind one.

"More pressing matters bring us together today," the Emperor droned on. "Larkin, it has upset me greatly to add your sister to the list of missing persons. Usually some sort of remains can be found in the event of a beast attack, but none were found of Lilith Oak.

"When Lord Alexaus sent me word of your situation, I thought it best to bring you here to discuss your thoughts and insights on the matter. It pains me deeply to lose a blacksmith, as those of your kind are rare and few. Maybe you can help me to understand what is going on in front of our very eyes, in our very towns." The Emperor's onyx gaze narrowed with expectancy.

Lord Alexaus was more a Plebeian than a member of the Elite, but Larkin didn't dare state his opinion. He addressed the Emperor with veneration, "Your Majesty, I cannot speak for my parents, as they are no more, but I am certain that they would be as grateful as I am that you are concerned in regard to my dear sister's disappearance. She was very proud of her work by the forge, as proud as we were of her intelligence and her will to persevere."

Larkin forced his voice to evoke an air of confidence that he hoped would win his freedom. "It breaks my heart that she is gone. When her fiancé and I failed to discover any remains within the ashes of my father's shop, I searched high and low for days, but I found no trace of remains."

"Well," the Emperor intoned, stroking his beard pensively, "she must have been eaten."

"Lilith goes hunting in the wilderness for days at a time," Larkin argued. "I stopped worrying about her when she returned unscathed for the hundredth time."

Obadïa's eyes narrowed with shrewd interest. "Indeed."

With a sharp intake of oxygen he prayed no one noticed, Larkin continued, "This harvest has been the most trying that I have ever experienced. I have been doing all that I can to produce enough provisions to keep myself and Lilith alive for the coming winter months, as well as produce a sizeable cut for you in the spring. Then, when winter sets in, I plan to rebuild the forge in hopes that Lilith will return of her own accord. And if not, then I will search the land high and low for my last remaining kin."

The Emperor's deep-set eyes bulged from his crimson face. "You couldn't *possibly* believe that you could traverse these lands alone in search of your sister? You would, without the slightest doubt, fail. Fatally. A mission such as that is utterly asinine and is doomed before it begins."

Larkin shrank back.

Obadïa leaned back in his throne. "Can you wield any weapons with skill? Surely your father deemed it important to instruct you on what it takes to protect yourself and your home. He was a master blacksmith, as your sister came to be." The Emperor's tone bore a hint of condescension and Larkin bit his tongue to ignore it. If he let his pride get the best of him now, it would cost him his life.

Larkin stuttered over his words, "Absolutely, Y-Your Majesty. My father taught me swordsmanship, but I never cared much for it. It was Lilith who held more of an interest in those skills. She doesn't know how to wield a blade as well as I, but she was the most accurate archer I've ever known. My mother taught her, of course. They were great huntresses. When times were tough and the quails failed to produce, they would provide."

The Emperor continued to stroke his beard in rhythmic intervals. "Was Lilith equipped with her bow when she disappeared?"

"No, Your Majesty, she was not. That's why I have been so worried about her, she has no means of protecting herself." Larkin lowered his gaze to the polished floor, aware of the Emperor's eyes studying him. If he were to convince Obadïa that he was indeed speaking truthfully, he needed to maintain constant eye contact, but he couldn't muster the courage. His position was as precarious as they came. If the Emperor deemed Larkin untrustworthy, he could be on trial for the murder of his sister. He had no alibis. No proof of his innocence.

The Emperor smirked, cocking his head. "You do not think it possible that she fell in love and ran away with another man? Someone other than her fiancé?" Obadïa heaved an arid chuckle, amusement twinkling in his dark eyes. "You see, my lad, I know women. I know their character. One is not so different from the other. They can vex men like nothing else, yet they care so little for us in return."

Larkin bristled. "No, absolutely not!" He'd never considered the possibility. Lilith didn't spend enough time socializing to have built a solid relationship with anyone beyond mere friendship, and her bond with Jude was unbreakable. "No, that is not a possibility. She must have been attacked by those wretched beasts!"

"Very well then, Mr. Oak. The paltry amount of information that you have granted me today is very... *displeasing*. I must say that I do believe your accounts to be true. However, I am ordering you to remain here in the capital while we investigate your sister's disappearance. You will be given comfortable accommodations throughout the duration of your stay."

The Emperor gestured to the soldiers surrounding Larkin. They unbound his wrists and began to shuffle him away from the dais. Larkin nervously bowed and gave his thanks before following the soldiers out of the throne room.

To Larkin's surprise, he was granted rooms of such opulence, he didn't want to go home. The bed was larger than his bedroom. The windows spanned from floor to ceiling. He had a view of the entire west end of Kenora, candle lights twinkling like stars across the horizon.

After indulging in a bath and a few chalices of the richest claret he'd ever tasted, Larkin dozed off into a world of his own devise.

13

DISCERNMENT

Lilith awoke later than usual, her suit clinging to her skin, moist with sweat from night terrors. Her thigh was bandaged tightly, but she had no recollection of anyone wrapping it. Though she failed to survive totally unscathed, she was proud of the way she fought.

She unwrapped and inspected her wounds. The stitches were pulled taut. The flesh along the edges was soft, red, and swollen. Out of curiosity, she flexed her quads to see if it would hurt, and winced, instantly regretting it.

Carefully removing her destroyed suit, she re-wrapped her thigh and slipped her legs into a fresh pair of breeches. Then she donned the daily cream-colored blouse and tightened her leather belt around her waist. Finger combing her tangled tresses, Lilith attempted to smooth out her appearance, though there was little she could do to mitigate the dark circles around her eyes.

The scent of burnt bread and eggs wafted up to her

bedchamber. Down in the kitchen, Julius and Ambrose murmured to one another. As she descended the staircase, the men looked up at her with evident concern. They both wore dishevelled hair, the only indication that they hadn't gotten a full night's sleep. Olga was the only other person in the kitchen.

"You will be relieved to know that Arduen and Quintus have gone for a walk together. They have matters of their own that they must attend to." Ambrose spoke with an air of disapproval, not his usual joyful disposition.

Without greeting her, Julius trained his focus on the remnants of his meal. Did he no longer care for her? She feared that her rebellious act had left her comrades less than pleased. Her earlier notion of pride now eroded into shame.

"What you did last night was brave, Lilith," Olga said, casting a stern glance in her direction. "It was also ignorant and disrespectful."

Lilith struggled to lift her eyes from the meal Ambrose set in front of her. "I'm aware. I won't be disobedient again." Forcefully, she swallowed a few bites. What was Arduen going to say? Suddenly sick with guilt, she set down her fork.

Olga moved closer to Lilith to speak more privately. "You must remember that your relationship with Arduen is the most important. Therefore, you must make an effort to get to know him. Being honest with one another is the best way to achieve connection. He is far more sensitive than he appears to be. You may well be surprised by his graciousness."

Lilith met Olga's gaze. "I've never been disobedient to my parents. I never had to be. Here, it feels like time doesn't move and I'm impatient. I want to be better. Capable. Reliable. I have been overcome with a passion and desire, but I don't know *why*. I don't understand it. Is it from within myself or is it part of this gift from above? Help me understand what *drives* me!" She implored the Oracle with her stare, her hands gripping the table so tight, her knuckles were stark white.

Olga's dour expression transformed into one of empathy and understanding. "My dear, what you are feeling is a lust for revenge. You have lost much to Spiro. I understand why you feel the way you do. Surely you must want to expedite your training so that you may return to your brother. Trust me when I say, Arduen understands that better than any of us."

Lilith fought back tears. She'd never spoken of the devastation of the loss of her parents—not even with Larkin. Sure they'd mourned together, in their own way. They'd supported one another by bottling everything up. Corked it so that none of the grief could spill free, staining what good remained in their simple, Plebeian livelihood.

"There is no shame in feeling such sadness," Olga whispered. "We will lose those that we love—if not everyone—for no one can live as long as we do. It will never get easier. No amount of experience can help us feel the loss of a loved one any less, it can only help us to be fearless when we do love."

"Can you tell me, is my brother safe?"

Olga patted Lilith's cheek gently. "He is in good hands, living very comfortably. I can see that he misses you and he worries that you no longer walk upon this earth."

"I will visit him once I graduate," Lilith resolved. "I will work hard to make him proud of me."

"I believe he already is," Olga said.

The front door burst open and in stormed Arduen and Quin. Lilith's eyes dropped to her lap, to the bulge of the bandage beneath the fabric of her breeches.

"Lilith," Arduen acknowledged her curtly. "Off to the study." When she didn't move with immediacy, he added brusquely, "Now."

"I TOLD YOU NOT TO GO," ARDUEN SAID, CUTTING STRAIGHT TO the point. "That was a strict order." His voice was grim, but not exceptionally vexed. Perhaps he'd spent the night mulling over it. Perhaps he'd realized that he wasn't her father; he couldn't rule over her. "I didn't deny you because I deem you incapable but rather because you have little experience fighting a real enemy. You are not ready, Lilith."

She bowed her head. "I'm sorry, Master. I wasn't thinking, and I struggled to reason with myself. I've had this powerful angst as of late. This *drive* toward the unknown. I was talking with Olga and she advised me to be more open with you. I'm trying to do that but it's not in my nature to be free with my thoughts." *Nor my feelings.*

Lilith stared at a particularly interesting knot in the wood of the desk. Arduen's lingering gaze was palpable.

"This injury will stunt your training," he said at last. "But we can work around it."

"Yes, Master." Lilith gulped. "But what of my punishment?"

Arduen's grimace softened into a meek smile. "I believe you've already been punished. But since you cannot train, you will accompany Olga to Kynös. It's where we gather supplies and food, as well as where we keep our steeds boarded. You will help Olga retrieve our horses."

Lilith arched an eyebrow. "Why are we in need of horses?"

"Because we've been summoned to the capital by the Emperor himself. We must travel to Kenora anon."

Of course she'd never been to the capital, but a part of her recoiled at the idea of travelling so soon. She'd only just begun to settle in at the Frourío, and now Arduen was upsetting her life again.

Regretfully, she inquired, "When do we leave?"

LILITH TOOK A FEW MOMENTS TO HERSELF. SHE NEEDED TO cleanse the aftermath of battle from her skin. The hot water was abrasive on her wounds, but keeping the area clean was her first priority. Soaking in the tub had left her feeling ten pounds lighter and her chest no longer seemed reluctant when she inhaled.

Once she was dressed, Lilith met Olga near the Forest's edge. The Oracle had been watching Quin and Julius training. The men appeared to be meditating. The two women stood and observed, the silence punctuated by the lilting birds, rustling leaves, and the shushing of the sea's rolling waves. A plethora of questions arose in Lilith's mind, but she refrained from impinging upon the moment's tranquility to voice them.

Julius sat directly across from Quin, legs folded beneath him. Their hands were placed flat upon their knees, their chins set firmly against their chests. With eyes closed, they chanted verses unknown to her.

Olga jerked her head in the direction of the pathway, and Lilith followed her lead. Once they were far enough away that conversation wouldn't disturb Quin and Julius, Olga began to explain. "They are communicating with the Gods. That is something you will be able to do when you are closer to graduating."

Evidently confused, Lilith queried, "I thought only you could speak with the Gods?"

"They do not speak with Them such as I do. There is power in spiritual connection. When two Divines connect and call to one God, they can communicate just as clearly as you and I are currently. The only contrast to the way in which we are communicating right now is that the Gods choose to convey Their messages through images and emotions. They do not exchange information through simple words but rather notions, visions, and intuitions."

Lilith tried to envision the nature of interaction the men were experiencing, but it remained elusive.

The pines' boughs swayed on the late-autumn breeze, their soughing strident. Since her Anointment, the earth and its strange beings had become uncomfortably lucid. She allowed a shiver to roll through her.

THE TOWN OF KYNÖS WAS DIRECTLY EAST OF THE MEGÁLOS, STILL inside the confines of the expansive Forest. Lilith enjoyed Olga's company. The old woman was as maternal as she was wise. On many occasions, she would stop Lilith and introduce her to a rare plant or animal that stumbled along their path.

Lilith asked, "Were you ever married, or do you have a family of your own?"

Olga was quiet as she pondered what information she would share. Lilith wondered, after a significant amount of silence, whether the woman would reveal anything at all.

"I never married," she finally said, "though I did have a lover that I considered my spouse. I still believe that he and I would have lasted an eternity, as my love for him still burns deep within." She held a slender hand to her chest, her eyes staring blankly into the distance. For a love to endure long after death was extremely rare. How great it must have been. *Pràgma*—everlasting love.

Lilith sighed heavily. Her parents had been *Pràgma*, too.

In that moment, she found herself strangely thankful for the distance now placed between herself and Jude. She didn't love him as passionately as a spouse should, and she hoped that he would find another in her absence.

Quietly, Olga addressed Lilith in a much more sullen tone, "Be careful who you love. Guard your heart with intent, lest you go mad with the fear of loss before you must suffer the pain of loss itself!"

⊚ ⺵ ⸺ ⋔ ♭

THE TOWN OF KYNÖS WAS SLIGHTLY SMALLER THAN UTICA. THE houses stood tall with plaster-covered walls and round windows. The streets were astir with Augustans running their errands. The two women made their way into the town, passing by two guards. Olga greeted them with familiarity but carried on without preamble.

As they veered from the main thoroughfare, the voices of the townspeople rang in Lilith's mind as though they were standing in close proximity. She made a quick observation of Olga, but the Oracle didn't seem to be disturbed by the clamor. Lilith focused on drowning them out, but the attempt was in vain.

Olga's eyes narrowed shrewdly upon her. "You're listening to them." It wasn't a question.

"Yes, I've never experienced this before. I can hear everyone at the Frourío but not this loud. This…" Lilith waved a hand through the air. "Does it not bother you?" She winced as unknown, incensed voices assaulted her mind. They were so insistent, she could *feel* their ire.

"Not quite. I've learned how to mute it," said Olga. "This is all part of your teaching, but that is Arduen's place, not mine. However, since this has caused you discomfort, I will help train you in this aspect. Just this once."

Lilith turned to Olga expectantly. The old woman grasped both of her hands and said, "Focus on my eyes alone. Take note of every detail you can."

Doing exactly what she was told, Lilith began to examine Olga's eyes closely. Every color and speckle she could make out from an arm's length away.

"Do you hear them now?"

Silence.

Lilith gawped. By focusing on another task, the voices were almost completely diminished. When she focused back on the voices again, they overwhelmed her, forcing her to cover her ears, but of course that did nothing. Then she tried inspecting her boots, counting the mottled spots of dirt decorating the leather. A moment later, the voices were quieted. Lilith repeated the process several times before she was confident that she would be able to silence the din at her will.

"It takes some time to adjust," Olga said. "A bit of practice, but you will learn to do it almost instinctively. It is a lot of information to take in at times, but I'm not concerned about your veracity. You seem open-minded and critical enough to think for yourself.

"I am not bothered by the noise; I rather enjoy listening in on the latest gossip." Olga giggled. "I know what the butcher has been up to and how everyone's business is going, and I don't even have to ask a soul." She beamed at the cluster of buildings.

Intrigued, Lilith attempted to focus in on several different conversations. When she heard something that snatched her interest, she would try to focus in on it. It wasn't long before she acquired a significant amount of control over her senses.

"Is there a name for this gift?" Lilith asked.

"It's called Discernment."

THEY STOPPED AT A MANOR WITH A LARGE BARN BESIDE IT. LILITH assumed this was the family that took care of the Divines' horses. Olga was preoccupied with the noble who owned the place. He was hunched over a cane fashioned from dark wood. His loose robes were slightly too long for him, as if he'd shrunk in his old age. He seemed amicable enough, though he wasn't inclined to give Olga what she bargained for.

"I had to barter another horse from him," Olga explained. "He didn't fancy the price we set, but we pay him well enough every month. I thought Arduen had taken care of the matter, but the old man must have forgotten their conversation. His memory escapes him far too often these days."

The man disappeared and returned shortly with the horses. Olga handed over the reins of a beautiful chestnut gelding to

Lilith, which she received with excitement. "This is Skydancer," said Olga. "He's yours now."

Lilith patted Skydancer's neck and chattered to him while she waited for Olga to tie up the horses.

Once seated atop Skydancer, Lilith attempted to block out the voices, but to no avail. A woman's screams of agony pierced her thoughts until her own abdomen began to cramp. Alarmed, she wrapped her arms around herself and began to focus on her breathing. She managed to drown out the other voices but couldn't escape the woman's squalls.

Flames speared through her core like fresh-forged steel, and Lilith was inundated with searing pain. It was every-where. Inhabiting every crevice of her body. Trembling, she cried out in anguish.

Olga traipsed over slowly so as not to startle Skydancer, but she was too late. The horse had been disturbed by Lilith's displeasure. He reared and bucked her off. Lilith fell to the ground with a thud. Gasping for air, she skittered away from the horse, continuing to hold herself together. The pain became crippling, her vision flashing red.

Hands cupped her head and held her firm. Olga's voice perforated the torturous pall that had settled over her. Ever so slowly, the pain subsided, leaving Lilith's body numb. She panted, staring up at Olga, confused and wanting an explanation.

"I ... couldn't ... stop it," she managed to say between gasps of air.

The Oracle shook her head and muttered a curse. "You must have senses far more mature than the average Divine of your level. You need instruction as soon as we return." She helped Lilith rise to her feet.

"Calm your horse," Olga ordered. "Develop a relationship with him so that he will be faithful to you. I will keep a mental shield around you until we are well away from town." Though Olga spoke with authority, there was a gentleness to her words, a form of empathy for Lilith's situation.

Develop a relationship. Gods, hadn't she figured out Lilith doesn't excel at that?

Lilith took Skydancer's reins and cooed words of comfort into his twitching ears. The horse was of a gentle disposition and he took to her again within minutes. Though she was sore from the fall, Lilith managed to climb up into the saddle. As she waited for the Oracle, she contemplated the possible reasons why Arduen hadn't schooled her in Discernment. It seemed almost cruel to let her walk into a town, ignorant of such an ability.

When Olga was finished and the other horses were tied in tow, they began their journey back to the Frourío. Eager to escape Kynös. Lilith spurred Skydancer to a trot.

◎ ⑥ ⤳ M ◊

Upon their return, Olga and Ambrose led the horses to the small stable. Lilith, anxious to speak with Arduen, ran inside as quickly as her sore limbs would allow. When she burst into the kitchen, she nearly startled Quin and Julius out of their seats.

"What's wrong, Lilith?" Quin inquired.

"Nothing, Master... Is Arduen here?" She was short of breath.

"He's taking a walk along the beach. Is everything all

right? Is Olga hurt?" Quin took a few steps in her direction, but before he could reach her, Lilith ran out the door again.

Julius sprinted after her, heedless of Ambrose and Olga who were on their way inside. Being nearly a foot taller, he had little trouble catching up to her.

"What is going on?" he demanded, placing a firm hand on Lilith's shoulder, spinning her around to face him. She winced with pain; the ride home had proven to only worsen her bruises and she worried about the sutures in her thigh.

"I need to speak with Arduen now," she said irritably.

"Are you hurt? What's happened?" Julius held her in place.

She scowled. "I've just experienced something terrible! I don't think I was supposed to..." She struggled to mask the anxiety in her voice.

Julius waited patiently for her to elaborate, and when she didn't, he pressed her for answers. "I have to find Arduen," she said again, annoyed. "You can come with me if you wish, but do not stop me."

She spotted Arduen about half a mile down the beach. Lilith and Julius set off in his direction together, slipping in the soft sand. Julius lent his arm to her for support, and she accepted, too exhausted to refuse.

When they met, Arduen was the first to speak. "How was your tr—"

"What is Discernment? And why have you left me in the dark?" Lilith didn't bother to dilute the resentment seeping into her voice.

The creases on Arduen's brow deepened. "That is beyond your skill level, Lilith. If I had thought you needed it, you'd have been instructed."

Lilith let out the breath of air she'd been holding in. "I have experienced it today and it has caused me a great deal of pain. Including getting bucked off a horse, while birthing a child that I didn't conceive!"

Both Arduen and Julius looked at her incredulously. Wide-eyed. Open-mouthed. Julius placed his hand on her back, try as he might to comfort her.

"You must tell me what happened—*exactly* as it happened —leave out no details," Arduen demanded.

So Lilith recounted the experience from the moment they arrived at Kynös. Arduen listened intently to every word, nodding occasionally with fists set on his hips.

When Lilith was finished, he placed a hand on her shoulder and brought his eyes level with hers. "You are maturing with accelerated speed. We have much to cover. Yet you're injured and you need rest."

"I need guidance," she countered.

At her mulish glower, he conceded. "Tomorrow, we'll discuss subjects that I deem you ready for. I am sorry that you have experienced this; if I had thought this level of Discernment possible for you, I never would have sent you to Kynös."

Arduen scratched his head, seeming as perplexed by the situation as she was. "It seems that Constantine is smiling down upon you, though it may feel as though He is punishing you." He smiled pitifully. "If anything, take solace in that." Then he dismissed the pair.

Lilith was too exhausted to argue and she let Julius escort her back to the Frourío. They trudged through the sand, arms linked.

"It seems like an awful cruel way to smile upon someone," Lilith deadpanned.

Julius chuckled, the low timbre of his mirth sending vibrations up her arm. "The horse must have thrown you pretty far," he observed. "We should check on your wound, just to make sure that your sutures are holding up."

Once they reached the Frourío, Olga followed Lilith to her bedchamber and together they cleaned her wound and changed the bandage. When they were finished, the Oracle made her excuses and bid her good night.

Lilith lay on her bed, far too exhausted and sore to do much else. What would life be like if Spiro and his minions never existed?

Nightly, she'd taken to soothing herself to sleep by replaying fond memories of Larkin behind closed eyelids. She clung to them as if, in this aberration, all vestiges of him would evanesce.

14

TENEBROUS AND TWISTED

Lilith met with Arduen an hour earlier than usual. Ambrose delivered their breakfast to the study. The sun was just beginning to rise, emitting barely enough light to work by. Arduen lit an oil lamp and set it in the centre of the desk before he proceeded with the lesson.

He explained that excessive prayer could be misconstrued by the Gods as a request for accelerated abilities. Lilith prayed daily, following her morning lesson, no more than what was expected of her. Arduen was convinced that she was being privileged by Constantine, but she had never prayed to Him verbally, but rather *basked* in His presence.

"Today we will practice controlling Discernment," Arduen said. "I will explain to you what you must do, and we will practice this with the sea and the creatures that dwell therein." He gestured to the expanse of azure that consumed the view from the window.

He explained that Discernment was an ability that all

Divine gradually acquired in the first few years of their training. Julius had experienced Discernment at an early stage as
well, though he didn't engage in another person's physical
feelings or sensations—that level of skill took many years to
develop.

"Discernment," Arduen began, "is the ability to connect
with others. It serves many purposes for us. One being that we
can connect with the people that we serve and protect. We can
sense their emotions and intentions, thus understanding political and hostile situations with an unbiased mind. It serves
another purpose in battle; it enables us to know all that tran-
spires on the battlefield, and also to be highly aware of our
surroundings. You will be able to sense when someone is
attempting to attack you or when a comrade has been injured.
With Discernment, no one will ever be able to sneak up on
you."

So that was how she was able to sense Julius and Ambrose
before she'd seen them on the night of the raid. Unbeknownst
to her, she was experiencing Discernment. Thankfully, she
didn't partake in the pain of the dying beasts.

"For you, it seems that controlling it will be the main struggle," Arduen said. "And our first priority. You must learn to
block out the din that assails our minds when we encounter
crowded settings. When we must travel to cities, it's important
that this becomes second nature to you." He strode to the
window and beckoned for her to join him. Clearing his throat,
he began to instruct her on how to reach out with her mind.

With her eyes closed, Lilith took a moment to try this. The
sound of the sea was a calming, a rough vibration, nothing like
the roaring tumult of the townspeople of Kynös. She kept her
eyes shut, aware that Arduen was observing her intently,

waiting for an indication that she was either failing or triumphing.

"Are you within the sea's brawl?"

Lilith grinned. "I believe I am."

"Good. Now I want you to feel the water for other entities, for beings foreign to you. Try to connect with them like you did with the woman in labor."

Acquiescing, Lilith expanded her mind until she could feel the presence of the foreign entities. There were several immature and primitive emotions—elation, anger, urges, determination—that rippled off of them to the rhythm of the undulating waves.

"Have you done it?" Arduen asked, perforating the silence. Though his voice was soft, his rich timbre pulled her back to him. Lilith managed a slight nod, afraid to lose focus. "Good," he commended. "Now I want you to close it all off, until you can barely sense the sea."

Focusing on one creature only, she attempted to diffuse the rest from her mind. It took longer than she'd anticipated before she found success. Once she did, she began to back her consciousness away from the singular entity.

"Focus on something separate from the sea," Arduen advised. "Something in this room or the Frourío itself."

Lilith began to focus on her own body. The floor beneath her feet, the stones that constructed the walls, the iron structures of the light fixtures. She began to repaint the exact image of one of the sconces in her mind, envisioning exactly how the glass panels sat within the intricate iron borders. The sound of the rushing waves dissipated.

Lilith opened her eyes, satisfaction blossoming into a smile. "I've done it, Master."

"Good." Arduen clapped her on the shoulder, his touch firm but benign. "I want you to practice this every morning when you rise."

They sat down at the desk. Tomes were spread across its surface as if someone had been conducting heavy research.

"How often do you pray to Constantine?" he asked suddenly.

Lilith shrugged noncommittally. "Every day before lunch," she answered honestly.

Arduen furrowed his brow, lost in thought. His hand tapped his ankle, which he had rested over his knee. He stroked his short beard, lips pursed. "We shall pray together today. It's best that we do this outside in nature."

"Yes, Master."

"Let us go to the beach."

⌾ ⍥ ➴ ⋔ ◊

"SIT YOURSELF IN FRONT OF ME, LEGS CROSSED," ARDUEN instructed. "Align your feet with mine. Lay your hands, palms down, on your knees. Close your eyes and lower your head. It's a vulnerable position, but it is necessary. We are displaying to Constantine that we want Him to join us."

Lilith obeyed, wincing at the sharp pain in her thigh.

"Relax, Lilith."

Moments passed, neither Divine uttered a word. The only sound was the rushing of the sea. The waves had picked up and were almost touching them as the water smoothed over the sand.

Thankful that nudity was not a requirement for communal prayer, Lilith peeked through her lashes and studied her

Master. His head was downcast, his hair obscuring his eyes from view like a curtain of molten gold. She closed her eyes quickly, still unable to feel a presence from any God. Her heart pounded in her ears as the cold water brushed her leg. Hills rose along the skin of her arms, short hairs reaching for the clouds. She shuddered, then gulped a deep breath to brace herself for the next cold wave.

It wasn't long before Arduen lifted his head. Lilith started at the motion. Her heart began to pound again, reminding her of the beasts' mating ceremony. Her cheeks flushed, abashed, and she was grateful that Discernment didn't involve reading another's mind.

"That's enough for today."

Dark clouds began to gather in the north over the sea. Wondering if the northern continent experienced the same gale approaching them, Lilith barely noticed Arduen's proffered hand. She let him pull her to her feet, avoiding his eyes. The lesson should have brought them closer, but she'd never felt more distant.

"Thank you," she said warily.

"Now we will have lunch."

Lilith followed him to the Frourío meekly.

"And after," he called over his shoulder, "since you are still injured, I will show you how to properly wield Aether."

FOLLOWING THE MIDDAY MEAL, ARDUEN AND LILITH MARCHED into the towering pines through which they first arrived at the Frourío. The storm that raged during lunch had abated slightly, though the air was thick and damp, and rain still drizzled. Arduen had requested Lilith change into her plated leather suit—the only one she had since she'd destroyed the other one in the raid. The suits stuck to their bodies, outlining their figures, lines and contours of muscle stark on them both.

Arduen didn't seem to take notice, he was focused on finding the best location to practice. He cautioned Lilith to stay where she was, concealed within the trees, then he continued to tread into an open glade. With her arms wrapped around her rib cage, she waited. Her eyes followed her Master's movements in the distance, but she quickly became ensnared by dark thoughts.

For Lilith, the pain of losing those closest to her was not foreign, it was reality. Larkin was her only living relative. It would be years before she could see him again. He hadn't written her, which she knew was unusual, but Arduen and Olga both assured her that Evös returned with no response. Her chest grew heavy with a dull ache and her throat began to swell shut, but she didn't reveal to them her worries.

Immortality was not a gift from the Gods, but a curse. What if it took Larkin a lifetime to forgive her? What if she couldn't find comfort with the other Divine? What if she could never see Arduen as a fatherly figure? She was content with her relationship with Olga, for the old woman reminded her of a wise-minded grandmother. Yet her age was so great, could she survive a war if it was to come? And what if Lilith was the only Divine to survive?

No, unlimited years was a gift of the cruelest kind.

An involuntary whimper escaped her lips and Lilith placed a trembling hand over her mouth. The rain would hide her tears from her Master's sight, but he would hear her sobs. And through Discernment, he could feel her lament.

Arduen distracted Lilith from her devitalizing thoughts as he paced back and forth, head downcast, hands clenched into fists at his sides. What he was doing, she hadn't the faintest idea. She sighed, the minutes melting together seamlessly and without distinction.

"I earnestly discourage unsupervised training of Aether," Arduen began, his voice muffled by the rain. "Lest you swallow yourself into the void. It is the most unforgiving gift, and therefore, the most precarious to train. We will get through it, but it'll take some time, which is something we don't have much of. If we expedite the process, you will not be as confident as need be."

With his arms splayed, palms supinated, Arduen dropped his head back and closed his eyes. Within a few seconds he was enveloped by the same cloud of enigmatic darkness she'd witnessed twice before. Except that this time it was a gargantuan display, and Lilith struggled to simply observe it. The strength of wind that emanated from the blast forced her down onto the grass. Shielding her face with her hands, she could scarcely make out Arduen's figure. He swung his arms with stealthy grace and shards of Aether shot out of the abyss like flaming arrows. The colossal void rose up into the sky.

Every muscle in Lilith's body tensed as she watched the performance, and when her nerves heightened, she began to wish for its completion.

When Arduen finally yielded, the cloud shrank until it vanished around him, almost as if he absorbed it back into himself. Lilith stared as her Master twisted to face her and dipped into a magnanimous bow. He approached her then, short of breath, but well and sound.

"That was amazing..." She couldn't conceive any other words to describe what her eyes beheld.

"Indeed, it can be when wielded with accuracy, but that will take time." He gestured behind him. The grass had been completely eradicated, leaving behind cracked, desiccated earth. "As your lungs draw breath, your heart pulses with blood. So, too, does Aether flow in your veins."

He lifted her to her feet, not unlike a father would his child. When she stood, he didn't release his hold on her, his steel eyes fixated on her with concern. Lilith averted her gaze and attempted to pull her hand from his, but he refused to relinquish his grip.

"What is the matter, Lilith?" he asked. "I can see you've been upset."

"I'm fine," she lied, turning away, but he didn't let go. "Please," she pleaded. "I'm fine."

Without releasing her, he said softly, "I am not only the one whom instructs you in battle, but I am also the one to whom you are to confide in. Do not shy away from me, Lilith." A finger stroked her damp cheek. "I am here for you whatever your needs be. I know I can seem hard, strict at times, but there is no one here who can understand you like I do." His tone was gentle. It awoke a strange desire in her, but for what, she didn't know.

Lilith wanted to speak aloud all the problems she'd kept concealed for years, but still she refrained.

"I can't," she said softly, and he let her go.

Later that evening, following dinner, Lilith returned to

her bedchamber where she argued with herself within the confines of her tangled mind. She needed a distraction.

She exited her room quietly and proceeded up the stairs to the study. As she entered, she noticed the sconces were lit. She had company.

The large door creaked, betraying her arrival.

Arduen lifted his head from a derelict tome and greeted her with a feeble smile. "Hello, Lilith. What brings you to the study at this hour?"

"I'm searching for a book," she said mildly. "Perhaps a storybook, if one exists here." She didn't advance into the room. She hoped that he would direct her to the appropriate shelf.

When Arduen returned his attention to his studies, Lilith began to peruse the shelves for a suitable book, the tension in the room mounting on her shoulders. The pressure swelled, her muscles taut like a bowstring. Tempting her to break. Tempting her to speak.

Not now, Lilith. Not now.

A lump swelled in her throat. Unbidden and insistent. *Let it out.* But she couldn't. She wouldn't.

The moment the words spilled out, desolation pervaded the chamber like a dark shroud. "I saw her body," she blurted, keeping her gaze locked on the spines of the books before her.

Arduen's eyes drifted up to her. She could feel his ice-cold irises boring into her.

"My brother found my mother hanging from one of the oaks outside Utica. He didn't want me to see her, but I had to." Lilith recalled her mother's lifeless face, the deathly pallor of her skin. The image pierced her brain, her heart becoming a stone lodged in her throat.

"My father perished in the Battle of Elïath. I never saw his body; he was never returned to us. His death was the reason for her suicide." A shuffle of paper. The slightest groan of wood against stone.

"I wanted to see her before we buried her." Her face heated. This was the first time she'd ever spoken of her mother's death to anyone. "We weren't enough for her!"

Tears streaked her face as she turned to the desk, though Arduen was no longer seated. He stood an arm's length away, hands stuffed into the pockets of his breeches, a grim expression coating his features.

Lilith bit down on her lip, trying with all her will to maintain composure. To quell the rising tide of sorrow. Never had she spoken to anyone so openly, she'd never known how to.

"My brother and I never spoke about losing our parents. We didn't set any boundaries about what was okay to speak out loud and what wasn't, we just never did. We never shed any tears in front of one another, we only continued on with our lives. The difference was that there was no help making ends meet… and the two vacant chairs at the dinner table." She loosed a long-stifled sob and covered her face with her hands, weeping until her abdomen began to ache.

A large hand fell upon her shoulder and she was pressed into a wall of warmth. Though she found comfort in his arms, the gesture only caused her bawling to intensify. Arduen began to speak the same words Julius had the night she was injured in the raid. With each syllable, her body relaxed.

"You must know that I am always willing to listen to you," he said, pulling away slightly to look into her face. Lilith lifted her gaze with reluctance. The candlelight deepened the sharp edges of his cheekbones, his jawline. He appeared so young for someone so old.

"It is so important that we thoroughly understand each other, Fledgling." His baritone was soft, affectionate. He tucked a stray strand of hair behind her ear. Before releasing her, he added, "I have had my share of losses as well."

Lilith expected an elaboration, a confession of his own, but her Master remained silent. When he returned to his book without another word, she was left befuddled, wondering whether she would ever truly know him.

But maybe Arduen was so antiquated, he was no longer attuned to human emotion. Maybe after so many years, all that remained was atavistic intuit. Senses that propelled and repressed, but never indulged. Maybe he'd become immune to the visceral feeling of loss, having likely endured so much of it.

Grief was a narrow path, tenebrous and twisted, best tread in isolation. And yet, for the first time in years, Lilith was pining for a hand to hold. A voice to guide her. And though her hand was outstretched, she still walked alone.

15

REUNITED AT LONG LAST

Rhéa DaSylvà graced the hallways of the Emperor's castle with her elegant gait. Servants and legionnaires alike turned to gawk and assess, to take in the exquisite sight of her. It was inevitable to become a spectacle when your veins thrummed with undeniable, celestial power.

The bland stone walls had become her new home. Her voice trilled a melody that had become her new favorite, as the aroma of human flesh drifted and coated her nostrils like scented oil.

Rhéa had succeeded in sending Selene—a naïve Enchantress of seventy years—back to the Obsydían Marsh. Whether her mother had vouched for Rhéa or not, she didn't doubt that sending a younger Enchantress was a blatant insult from the High Enchantress—an insult directed at *her*.

The young Enchantress balked at the sight of Rhéa, her pale-blue eyes bulging. Rhéa managed to convince Selene that there had been a change of plans, and Selene handed over the Imperial decree and scurried off into the eastern horizon.

In the heat of the moment, Rhéa cared not if Selene told the High Enchantress. After attempting to make a fool of Rhéa and her mother in front of the Council of Thirteens, she could go to Hades. Though, Rhéa reminded herself, Ophelía likely had a place reserved in the underworld. *If* the ancient woman would ever die.

Rhéa dipped her head and breathed a spell. Elder Tongue danced in her ears, mingling with the autumn breeze. Her eyes began to burn as the spell to alter the color of her irises took charge. As a member of the Ilíos coven, Rhéa's eyes were golden. When she wanted to keep her identity hidden, she only needed alter them with magic. With irises like midsummer oak leaves, Rhéa would be undetected by any veiled enemies.

There were four covens that the Enchantresses were divided into. An Enchantress was either born into their coven or chose their coven when they found their way to the Marsh.

Enchantresses of the Asimí Fléves—the Silver Veins—bore irises of silver. The Nychta Skiá—the Night Shade—possessed violet irises. Ophelía was of this coven. Her lineage was valued highly as she'd been bred from a long line of Enchantresses born within the borders of the Obsydían Marsh. The Ápeiro Astéri—the Infinity Star—bore irises of a pale blue. Renowned for their wisdom and intelligence, it was no wonder Selene had balked at the sight of Rhéa. Poor little dove.

Though the Ilíos coven was praised for their healing gifts, they were also known for their stubbornness. If an Enchantress of the Amalthea Star had her heart set on something, it was hers.

When Rhéa arrived at the golden doors to the castle, two soldiers of the Emperor's Frourà—the Guard—stepped forth to question her. Rhéa just held up the decree and flashed them a saccharine smile, convincing them of her guilelessness. They'd spread the doors wide for her. As she entered, she was well aware of their stares on the back of her pretty little head. If only they knew how many years she'd endured upon the earth.

Meeting with Emperor Obadïa had gone just as she'd imagined. His Right Hand, Captain Vaughn, stood protectively by his master's side. No sign of the vulgar Crown Prince, which evoked a sigh of relief from Rhéa.

Listening with keen ears, Rhéa ignored the nonsense that prattled out of the Emperor's mouth, his yellow-gold teeth a visible emetic. She feigned interest in his tawdry words, waiting with a patient façade. Dismissed with a servant to escort her to her new chambers, Rhéa took off after the servant with nothing but a dip of her delicate chin in His Majesty's direction. No Enchantress would ever bow to the Empire.

Rhéa had been invited to dine with the Emperor that evening. Naturally, upon soaking in the sunken marble bath that accompanied her bedchamber, Rhéa readied herself for the evening.

Her chiton dress was sage green, lace embroidering the hems, while the middle hugged her torso tightly, outlining her curvaceous figure. She let her dark hair fall over her shoulders like incandescent moonlit waves of the Galatëa. Her new emerald eyes smoldered back at her in the mirror's reflection, so familiar, it was jarring. She was tempted to scry her mother, to see for herself if the Obsydían Marsh had adopted a hostile environment since her little scheme, but she refrained. She would allow nothing to ruin her evening—her *reunion*.

The high table was completely concealed beneath a mass of trays piled high with delicacies. *Pasteli* and other honey-doused pastries sweetened the atmosphere. It was beyond her why the Emperor had cleared a space for her at the high table. Formality was unnatural to her, and she knew what the courtiers thought of her: a dirty, rutting witch.

Rhéa ate well, famished after her ride to the capital, though she managed her manners around the Emperor and his noblemen. Captain Vaughn, the Emperor's Right Hand, watched her every moment, his eyes settling on her with a roguish gleam that she found quite disturbing. Rhéa returned his gaze with equal intensity, and she took great pleasure in watching him bristle and quake. When he broke—and he did every time—he looked back to his master in submission. *What a fool.*

Rhéa scanned the crowd for her beloved. He was the General of the Agemas, the highest ranked regiment in the Emperor's Milítia. Only the Agemas were granted permission to dine in the Great Hall. All other soldiers of the Emperor's Milítia and Frourà were sequestered to the mess hall, down under the castle with the barracks.

Over the cluster of heads, she caught sight of dark hair and olive skin. Heat speared through her at the sight of her husband. His hair fell to his broad shoulders, the same shoulders she'd gripped through the night, through the trials and pleasures they'd endured together. Too many years had passed since she'd held him.

As his gaze met hers across the Great Hall, the Enchantress preened. By the intensity of his gaze, she knew nothing had altered between them. Miles's eyes narrowed into slits and he rose from his seat, surrounded by his warriors.

Rhéa wanted to wait, to listen to the goings-on of the Empire, but she couldn't restrain herself any longer. She rose, making excuses along the lines of "a healer needs a long night's rest," and bid her company farewell. Not one of the courtiers objected, not even Captain Vaughn's, whose eyes followed her until she at last exited the hall.

The corridor was barren, only two Frourà soldiers were stationed outside the doors. She nodded a greeting to them both, and they flushed at the sight of her. She smirked, satisfied with their reaction before she trailed the scent of her betrothed.

Rhéa's slippered feet were silent upon the carpeted hallways. She turned a corner, convinced she was close, and was immediately shoved into a wall.

This wasn't an attack. No man would cradle the head of a woman they were about to harm. She welcomed the assault of lips on her skin. His hands tore through her thick hair, cupping her head gently.

Rhéa pushed him back slightly. "Mi—" her voice rasped, but she stopped herself from saying his name aloud, her chest heaving.

His emerald eyes were dark, hooded and heavy as they settled on her. Oh, it had been far too long since they held one another… savored one another.

"Ly—" he began to breathe her name, but she cut him off with a smothering kiss.

"Rhéa," she corrected him. He nodded and, lowering his face to hers, and continued to kiss her.

"Your eyes," he said against her skin.

Rhéa uttered the spell. Of course her husband wouldn't want to gaze into a mirror image of his own eyes. He'd want his wife, whole and true.

Her body burned under his touch as he continued his worship, but she couldn't forget that the Emperor had spies seeded everywhere in the castle.

"Take me to your chambers," she said. A request that didn't take much convincing. He grasped her hand and pulled her along.

RHÉA COULD SPEND FOREVER LIKE THIS, LIVING IN A CASTLE WITH her husband by her side. It'd be difficult to return to the Obsydían Marsh—she'd known all along that it would—but Ophelía would hunt her down if she didn't. Rhéa had left the Enchantresses once before. Escaping twice? That was unheard of. A sworn Enchantress was only ever allowed to leave the Marsh for twenty years, which she'd breached. The repercussions would be dire. But lying beside her husband could convince her that it would be worth it.

After snoozing in her husband's bed all morn, Rhéa returned to her own quarters to clean up. A young servant girl arrived to escort the Enchantress to the chambers of her new patient. From what she'd gleaned from the servant, the young man was being questioned by the Emperor for withholding information about a significant investigation.

The raven-haired servant halted before the chamber door and signalled for Rhéa to enter. Two Frourà soldiers stood vigil outside. As the servant grasped the door handle, the sleeve of her robe fell away, exposing a medley of colorful bruises along her forearm.

With guards sanctioned nearby, Rhéa lowered her voice. "What on earth happened to you?" When the girl didn't deign to respond, she added, "Have you been training with the men?"

When the girl paid no heed to the jest, Rhéa pulled the girl inside her patient's chamber and whispered discreetly, "I can heal those for you, and make the one who did this pay…"

The girl leaned away from Rhéa and shook her head with such vehemence, the Enchantresses flinched.

"It won't cause you any problems, I promise you." She was nearly pleading with the servant.

"I can handle myself, mistress."

Rhéa digressed as the girl retreated. Whatever was going on here, it was a matter meant to be dealt with later.

When she strode into the chamber, she met nothing but darkness. Only a few of the sconces were lit. It took her eyes a minute to adjust. In the gloom, a young man lay face down on the bed, shirtless and exposed.

She pulled a chair up to the side of the bed and studied his ailments. His face was concealed, but his scent washed over her, *through* her. She knew him, or had known him, and she was here to help.

His back had been whipped clean of flesh and a multitude of welts decorated his limbs. Heartsore, she began to form the spell in Elder Tongue. The magic needed a moment to gather its strength before it took hold.

It was only when her gaze fell onto the slaughtered flesh of the young man that Rhéa began to wonder if she'd commenced digging her own grave three decades ago, and only now was she to lie in it. Now she was to atone for it all, make everything right by her loved ones, all before Ophelía's hands contracted around her neck.

Rhéa shook her head clear. She was an Enchantress of the Ilíos coven. Grappling for governance of her trepidations, she cursed herself silently and sifted through the contents of her pack. Withdrawing a vial, she wasted no time. She poured the contents over the young man's back. His torn flesh began to sizzle and bubble like boiling water dyed crimson. When the skin had once again graced his back, unmarred and flawless as a babe's, she gently rolled him over.

Her breath hitched. His chest had been branded with sigils in Elder Tongue. The Emperor believed that marking any suspect with the ancient sigil of truth would summon forth the answers he desired. The only issue being the lack of magic, the lack of spoken Elder Tongue, and the lack of an Enchantress. Rhéa pleaded to the Stars that the Emperor wouldn't realize this. She could never partake in torture.

As she began to heal his burns, she sang the spell to life. "Câstré," she sang. "Víínn. Duínn vledreè."

The room began to buzz with energy as her voice caressed the stale air within. It seemed almost as though another voice melded with hers, singing to the ancient rhythm in a familiar baritone.

"Thank you, Mother."

Rhéa froze. She drew herself farther from the bed into the veil of the shadows. She didn't dare cease the spell lest she be forced to begin anew.

Gazing down upon the man, their eyes met. The Enchantress shushed him and released a silent blast of energy while she continued to sing. She would need to alter the color of her eyes if the green disconcerted her patient so.

At the culmination of her power, the young man succumbed to its majesty, lured into a deep sleep. He'd likely forget the occurrence, that he had glimpsed something within her.

"Sleep deep, sweet Larkin," she said.

The man didn't stir at the mention of his name, only a peaceful expression washed over his face.

16

GUIDANCE FROM WITHIN

"It seems that I've neglected to teach you about all the ethnic groups that call Augusta their home." Arduen began the lesson as if the moment they'd shared the previous evening hadn't transpired at all. "You must be equipped with as much knowledge as possible about each of the races. Though we are not sworn in fealty to any particular race or throne, we do have obligations to protect all of them."

Arduen met her gaze. The whites of his eyes tinted slightly red as if he hadn't slept in days. Was he all right? She wanted to ask but refrained. It was appropriate for him to ask her what was on her mind, but it was not the same in reverse.

"There are the Emperor's Augustans, those who inhabit the many towns and cities we see on our map. Though you have not travelled the lands overmuch, you know all that you need to about that group of people. I have also taught you briefly about the Enchantresses and their home in the Obsydían Marsh. Then there is the Walabeän Colony, they are located in the Isles of Nysía, northwest of the Frourío." He pointed at a group of four small islands not too far offshore, the parchment of the map crinkling under his fingertip.

"It is important that you know about the reclusive community that inhabit the Orösía Mountains. We have seldom ever communicated with them, as most are not fluent in Modern Tongue. Nonetheless, when Spiro does intrude upon their territory, they will call for us, as everyone does. They are a settlement of tribes, but they are formally called the Vunósoï."

Lilith observed the lumps on the map that indicated the Orösía Mountains. She'd always hoped to travel there to see the massive mounds of land for herself. But for now, the small knolls on the outskirts of the Forest would have to suffice.

"Now, not all myths are fiction, and not all beings live on land." He stood at to the window, his breath fogging the windowpane as his eyes surveyed the view. "There are races living beneath the waters, beyond the shores that surround this continent. They are to be feared as well as protected.

"The Sirens is what we call them, though they have bestowed another name upon their kind: the Ophïon. We rarely witness their presence upon the earth, though they can survive on land or Undersea. Humans have become quite hostile toward them in recent centuries, so we can only assume that King Aegæon is not too keen on assisting in our war against Spiro. Their home remains unaffected. Their waters are peaceful and teeming with life. I only hope that it remains this way."

"Do the Ophïon believe in the Gods?" Lilith asked. "Has there ever been a Divine Siren?"

Arduen was contemplative as he returned to his seat, chewing on his bottom lip. "No and no. They worship separate Gods, and unlike the Enchantresses, they do not acknowledge our Gods, nor do they fear Them." He sighed and leaned back in his seat. "They keep to themselves, which is best. They aren't the… most amicable of folks. They discriminate against us, as well as their own kind."

"What Gods do they worship?"

Arduen stroked his short beard as he pondered her question. "They worship Tethys and his Goddess bride, Eidothea. Though I cannot recall their parables, they are very pious beings."

"I wonder what it would be like to live under the sea," Lilith mused.

"Yes, I do too. I've only travelled to their domain once. They live in buildings carved from coral. It's hauntingly beautiful. It seems as though there is always music thrumming through their halls."

While Arduen allowed Lilith a moment to mull over what he'd taught, she took the time to observe him closely.

Would he ever close the gap that remained between them? She so desperately wanted to excel in her training, if only to graduate and return home. But there was something about her relationship with Arduen that gave her pause. Her heart seemed to expand inside her chest, and as she thought more and more about leaving, the dull ache only intensified. He encouraged her to grow closer to him, yet no matter how much she pushed back, he never yielded any of his own struggles.

What had he thought of her when she poured out all her pains into his hands? Did he pity her, or did he understand?

When Arduen's gaze returned to her, Lilith forced a faint smile.

"That's enough for today. Let's pray together now."

FIVE YEARS. IT HAD TAKEN JULIUS FIVE YEARS TO NEAR HIS graduation. Day after day, he excelled at every aspect of being Divine. Would she ever graduate? There were days that left her hopeful and there were days she succumbed to nauseating anxiety.

It had become evident in her training as well. Her body had been pushed past its extremities. Where once she'd felt strong, she now felt boneless. Left to flounder up the spiralling staircase to her awaiting bed every night like a sack of bones. Arduen did his best to spur her on, to speak words of wisdom and encouragement. But despite the slight moments of respite, Lilith surrendered to her berating doubts.

"You must believe in yourself, Lilith," Arduen said. "Cast away all of your worries for they will not ward off the outcome. They will only make the path to the future more insufferable."

Lilith lay on the ground, her body aching from the countless bruises her Master's wooden sword had inflicted. She wasn't angry with him for hurting her. It was better that he show her no mercy, for how else was she going to convince herself that she could prevail?

"Let's go again," she said indignantly.

Arduen lowered the practice sword. "You've had enough for today. Go and get cleaned up for supper." An order.

"I can do this," she insisted. "I have to do this!" She rose to her feet, wincing as she did.

Her Master sighed and shook his head. "Lilith, there is still much to learn and you're in no mental state to spar. You are letting your emotions cloud your judgement. You can't focus as you should."

At the sight of her crestfallen expression, he added, "It's dangerous to push a Divine too far, especially a novice. You're too emotional, and that can be lethal for all of us. Therefore, we are done." Arduen retrieved the wooden sword from her hand and she argued no more.

THE AUTUMN BREEZE FILTERED THROUGH THE OPEN WINDOW, A cool caress on her bare skin as Lilith knelt into prayer position. On the floor of her bedchamber, she let the presence of Constantine wash over her. For the first time, she was compelled to speak—to plead—for guidance. Assurance.

"Constantine," she began, "I have spent many days seeking You—seeking knowledge—yet I am losing faith. I am losing faith in myself. I need guidance greater than Arduen can grant me. I need guidance from within. It seems that I am not strong enough, and Spiro could attack at any moment. I'm afraid that I will not survive battle." *Not if my father failed to.*

"I need You to help me to understand and see what it is that I cannot on my own. Lest I perish and You're forced to start anew with another." Lilith let her words fade away as she lay there, vulnerable. Her God's presence washed over her, but she didn't perceive a response. With a disappointed sigh, she rose to her feet and dressed herself. It was time for supper.

The kitchen was alive with excitement as Lilith entered the large chamber. No one seemed to notice her, they were too focused on whatever the cause of commotion was. She seated herself as Olga took notice of her presence.

The Oracle slid toward her. Lilith had never witnessed Olga in such a cheerful state. "I have just shared the news!" she exclaimed. "We will be joined by another noviciate! He will arrive tomorrow. His name is Felix, and Wren will be his Master."

"Ah, I haven't heard from Wren in what feels like a hundred years!" exclaimed Quin. "Have you, Arduen?"

Her Master laughed and shook his head. "Last I heard, he went off to rusticate overseas in Dalegonè. I haven't heard from him since."

Quin chuckled darkly. "I'm starting to think he was the smartest of us all." Arduen joined in his mirth and Lilith focused in on his timbre.

"You don't mean Lord Wren, do you?" Julius cut in. "My father appointed him lord over the northeastern province of Dalegonè. My father told me he was Divine, but we didn't have much time to discuss before I left."

Lilith's attention fell on her colleague with shrewd interest. What position did his father hold in the Dalegonian government to be able to *appoint* lords?

"That would be him," Quin confirmed. "Many Divines become lords or dignitaries in their retirement."

Arduen jabbed an elbow into Quin's side. "Politics give the lazy ones a sense of duty and purpose." He didn't seem to be particularly fond of Wren, though Lilith was unsure if the others could sense it.

Quin scoffed. "He was never one to endorse warrior women, so be wary of him, Lilith. Do not take his words to heart." He placed a reassuring hand on her shoulder and squeezed once.

Lilith was used to censure. Since assuming her father's role as Utica's blacksmith, she had no issue claiming roles that were dominated by men. In fact, she prided herself on her ability to master those roles. Besides, what did one's reproductive purpose have to do with how they chose to make a living?

"You don't have to worry about him, Lilith," Arduen added. "He was always afraid of the Aether wielders, so he won't give you much grief." He winked at her.

"This will delay our trip to the capital," Olga added. "Hapless, but under the best circumstance. Emperor Obadïa will have to wait."

"Wren is quite the old brute," Quin said on a sigh. "This shall make for some interesting sparring. You must ensure you get out with us, Ambrose. You won't want to miss Wren's skill with a blade."

"If he's retained any," Arduen added caustically, and the kitchen erupted into a symphony of laughter and chortles. Lilith delighted in it.

"And what is this new Divine's element?" Julius queried.

Olga grinned. "He was Anointed by Thëo, God of Earth."

17

MORE BURDEN THAN BLESSING

Through clenched teeth, Lilith cursed as her arrow whistled through the air right past her target. She hadn't had much practice in the past few months, leaving her less than apt with a bow. After spending so many days berating herself for her shortcomings, she spent an equivalent amount of time coercing her mind to become more understanding of herself.

Before she let her doubts besiege her yet again, she nocked an arrow, raised her bow, aimed and released. She missed the entire target by an inch. She dispelled the frustrated breath she'd been harboring with a *whoosh*. The breeze rustled through the remaining copper leaves, camouflaging another stream of colorful curses.

"You need to expel all the air in your lungs before you take aim and release." Lilith didn't have to see Julius to know the voice belonged to him.

"I seem to have forgotten…" she said dryly as she took aim

again and released; this time she hit the target. Not a bullseye though.

"Much better!" Julius took up position beside her, his own longbow in his hands. He smiled down at her as he nocked an arrow, aimed, and released. Bullseye.

Lilith grinned at him, struggling to seem unimpressed by the accuracy of his shot. "How long have you practised archery?"

"Since I was a child. It was important to my father that I knew how to wield an assortment weapons, lest I ever found myself in a life-threatening situation." He nocked another arrow but kept his bow lowered, waiting for Lilith to take another shot. She did and hit the outer edge of the target again.

Inviting conversation, she asked, "Do you have siblings?"

"No," he replied shortly. When she decided better of inquiring further, he added, "My younger sister died shortly after birth and my mother didn't want to bear any others, since she'd produced a suitable heir already. My father loves her enough to grant her every wish."

Lilith inclined her head and said gently, "I'm sorry." *His father's heir*. What was he the heir of? His father had given Wren the status of lord, so he was certainly of high status. She straightened her posture instinctively. Julius could be of noble birth! She fell silent and refocused on her form, not pressing him to divulge any more of his personal life.

"Don't be. Death is a vital part of life, however contradictory that may seem." He laughed hollowly and echoed her question, "Do you have any siblings?"

Lowering her bow, she answered, "I have an older brother." She hesitated to explain further. Her family situation was complicated enough, she didn't want him to know how damaged she truly was.

"Are you close with him?"

"I was…"

Julius arched a dark brow. "And you are no longer?"

"Well, I'm here now," she explained. "It's difficult to be close."

As he spoke, he fired another arrow. "I don't see how physical distance can translate into being distant from someone." Bullseye. "I consider myself close with my father, yet I am many miles from him." His understanding of closeness was intriguing, and Lilith welcomed the new perspective.

"You haven't seen him since you came here?"

"No, I have not. We cannot write either, as there are not many birds that can survive the journey overseas. And I wouldn't trust a common courier, not that I'd be able to find one willing to travel to Xanthë."

"But you consider yourself close to him still?" After five years. She didn't attempt to mask her confusion, she wanted to understand.

"Yes, because life is long, and I won't be confined here forever. I'm nearing graduation now; I can return home to him as soon as I am deemed worthy. I assume that he and I will pick up where we left off. Nothing will have changed between us." He finished his short explanation with that endearing smile, never lacking in charm.

Julius was just another person she would have to say goodbye to, Lilith reminded herself. The more she thought about her immortality, the more the coming years terrified her. The Divine were of the opinion that they were family, yet they were scattered across the world, separated from one another unless situations proved to be hostile and their services were needed. It would not be wise to get attached to anyone here—even Arduen.

To love is to lose.

Lilith lowered her gaze until it rested upon Julius's scarred forearms. Though many other women would be of the opinion that his scars were unattractive, even grotesque, she found them to be warranting of respect and admiration. A blush suffused her cheeks when he noticed her attention.

Julius smiled, his eyes flashing to his scarred arms. "Don't go playing with elements unsupervised." He raised his bow and released another arrow. Bullseye, yet again.

Determined to do the same, Lilith nocked an arrow and raised her bow into position. She exhaled as he instructed, squinted as she aimed, and released. It pierced the heart of the target.

Bullseye.

She turned to Julius, beaming. His eyes softened as they met hers. "You're a natural archer."

Returning his bow to his back, he made to leave. Before he left her alone, he said, "Do not let yourself grow so hard, Lilith. You may think that letting people go will make you stronger, but it is not so. You'll only become the cause of your own misery. Realizing and accepting every situation as temporary will help you to pull through."

His eyes pierced her over his leather spaulders. "You may surprise yourself. Strength is not determined by will, or muscle, or dexterity, but rather by perspective. You only have to avert your eyes slightly to transform your outlook completely."

AT THE MIDDAY MEAL, LILITH KEPT TO HERSELF. SHE NOTICED THE way Julius held himself at the table. How utterly polite his manners were. It struck her like a backhanded blow. Could he be the Crown Prince of Dalegonè?

Keeping her sight deviated, she focused on the scraps of meat in front of her, pushing them around her plate, no longer interested in her meal. Her colleague was a *prince*. He probably already had some experience in the training that they'd been undergoing, at least intellectually. It could take her even longer to graduate than the five years it had taken him.

Dismayed, she didn't lift her head when the door burst open and two tall figures sauntered in. Winter in northern Augusta was frigid, but an even colder torrent followed them here.

Lilith was the only one who refrained from standing to greet the newcomers. After a brief introduction, in which Wren granted Lilith nothing but a terse tilt of his head, they all took their seats at the kitchen table. The new noviciate, Felix, cast her a nervous smile as she passed the plate of roast beef to him.

They spent the rest of their meal listening to Wren vaunt of his travels and subsequently of his many excursions with King Faustus, ruler of Dalegonè—and Julius's father.

Confirmation rushed through Lilith like a cold deluge. He *was* a prince. A crown prince. All this time, she'd been speaking to royalty!

Wren regarded Julius with the semi-formal title, Prince. He did absolutely nothing to conceal his affection and admiration for Julius. He even went so far as to inform him that his father was getting stronger, whatever that meant. Julius only smiled appreciably, politely, and said very little.

After everyone was finished their meals, the Masters displayed no inclination to stand and get along with the afternoon's usual events. Arduen announced to the noviciates that because of the new arrival, they would forgo the usual training in the sparring field and allow them to get acquainted with one another—much to Lilith's annoyance, she was eager to excel.

"Well," said Julius, "why don't we go outside and walk along the beach?"

Felix only shyly mumbled his assent before following Julius to the door. Lilith remained seated, unsure whether the invitation was extended to her.

Julius turned to her and asked quietly, "Will you join us?"

Reluctantly, she followed. For who was she to deny a prince?

⚬ ⚬ ⚬ ⚬ ⚬

THE THREE NOVICIATES WALKED TOGETHER ALONG THE BEACH. The sand had grown tense from the brisk late-autumn climate. The sea's waves were larger than usual, their white caps appearing and disappearing across the horizon. Lilith found the motion of the waves calming; she didn't avert her gaze from its beauty when the men began to converse.

Julius spoke first. "Where are you from?"

"I was born in Calydon, but I was orphaned very young as my mother passed giving birth to my twin sister, and my father fell in the second battle of Dodöna. So I was sent to

Argolïs with the other orphans from my town." Felix's tone was sombre but he spoke with confidence.

The Battle of Dodöna. Felix had lost his father to the cataclysmic battle that was the predecessor to the Battle of Elïath, which occurred almost a decade later—the battle that had claimed her own father's life.

Felix asked in turn, "Where are you from? Both of you."

Lilith gestured for Julius to speak first, so the prince cleared his throat and loosed a lengthy sigh. "I hail from Dalegonè's capital, Xanthë. I was born and raised there."

"Wren said you're the Crown Prince. He speaks so fondly of you. That's a rarity." There was no hint of hesitation in his words. The boy was so innocent.

"Yes, my father is the King of Dalegonè." Julius displayed no sign of arrogance in the statement.

"Do you have siblings?" Felix seemed fascinated by Julius's heritage, and for a moment, it was as though Lilith was listening in on a private conversation.

"Unfortunately, I am an only child."

"The Fawkes Dynasty," Felix remarked wistfully. He seemed in awe of the presence of royalty. And if Lilith was honest, she was too.

"Yes," Julius answered absentmindedly.

Julius Fawkes.

"I haven't heard much about your country," said Felix. "But I have heard that your father is highly esteemed and beloved by your people." Such an education was surprising for an orphan. Lilith, having had a decent education, had been taught the basics about Dalegonè, its people and culture. Though she possessed a very fragmented vision of what Julius's upbringing would have looked like.

"That is a statement that would tickle my father's ears," Julius mused.

"You can wield Fire?" Felix asked, brows pointed to the sky when Julius nodded humbly. "Incredible!" he gasped. "I'm glad I wasn't blessed by Xander, no offence. I heard Fire is a bloody bitch to wield."

"Indeed, it can be." Julius held up his hands, showcasing the intricate swirls etched into his skin, decorating his fore-arms. Felix blanched, almost reaching forward to grasp Julius's hands, as if his glimpse couldn't have been close enough.

Felix dropped the subject and turned to Lilith. "And what about you?"

Her eyes remained focused on the sea. "I wield Aether," she responded primly.

"And where are you from?"

"I am from Utica." She didn't bother to elaborate on her heritage or her childhood. Not that she didn't want to, but she wasn't sure how. Spending so much time in one place didn't make for interesting tales and conversation, or for meeting new people.

"That's not far from Calydon!"

Lilith smiled at him kindly. He was modest and positively eager for greater knowledge. If only she could be so light-hearted. She only wished she'd had nothing to lose when Constantine had Anointed her, maybe then she would have been as excited to leave home.

"How old are you, Felix?" she asked.

"I'm sixteen, and you?" His glance flitted between them both.

Julius answered first, "I am twenty-two."

"And I'm eighteen," Lilith chimed in, finding her mood had improved since she'd first set out with the boys.

Felix nodded his head in appreciation, his mousy brown hair falling over his forehead. "I'm glad that I'm the youngest, it just means you two will have no choice but to help me catch up."

Julius laughed at the remark and Lilith managed to cast a closed-lip smile in his direction.

"Sixteen, aye? That means you've been released from the orphanage only this year," Julius observed. "What have you been doing in Argolïs since you've been a free man?"

Felix considered the question for a moment. "I had to find a job immediately. There isn't enough room to remain at the orphanage, so once your sixteenth birthday arrives, you're basically thrown out the door. No feast. No celebration. It didn't feel like freedom when night fell and I was searching for a safe place to rest my head, especially without the drachmae to pay for it."

Lilith had spent many nights out in the wilderness by herself with nothing but a bedroll and her bow. But that was entirely different from spending an evening in the streets of a large city, astir with vagrants and criminals.

"But you survived…" Julius said, spurring on Felix's story.

"I did. I was able to locate an inn that set me up in a small room—more like a cupboard—and allowed me to stay until I found a place of my own. I had to pay them back, of course. They were more than generous, and they fed me too. For *free*." His tone was so sanguine, Lilith was ashamed of her recent dismal demeanor.

"I found a job in the mines and worked away my days. I was up before dawn and home after dusk. I paid the innkeepers every night and they continued to feed me. They became like family. I am beholden to them, and one day I will return and repay my debts owed to them." Felix placed a fist over his heart.

"The likeness of that generosity is a rarity in any city," Julius noted. When he cast an expectant glance her way, Lilith smiled agreeably.

"What was it like to have thought your life was over, only to wake up and realize you're fine?" Felix glanced between them both.

A shadow blanketed the prince's face, but before she could inspect it any closer, it passed.

Lilith hesitated. How could an experience like that be put into words? It couldn't. She'd never spoken of the event to anyone and she'd rarely thought about it, especially what it had *felt* like.

"Well what was it like for you?" Julius cunningly deflected the question, not to Lilith's surprise. You don't survive court if you aren't cunning with your words and how you order them. She doubted anyone ignored the Crown Prince.

"I was just working as usual, pickaxe in hand, when I heard screaming and a rumbling that seemed to almost come from within the stones. It was so violent. Then everything went black." Felix dramatized his story like a fantastical tale.

"When I finally came to, I was lying among the bodies of my fallen workmates. I was covered in blood, completely drenched. It had coagulated on my skin, my clothes. I guess they assumed that I was dead as well. Then an official noticed me. He carefully lifted me to my feet, calling for assistance. I was cared for, courtesy of my employers. When they discovered that I had no wounds, not even a bruise, the questions sprang up.

"Of course I had no idea what had happened and I couldn't answer any of them. I spent days being questioned by the Emperor's Frourà, who were sent to investigate the accident. They kept me in a tent and I just pretended to be a mental vegetable. I pretended that I didn't know my own name or where I lived or that I was even employed in the mines. They believed it.

"Then Wren showed up one night and explained everything, and it all made more sense than mere luck. So I fled with him, and it took nearly a month of swift travel to make it here."

The story left a whirlwind of near-deafening thoughts swirling in Lilith's head. Visions of blood and gore flashed behind her eyelids, and she stiffened at the morbidity of them. She looked out over the sea, hoping the beautiful sight could cleanse her mind of the horror.

What unnerved her more was the fact that she was slightly comforted by the shared trauma. Was that selfish? Was that what Arduen meant by all Divine becoming family? Only through shared experiences and understanding?

"Very interesting..." said Julius. He'd gone unusually distant himself.

Felix continued speaking with enthusiasm, "I honestly didn't know what it meant until Wren told me all I needed to know on the way. He told me all about our individual gifts and how we work together, like an army, like the Emperor's Milítia. Then he told me we can live forever. Of all the gifts, that's what I most look forward to: raising mountains and living on them forever!" He was guileless, and though Lilith found her new colleague amiable, she admired his innocence most. But his openness to discuss sensitive topics was unsettling.

With the promise of unlimited days, the simple luxuries of life became meaningless. It seemed all too easy to become insensate to deeper emotion, to the visceral notions of life. The thought was repulsive, sparking an unprecedented fear that shadowed every thought.

"I think," she began without inflection, "that immortality is more a burden than a blessing." With a curt goodbye, she made her way back to the Frourío.

"She's prickly," she heard Felix say as she stalked away.

SUMMON AND STIFLE

Out on the eastern edge of the training field, Lilith released arrow after arrow. With every shot, she hit her mark.

Utterly pleased, Arduen grinned at his noviciate. "Well done! Practice has paid off." He held out his hands, gesturing to the bow and quiver, and she handed them over before retreating a few steps at his command. "Now to make this more difficult…"

Lilith watched him with narrowed eyes, bracing herself for a release of Aether, but Arduen had other ideas. He displayed an array of moves so stealthy, with inhuman speed and deadly accuracy. Whenever he faced the target, he fired and hit its centre. Every twist and turn and jump, he deftly pulled an arrow from the quiver, nocked it, and sent it soaring toward the target, always in graceful unison. She had never seen anything so impressive, and she instantly lusted after the skill.

Arduen, noting the astonishment gleaming in her eyes,

produced an esteemed bow. "That is what I want you to begin practicing for the next hour. Do not expect to master it today. This took years for me, but it definitely prepares the archer's mind for the true complexities of battle." He studied her for a moment. What had he perceived?

"Yes, Master," Lilith cooed, a faint smile tugging at her lips.

He mirrored her smile. "Tomorrow we leave for the capital. I expect you have practiced Discernment. You need to be able to handle the din of Kenora."

"I practice every evening with the sea. I feel and explore every crevice, every creature, and I mute them out one by one."

Arduen seemed pleased with her answer. "I don't believe you'll have any major problems then, but a city the size of Kenora will still be a shock. It'll be eight days of travel. I suggest you pack tonight."

"Yes, Master."

He waved a quick goodbye, and Lilith bit down hard on her bottom lip as he crossed the field. She had a new problem; she possessed no presentable clothing to wear in the Emperor's presence. She resolved to ask Olga for any spare garments that would be considered presentable.

Another figure strode in her direction in the afternoon sunlight—Julius. Lilith's cheeks burned as she observed his stride, the surety in each step, the power he exuded. His features were elegant and gentle, yet he possessed such a masculine air.

Lowering her gaze, she prayed for composure as he approached. She couldn't stand for any distractions, not now that she was beginning to excel. Larkin was waiting for her in Utica. She couldn't throw that all away for a man she just met.

"Arduen said you hit every target dead centre!" Julius beamed at her.

"I did," she confirmed. "Thanks to your seasoned expertise, *Prince*."

Julius winced slightly at the use of the title and shuffled his feet awkwardly, the first time she'd ever witnessed him appear uneasy. "I'm glad," was all he said.

Lilith was reluctant to begin attempting to master a new skill with him there to witness, so she waited for him to speak. When Julius brushed a stray curl from his eyes, she resisted the urge to reach out and assist him.

"I just wanted to ask you about what you said yesterday afternoon..." He didn't look up from his hands, clasped tightly around the blade of his wooden sword.

Unable to form coherent words, she arched a brow and waved him on.

"You mentioned that you think immortality is more of a burden than a blessing. I want to know *why* you think that." He looked into her eyes, Xander's Fire smoldering in his gaze, and she thought she could glimpse a sense of sorrow within the flames.

Lilith tore her eyes from his, needing to sever contact while she organized her thoughts. "It's just unsettling knowing that I will outlive the ones I love most." She paused to consider the information she was about to share with him, but when she glimpsed the vulnerability that coated his fine features, she resolved to lower her barriers as well. "I can't stand to imagine a day where I will have to watch them go—those I love. And if I don't watch them pass, I will grieve just as fiercely when the realization hits me. For surely when a century passes, they will be gone. I don't have parents to say goodbye to, but my brother"—she choked on the words—"my brother is my only living family, and I can't stand the thought of life without him. He grounds me. Who will I be when he's not here to remind me of who I really am?" She bowed her head, closed her eyes, willing the tears to subside.

Julius stepped closer to her, though he halted at a respectable distance. "I understand..." He heaved a wavering sigh. "I have also had similar thoughts. I can't imagine being without my family and those who faithfully serve us. I cannot imagine living under a monarch who does not age or die. I don't want to be king, yet due to my love for my people, I am obligated."

Lilith considered his words carefully. Julius was his father's only child and the responsibility of ruling Dalegonè would be passed to him in the coming years. Yet she'd dismissed the thought of Julius ascending his father's throne because he was Divine, and Divinity superseded all other responsibilities.

Sounds of Wren and Felix sparring drifted over to them on the breeze.

"What do you think of Felix?" Julius asked.

Lilith followed his gaze. "He's kind." She should say more, but she couldn't. If Julius was asking Felix what he thought of her, he'd say *'she's prickly.'*

"Go easy on him." Julius patted her shoulder, her stomach flipping at his touch. "He's young, and since he didn't have much to lose before this, coming to live and train at the Frourío is a blessing, not a curse."

"Right," she said.

"He doesn't have anyone to miss," said Julius. "Not like we do."

Together they made their way through the training field. As they sauntered toward the looming tower, they paused to witness Felix's first training session with Wren. His tawny skin was coated in sweat, but nonetheless, his face was locked in a determined grin. Lilith couldn't help but giggle, which she stifled at Wren's glare.

"Hello, Lilith," Felix greeted her with evident cheer. "Care to demonstrate your skill with the blade?"

She held her hand out to Wren, indicating her intention to accept Felix's offer.

A scathing laugh escaped Wren's lips. "I would rather my mentee learn from someone more *capable* with a blade. Prince Julius, would you care to spar with Felix?"

Julius shifted uncomfortably, clearly unsure whether to accept and help Felix or to defend Lilith's honor. He chose the latter. "I would, but I've had enough sparring today. I must send my prayers to Xander before we sup tonight." He cast a warning glance at Lilith before politely bidding them farewell.

Wren paid Lilith little heed as he turned back to his noviciate. Lilith scoffed and made to leave before Wren's voice halted her.

"If you are wise, my boy, and wish to survive the oncoming war, you will train only with men who are skilled and honed warriors." Wren raised his voice. "Do not tarry with women who should be warming our beds and raising our children."

That was enough to set Lilith off, but she couldn't lash out, she couldn't retaliate. Wren was a Master, and it was expected of her to treat him as such. She turned to face them, a mocking, saccharine smile spreading her lips. A single vein throbbed on Wren's tanned forehead, noticeable under beads of sweat.

Lilith approached Felix and said, loud enough for both men to hear, "If you are wise, my boy, and wish to survive the impending war, you will train with smart yet fierce women who are blessed with the skill to both summon life and *stifle* it."

Wren flushed at the impertinence lining her riposte but quickly masked it with a dignified jut of his chin. A slight grin settled over his feline features. A grin that Lilith noticed did not reach his eyes.

⚬ ⚬ ⚬ ⚬ ⚬

LILITH RETURNED TO HER BEDCHAMBER AND CHANGED INTO CLEAN breeches and a freshly laundered blouse. She dried her long hair with a towel before braiding it back out of her face. Arduen had told her to pack, but she had very few belongings, so there was no pressing need.

She lounged upon her bed, casting her mind out into the oscillating waves of the sea. She hummed a tune as she investigated the many creatures that populated the sea's depths, trilling delightedly when she discovered an unfamiliar entity.

Reverberations thundered through the walls of the Frourío. Dust scattered on the floor. Lilith jumped off her bed in alarm as the door to her bedchamber burst open.

Arduen, red faced and irate, stormed in, slamming the door behind him. When he faced her, his glare shot awls.

Lilith's heart pounded. Blood rushed to her face as her Master closed in on her. He'd never been this angry, not even when she disobeyed his orders and joined the boys on the raid. Not even when he found out she'd been injured because of her foolishness.

Arduen's baritone cracked through the air like a whip. "I do not want to hear that you have disrespected a Master in this hold. I *never* want to be this humiliated by my own noviciate again! You will learn to hold your tongue against those who are elder and wiser than you. Am I understood?!"

Lilith bit back the retort on the end of her tongue, but her silence only incensed him further. He was practically seething. Mustering courage, she defended herself. "He wouldn't let me spar with Felix because I'm *female!*"

Arduen raised his hand to silence her and she froze with parted lips, nerve faltering.

"I do not care!" he spat with explosive impulse.

She pursed her lips, beseeching them to cease their quivering. She tried to formulate the words to make him understand her. He had to understand. "Arduen, he *humiliated* me!" She implored him with her gaze. Her voice shaking, she barely managed to whisper, "You must understand."

"I am your Master!" he bellowed, his glower inciting tears.

Lilith shied away from him, ashamed of the fear that coursed through her body. With a hand covering her mouth, she knew, with his Divine senses, that he could see her trembling. Her stomach became leaden with so many mixed emotions, she couldn't begin to comprehend all of them.

Lowering his voice, Arduen adopted a softer, gentler tone. "There are rules in place here, and respecting your Masters is the first and foremost of those. Break that rule and you will face the consequences, and they are *dire.*"

She was still unable to face him, fearful of another turbulent harangue. Choking on her sobs, she could only produce a nod. When he remained unmoved by the action, she was forced to say, "Yes, Master."

Arduen relinquished an exasperated sigh as he scratched at his head. He opened his mouth as if to say something, but clamped his jaw shut and angled toward the door. Before he left, he turned back to her and said gently, "Dinner is about to be served."

Lilith didn't move until the *click* of the shutting door sounded and the thumping of Arduen's retreating footsteps faded. Chatter rose to meet her ears from the kitchen below, but she refused to join them. For they'd heard what had occurred, and she had no intention to sit among them with a tear-stained face. But mostly, she refused to give Wren the satisfaction.

She took to her windowsill and sent her consciousness soaring toward the sea's depths. She became one with every pulse of every heartbeat of every creature beneath the blue surface of the Undersea. The waves reverberated through her veins. Saltwater sluicing through her arteries.

Lilith sucked in a ragged breath, willing herself to leave the confines of her bedchamber and swim beneath the sea's surface.

YOUR TIME HAS COME

Larkin woke with a start as two strong hands gripped his shoulders and dragged him from the comfort of his bed. He groaned but did not resist; it was the same routine every day. Though the healer visited nightly to mend his crippled limbs, a sense of lameness still lingered.

Every day the Emperor's soldiers retrieved him. He was taken to a torture chamber for questioning. They wanted answers he didn't have. Though he screamed the truth, they wouldn't believe him. They were relentless with their sadistic tactics.

The Frourà legionnaires threw him to the floor and began to bind his wrists and ankles. This time they used rope, a pleasant contrast to the usual harsh iron shackles. They bound his hands to his feet, his face pressed firmly to the plush carpet beneath him as they proceeded to tie his limbs, his back arching uncomfortably. He didn't voice his discomfort as his muscles stretched taut. The soldiers fed themselves on unpleasant noises, they would only become more ruthless the more he protested.

They settled themselves into formation around him. They didn't speak once during the process—they never did. They just grunted, their touch callous, their armor jingling a macabre melody.

Larkin closed his eyes and let his head sag as they made their way out of his chambers and back down to the interrogation vaults beneath the castle.

They carried him through hallways, deep crimson carpets fading into gold. This wasn't the usual route. It was taking them far longer to reach their destination than usual. The soldiers had never strayed from the path. They moved through the servants' passages, keeping as discreet as possible.

Heat seared through Larkin's aching limbs. What was the reason for the alternate route? Had the Emperor finally ordered his execution? Every step the soldiers took ripped at the skin around his wrists and ankles. Hot blood dripped down his arms, globules visible on the stone floor, forming a trail behind him. Larkin grimaced at the pain, but his thoughts wouldn't deviate from his possible execution.

"Excuse me, has there been a change of plans?" he dared to ask.

"Your time has come, Larkin Oak," said one of the legionnaires. The other soldiers grunted their laughter, guttural sounds of heartless warriors.

In one swift movement, the soldier to his right shifted. Worn, black leather boots entered Larkin's line of sight. Then sharp pain lanced through his skull and everything went black.

2 0

ORPHANS AND BASTARDS

As the Divine prepared for the trip to the capital, Olga gifted Lilith a leather pack. The Oracle had procured a selection of chiton gowns from Kynös, of which she let Lilith have first pick. At the woman's munificence, Lilith couldn't help but feel she'd been foisted upon them with little to offer in exchange.

Lilith packed a clean set of breeches and a tunic, along with fur-lined leathers that Arduen had given her for when the temperatures dropped to near-freezing. They still hadn't spoken since his steaming tirade, and she wasn't sure she was ready to reconcile.

It was a lengthy trip to the capital and in the cold late-autumn weather, they wouldn't be able to bathe before they reached their destination. Lilith chose to ride in her leathers as they were the most comfortable, and flexible, should they encounter enemies on the road. Olga gifted her a new cloak, a woollen himation suitable for winter, of which she clasped at her clavicle. The large hood would shelter her from the bite of freezing rain—and prying eyes.

They raced through the day, only stopping twice to eat and let the horses rest and drink. Arduen and Quin mapped out the journey, every resting location predetermined by their combined experience and wisdom. Dark clouds dominated the southern sky and Olga estimated that they would enter the gale by midday.

Felix often broke the silence with questions about the Emperor or the purpose of their meeting, or even the role of the Divinity in politics. A topic which Lilith found exceedingly interesting.

"We are the disciples of the Gods," Arduen replied. "So naturally, if the Gods are considered above royalty, then so are we. We were created to serve and protect all the inhabitants of this world equally, therefore no oaths of fealty may be granted."

"What if they forced us to swear an oath?" Felix asked. "What if, for instance, they were to drug us and use force?"

It was Quin who responded first, "Then we let them kill us. We do not swear any oaths. Death would be the only option as the Gods would smite us down for sacrificing our freedom, the one most important gift from above."

"No political leader would ever be so foolish as to drug one of the Divine," Arduen added. "For even a drug couldn't diminish the powers we contain within. Substances would merely *confuse* rather than *diffuse* our gifts. They could cause more catastrophic outcomes, obliterating everyone involved, even ourselves. No. No ruler has ever been so injudicious.

Attempting to conquer a Divine would be the most strident affront to the Gods, and They would punish not only that individual, but likely damn their entire dynasty."

"But how do we know that the Gods will smite us down for declaring allegiance to a ruler?" Felix inquired.

Lilith cringed as Wren's voice rose from the silence. "We know that They will because They've done it before. We've had a few situations where a Divine was manipulated into swearing fealty to a crown, and every time they were struck down by the wrath of their God. No Athánatos Star for them!"

"But I thought every Divine was due to receive their own Star?" Felix groused.

Arduen chuckled, amused by the boy. "We all do but only if our actions are honorable."

The sky darkened, shrouding them in the heart of the gale. Frozen rain began to pelt them mercilessly.

"Well throw me to the Maw of Hades!" Felix burst out. "Our bodies are parting the airborne piss!" He waved a hand through the mist with a dramatic flair.

Wren swatted his noviciate with a muffled curse. It was blasphemy to call the rain Gods' piss. In Felix's defence, the rain was thick enough to wade through and mighty irritating.

Lilith harnessed her snigger. Her eyes drilling into the back of Wren's head. A lopsided grin split her lips as she imagined all the ways she could force him to fall from his steed. How she could coerce the horse into rearing and bucking him off. She amused herself in this manner until they made camp for the evening in the confines of the Forest.

There was a small pond within the trees close to the camp. The men bathed first, using cloths to wash themselves as it was too cold to swim. Olga and Lilith took their turn while Arduen and Quin made a quick stew over the campfire. Julius, Wren, and Felix tended to the horses' needs.

The pond seemed to glow in the moonlight, embodying an emerald hue from the trees that encircled it. It would have been a welcoming sight if the air wasn't so chilly. Olga removed her clothing, exposing smooth bare skin to the brisk air. Lilith couldn't help her curiosity as she studied the woman. Her body was lined with lean muscle, proof that she was still a fierce warrior. She appeared to be a woman in her early forties, but as the Oracle, she was the eldest living Divine.

"You have a beautiful skin tone, Lilith." Olga said, the expression on her face letting Lilith know that she was aware of her studying eyes.

"Thank you," Lilith replied, embarrassed. Her skin bore a tawny undertone, as if she spent all her days being kissed by the sun. She'd never thought her skin to be exceptionally beautiful, but it was clear of blemishes. Her father and brother were born with olive skin, and Lilith had often imagined herself growing into such a complexion.

"Oh, to be young..." Olga cooed into the darkness.

The Oracle pulled several bars of soap from her pack. Rolling one bar between her hands, she passed the second to Lilith. After she lathered the suds onto her skin and massaged it in, Olga dunked her cloth under the water and rinsed. Lilith followed suit. Once they were finished, they donned clean attire and packed up their belongings.

For a short moment, Olga scrutinized Lilith's outfit, her usual blouse and breeches. "We really need to get you more clothing, my dear," Olga said. "I will send one of the Emperor's servants to gather the supplies we need while we are tending to our business with the Emperor."

Lilith thanked her, though she didn't want more reasons to be beholden to the Divine of the Frourío.

When they were finished bathing, Lilith asked Olga to tend to her matted braid. As the Oracle worked, she asked, "What is the capital like?"

"It's crowded and busy. There are people who live in such odious conditions and then there are those who are foreign to them, those who are surrounded by nothing but opulence."

"What of the Emperor and the other nobles? What are they like?"

Olga seemed to consider her words wisely, for it took her a moment to respond, in which time she braided Lilith's long hair down her back. Lilith closed her eyes in contentment as Olga's long nails gently grazed her scalp.

"The Emperor is well versed in politics and is used to getting what he wants, he's used to favoritism. Be wary of him. Thankfully you do not have to deal with him, or his sycophantic courtiers, without our aid. You will never have to confer with him much more than a simple greeting and farewell. As for his son, there is much to caution you about where Prince Oríon is concerned. I would keep your distance entirely."

"And what of the others in the court?" Lilith probed.

Olga briefly summarized the tension within the court. Quarrels and bouts between certain noble families and the Elite class that seemed to have been passed down through the generations.

"There isn't much that you need be concerned with, Lilith. Arduen and I will handle most of the affairs and take the lead in the discussions. That has always been the way. Arduen will always have your best interest in mind, however harsh he may seem at times." Olga flashed her a pointed look.

Lilith hung her head and kept to herself. The last topic she wanted to discuss was her Master.

When they sauntered back to camp, the men looked up from the campfire as they entered the clearing. Lilith rushed to Skydancer's side to give him some attention before she went to sleep. Seating herself between Olga and Quin, she kept her eyes diverted from both Wren and Arduen. She could sense Arduen's gaze, and despite her will to ignore it, her eyes rose to meet his. Her Master's lips quirked into the slightest smile. It did little to assuage the contention between them. Her mind had been cloven by his diatribe, and she needed more than a smile to stitch it back together.

It would take a God to mend the rift that now divided them. Unease still lingered where her Master was concerned, and his thunderous footsteps echoed in the chamber of her mind for the remainder of the evening.

◎ ◌ ⤳ ⋔ ◌

THE DAYS MELDED TOGETHER LIKE ORE HOT FROM THE FORGE. They awoke at first light, and after a quick meal of cheese and bread, they set off toward the capital.

Lilith patted the side of Skydancer's long elegant neck, her eyes peeled for any sign of danger. Her comrades fell into formation on the road ahead of her.

Arduen's expression was inscrutable as he steered his mare

to fall in alongside Skydancer. Whenever she met his watchful gaze, he offered her a meek smile which she shied away from every time.

After a few moments of shared silence, he finally spoke, "Lilith, I want to talk to you." *About the other evening.*

She offered a reflection of the faint smile he'd given her in response, an attempt to dispel the hurt still embedded inside her chest. "It doesn't matter anymore. I've become aware of my place, Master," she intoned, no venom slithering in her voice.

Another awkward moment of silence stretched between them.

There *was* more that she wanted to say. She'd be damned to allow Wren to sow discord in their relationship. Disunity would only hinder her progress as a noviciate. And the faster she excelled, the sooner she'd be reunited with Larkin.

"How can you ever expect me to have confidence on the battlefield when you berate me for defending myself?" Arduen gave no answer and she feared she may have stepped out of line again.

Her Master bowed his head, his expression speculative, and when he returned his gaze to her, his eyes were full of remorse. "I am sorry, Lilith," he said, tone soaked in penitence.

Lilith couldn't form the words to forgive him, though she already had. Drawing Skydancer closer to his mare, she reached for his hand. His fingers wrapped around her fist; her hand so small in his.

"You cannot be blamed," she said. "I don't think you meant to hurt me." Would this be enough to draw him from his shell? Would it be enough to mend what had been riven?

"I did not, no. Of course I didn't. Seeing you so disheveled broke me." He chuffed. "I am as new to Masterdom as you are to Divinity. I hope you can understand that we are both learning to assume new roles." He gave her hand an affectionate squeeze. "I never want to hurt you, Lilith. I don't enjoy this friction either. I was angry, and I lashed out at you. I apologize."

"I understand," she whispered.

"Thank you," Arduen said. "I hope you can forgive me. I didn't handle the situation as I should have. I should have defended you and I failed. For that, again, I must apologize. I never want you to feel inadequate, for any reason. You are just as strong and skilled as any other young Divine, and you will be quite capable in a few years' time. A force to reckon with, I assume." He chuckled breathily. He was nervous, and for whatever reason, she was comforted by it.

"I forgive you," she breathed, and exhaled a mountain of pressure. The lump that had taken residence in her throat finally dissolved.

"My relationship with Wren has always been brimming with animosity," said Arduen. "However, in recent decades we have grown to withstand each other."

Lilith couldn't help the smirk that blossomed. "Because you've had a sea to separate you?"

Arduen huffed a laugh. "He is the truculent sort. But there are reasons he is the way he is." His voice dropped an octave, and he gave her hand another squeeze. "Seeds have been planted that have sprouted into daemons. There is no cure for such misery. It would be best to steer clear of him. Understood?"

"Yes, Master."

THERE WAS A SLOW SHIFT OF CONSCIOUSNESS. IT STARTED AS A recognition of sorts, as Lilith distinguished several entities nearby. After a few hours of this, the company became uproarious in her mind. They were close to the capital. Thousands of people lived in Kenora, and the thought that she would have to block them all out was daunting. It seemed impossible. Lilith longed for the sequestration of the Frourío and the calmness of the sea.

Practicing her control of Discernment had strengthened her ability to drown out the consciousness and sensations of other beings around her. But the simple minds of tiny sea creatures paled in comparison to the complex minds of humans.

The group of Divine galloped toward a large knoll. Quin and Julius crested the hill first and halted, taking in the scene before them. The other side of the knoll fell much steeper and the land all around for miles was sunken in, almost as if one of the Gods had indented the earth with His massive fist.

Kenora lay in the centre of the crater. The Emperor's castle stretched up from the cluster of bleached roofs. The city appeared as a jagged horizon, minarets rising into the sky; all of the structures dominated by the Emperor's whitewashed castle; all of the buildings constructed of the same ivory stone.

Lilith followed Arduen's lead around the knoll and through a minuscule valley, where the main road cut through the mound of earth, winding toward monumental wrought iron gates. They passed underneath the archway to be met by a wall of stench, a concoction of offal and body musk.

Trumpets sounded through the streets. The dwellers of

Kenora, a wondrous range of poor and wealthy, of Plebeian and Elite, bracketed the main thoroughfare leading to the castle. The only trace of color was the wilted blooms in window boxes.

Scanning the crowd, Lilith ignored the fingers pointed in their direction, the shouts of admiration and joy that emanated from the throng. The Augustan flag, a royal blue that faded to a brilliant gold, symbolizing the union of Western and Eastern Augusta many centuries past, swayed in the breeze, suspended from the uppermost windows of every house and hovel alike.

The Plebeians of Kenora were dressed in traditional styled chitons, the hems of which were darkened with grime. Only the wealthier could afford a cloak. The slaves, darting about in the shadows performing various tasks for their masters, were better garbed than the poorest Plebes. Even in the colder months, women wore peplos with long flowing sleeves for additional warmth—but only those who could afford it. The less fortunate were forced to expose their limbs to the stinging elements, save for ill-fitting himations.

Lilith's heart plummeted as the underprivileged children ran out to greet them. Clad in ragged robes, they couldn't possibly be warm enough. They clasped on to the hands of their destitute parents; mothers and fathers who appeared as though they could be their grandparents, the lack of nutriment resulting in such cadaverous appearances.

Lilith surveyed the city folk with morbid fascination, the sight left her reeling with self-disgust. Utica didn't know poverty the way that Kenora did. Such depravity was foreign to her. Fear and pity eddied in her gut, cloying, sparking the urge to flee. The majority of the capitals' populace was deprived of even the slightest sustainable conditions, all owed to the Great Divine's campaign for the throne.

When the Emperor's castle came into full view, Lilith exhaled a shaky breath. Ominous and dull, the castle was many times the size of Lord Alexaus's manor in Utica. The stone was the same tasteless white, the towers extending into the cloudy sky like the talons of a mighty beast.

Several legionnaires from the Emperor's Frourà took their horses and led the Divine into the castle. When the large golden doors banged closed behind them, Lilith took a moment to reassure herself that she was a free woman. That she could walk out of the fortress at any moment, free of scrutiny and repercussions—except the ones that Arduen might bestow upon her.

The armored legionnaires didn't speak as they ambled along a plush vermillion carpet that devoured Lilith's boots like sodden grass. She was suddenly conscious of her appearance, having forgone a proper bath in over a week.

They arrived at two polished wooden doors, the handles shining gold, sparkling in the light of the sconces. Lilith didn't waste time debating whether the handles were solid gold or not, the display of lavish decor had already convinced her that they were genuine. Two Frourà soldiers strode forth to open the grand doors, and when they did, the Divine cadre walked through without delay.

The large room was streaked by shafts of dusty light leaking in through the narrow windows that lined the oblong chamber. The glow accomplished little in lifting the grim atmosphere. Frourà legionnaires stood vigilant, straddling the crimson carpet leading toward a dais at the far end of the hall. Lilith's eyes followed the carpeted path until they settled upon a lone figure. Her heart leapt into her throat as she made eye contact with the man who created orphans and bastards.

Emperor Obadïa flashed them a malevolent grin. "Welcome, Divine."

CRYPTIC MESSAGES

Lilith strained against the instinct to gape, schooling her features into neutrality. She'd heard tales of Obadïa all her life, but she'd never anticipated that she would ever see the man face to face. Much less that he would ever come to know her name, or that she would be a liberated woman for the occasion.

Emperor Obadïa was striking, a hulking mass of a man. Anyone would have looked upon him with admiration, but years of battle had taken its toll. His Majesty was scarred from head to toe. Burnt, no doubt, by Spiro's vile beasts. He possessed such a venerable demeanor; Lilith fought the urge to drop to her knees in his presence. Though she'd done nothing deserving of punishment, she had to resist begging for his mercy.

The Emperor's dark eyes swept over each of them, Arduen being the only member of their group to earn a nod of recognition. When Obadïa's infernal glare rested upon Lilith, he halted. Arduen shifted his attention to her as well, which provided her enough confidence to divert her gaze from the Emperor and rest them upon her Master. A very slight reassuring smile spread across Arduen's lips, and with it, warmth seeped back into her limbs. She hadn't realized that she was shaking until Arduen tore his eyes from her.

"Your Majesty," Arduen spoke on their behalf, "we have grown in the past few months. A good omen in such miserable times."

There was a stretch of silence in which Lilith used to gather her composure. She forced herself to redirect her gaze to the Emperor. He'd ceased his stare, his eyes now focused on Arduen. His regal chiton was Augustan blue, with gold trim for the colors of a united Empire. When he spoke, his voice was deep and raspy, a complimentary addition to his overall overwhelming carriage.

"That is comforting indeed," Obadïa said. "My city has come alive with excitement. Your cadre is growing as well as my Milítia. We will be a formidable enemy when next we face Spiro on the battlefield."

The Emperor's eyes gleamed with pride as he scanned the group again, no doubt assessing every detail of their appearance. "I will have my men escort you to your accommodations. You may wash up and rest before our feast tonight. My servants will retrieve you when the hour is upon us." The Emperor turned back to his throne, a dismissal of sorts.

Arduen inclined his head in thanks and Lilith quickly imitated the movement. She gulped as the Emperor's glance lingered on her for another painful moment. What had he perceived of her to be so acutely interested?

AFTER SUBMERSING HERSELF IN A PRODIGIOUS GRANITE BATHTUB, Lilith asked Olga to brush and braid her saturated hair. Only once she was clean did she allow herself to collapse on the inordinate four-poster bed. The Oracle promised to wake her when it was time to don her gown and prepare for the banquet.

When Olga woke Lilith from her afternoon slumber, she groaned in protest and pulled the duvet above her head. The old woman only laughed viciously as she ripped the covers off of her, exposing Lilith, wearing nothing but a thin shift.

Olga began organizing their packs, amongst many paper bags. "You will be pleased to know that while you slept away the afternoon, I sent for a servant to collect various items from the markets. You will have new clothes to take home with you."

As pleased as she was to hear this, Lilith was distracted by Olga's words. *Home.* She should have taken comfort in the fact that she now envisioned the Frourío as her home, but it left her equally as disconcerted. Home had always been Utica. Home had always been Larkin.

Stealing a moment to admire her new clothing, Lilith had to clamp her jaw shut to keep herself from gaping. New leather breeches that were sinfully flattering lay across the end of the bed. Beside them lay black blouses of the finest spun cotton, black pearl buttons running down the length the garments. Lilith almost accosted Olga for the drachmae it must have cost her.

"Thank you, Olga."

The Oracle grinned as she sorted through the bags, folding

garments in separate piles. No doubt she had the servants pick up some clothing for Felix as well. "We must prepare ourselves for the banquet."

Obeying her request, Lilith retrieved the dress that Olga lent her. It was a simple chiton gown, and she wasn't familiar with tying off such a dress. She made her way to the floor-to-ceiling mirror and inspected it. It was a floor-length golden fabric, deep violet stitching decorating the hem.

Olga assisted Lilith in donning the gown, tying it around her middle, accentuating her figure. Straps coiled around her chest elegantly, leaving her arms exposed. Once the Oracle was satisfied with the fit of the gown, she left Lilith to prepare herself. She traded her usual boots for violet slippers to match the detailed stitching.

With tears in her eyes, Olga beamed at her. "You are the epitome of lovely!"

Lilith blushed as she scrutinized her chest. "I think my *donas* are a little too exposed."

Olga cackled. "Fortunately for you, that is the prevalent style in Kenora."

Though the material wasn't particularly diaphanous, the muscle she'd gained since her Anointment was blatantly visible. The lines that cut through her abdomen, and the multiple slight curves that made up her arms, were stark in the dim lighting. As much as she'd always admired and valued strength before beauty, it wasn't until this moment that she realized strength *was* beauty.

"What should I do with my hair?" she asked Olga.

The Oracle had outfitted herself in a gorgeous crimson chiton gown of silk, similar to Lilith's. Her slippered feet tapped against the slate floor as she hurried to tend to Lilith. Olga stood at her side and gazed into the mirror. After a moment of intense consideration, she unfastened Lilith's long hair from her braid and let it fall in gentle waves.

"Down is always best," she said as she ran a comb through her tresses. Olga then braided Lilith's fringe and clasped the two plaits at the back of her head. When she was finished, Lilith appeared no less than royalty.

"How is that?" Olga asked.

"I couldn't have done it better myself."

The two women stood side by side before the large mirror. As her eyes inspected their appearance, Lilith let a satisfied grin spread her berry-stained lips. They looked so lovely, no one would ever suspect how lethal they truly were.

◎ ʊ ∽ ⋔ ◊

Outside the large wooden doors of the Great Hall, the Divine gathered, clad in full regalia. The men each wore a chlamys, warrior musculature on full display, faces clean-shaven.

Lilith, plagued with anxiety, kept her face downcast. A warm breeze enveloped her, and she lifted her head to find her face inches from Julius's.

The prince's sable curls were luminescent, the blunt ends brushing against his broad shoulders. She noted the smooth, elegant planes of his face as he smiled down at her.

"You are beautiful, Lilith."

Caught off-guard by the compliment, she regarded him with wide, kohl lined eyes. But she quickly lost herself in his.

Julius's irises were the color of the sky just before the sunset. Her skin blazed. She was forced to avert her gaze to the polished silver brooch that secured his cloak to his chest. But even that was futile. In his chlamys, most of his chest was visible. His arms—

"Thank you," she said, cutting off her sensuous thoughts. "You look very handsome." Indeed, he was. *As always.*

Julius bowed his head in thanks, but his gaze lingering on her for a moment longer. He lowered his voice so only she could hear him. "I don't concern myself with any eyes but my own, and neither should you."

Lilith knew what he meant, that she should not let the Emperor's proprietary stare disconcert her as it so obviously had. She returned his sweet smile one last time before the great doors swung inward and a small page boy announced their arrival.

Emperor Obadïa was already seated at the high table, accompanied by his courtiers. Lilith observed each attendee, recognizing the young man who was seated adjacent to the Emperor as Prince Orìon. He didn't seem as ill-tempered as Olga had implied.

Olga had told her that decades ago, when the Emperor was young and strong, he'd taken many consorts and refused to claim a bride, refused an Empress. Eventually, he became besotted with a young woman and all his old resistance became history. He married her and made her his Empress. A year later she bore Orìon, and the struggle of childbirth claimed her life. Olga believed this was the reason Emperor Obadïa had become so stern, had hardened his hand, and also why his heir was a callous brat.

Lilith seated herself between Olga and Arduen, directly

across from Quin and Julius. Wren and Felix assumed the end seats, and she envied them for their close proximity to the only known exit in the room.

Lilith smiled saccharinely at the hollow platitudes directed her way, until her cheeks beseeched her for release. The lords were evidently supplicants basking in the Emperor's presence.

When the Emperor spoke, the entire company was doused in silence. The only remaining sound was his deep voice; it crackled like burning embers. "Welcome to Kenora. I am pleased to host you here in my home. To my left is my son and heir, Prince Orìon. To my right is an Epistaí of mine, my Right Hand and Captain of my Frourà, Vaughn." The handsome man leaned over the table and dipped his chin in greeting. The Emperor quickly introduced the many courtiers that had travelled to the capital for the occasion. No ladies joined their counterparts.

Lilith leaned in to Arduen as she observed the wide face of Captain Vaughn. "What is an Epistaí?"

Arduen whispered, "A person of importance to the crown. Most every captain or general is granted the title."

"The lords don't receive that title?" she queried.

"No," he said, "because they don't remain in Kenora and serve in the Emperor's presence." She nodded her understanding as they drew apart.

"I would like all the Divine present to know," a rail-thin man announced, "that I have instructed my most revered blacksmith to forge fresh armor for you all." He waved a frail arm through the air. "In the event that there will be a battle that awaits us in the near future, our Divine shall be protected. Please allow my servants to take your measurements before you depart."

Quin tilted his head, his expression blank. "Thank you, Lord Malos, but I must remind you that our skin must breathe during battle. If we are to summon our elements, I cannot, and I cannot have my noviciate, suffocate within a suit of armor. If our element cannot escape, Xander's Fire could very well burn us alive. We must thank you for your generosity, and also warn you that we may only be able to accept a few pieces of the suits."

Lilith shuddered. The thought of being sucked away by her own power was terrifying.

Lord Malos bowed his head and said kindly, "I will notify my blacksmith when I deliver your measurements. We can discuss later what your specifications shall be."

Quin thanked Lord Malos again.

Prince Orìon joined the discussion then, glaring down the long table to meet Arduen's gaze. "You and your mates will be honored to have the greatest blacksmith in all of Augusta forge your suits. He very well may be the only fucking reason you survive Spiro's wrath."

Lord Malos paled, his jaw snapping shut with an audible *crack.*

Orìon would have been handsome if he only wiped the permanent sneer off his face. That smug grin loitered on his lips. It sent spiders crawling down Lilith's spine. As his eyes met hers, lingered, she chafed under his insolence. She repositioned herself behind Olga, slipping out of the heir's line of sight. Arduen only smiled at Orìon, altering nothing of his demeanor, emitting no infirmity by the evident threat that underlined the heir's words.

"Where is General Achilles?" Orìon regarded his father, his

voice taking on an air of reverence of which Lilith didn't think him capable.

Emperor Obadïa released a heavy, exasperated sigh. No doubt a dramatic gesture to sow disrespect for whoever General Achilles was. "He has been excused for his dereliction of duty."

"Ah," Orìon sneered. "The Enchantress has left our general bereft of good sense."

"So it seems," the Emperor waved his heir off. "Liakos," he called to one of the courtiers down the table. "You may speak."

Lord Liakos stood to address the Divine. He appeared rather fragile for a man of great power. If this man was a warrior, it was battles of intelligence he dominated. With a voice like liquid silk, he said, "It is my responsibility to ensure the safety of those dwelling within my territory. Thassös is not the closest city to Kenora, but it has been touched by the carnage of battle more than any other." His tongue slid across his dainty lips. "I assume you will understand my concern when I ask, what precautions will be taken to ensure that my civilians remain unharmed?" His eyes fluttered expectantly between Arduen and Quin, narrowed with such scrutiny, Lilith shied from him.

"I believe that is a matter for you and Your Majesty to discuss." Arduen spoke with clarity and confidence that brooked no question. "We serve and protect all of Augusta, but we are not rulers by any means. We will be conscious of our actions during war, no harm will come to any of your subjects, so long as we can help it. But it is imperative that our focus be solely on Spiro. If we can force him to yield, then we may end the conflict that's stifled Augusta for the past century. However, there will be further casualties."

Lord Liakos couldn't seem to tear his glower from Arduen. Umbrage left his skin flushed crimson. He was vexed, no doubt, by the way Arduen had made his concerns seem insignificant, even doltish. When Liakos finally yielded, he crossed his arms over his chest, and released a blast of air through his thin nose. He locked eyes with another lord positioned across from him, no doubt sharing a silent conversation. Just how many cryptic messages lingered behind that gaze?

Servants poured into the hall carrying platters piled high with food. Lilith's stomach vibrated with a growl as the scent of roasted meats wafted through the air. She was relieved that the distraction of a luxurious meal would likely stifle the tense conversation.

Emperor Obadïa rose from his seat; his height still left Lilith feeling elfin. He recited prayers of gratitude to each of the Gods before he gave the approval to begin the feast.

Lilith dug in as respectfully as she could, mimicking Olga's manners and following her lead. Stuffed quail made her mouth water. Each tray consisted of a meat surrounded by mounds of olives, grapes and nuts.

As they indulged, the Emperor's watchful gaze lingered on every attendee, including her. Lilith felt his attention. She lifted her face to meet his. Obadïa smiled faintly, though it was not a welcoming expression. His eyes remained dull, dark, insidious. The jewels that glittered across his knuckles flashed as his hand grasped a chalice of claret. His crooked, near-predatory smile faded as a courtier grappled for his attention.

Lilith's skin burned, blood rushing beneath, as if it was

eager to burst free of its prison. She prayed to Constantine that Obadïa couldn't detect how deeply he'd unsettled her. Did her fear linger in the air like steam? Did he take pleasure in watching her wither before him? Steeling herself, she cast the vision of the Emperor's hungry eyes from her mind. What was he imagining when he looked at her? The beautiful gown falling to the floor at her feet?

"Tell me, Arduen, what are the names of your newest additions?" The Emperor asked. All attendees shifted their focus to her Master.

"Our newest addition is Felix Dynamis," Arduen said. "He has been Anointed by Thëo. It has been many centuries since we received a new Divine of Earth. Thank the Gods that Wren is still alive to mentor him." Lilith grinned at the sly hint of a slice at Wren's pride, though the man elicited no reaction to Arduen's words.

"You have met Julius Fawkes on several occasions, so that leaves my noviciate," Arduen glanced over at her with brimming fondness, "Lilith Oak from Utica."

"You don't say…" The Emperor looked over at his Epistaí with an expression of incredulity. Captain Vaughn seemed equally alert. Lilith reached for Arduen's hand, grasping it firm under the table.

"Can you clarify your statement?" Arduen asked, his thumb tracing comforting circles on the back of her hand.

The Emperor turned his back on them. Only then did it occur to Lilith that he seemed almost nervous himself. When Obadïa addressed them again, he spoke slowly, "In the event that a smithy is destroyed and the blacksmith's remains go missing, it becomes the Empire's duty to investigate." The Emperor paused to consider his words with care.

Lilith's skin prickled.

When Obadïa continued, his words were slow and calculated. "That is why I had your brother, Larkin Oak, summoned to Kenora. He has been questioned as to your whereabouts, but all evidence was incriminating in his regard. I..." the Emperor's voice faltered.

Arduen's hand shifted under Lilith's and he grasped her firmly, holding her still. His massive hand engulfed hers in its warmth, calluses scraping against her softer skin.

Larkin was in the capital! In the same building she was! At the same exact moment!

"It is unfortunate," Obadïa continued, "but Larkin Oak has been declared guilty of arson and subsequently, murder. He was sentenced to death."

Lilith ripped her hand free of Arduen's grasp and rose to her feet in alarm.

Obadïa finished briskly, "And he has paid for his crimes this morn."

"You did *what*?" Lilith shrieked.

A shock wave of Aether careened through her body, the force of it causing her to flounder uncomfortably. *Hold it in. Hold it in.* Her chair toppled over behind her with a clatter as she stumbled. Olga and Arduen rose out of their seats just as quickly, the Oracle attempting to calm her, but to no avail.

The room spun. Lilith began to hyperventilate.

Words were exchanged between Arduen, Quin and the Emperor. Losing all sense of time and space, Lilith toppled into a wall of warmth, the familiar scent of burnt wood and spice washing over her.

Arduen.

She couldn't see him through her tears, but she knew she

was in his arms. Beyond that, Lilith could discern nothing of what he said to her, the pounding of her heart and the rushing of her grief muting all other sounds and sensations.

Ever since the Almighty had stolen her breath, she'd never truly felt alone.

Until now.

SILK SHEETS AND STRONG ARMS

Following a long nap, dinner, and a decadent slice of honey-drizzled bread with her husband, Rhéa set off to tend to her patient. At times, she had to remind herself that he was the reason she was here. It was difficult to remember her purpose swathed in silk sheets and strong arms.

Slowly making her way through the vast corridors, the Enchantress kept her eyes peeled for those she'd pinned as the Emperor's spies. She was sure that the Màtia—the Emperor's Eyes—was the sole reason her husband had been excused from the welcoming feast for the Gods' Divine.

Another war.

Rhéa scoffed at the thought.

The Enchantress dreaded the time of day she trekked to her patient's chambers. Without fail, without relent, he was worse with every setting of the sun.

Dread knitted her entrails.

Maybe that's why she hadn't been chosen. As an

Enchantress of the Ilíos coven, her power was most influential when the sun reached its zenith. Selene was from Ápeiro Astéri, Enchantresses of the Infinity Star. Their power reached its culmination under Starlight. Perhaps Ophelía had based the decision upon what would be best for the patient.

Rhéa sighed in guilty defeat.

The hallway to her patient's chambers was unusually still. There were no guards, not one Frourà sentinel vigil outside Larkin's door, as they always were. Had he been kept late? Had he confessed to his crimes? She shook the morose thoughts from her mind. This young man was no murderer. She could see it in his eyes.

She knocked on the door once… twice… thrice. No answer. No call from within. Wrapping her palm around the door handle, she listened. No approaching footsteps sounded from behind the door. There was no rise and fall of her patient's breath beyond.

The Enchantress was alone.

Rhéa pushed the door in. "Híne," she hissed, directing the magic to the sconces. They flared to life in response. The chamber became illuminated before her, and there was no one within.

Frantically, she searched the bathing chamber and the wardrobe. No one was there. In a panic, Rhéa stormed from the room in the direction of her betrothed.

NOTHING TO LOSE

Lilith awoke to swollen eyes and a face to match. Arduen sat in a chair beside her bed, his head propped on steepled fingers, still fast asleep. Olga snored on peacefully beside her, muttering about efrits in the night.

Arduen stirred as Lilith sat up. He reached out to cup her face, his expression one of paternal concern. She leaned into his touch, closing her eyes to ward off the onslaught of tears that threatened.

"I was worried you'd never fall asleep," he whispered. "We will leave as soon as Lord Malos's servants arrive to take our measurements." He said no more. For what was there to say? There was no use in asking how she was, of course she was a wreck. Whatever goodness she'd possessed rendered flotsam on a lazy, post-storm tide.

Lilith gathered her things, dressing into a beautiful new black tunic and breeches. Olga even bought her new boots which accomplished little in raising her sombre mood. New attire wouldn't make her feel like a new person. It wouldn't meld together the pieces of her shattered heart.

There was a knock on the door and Lord Malos's servants filtered in to take their measurements for the new armor. Olga denied them several times, stating that she already possessed a suit of armor. The servants just shook their heads and prodded her to stand still. Lilith acquiesced mutely and allowed her body to become pliable as the servants carried out their ministrations.

⊙ ⑤ ⟿ ৶ ♭

FINALLY MOUNTED, LILITH ONCE AGAIN TOOK UP THE REAR AS their party left the capital behind. She was relieved that Olga and Julius had given up coddling her. Perhaps Arduen had told them that she needed space to sort through all the fragmented pieces of her mind. Her life had been uprooted by the Gods, now destroyed by the Emperor. It would be a long time before she considered herself even remotely all right.

Rage boiled in her blood. Larkin never would have started the fire. It couldn't have been him. He loved her. Through and through. Larkin was a candle in the wind, a flame in the breeze, still alight after all that assailed him. There was not an ounce of malice in his body. No jealousy. No corruption. Just love and sadness. A mirror of her own soul, her own heart.

How long had he suffered under the Emperor's sadistic interrogators before they'd given him release? Had he been sequestered to torment the entire time she'd been training at the Frourío? Did he feel jilted by her disappearance? His silence to her letter finally made sense. Lilith prayed that he didn't die thinking she didn't care for him.

The clouds threatened to dispel their contents upon the land beneath. Lilith frowned; the weather seemed to correlate well with her mood. The mass of impending obsidian clouds was a symbol of a dark omen, a mere vision of what their future would hold.

"Lord Liakos doesn't seem to be very fond of us..." Felix acknowledged.

"He's been trying for years to enact some sort of decree to bind us," Arduen stated. "He views our powers as weapons of mass destruction. What he doesn't realize is that the Gods rule over us and we answer to Them only. That is why I believe his health has been failing him, his lack of trust for the Gods' disciples is an affront to Them."

"That makes sense," Julius said. "He is so frail, but he can't be much older than his fourth decade."

Arduen chuckled. "The Gods can be cruel at times. Who knows how else he may have insulted Them? He could be a non-believer. He could be in league with Spiro."

"He seems cowardly," Felix stated. "I bet if Spiro came to his doorstep, Liakos would yield his land and his power to the Great Divine just to save his own skin. Sell his people. His Majesty's Empire."

"Some people don't deserve the power that is bestowed upon them," Arduen said. "Thankfully our Gods are actively present in the goings on of Their world. Justice will be had."

Lilith was too distracted by her own thoughts to participate in the discussion. Her eyes were peeled, constantly scanning the landscape for any flicker of movement, any sign that her brother was alive. So much of the uncanny had occurred in the recent months, surely her brother could survive. Perhaps he'd been Anointed, too.

Silly girl! He's gone. Let him go. You are alone now.

Lilith thanked Constantine that she had Skydancer beneath her, else she'd be on the ground, incapacitated. Her only living family member had now been sundered. She was truly alone in flesh and blood. Bound to walk the earth for all eternity, the last living, breathing Oak.

She didn't notice Arduen next to her until he reached over and took her hand in his. There were dark shadows beneath his eyes, making the blue of his irises paler.

Squeezing her hand affectionately, he spoke into the distance, "I am sorry about Larkin." He patted his mare, the gesture more of a comfort to him than to her.

"He is the only family I had left to live for…" She watched as Skydancer nudged Arduen's mare affectionately. A sight that would have once made her beam now elicited nothing.

"You can brood over it—and I don't blame you if that's what you choose to do—or you can decide to see this differently. You are the only one capable of controlling how this situation affects you. Choose, if you so wish, to go down with this ship, miserable and desolate. Or you can use this to fuel you."

Her heart felt like a stone in her chest, cold and unfeeling.

"Right now, you are Spiro's most fearsome enemy," Arduen said, his eyes set on her fiercely, as if beckoning her to challenge his statement.

"How?" Lilith shook her head, baffled, and raised her hands to the dark skies above. "How can I possibly be fearsome? I have nothing!"

"That's exactly why." A flicker of a smirk graced his lips. "You have nothing to lose."

A HEART OF STEEL AND FIRE

Waves crashed onto the shore, splashing Lilith's bare feet. Winter had finally descended upon the Frourío. Having woken up in the dead of night, numb and restless, Lilith made her way down to the beach wearing nothing more than her nightgown. She'd been drawn to the waters with the hope that whatever lay beneath the waves could ease her mind and heal her heart.

Lilith stepped into the sea until it rose to her knees. The water was gelid, but she didn't elicit a reaction, not even a wince. The moon was full and bright, illuminating a wavering line upon the horizon, shooting straight at her like a spotlight.

The waves rose high, reaching for the moon, and folded in on themselves as they crashed down. The echoes of their wrath nearly pushed Lilith off her feet. If she let them, would the sea carry her away? Could she become one with them? Sell her soul to the Undersea?

The Galatëa furled and unfurled as she scalded the waves with her gaze. Swiftly, a swell rose into the sky, its gargantuan size blocking out the light of the moon. Lilith inspected its beauty as the edges of the wave were illuminated by the stars. As it crested and crashed down, it glimmered with celestial light. The wave rocked the sea that birthed it, and the water stirred like a mighty beast that had just woken from a slumber.

Lilith was knocked off her feet against her will, the frigid waters laying claim to her. Every muscle in her body tensed, flexed, determined to gain purchase. Her fingertips scraped against the sand and stones until there was nothing but water. Until she lost sense of direction entirely.

She let the sea take her. She let the waves mold her anew. It washed away her fears. Froze her heart and forged her a new one. A heart of steel and fire. A heart of ether and wind. A heart that could never be broken.

When the sea finally spat her out, Lilith crawled onto the beach, water seeping from her lips. As she lay on the sand, soaked to her very core, she was convinced she'd been granted a new soul.

A new determination.

A new purpose.

◎ ☺ ⟿ ♏ ♖

A FORTNIGHT HAD PASSED SINCE THE DIVINE RETURNED FROM THE capital. Two weeks since she'd learned of her brother's misfortune. Fourteen days she'd pushed herself to her extremities in an attempt to forget. Fifteen long, restive nights.

Having spent her morning burning off her anxiety with a

long run through the Megálos, Lilith stood in the fresh snow under Arduen's watchful gaze.

This was a test. A test to determine whether she was fit to participate in battle or remain on the sidelines. Truthfully, Lilith was uncertain whether she wanted to fight. The competence to control Aether remained elusive. Where war was concerned, fear tugged at her chest and gnawed at her entrails, begging her to recede.

After almost an hour standing outside in the frigid winds, Lilith released a surge of Aether so powerful, the entire Forest erupted. Whatever birds had remained north in the Megálos took to the skies to flee Constantine's might.

Lilith grimaced as she gained control of the blast, aware of Arduen's presence, reminding herself what she needed to do to keep him safe from her wrath. She parried a blow from her imaginary enemy and blasted it with her dark abyss. Then she twisted and shot arrows of Aether from her palms, lightning fast.

In her mind, Arduen's instructions repeated: *Shape it with your fingers. Tensing your arms will help to mold it. If you imagine a shape within your mind, you can construct it with Aether.*

Violet flashes threatened to blind her. Lilith let a grim smile spread across her lips, a grin that she knew would terrify every last one of Spiro's beasts. The scene in front of her was as beautiful as it was horrifying, and it took every ounce of focus to keep herself sane and governed.

As your lungs draw breath, your heart pulses with blood. So, too, does Aether flow in your veins.

She commands Aether, *not* the obverse.

Darkness swirled through the air, concealing the snow-covered meadow from sight. She'd let the abyss grow to a heinous size in order to prove that she could wield it, subdue it, command and dominate it.

Suddenly aware of Arduen's call from behind her, she siphoned the element. Her body began to tingle and twitch as the power cascaded into her. The worst part of releasing Aether into the world was harnessing it.

Lilith was overcome with a burning pain. It lanced through every limb and seared every crevice. She became disabled by its unyielding force and fell to the snow, paralyzed. When the soothing hand of her Master finally grazed her, she knew all would be as it was meant to be. She would be all right.

Arduen absorbed what remained of the chaos that she'd unleashed, and calm settled over the glade.

When the world had returned to its former normalcy, and the sky was once again a deep indigo, she opened her eyes. Her Master stood above her, a contemplative cast consuming is features.

"Did I fail?" she rasped.

Arduen shook his head and barked a hollow laugh. "You are powerful, indeed, but we have much to work on."

Lilith groaned as he eased her onto her feet. "If I die because of you, I'll come back as a revenant and make the rest of your immortal days a living Hades." Her comment was met with rumbling laughter.

After some time, she asked, "Am I fit for war?" Not entirely sure what she wanted to hear, she still needed to know, lest the anxiety gnaw at her any longer.

"Let's just see how well you fare with your swordsmanship... *then* I will decide." Arduen wiped the snow from her suit, steadying her with a strong hand on her shoulder.

"Yes, Master."

JULIUS DROPPED HIMSELF INTO THE SEAT ACROSS FROM LILITH, HIS plate piled high with food.

"Finish your meal. You're testing today." There was an authoritative undertone to his voice that set her on edge. But when she met his gaze, the outer edges of his eyes crinkled as his face lit up with a grin, and her irritation abated.

"Says the man who has yet to finish his *own*." Lilith glared at him, a smile quirking to life.

Julius was four years her elder, but he acted like a decade divided them. The way he held himself together, remained stoic, even when everything around them was not as it should be. Lilith couldn't resist herself; she admired his demeanor, and if she could, she'd adopt it. But some deep, stubborn part of her just wasn't ready to be at peace.

"Alas, you are right, and I am wrong. Whatever will I do without my dear Lilith to correct me when I fall short?" He leaned back and fanned his face in a sardonic charade.

Lilith bit back her mirth. "You're an entire foot taller than me. You'll never fall short unless someone removes your legs."

The prince scoffed, and picked up his fork and knife with vigor, his tapered eyes locked on hers. "Well let's hope that doesn't happen, aye?"

Lilith cackled, the laughter warming her stomach, releasing the tension in her chest.

Gods, it feels so good.

"You'll do well today. Don't be nervous." Julius assumed his usual mien and began to cut at his meat.

"I didn't succeed in my elemental testing." Lilith picked at the mashed potatoes on her plate. Usually Ambrose's food was bursting with flavor, but today it was bland. It had to be her nerves.

"But you didn't fail either…" he insisted, a dark eyebrow arched.

"How do you know? Did Arduen tell you?"

"Arduen boasts about you like you're his pride and joy," Julius said. "Of *course* he told us how well you did."

Arduen's initial reaction didn't convince Lilith that her progress had pleased or impressed him at all. With a wry smile, she sipped the remainder of her tea and continued to pick at her meal, satisfaction blossoming within her.

LILITH SWUNG OAK WITH ILL INTENT AT ARDUEN'S EXPOSED NECK, slicing down to collide with his own blade. This was their first real attempt at a duel bearing steel. He had deemed her a competent enough *swordswoman*, so he opted to test her.

The other Divine slowly filed in to observe the duel. Lilith paid them no heed, refusing to break her iron grip on Oak. She needed to prove that she was prepared for battle, with or without Aether. When she had come to the conclusion that she longed for battle, she didn't know, but the thought of Arduen and Julius fighting without her was tantamount to marching into the fray at their sides.

They duelled with snow whipping up around them, a flurry of white. With every move, it sprayed forth. No amount of inclement weather could halt the progress of the Divine. Fortunately, winter only lasted a few short months in Augusta.

Lilith twisted away from Arduen's reach as he swung side-ways, blade directed at her abdomen. As she spun, she caught

Julius's hazel eyes, and she forced herself not to preen under his gaze.

Finally, as if he'd yielded to her, she landed the blow that would have ended the bout fatally for Arduen, had she not halted her blade mid-air, a hair's breadth from his neck.

Her Master cast her a satisfied grin and held his hands up in defeat. She knew he'd let her win, but only because he deemed her worthy of battle.

Lilith was ready.

Their audience applauded. Everyone, Lilith noted, except Wren—whom she paid little consideration.

Julius approached her bearing a painfully handsome grin. "Care for a challenge, milady?"

Lilith cocked her head and peered up at him, hoping that she appeared as confident as she felt doltish. "Hmm..." She pretended to consider his offer for a moment. "I *guess* I can spare some free time for you," she said coyly.

He only chuckled as he took his place across from her, already assuming a defensive stance.

Aware that Arduen and the others were still standing idle to observe, Lilith sucked in a deep breath and charged. She landed Oak upon Julius's blade, Orphëus. The clang rang in her ears long after they separated, retreated and charged again.

She parried Julius's blow, twisting away from him deftly. She stopped herself halfway through only to reverse and charge again from the same direction. He jumped back in surprise. His reflexes were catlike though, and soon he would predict her every move.

Pivoting, Lilith narrowly escaped his blade. She indulged

in the *whoosh* it made as it sailed over her head. An exultant grin split her lips as she caught the scent of victory.

Finally, she was getting it!

Julius dove down with astounding aggression, and Lilith lifted Oak with both hands, preparing to block his blow. As if he'd been watching her movements in slow motion, he corrected his posture with inhuman speed and cut downward, locking her blade between his and the ground. With one flick of his wrist, Oak sailed into the air, disappearing under a white plume of snow.

A second later, Julius's muscular arm was wrapped around Lilith's chest in a secure embrace while his other brought Orphëus up to her exposed neck. She could feel his hot breath caressing her cheek as he panted, the edge of his blade barely an inch from her vitals. His heart thundered against her back, and for a moment, she didn't want him to release her.

Lilith went limp in his arms, daring him to hold her still, her life in his hands. "Constantine take you, *Prince*," she gasped, and Julius lowered his sword and released her.

Horror struck her as her knees sunk into the powder. Everything had become obscured by white. She hadn't intended to lose control of her body, but something had stripped the sovereignty from her.

Some *thing* had pilfered her.

Screams and incoherent shouts erupted. The ground quaked vigorously beneath her. Still Lilith's senses denied her access to sight. She couldn't help them. She couldn't see them.

Hands reached for her, but they were ripped away forcefully. Ice rushed through her body. It abraded her skin, freezing her extremities. The cold carried her away like the hands of a God. Suddenly she was weightless. Floating drift-wood in the Galatëa.

Maybe Julius had sliced her neck. Maybe this was what bleeding out felt like, and Constantine had come to claim her. Maybe this was what it felt like to perish as a Divine, for her body to be swept up and consumed, only to be constructed into a glowing Star reflecting what she'd once been. When her eyes opened, she would be watching her comrades from above.

Lilith let the cold devour her, the screams and shouts of panic finally subsiding as she gave way to polar turbulence. The frigid surroundings evaporated to make way for searing warmth. She opened her eyes.

It was Julius, his raven locks a halo rimming his beautiful face, his body limned with gold.

Xander's Fire.

Lilith finally came to in a panic. She gripped the prince as he wrapped his arms around her and surged upward. Together they broke the surface of the Galatëa. She gasped for air before realizing she had never needed it. Alarm settled upon her as Julius braced her head between his palms. She wrapped her legs around his waist to remain aloft, her arms clasped around his neck.

"You're all right!" he yelled over the tumult. She wasn't certain whether he was intending to convince her or himself. All she could do was nod vehemently, her body shuddering violently in his arms. She held fast to him as he swam back to shore.

Lilith spared a glance toward the Frourío, where everyone stood, soaked and flustered. She wondered what could have caused the calamity as Julius emerged from the icy sea, bearing her in his arms.

Closing her eyes, she rested her head on Julius's chest as Arduen ran to them, his arms outstretched like a concerned father reaching for his infant. Worry varnished his features as he brushed her soaking hair back to inspect her face.

"What happened?" Lilith rasped.

"One of our noviciates has been blessed by Kyril."

KYRIL'S WATER

Arduen stood before the hearth clothed in dry trousers and a tunic. Before him, the others sat in bleary anticipation. Lilith amongst them, her freshly plaited hair still damp, her bones still brittle from the gelid sea.

"I have enough faith, judging from the immensity of that wave," said Arduen, "that whoever commanded it has little power left to cause significant harm." He indicated the wooden goblet in his hands. "Especially with the meagre amount of liquid in this goblet."

His gaze swept over the three young Divine, his eyes pausing on each one of them as if he could Discern who'd been blessed by Kyril.

"Doesn't Olga know who's been blessed?" Felix nearly whined.

Olga interjected, "I only know the God who has Anointed

and the location of the Anointed. I do not receive any other details for those who are already Divine."

Felix twisted his lips into what resembled a pensive grimace. "We died to become Divine. Mustn't we die to become Anointed again?"

The Oracle answered, "Once a you are Divine, any of the Gods can Anoint you at Their discretion."

Tense silence permeated the room.

Arduen offered the goblet to Felix first, who immediately cast a wary glance at his Master. The entire room remained tight-lipped. After holding the cup for several long minutes, Felix received a nod of approval from Wren before he passed the goblet to Julius. He relinquished the cup as if it spewed worms.

Lilith watched closely as the prince grasped the wood with long, elegant hands. Julius was calm, even tranquil, as he lowered his eyes to the goblet. Dread filled her as he raised the cup and proffered it to her.

As she reached for it, her gaze caught Julius's. Solicitude was writ in his expression so transparently, it might as well have been inked onto his skin. Lilith immediately averted her eyes and focused on the goblet in her hands. Wrapping her fingers around the wood, she fixated her gaze on the intricate carvings along the upper rim, praying the water to remain still.

It can't be me. It can't be me. It can't be me.

There was nothing. No hint of power, not like what she experienced when she wielded Aether. She knew what it felt like to summon forth the elements, to release a blast of a God's own fury. This wasn't it. Absent was the rushing of blood in her ears, the inexplicable emotions that threatened to tear through her chest and become another living, breathing, walking beast.

Nothing but exhaustion remained. It swept through her like a palpable gust. Her stiff limbs beseeched her to rest. Her head, leaden with fatigue, throbbed ceaselessly. But she dared not move, lest she disturb the water that remained so still inside the goblet. She could have sworn it had frozen over from the cold that seeped from her skin.

After all she had to cope with since their return, the responsibility of learning a new element was not one she wished for. No. Lilith was certain no God would bless her with another power. She was only just beginning to make progress wielding Aether, controlling it, molding it to her will. Why would They burden an inept student with another element to master?

Finally, as if the Gods Themselves struck her across the face, Kyril's Water began to swirl.

Lilith's hand went slack, nearly dropping the goblet, but Arduen reached for it, catching it before it left her fingers. When he wrapped his hand around the cup's girth, the Water stilled. Its surface resembled a sheet of ice once again so suddenly that Lilith thought her eyes may have deceived her. She was freezing, exhausted—in shock, no less.

The room remained silent. Every Divines' eyes focused on Arduen as his own flashed from the goblet to his noviciate. He dropped to his knees at her side, his gaze resting on her. Lilith looked into his eyes, imploring him to take this burden from her. Nothing less than affection swirled in those icy irises, but nothing he could do would reverse what the Gods had done.

Petrified by the goblet and its contents, Lilith could only gawk at the wood. She gave a mulish shake of her head as

Arduen reached for her wrist and placed her palm against the surface of the wood. Upon her touch, the Water resumed its eddy, and a chorus of gasps sounded throughout the room.

Lilith had been blessed by Kyril.

"That settles it then," Arduen said. "Congratulations, Lilith. You are the first Divine in over a century to wield more than one element."

No.

It was impossible. Who was she to earn greater favor? Lilith remained seated, transfixed by the flickering flames and listening numbly as her compadres made varying remarks.

"What an *honor*…"

"Brilliant…"

"What kind of soul you must possess!"

Lilith only stirred when Arduen's hand grazed her shoulder. Gazing up at him, she lacked the energy to mask the fear from her features.

"What happens now?" she whispered.

Arduen smiled down at her, then wrapped an arm around her shoulders. "We summon another Master to instruct you in Kyril's Water. We keep training. We persist and pray that this war will be over soon. We will prevail. I don't know how to begin to convince you how utterly honorable this is. You're the first Divine the Gods have entrusted with such power since Spiro."

"That doesn't help me feel better," she grumbled.

"No," Arduen replied, "I don't think there is much that can make you feel better. Not right now. But I want you to know, power like this, it's isolating. Spiro went mad with *Philautia* because he had no one to share that power with. None of us had been blessed by more than one God. We could never understand him. No one could." He paused to lick his lips, a vein in his brow bulged. "That loneliness, mixed with misunderstanding, it threw him over the edge. Past the brink of return." He took her hand and held her fist against his chest, atop his heart. "I won't let that happen to you."

Lilith wanted to believe him. Gods, she wanted Arduen to take care of her forever. But that wasn't possible, was it?

"Who will be my new Master?" she asked.

He released her hand, a tense sigh escaping his lips. "Zurí. Spiro's past partner."

"His Philías?" *Shield-mate.* A partner in battle. If anyone understood Spiro's dexterity, it would be Zurí.

"No, his *lover*."

⚬ ☼ ⟿ ᛗ ♦

AFTER AN HOUR OF DISCUSSION AND PREPARATION FOR ZURÍ'S arrival, Lilith finally released the tension that had ceased her body. She allowed Arduen to bear her weight, her shoulders and arms slack at her sides as she leaned against him. It had taken its toll, sitting with the others as they discussed what would need to happen to accommodate her new gift. As she sat there under the façade of tranquility, her mind was a rattled heap of consternation, bellowing absurdities only she could hear.

How was she going to master Aether *and* Water? Her ability to control Aether was precarious enough, but to wield *two* elements amidst a cluster of allies and enemies? She would be lucky if she was capable enough to summon even the slightest shard of power without stabbing the wrong target. She shuddered at the thought of causing the deaths of good men, men who had families… How could she cause another daughter the same pain she'd suffered for years?

As if sensing her internal conflict, Arduen wrapped an arm around her, inviting her to fall into him. Pressing her cheek against his chest, she closed her eyes, her body still trembling. She was relieved that her comrades had recovered from the tsunami she'd inflicted upon the Frourío, but still she remained agitated.

Stealing a quick glance around the room, it seemed as though everyone had thawed since the incident, though their faces were still pale, sallow. Nothing could rid the incessant chill that seeped through sinew, penetrating deep into the marrow of their bones.

Lilith never prayed to Kyril, God of Water. Not once. She'd never asked any of the Gods to bestow even an ounce of greater power. She wasn't advanced enough in her training to handle any more. Yet here she was, becoming more and more like Spiro. The thought bore down upon her like a swollen, oppressive cloud.

There was no escaping her responsibilities, however ominous they may be. She would have to establish a capable harness of both elements, and she needed to do it quickly. There was no buying time, Spiro would attack when it was most convenient for *him*. Lilith needed to hustle if she was going to be fit for battle anon.

After a gruelling conversation in which Olga and Arduen determined how to best continue Lilith's instruction, they escorted her to her bedchamber, but she was reluctant to be bereft of Arduen's warmth.

The Oracle led her up the stairs. She seemed to be worried

about Lilith's physical state, commenting on how ashen her skin had become.

When Olga was about to take her leave, Lilith asked, "How did Arduen know that it was a noviciate that had been blessed by Kyril, not a Master?"

"Because a Master would recognize the new ability the moment we were Anointed by another God." And with that, Olga bade Lilith good night and closed the door behind her.

◎ ☺ ⤳ ⋔ ◊

Lilith sprinted through the dense trees, hot on Rally's tail. She could see him clearly now as he weaved through the mossy trunks. She was gaining on him. He must be hurt. Forcing panic aside, she pushed forward.

When she was younger, she used to stretch her hands far out in front of her, as if she could reach and grab hold of air and pull herself along faster. She began to do just that when she came to an abrupt halt.

Were her hands always so large? Was that hair?!

Lilith examined her hands in horror. She was not herself. Stricken with alarm, she grabbed at her torso, at her breasts and belly. She had no breasts. Had she not eaten enough this month? Was she ill?

Sauntering on in a panic-stricken delirium, she found herself before a small pond. She knelt beside the water, careful not to disturb its glass-like surface, and leaned over to examine her reflection.

No, his reflection.

She was Larkin. Utterly confused, Lilith sat back on her heels, dazed. How this could have happened? This was impossible! But her mind still belonged to her, not him.

Lilith leaned forward again, needing to confirm that she was indeed her brother. As her shoulder-length dark hair came into view, she noticed a shadow stirring behind her. Watched as it transformed.

It was green as the leaves that were cloaked in darkness. Yellow eyes slit open to gaze at her reflection. Two large lips she hadn't noticed parted to reveal long sharp teeth. The teeth of a predator.

The teeth of a beast.

Lilith dared to scream for help but it was too late. The monster gripped her brother's shoulders, blood already oozing from the holes where its talons had dug into her flesh. His flesh.

The beast pulled her back into the night. Lilith could only scream as the monster tore her away from Larkin's reflection. But it wasn't his talons that she felt boring into her gut, into her sides, tugging her limbs in every direction.

No, it was Water.

The deluge had come for her. It pulled at her and beat her down upon the rocks at the bottom of the sea. She tried with all her strength to swim to the surface, but her body failed to shift in accordance with her flailing limbs.

It was alive. A beast of fluidity.

Lilith whimpered, bubbles clouding her vision. She was going to drown, and if the Gods didn't let her die, she would be confined to the Undersea for eternity. Letting go, she relinquished all hope that reinforced her drive to live, and she relaxed her limbs, letting Kyril's Water have its way with her. With Larkin.

The sea stilled at last as if reacting to her sudden yielding. As if it only wanted to play with her. After a moment of peace, Lilith began to rise toward the light. But the moment her body began to move, so did the vast Water surrounding her. Whatever sick game it played, she wanted no part of it.

The current picked up until she was forced into hard rock. All she could do was let loose a scream as the rock neared Larkin's face. Her face.

◎ ⑤ ⤳ ⋔ ◊

"LILITH!" JULIUS'S VOICE BROKE THROUGH HER NIGHT TERROR AS he shook her, his hands gripping her shoulders exactly where the beast had only moments before. "It's okay, Lilith." Julius encouraged her to lie down again as she tried to force herself up. She let him guide her down.

The prince sat on the edge of her bed, his hazel eyes smoldering in the moonlight, the moonbeams illuminating his silky black curls, his dark-golden skin lucent.

She heaved a sigh and closed her eyes, praying that the beast wouldn't be waiting for her behind her heavy eyelids. When there was no evidence of its existence, she opened her eyes again.

"Did I wake you?" she asked, suddenly self-conscious. His bedchamber was on the floor above hers.

Julius hesitated. "No, I had come to see if you were still awake. I can't sleep, and I have a request for you." When she didn't respond, he continued, "I just wanted to ask if you can swim. I know you grew up inland, so it wouldn't be surprising if no one taught you…" He paused as if wary of insulting her. "When I swam out to you, it was almost like you had given up, but then I realized that you may not be able to swim to shore yourself."

Lilith took no umbrage at his query. Julius was well-educated, being a prince and an heir to a throne. A great throne.

"No, I can't swim," she confessed. "But I guess I can just

move the Water out of my way now." She released a withering laugh but he didn't join her.

"Yes, but it will take some time to learn how to do that. I know we are Divine—we are able to breathe as any of the oceanic mammals do—but I still worry that without the skill to move within Water, you will become prey to the many creatures that lurk beneath the surface." He gazed down at her with an intensity Lilith had only glimpsed a few times in her life.

Julius was truly afraid for her, and it was he who had dove into the sea to retrieve her when she was swept away. The voice in the back of her mind beseeched her not to open up to him, not to let herself fall for a prince whose destiny lay across a sea.

"It's winter, Julius. How will you teach me to swim?"

"I wield Fire," he reminded her. "You never have to fear the cold when you're with me."

"All right." She yawned. "I agree to let you instruct me." She rolled over, hoping that would be enough to communicate that she needed to sleep.

His only response was, "I look forward to it," before he rose from her bed, somehow leaving her room darker than it had been before.

A WELL OF POWER

The Masters seemed exceedingly proud of Lilith for her second Anointment, but not one of them asked her how she felt about it. If she was honest with herself, she was afraid. Now that she was a walking, breathing target for Spiro, she had to be all the more equipped to face him.

It was difficult not to notice that Wren didn't participate in these particular praises, though he was indeed present. He would roll his eyes or raise his eyebrows mockingly. Lilith did her best to ignore his obstinance. The man was not fond of women with power and that may well be his downfall.

Despite the shift in atmosphere and the Masters' regard toward her, Lilith felt little difference. A slight uneasiness swept through her, the return of that fear of failure that had haunted her during her first weeks at the Frourío. She did sense something greater within herself. As if part of her being had opened up, had expanded to accept *more*, but the power was not roiling beneath her skin like Aether did.

"Zurí will take another week to arrive," Arduen said. "Until then we will continue with our training. We must remain focused on your entire arsenal." He seemed flustered, whether because there was more on his plate with her new blessing, or because he would now have to work alongside Zurí to guide her. Either way, he'd kept her too busy to let the weight of Larkin's death sunder her.

Not death. Execution.

Lilith dreamt of Larkin every night, but with Arduen's aid, she survived each day. But grief hit her like a backhanded blow when she turned in each evening.

Felix seemed most exuberant about Lilith's new blessing. She'd often catch him studying her when she wasn't looking, and when she met his gaze, he'd beam at her in awe.

"It seems like your well of power has expanded." Wren said to her with the least amount of enthusiasm she'd ever heard from him.

Lilith seated herself on the floor beside Julius. Following supper, the noviciates often played card games on the rug before the hearth. Another distraction she was grateful for.

"It would have all been for naught, had *I* not saved you." Julius smirked, his eyes twinkling playfully as he elbowed her shoulder. She gawked and nudged him back.

"A well of power?" Felix chimed. "That was a *latrine!*"

Lilith and Julius exchanged incredulous glances before bursting into fits of laughter, inducing a stream of tears from them both. Wren dropped his face into his palms, though Lilith could see a wry grin through his beard.

"Someone get this kid a dictionary!" Julius said through heaves of mirth, tears streaming his cheeks. Felix looked between them all with a bemused expression blanketing his face.

"I think he meant *ravine...*" Lilith mused, "but I could be wrong."

The howling ensued until reality settled over her like a pall, and she was forced to face the gravity of her situation again. She could do very little to conceal the wariness that flooded her. Arduen had become the only person who could ease her anxiety. How he did it, she hadn't the slightest clue, but she was forever grateful to her Master.

"Come with me to the rooftop," he said one morning.

"Why?" she asked. Lilith hadn't realized that they had access to the roof of the Frourío.

Arduen sighed, rolled his eyes, but she could tell he was amused. "If you'd like to find out, you best cease your inquisition and follow me."

Allowing for a slight smile to tug at the corners of her lips, Lilith pulled on her thick winter himation before following her Master up the spiral staircase. Climbing the stairs was a workout in itself, but the two Divine were barely affected, their breathing steady, if even relaxed. Lilith silently praised her morning runs.

When they reached the uppermost landing, her eyes settled on a wooden ladder leading up to a small latch door. Why hadn't she thought to explore beyond the study floor?

Arduen climbed the ladder first and pushed the latch door open. The pale morning sunlight poured in and bathed the dusty hallway in gold.

Following his lead, Lilith squinted as she hoisted herself up onto the rooftop. The air was brisk, it stung her cheeks until her eyes watered. She drew up her hood and strode to Arduen's side. Together, they glanced out at the Galatëa Sea—the sea that she could now control.

Arduen began to instruct her in a gentle voice, "Aether is not just for means of slaughter and damnation. The gift possesses a greater purpose." He flashed her a sidelong glance. Lilith had become used to him studying her to see whether she was paying attention. Wrapping her fur-lined cloak tighter around her shivering frame, she waited patiently for Arduen to begin his demonstration.

Dispelling a breath through his nostrils, he held his hands out to his sides, palms supinated. Lilith studied him closely. Even with his eyes closed, she knew that he was well aware of her gaze. There truly wasn't much that he wasn't aware of.

Warmth was sucked from her bones as a cool darkness settled over them. Lilith turned her attention to the horizon. An impending gale raced toward them at an alarming speed.

"Master," her voice a plea as she gripped his arm, "maybe we should do this another day." But Arduen made no inclination to respond. He stood still as ever, eyes clamped shut, palms facing the sky. Unflappable amidst chaos, a wry smile tugged at his lips.

The storm held no active electricity and Lilith couldn't glean any thunder rolling within the burnt clouds. She relaxed slightly when she noticed its change of direction, heading east toward Kynös. The sky slowly transformed into a magnificent violet shade. Clouds softened into a gentle pink, the horizon a deep royal blue. Lilith gaped at the brilliance of it.

"It's you!" she exclaimed. "You're commanding the skies!"

Arduen finally opened an eye, winked, and flashed her a dignified grin. "Indeed, I am," he said. "And you can, too."

Lilith glanced out at the sea with wonder.

"Not every Divine gift is meant to bring destruction. The Gods intended for us to create as much as to destroy… on Their behalf, of course."

"How can I do this?" She was unable to mask the wistfulness in her voice.

"It takes years to master, but you can start by forming and moving clouds, changing colors slightly. It all depends entirely upon what is in *here*." He tapped her chest. "The sky becomes a reflection of your emotions when you open the door and allow it inside."

"How do I *open* the door?"

"You must release all pretence," he said. "You must sunder your inner barriers and boundaries. It takes patience and many attempts, but once you are successful, it'll become easier every time. More satisfying, too. This can be helpful in battle, but I think it's best in times like these, occasions when we need inspiration and motivation—hope above all else." He cast her a knowing smile and grazed her shoulder affectionately with his.

"Can we change from night to day?"

"There are limitations," he said. "We cannot change the course of the sun and moon and we cannot move the stars, though we can certainly conceal them." Arduen turned to face her, and Lilith followed suit, their breaths were no more than clouds between them.

"As I've said before, Aether is an abyss that sucks the life from our enemies, from any who come into contact with it. It cleaves the soul from the body. Renders the physical nothing more than a charred heap of near-dust. It can be shaped and formed in many ways, but that is not all that it can do."

Arduen gestured to the sky with a wave of his hand. "Aether is also the atmosphere above us. We have been blessed with the ability to shape the sky as we see fit, to mold it to reflect our deepest emotions."

Lilith stared out at the sky long after her Master had left her there. His alterations slowly returning to what they once were, no doubt because his attention was now directed elsewhere.

Her eyes wandered to the gale off in the distance, dissipating slowly. Lilith laughed to herself. She breathed deep and closed her eyes. Opening up her heart would be the toughest task she'd attempted since arriving at the Frourío, but she was determined to master this art. For that is what it was at its core: art.

For the first time since she'd been Anointed, she now had the means to express herself. And because of this, she no longer regarded her journey as insurmountable.

◌ ◌ ◌ ◌ ◌

As Lilith and Julius set out for the beach, Lilith honed her courage and yielded to the adrenaline that coursed through her veins, numbing her muscles, causing all senses to become lucid.

Julius instructed her briefly and concisely as they stood ankle-deep in the frigid waters. Broken sheets of ice floated on the calm surface as they waded in deeper. He chose a day where the winds were not so harrowing and the temperature not quite as glacial. He noted that he'd determined to cancel the lesson that morning when the sky clouded over, but thanked the Gods that it cleared miraculously. She stifled a giggle.

"I will draw upon Xander's Fire to heat the sea," he said. "I want you to let go of my hand *only* when I tell you to. Don't worry, I will not let go of you. We have but an hour before the tide shifts. Let's make the most of it." He addressed her like a king, assuming authority, his countenance demanding obedience and respect.

Julius continued in the same manner, "I will keep my mind open to our surroundings to ensure our safety, watchful for predators. I want you to remain closed off so you can focus on my instructions, got it?"

Lilith nodded her comprehension, eager to get deeper into the warm waters, eager to learn, and equally eager to jump into her bed once it was all over.

Julius gripped her frozen hand, entwined his fingers with hers, securing her to him, their arms tethers, their grips fetters. Heat seared her cheeks at his calloused yet gentle touch. She knew that the heat came from within her, not his own scalding skin. He raised his free hand and released a blast of Fire onto the water's surface.

They waited in silence as the flames danced, swirling delicately as smoke rose to the sunset sky.

After a moment, Julius prodded Lilith to join him as he stepped forth into the sea, tugging her after him. The waves rose to his neck, leaving her forced to attempt to tread.

The water was warm, much more comfortable than she'd anticipated. Julius let her feel the water, he let her body sort through its own instinct to survive. Then he swam closer to the shore, stopping where the water met his hips and her navel, and dipped under the surface, still grasping her hand in his.

Unable to tear her gaze away from him as he rose up out of the water, Lilith watched in fascination as droplets rolled down the gentle curve of his cheekbone, over his sensuous lips, his strong chin. She had to restrain herself from wiping it away, to feel his soft skin under her fingertips, from experiencing what those lips felt like. She noted the curve of his throat, the manly mount at its centre, exaggerated as he craned his neck. The short distance between them grew taut.

Julius wiped his eyes and smiled encouragingly, gesturing for her to dunk as well. Lilith acquiesced. Rising from the sea, she became self-conscious—there was no way she appeared half as elegant as he had.

Every muscle trembled nervously as he wrapped a strong arm around her waist. "Now," he said, his tone firm with authority, "I want you to move your legs like such." He indicated for her to follow his gaze, and she glanced down at his long legs. His toes still touched the sandy bottom of the sea, but his knees moved in and out. "Mimic my movement as best you can," he instructed.

Loosing a breathy laugh, Lilith struggled to keep her legs moving as he instructed, banging her knee against his at times. They bobbed in the waves.

The first task was not to control Water but rather to survive it. She'd never swum before, never deep enough that her feet couldn't touch the bottom. Julius had swum her out so far, she had to remind herself that she couldn't drown. He could touch the bottom, and he wouldn't let her drift away. She was safe with him. The prince grew up on the coast. He'd been taught rescue and recovery, a skill set to accompany his warrior arsenal. He was trained by the best in Dalegonè. And with his new skills as a Divine, he wouldn't let harm come to her.

"Mimic the movement of my arms with yours." His gaze panned her body. "Yes, just like that!"

Lilith studied his form and tried her best to mirror him. She remained amenable as he instructed her, correcting her often. He used his own hands to fix her form and guide her limbs. Flames erupted beneath her skin despite the gelid temperature. Julius only ever paused when he needed to heat the sea around them.

When they retired for the evening, Lilith struggled to cast out the vision of Julius rising from the sea. How magical he appeared as the water's surface broke for him. But she shouldn't look at him like that. Certainly not when she had a fiancé of her own.

Julius commended her progress as he led her inside. Lilith couldn't help but admit that she looked forward to her next lesson with the prince, whilst guilt stabbed at her chest with a vengeance.

With a sigh, she relinquished her worries and shut her eyes, and gave in to her mind's conjuring: old memories of her and Larkin chasing each other through the narrow streets of Utica.

YOU ARE MY ENTIRE UNIVERSE.

SEMANTICS

It was late one evening when Rhéa was summoned to attend to Prince Orìon's needs. Apparently, he had an incident with the Imperial hunting dogs and requested an Enchantress's touch to heal the scratches.

Stars bless her now.

Paying little heed to her unsettled nerves, Rhéa checked her appearance in the mirror. She took her time as the servant waited, impatiently tapping his foot on the marble floor. The servant was beyond intolerant. He only allowed her enough time to acquire a cleansing tonic from her pack. Rhéa hoped that Orìon's wounds were shallow enough that she wouldn't need anything else.

"It is time," the servant's husky voice demanded.

Once satisfied with her appearance, the Enchantress followed the servant into the chilled hallways. Her corridor bore gaping glassless windows that were open to the elements. She cursed them daily. The howling of the winter winds disturbed her sleep and scolded her when she dared leave her chambers.

Coming to a halt in front of two grand oaken doors, two Frourà sentinels parted to allow for the servant to open the door. He gestured for Rhéa to enter the chambers. As she passed, the servant muttered, "One cry of anguish from the boy and you'll have these two to answer to." He eyed the towering masts of muscle bracketing the doorway. The soldiers didn't respond, but she didn't doubt the servant's threat.

"Please, come in," the prince's arid voice rang forth.

Rhéa leaned back into the servant and purred, "It couldn't be nearly as horrid as the cruelty I've faced in the *Marsh*." She felt warmly satisfied as the man's face paled at the mention of the Obsydían Marsh. Mortals feared the land ruled by the Enchantresses. The land that Rhéa would forever remain pulled toward, like the land possessed the lure of a lodestone.

Winking curtly to her rude escort, Rhéa entered the prince's chambers. Her shoulders tensed, the *click* of the shutting door sounding almost like a death sentence.

"About time," Orìon intoned haughtily.

Rhéa responded primly, "I came as swiftly as your servant requested my service."

The heir was similarly dispositioned to his father. He'd inherited many of the Emperor's distinguished physical attributes: his dark, deep-set eyes, his broad shoulders and golden mane. Orìon's skin was flawlessly alabaster, unlike his father's ocherous complexion. He held himself in the same esteemed manner, which always left Rhéa rife with hostility.

Orìon glanced at her from under heavy lids, the sole indication that he'd been drinking heavily. The suspicion was only confirmed as she drew nearer and smelt the whiskey on his breath, liquor she would never be able to afford. Why, when his country had been at war for far longer than he'd drawn breath, did he choose to squander the crown's riches on imbibing? Surely the drachmae used to provide the castle with such luxuries would have been better spent elsewhere.

The prince stretched his arm out to her expectantly, a silent demand to begin her craft. There were several scratches running streams through his otherwise spotless skin. The scratches weren't as narrow and stark as she would expect from a dog's claw. The abrasions were surprisingly deep, slightly jagged and… wider. Almost as if a fingernail were the assailant.

"Are you going to heal those or just gawk at them all day?" It wasn't a question, but a demand in disguise. The prince was far too used to getting what he wanted, when he wanted.

"I need to see if there is any lingering debris in the… *gashes.*" Rhéa was careful with her choice of words. She wouldn't put it past Orìon to strike her for dismissing his wounds as mere scrapes. "If a dog's claw has pierced your skin, there are many substances that could get into your bloodstream, causing you to become ill." She ferreted the cleansing tonic out of the pocket of her gown.

"What do you mean *if?*" Orìon's steely gaze narrowed viciously.

Cursing herself, Rhéa tempered her tone, the tension now stretching taut between them, threatening to snap at any moment. "I mean to say that these gashes are wider than I would expect scratches from a claw to be."

"It is not your business how I attained these wounds. Your

only *purpose* here is to ensure that I heal unscarred," the prince reprimanded.

The prince was morose, and Rhéa calmed herself by imagining all the curses and hexes she could place on him. *Later.* She would think of those things later. She offered a slight bow of her head in deference.

Orìon hissed as she dropped the tonic onto the cuts. He glared at her but didn't withdraw his arm. The sooner she cleaned him, the sooner she could heal him, and then she'd be free of the belligerent brat. The man who would someday be Emperor, likely in the near future. Possibly. But the possibility alone was enough to make Rhéa fear for her life, her husband and her children, and everyone else who called Augusta their home.

Ignoring the prince's glower, Rhéa began to sing in Elder Tongue. "Hyàss dinns teq toffáss." *Heal skin and sinew.*

He didn't flinch as her palm illuminated above his wounds with a glow as brilliant as the sun. It would have been brighter if the sun were indeed awake, but it was the Stars' time to dance in the sky.

Once the wounded skin had knitted back together, leaving only white lines, Orìon inspected his arm. "I said, *Enchantress,*" he spat abhorrently, "*unscarred.*"

Rhéa fought for equanimity under the scrutiny and simply responded with an excessively saccharine smile.

"Don't be smart with me," he warned.

"The marks will fade," she assured. "The skin is fresh, untouched by the sun. Once you expose it to the elements, it will be unnoticeable."

The prince only scowled and exhaled tersely. "It better be." The threat lingered in the stale air between them.

Rhéa waited for another command, but Orìon said nothing for some time. She resisted the urge to stand and leave.

"You may go."

The Enchantress rose to stand before him. Though she stood above him, it seemed almost as though he were the one staring down his nose at her. How a child could belittle a grown Enchantress was beyond her. She would have given her life savings to witness Ophelía and the prince alone in a room together.

"Why are you smiling at me? I have dismissed you!" he snapped.

The door creaked open behind her and she turned to leave. "What?"

Rhéa glanced over her shoulder, her eyes narrowing upon him in such a way, she knew it would derail him.

The prince stood, stomping a sandalled foot on the ground. He crossed his arms over his chest, showing off his beringed fingers. "You deign not to bow to your future Emperor?"

The light of the sconces flickered at her will, and a trace of excitement flared as she bore witness to him quiver.

"You should know, Prince," she mocked his earlier use of tone, "that you are not *my* Emperor. You are not *my* prince. The Enchantresses are free, we bow to no one." Though her words were exact, she kept her tone cool. "Have a good night, *Princeling*." She drenched her final words in venom.

Orìon allowed a slight puff of a laugh escape his mouth, then he approached her. Rhéa faced him head on as he lowered his nose mere inches from hers. She could feel his whiskey-breath kiss her skin as he whispered, "Is it really freedom if it is *given*?"

Rhéa clenched her jaw. Her fingers curled at her sides,

cupping air as if it were tangible, as if she could use it as ammunition. She was determined to leave the room without a target on her back, determined to leave the prince unaware of her presence within the castle.

Well, that had been ruined.

Holding her composure—if only to deny the prince the satisfaction of seeing her balk—she drawled, "Semantics." Spinning on her heels, Rhéa took her leave.

Navigating the vast hallways in solitude, a tremor ran through her limbs. Did Orìon know of her intimate association with the highest ranked general? She prayed to the Stars that he didn't. She needed to warn Miles of her encounter with Prince Orìon. Her husband would reprimand her for acting so crass, but he would know what to do. How to pacify the heir.

The halls were abuzz with servants rushing to and fro. The Enchantress dipped her chin in greeting to those who had shown her kindness. When she reached the corridor that led to her own private chambers, she noticed her door had been left ajar. Without hesitation, Rhéa stormed through the gaping archway.

Empty.

The large living chamber was empty, and everything was as she'd left it. The sconces were lit, and her bed had been made by the servants. She spun around, ensuring that no one awaited her in the shadows. It took her a moment to calm herself enough to sit down on the edge of her bed. She poured herself a glass of wine and sighed into the chalice, gulping down the rich claret.

A knock at the door sounded. The Enchantress jumped, spilling the crimson liquid on her chiton gown. Grumbling in irritation, she made to open the door.

The servant girl stood in the hallway, fresh towels folded in her slight arms. Rhéa swung the door wide for the girl to enter.

"I'm sorry to bother you," she said, her voice unusually faint, quivering ever so slightly.

Rhéa waved her inside and shut the door behind her. Turning back to the servant girl, the Enchantress inspected her as she moved. The girl was timid, her demeanor tainted with fear, more than ever before.

"What happened?" Rhéa inquired.

The girl tensed, cinched her bottom lip between her teeth. It was only when those dainty shoulders began to tremble that Rhéa approached the girl.

"I'm going to ask again, what happened?" She stroked the girl's spine comfortingly, as she had for her children when they awoke from night terrors.

The girl dropped the towels on the floor, as if her arms couldn't bear the weight any longer. "I'm tired," she croaked. "I'm so tired." She turned to the Enchantress. "I need to get out of here! Anywhere would be better than this Gods forsaken giant torture chamber."

"If you managed to get out of the castle undetected, where on earth would you go?" It wasn't a question to deter the girl from her desire to leave but to encourage her to think with reason, logic.

"I don't know," the girl admitted. "Hades would be a better alternative to this. I can't stay here!"

Rhéa sighed in defeat. She knew that tone well, it was resolute. "Hold on a little longer. I will help you find a way out. A *safe* way out."

"Aren't Enchantresses supposed to be dangerous... *cruel*?"

The girl shot a careful glance at Rhéa. "I don't know why I'm even talking to you."

Rhéa released a slight chortle at the statement. "We are not cruel until provoked." She flashed the girl a fiendish grin in the hope that it would inspire mirth, but the servant wasn't interested in jesting.

The girl trembled visibly. Rhéa pulled her to the bed and beckoned for her to sit. "What is your name?" Rhéa asked as the girl obeyed.

"Irís."

"You can stay here tonight, Irís, as long as you don't mind sharing the sheets with me." She chuckled. "A deep sleep is the best way to heal the heart and mind."

Irís's eyes shone with tears of evident gratitude, but she hung her head. "I can't..."

"Why?"

"They will notice my absence. They will punish me for dereliction of duty."

"Who will?"

The girl only shook her head in defiance. Rhéa noted her sunken eyes and wondered if she ever found peace when she shut them.

Irís placed a delicate hand on Rhéa's. "Thank you. For everything. I've rarely met anyone so generous and kind in this fortress."

Indeed, Rhéa thought to herself, this castle was a fortress of the coldest stone. The Enchantress smiled and glanced down at the girl's hand atop her own. A thunderhead blossomed in Rhéa's ears as she beheld her fingernails. The arcs of dark-crimson beneath them.

Blood. Undeniably so.

The prince's wounds were as she'd suspected: not claw abrasions but human fingernails. Irís's fingernails.

"How old are you?"

Irís murmured, "Seventeen."

Rhéa's temper sparked. Prince Orìon was preying on *girls*! "What did the prince do to you?"

Irís's gulp was audible. She knew, from the look of humiliation now adorning the young woman's face, that those scratches were not engraved upon the prince in pleasure. She grabbed hold of Irís's hand to inspect it more closely, confirmation heating her bloodstream.

"Stop!" The girl's response was strident enough for Rhéa to relent.

"You do *not* command an Enchantress, or a guest of the royal family," Rhéa chastised and the girl blanched.

The Enchantress grasped Irís's arm, though not ungently. "The prince will pay for this, but if you refuse him or hurt him again, he will not hesitate to have you punished. And Irís, the repercussions will be worse than death, I can assure you that."

"That is why I need to leave immediately," Irís cried, burying her face in her shaking hands.

"Give me time to sort it out, I will help you," Rhéa comforted. "Until then, I will heal whatever ailments they bestow upon you. I will do whatever is in my power to make the waiting period bearable."

Without an answer, Irís stalked to the door.

Rhéa followed her. "I don't know what causes Prince Orìon to treat women so callously, maybe it's the lack of maternal presence. But he will come to recognize his faults, or he will pay."

Irís nodded before she rushed from the room, her expression haunted.

After the girl took her leave, Rhéa refilled her chalice and stood before the mirror. She glanced over to her windowsill, still vacant, and speculated where Ezío could be. The eagle never went more than a day or two without gracing her with his presence. So unlike her familiar. When she reached out to him with her mind, her consciousness didn't merge with his as it should.

Something was very wrong.

Rhéa sang, "Se qu pevër seâte unt Vën, ahírr va setenté vuthé qu ontè va vuíll tèles." *By the power vested in me, align my vision with the one my soul seeks.*

Her mother's elegantly planed face appeared on the mirror's surface like rippling water. Rhéa beamed at her mother until the mirror settled, the spell took hold, and Tatiana's expression became vivid. It was an expression that she'd rarely glimpsed, but when she did, things were not as they should be.

"Why have you taken so long to scry me? Because you know I can't contact you?" Her mother's irate voice inflicted more shame upon her than any other. Indeed, the castle was warded against scrying from the outside in.

"I'm sorry," Rhéa pleaded.

"Apologies won't help us now." Her mother scowled, brow furrowed.

"What do you mean?"

"Ophelía has discovered Selene amongst Ápeiro Astéri. The High Enchantress knows that you intercepted Selene and took her place—*stole* her place."

Indeed, the situation was grave.

Rhéa couldn't summon to words the questions that

plagued her mind. For the Enchantresses, there were techni-cally no written laws but the rules were ironclad, and if they were broken, the foolish soul would suffer immensely. The foolish soul would endure torment for the rest of her immortal days.

"The High Enchantress," Tatiana continued, "has called for the Council of Thirteens to determine what course of action will be taken to right your wrongs. As your mother, I will answer for you, but know that Selene will be punished as well, and she is innocent."

The frenetic beat of her heart rushed in her ears. Invisible hands gripped Rhéa. She fought to conceal it but ultimately failed.

"I'm so sorry, Mother!" she cried.

"That's not the worst of it." Tatiana was growing ever more painstakingly enigmatic with her age.

Rhéa's blood froze. There wasn't much under the Stars that could be worse than being put on trial by the Council of Thir-teens, especially when you weren't present to answer for your crimes.

"The Emperor has informed Ophelía that he will be holding you in the capital, as you are the lead suspect in the investigation on the disappearance of Larkin Oak."

"Disappearance?" Rhéa shook her head. "They executed him! He was innocent!"

The mirror beholding her mother's lovely face, the four-poster bed, the intricate tapestries, all transformed into a blurry eddy. The floor wavered beneath her as she swayed, her head a faint cloud of compressed air. It took every ounce of energy within her to withhold the spell, to keep her mother present for another moment.

Tatiana's voice barely broke through her confusion. "You must leave, Rhéa. Flee while you have time!"

Rhéa didn't need to see her reflection to know that she'd taken on a deathly pallor. Her mother could see it, too.

"Why did Ophelía tell you? Why would she want you to warn me?" Reason began to filter into her mind once again. The ground stilled beneath her, though she remained feeble.

"You know Ophelía. Regardless of whether she favors you or not, you are her property, you belong to the Obsydían Marsh. She will not allow the Emperor to have his way with one of her own."

Rhéa believed it. She needed to return to atone for her own sins against the Marsh. It was her punishment to bear, not her mother's.

"I am on my way," Rhéa assured. "Tell Ophelía that I will answer for my crimes. I will pay the price. Not you. Not Selene."

Before her mother could respond, Rhéa released the spell. A moment later, the door to her chambers burst open and soldiers filed in, as if they'd been listening in the corridor. The chalice slipped from her grip at the sight of them, the dark liquid splattering the length of her gown. Rhéa looked down in amazement. Had she been holding it this whole time?

The soldiers said nothing as they took her by her arms. They were forceful but they didn't harm her. They led her from the chamber, leaving her belongings behind. They were the Emperor's property now.

"This won't be pleasant," one of the soldier's breathed in her ear, "so it's best that we go to sleep for now."

A bright spark of pain exploded in her skull, and everything went black.

SERPENT'S TONGUE

There had been a few incidents caused by Lilith's new blessing. During a nightmare, the tide rose high enough that the sea nearly touched the Frourío. Olga had come to soothe her, and the Oracle remained by her side throughout the night. By morning the tide had gone out, but the armory had retained sea water, which was difficult to remedy as Lilith was not yet disciplined enough to return it to the Galatëa.

Zurí arrived at the Frourío one blistering morning, gusts of snow wafting in through the front door in her wake. Ambrose loped off to tend to her stallion immediately, but not before he caught a glimpse of the exquisite sight of the Divine woman.

Everyone was present at the kitchen table. Hostility was high between Lilith and Wren as she asked Felix how he'd been getting along with his swordsmanship. The tension only grew increasingly taut as she offered to spar with him that afternoon. She obeyed Arduen's orders and ignored Wren's absurd misogynistic comments, and now she played at irritating him. She knew antagonizing the beast would provoke its wrath, but Lilith welcomed such commotion. It helped to keep her mind off of Larkin.

All at once the Divine of the Frourío rose to greet the notorious Zurí. The woman was strikingly tall, elegant and poised. Her back was ramrod straight and she wore a bodysuit similar to the others, though much more intricate details were woven into the leather. Her fur-lined himation hung loose on her frame, accentuating her sinuous figure. She was stunning, even with a slight scar marring the left side of her face. It made her appear distinguished and... *intimidating*.

Arduen broke free of the group once Zurí had removed her cloak. To Lilith's surprise, her Masters embraced in a familiar hug, Olga and Quin following Arduen's lead. Wren abandoned his meal to embrace Zurí as well. The woman finally smiled at them all, displaying straight, white teeth.

Lilith was entranced; Zurí was a vision.

Arduen waved Lilith over. She obliged sheepishly as Zurí's turquoise eyes met her own. Eyes that could kill a man with just one glance, but Lilith was not a man. She stretched her hand out to her new Master.

Zurí smirked contentedly and grasped Lilith's forearm. "Never did I presume the Gods would grant another Divine with greater power," she said, tone prim. "And here you are, young and beautiful, and... *female*. I look forward to getting to know you and fighting alongside you, Lilith."

Up close, Lilith could see the scar was stark against Zurí's ivory skin. Silver, as if it had done a lifetime of healing already.

Olga wedged herself between them. "I will show you to your bedchamber. We have so much to catch up on!"

"Very well," Zurí replied, though not unkindly. "While I am getting myself settled, you shall resume your usual schedule with Arduen."

"Yes, Master," Lilith whispered.

Zurí and Olga ascended the stairs, arm in arm, smiling wide as they chattered to one another like buntings.

"Finish your breakfast and meet me in the study." Arduen clapped her approvingly on the shoulder before following after the two women.

⊙ ⊛ ⟜ ᴍ ♦

As Lilith entered the study, Arduen was already seated at the desk. "I assume you studied last night… following your swimming lesson with Julius." It wasn't a question.

Lilith held her tongue. She was useless at lying. Larkin had always been the better liar. He was quick at devising a good tale and could muster up an impressive array of realistic expressions. If he was ever found guilty, it was always due to her lack of skill in the art. All that was needed to break her was a sharp raise of the eyebrows from her father, or a hand placed on her mother's hip as she inspected either of her children with those critical eyes. Lilith had always been the first to cave.

Arduen impaled her with his icy gaze. "You *did* review the chapter?"

She shuffled in place, her chair groaning in protest at the movement. "I was exhausted after my lesson. It slipped my mind."

Indeed, her second swimming lesson had proven to be quite taxing on her physically. Julius had relaxed her leash slightly, allowing her more freedom to move about. Lilith couldn't refuse him; the prince knew what he was doing. But the great sea was mighty, and still she struggled to fight off the terrors.

"I know you can't swim," Arduen said on an unusually exasperated sigh, "but you didn't even grant instinct one chance that day of the mighty swell… *your* mighty swell. You let those waters swallow you whole and you gave up." He took a firm hold of her hand. "Do not let the pain of losing the ones you love render you useless, Lilith. Do not let the fear of that pain stifle you."

She blanched, her chest tightening at his words.

Arduen sat back and opened the *History of Augusta* to the chapter on temples and began to read to her. When he was finished, he summarized, "Each temple worships one God only. Every capital of each of the five realms possesses a temple dedicated to the God of that realm."

"Why only one, Master?" Lilith interjected. "Why not have a temple worshipping all five Gods?"

"It is considered disrespectful to construct a temple that worships more than one God, for each God deserves Their own temple." He waited for Lilith to voice another question before he continued. "Those who live near a temple may visit daily to pray to that God or to worship in song or offering. Usually a male animal."

Lilith furrowed her brow. "Why a male animal?"

Arduen chuckled. "That's a good question. The animal of immolation must be male because the gender must match that of the God's. All the Gods are male. It would be a great insult to Them to offer a female animal. Not because the animal is female but because it is not the same gender as the Gods."

He steepled his fingers, leaning into the desk. "We believe the Gods can hear us, and indeed They can hear and see all. Many travel to temples to feel closer to their God, closer than they would in the comfort of their own home. Every town possesses a public house of prayer, but that is not a temple. Though they are usually fashioned after one of the great structures."

"That explains why there were never any sacrifices in Utica then," Lilith thought aloud. "Do the Divine partake in the sacrifices?"

"No."

"Why?"

"Because our lives are our sacrifice."

Lilith shifted in her seat uncomfortably. "Where is Constantine's temple?"

"The Temple of Constantine is northeast of Kynös, in the foothills. It is a very beautiful location. Many travel there just to behold its scenic magnificence." Arduen shuffled through his books and revealed a map of Augusta. "This is the Temple of Constantine," he said, pointing to the location.

"Will we be travelling there?"

"Yes, anon. Before you partake in any form of battle."

Lilith bristled. "Why?"

"Because you must travel to your own designated God's temple to declare your Dâs Thymó."

"Dâs Thymó?"

"It is your one wish," said Arduen. "Every Divine is granted one wish for their lifetime. So think long and wisely when you consider what it is that your heart desires most. This is the one aspect of our existence where we can truly be selfish."

"I guess I can't wish for resurrection?"

Arduen's expression darkened, but when he looked at her, recognition was stark in his features, for surely he had lost many loved ones over the years.

"I almost want to wish to never have to ask for one thing," Lilith said to change the subject. "I feel as though I could regret this for the rest of my life." Would it be wise to construct an Dâs Thymó that would not only affect her, but the rest of the world? It was a heavy burden rather than a gift, which seemed to be a trend for the life of the Divine.

"You don't have to come to any conclusions today," said Arduen. "But do spend some time considering it. I am always free to talk and help you decide, if you wish to share it with me."

Lilith dropped her gaze, her eyes settling on the desk before her.

"Do you have any other questions that you would like me to answer before we move on to prayer?"

Biting down on her lip, she asked, "How is it possible for the Divine of Aether and Fire to summon their element at will, without need of it pre-existing? As with Water, I need it to be present before me."

"The first Divine, Elïath, summoned his element for the first time. He didn't know how to wield it, how to control it. The Fire nearly annihilated his town. He burnt himself quite severely. It's a horrifying story, and many renditions have been written since."

An image of Julius's scarred arms flashed in her mind.

Suddenly Lilith was thankful not to have been blessed by Xander.

"The Gods communicated to him as They do to Olga," Arduen said. "Elïath had no one else to guide him. No one to help him make sense of the visions he was receiving and the voices he was hearing. One would assume they had gone mad, which he did. That is, until Sonös appeared. He'd been compelled by the Gods to travel to a distant city to meet the girl who could now wield Aether. Elïath and Sonös were the only two who could summon their element at will, as if it had taken refuge inside of them.

"There is no real reason why some elements come from within, but the ones that do are the most dangerous—the most deadly—even to the wielder. Bear that in mind every time you practice wielding Aether."

AT THEIR MIDDAY MEAL, LILITH WAITED FOR ZURÍ TO TAKE HER place among them. She kept her eyes peeled for the woman's fiery mane, but it was futile. The Oracle chimed about how wonderful it was to have another Divine home, but Zurí hadn't spent much time with them.

Home.

For the first time, Lilith took comfort in calling the Frourío home. There was nothing left for her in Utica. Perhaps a letter to Jude was in order, to sever what ties remained, but she couldn't bring herself to cast him off so carelessly. They were lifelong friends; he deserved better than that.

The tower had grown on her, along with its inhabitants, and

Lilith didn't want to leave. And maybe her Master was growing on her, too. He'd become a pillar of strength. A paragon of fortitude. Her world had crumbled, disintegrated beneath her very feet, but he resurrected hope. Arduen was the crenellation fortifying her resolve, shielding her from those who wished to sunder Constantine's noviciate. Hope flared at the thought. Yes, she could brazen her way through this with Arduen at her side.

Olga dropped her cutlery. Her expression inscrutable, her features frozen in place and the whites of her eyes exposed.

Arduen rose to his feet and rushed to her side. The room was silent, even Ambrose paused his clattering of dishes in the kitchen. All eyes were on Olga.

Was this what it looked like when the Oracle received a message from the Gods?

Olga murmured words indecipherable to Lilith. The rolling and lilting of Elder Tongue. Arduen knelt at her side, and Olga gripped his hands, her knuckles white.

"They are coming…" the Oracle muttered.

"Who is?" Arduen probed.

The veins on the backs of her hands threatened to explode, but Arduen didn't flinch or recoil.

"Spiro's beasts. They march for the capital." Her eyes were wide, her words coming in breathy gasps.

"I will send a message to the Emperor immediately," Arduen said. "As soon as he gives the order, we must march to Kenora. I will notify him that we have sent Quintus and Julius immediately." He nodded his approval, and Quin and Julius rose from their seats and rushed up the stairs, speaking calmly to one another.

Lilith frowned. Her bones had frozen stiff. She'd hoped, had even assumed, that when war would come upon them, they would all remain together. She couldn't help but fret over where Julius's path would take him.

"Lilith," said Arduen, his voice startling her from her torpor. "I want you to go pack your things. Once I send this letter, we are leaving."

"For the capital?"

"No, to the Temple of Constantine."

UNDER THE LURID WINTER SUN, LILITH HIT BULLSEYE AFTER bullseye, nocked arrow after arrow, gradually dispelling her anxiety. She refused to watch as Quin and Julius disappeared into the pines. Her own expedition had been delayed for a few hours as Arduen dealt with other tasks of importance.

Lilith rarely missed the target, even when performing absurd calisthenics. She'd reached a point where she was beginning to grow bored with her training. What she needed was competition, someone to challenge her.

The winter winds beat down on her as she trudged down the snow-dusted hill. Grunts and huffs sailed on the breeze to meet her ears. Wren and Felix were sparring across the field, the clang and clatter of their swords discernible over the shouts of instruction Wren bellowed at his noviciate.

Felix's jovial cheers were palpable even at a distance. His positivity radiated throughout the wintry Forest, his laughter near-infectious. Lilith couldn't help but admire the young man for his constant alacrity. She wished she possessed his level of exuberance.

She made to retrieve her arrows for the sixth time that session, taking mental notes of what she needed to work on.

As she turned back to her shooting post, she noticed Zurí standing in the shadows of the trees. Uncertain how long the woman had been there, watching, analyzing, and assessing her, Lilith blushed as their eyes met.

"How fares the great Lilith?"

Withholding her wince at the greeting, she replied, "I am well. And how fares my new Master?"

"I am well." Zurí approached, her long stride enviable. "You're a sure shot," she commended.

"Thank you, Master."

Zurí granted her a slight, closed-lip smile. "Please, don't stop on my behalf. Unless you would like to join the men?"

Lilith followed her gaze on the direction of the sparring field. "Wren won't let me join them."

Zurí scoffed and rolled her eyes, arms crossed over her full chest. "Don't listen to Wren. Some people never change, especially the immortal. Just tell him that your training is even more important than the boys', he won't argue with that."

"I tried once…" Lilith began hesitantly.

"And?"

"Arduen scolded me for talking disrespectfully to a Master, even if I wasn't entirely in the wrong. Wren has said some pretty disturbing things to Felix."

Zurí raised one perfectly groomed eyebrow. "Regarding…?"

"Something along the lines of women shouldn't be on the battlefield. That our place is in the home, raising children and tending to our male counterparts." She omitted the *warming of their beds* part. Lilith would never forgive Wren for the rift it had caused in her relationship with Arduen. Even if it had brought them closer in the end.

Zurí's laughter trilled. "He has a rutting serpent's tongue. He can't help it."

"Has he always been so openly opposed to women bearing arms?" Lilith asked.

"Not always. He is older than I, but when I was a noviciate, he was a Master to a beautiful young woman named Cordova. She was talented and soft-hearted, possessed a natural lust for knowledge. She was truly resilient. She graduated and decided to remain at the Frourío. Times were tough, and Spiro's situation was parlous. We could see the Dark Age forming, but we could do nothing to negate it. Not one of us could humble Spiro. The Frourío seemed like the safest place for all of us. Many were left broken after Spiro betrayed us, and I only had Cordova left of those I studied with. She and I were close, like sisters, and Wren was like her father."

Zurí's choice of words jolted Lilith. *Like her father.* Is that what she wanted from Arduen?

"Then one day," Zurí continued, "Olga announced that there had been an attack. Several Divine attempted to take on Spiro and called for our aid. They were defeated by the time we arrived on site. We lit their Stars, singing the Hymn of Divination, one after another, exhausted and heartsore.

"Suddenly, out of nowhere, beasts appeared, rising from the blood-soaked soil. They caught Cordova off guard and slit her throat. It all happened too quickly for the Oracle to heal her. Wren held her as she bled out." She drew a semicircle in the snow with the pointed tip of her boot. "He will never be the same."

Lilith swallowed, eyes squinting to inspect Wren from across the field.

"On several occasions Wren has begged me not to march

into battle with them. He won't take a female Divine as a Philías, or as a noviciate. He just can't bear to watch our demise." Zurí's luminous eyes were silver-lined. Lilith could only imagine the atrocities that those eyes had beheld.

"Be patient and forgiving of others, Lilith. Especially those with elongated years. There are likely many hardships they've been forced to face, hardships that you will come to understand one day. There is almost always a cause for someone to act so… callously, for seemingly no reason."

How had she never considered such a loss could have bred Wren's disapproval of his female counterparts? Sympathy welled within her. She was no stranger to grief.

"I am done with archery for the day," Lilith said. "Would you like to spar with me?"

Zurí cast her a sidelong glance. "Actually, I would rather begin instructing you on the commanding of Kyril's Water."

⚬ ⚬ ⚬ ⚬ ⚬

LILITH'S SECOND ATTEMPT AT COMMANDING WATER HAD NOT been as beleaguered as she'd originally presumed, and the lesson itself wasn't cursory. Zurí had been far less enigmatic than Arduen, and far more overt. She'd escorted Lilith to the armory, now dry thanks to her.

Their breath turned near-solid in the air. Lilith strained to control the Water inside a silver chalice Zurí had placed on the table. When she failed several times to cause the liquid to do anything other than eddy, she asked, "How is Water going to be useful in battle?"

"The earth is made of Water, as are the men who dwell upon it. Use that to your advantage."

Lilith pondered all the possibilities and still came up short.

Zurí must have been able to read the confusion on Lilith's face because she continued, "You can summon all of the moisture from the earth, but that can be devastating and place you in a lot of trouble, trust me." She rolled her eyes. "But observe the clouds and summon Water from them. Drown your enemies in a rainstorm." Zurí became electrified, her voice rising and falling with zeal, her hands fluttering in the air. "You can drain the fluid from the bodies surrounding you and you can use it to drown your enemies!" She made a crude gesture, and Lilith stifled a cackle at the sight of it.

"In order to be successful, you must learn how to be pragmatic. Logic will be what determines your success and failure. Get creative with how you summon and wield your gifts." There was a sparkle in Zurí's eyes. "Now continue."

Lilith obeyed. The Water swirled within the chalice, small drops splashing over the brim and onto the table.

"Now still the Water."

Unsure how to stop it, Lilith closed off her mind, emptied it, and watched as the Water stilled.

"That's it!" Zurí exclaimed. "Now wait until the Water is completely stagnant, and then command it to turn in the opposite direction."

Lilith waited patiently while the Water slowly swirled, gradually slowing before coming to a halt. After a moment, when the Water's surface had stilled long enough for Lilith to glimpse a clear reflection of the ceiling's oaken beams, she willed it into motion again. The Water obeyed almost instantly.

"Good!"

Relinquishing control, the Water grew still again. Lilith beamed at her new Master, but Zurí's eyes gazed past her.

Arduen approached the table. "I am pleased to see that you are excelling," he said.

Lilith only smiled slightly, awaiting his order to leave.

"Off you go, Lilith. Pack only what you need."

"Yes, Master."

ONE WISH FOR ETERNITY

For the better part of their journey, Lilith struggled to suppress her raging worries. The importance of this quest weighed down upon her immensely. She was acutely aware of how it would impact the remainder of her years, and she felt the pressing need to devote every thought to considering her Dâs Thymó.

Keeping her face downcast, Lilith trusted Skydancer to follow Arduen's mare, whom he often nuzzled affectionately. Tall pines reached high into the ocherous sky, the bottom shafts of their trunks barren of branches. The ground was dusted lightly with fresh snow as they galloped along the path. Lilith longed for open meadows streaked by streams that had long since frozen stiff, dotted only by slender firs—but the Realm of Elïath was far behind them now. The farther they rode from the Frourío, the landscape transformed. Small knolls swelled like frozen waves of a sea that seemed to roll on forever, leading her farther from home.

Arduen most often left her to her own thoughts, but when he did break the silence, it was with the purpose of bestowing upon her stories of old. Lilith listened in mute contentment, gleeful that he was sharing parts of his past—albeit, the most mysterious and joyful parts.

Her Master told her of his many escapades with Quin, Zurí and Olga. He omitted any stories with Spiro, but Lilith could guess a few of his stories involving Quin and Zurí was actually Spiro and Zurí. He told her that one harrowing winter, he traveled with Quin, Zurí and the High Enchantress in search of a rogue Enchantress, pregnant with a Magí's babe. He told her how Ophelía had made their journey far less beleaguered than it would have been without her. How she had formed the tree branches into small huts to shelter them from inclement weather and warmed them from within. How she had healed their horses so that they could travel excessively with few rests. How she had rolled a boulder-sized snowball with no more effort than a twitch of her finger, and it transformed into a flaming orb and trundled along the road before them, clearing the snow for their horses.

"I wish we could use magic," Lilith said, failing to siphon the wistfulness from her tone.

Arduen merely cast her a censorious glance before a wry grin stole over his features. "Aye." He matched her tone.

With one hand fisted in the reins, the other was clenched firm around Constance's hilt. Lilith had groused and griped until Arduen relented, allowing her to wield Constance over Oak. There was something so satisfying about always having her father's handiwork at her side, as if she carried a piece of him with her.

"The Temple of Constantine is nestled right over there." Arduen pointed to the northeast.

"Do you think we will have company?" She didn't mind if there were others worshipping while they went about the ceremony, but she couldn't deny that it made her slightly self-conscious. The idea of strangers bearing witness seemed to drain the intimacy from the moment.

"It's unlikely. There are no local towns," said Arduen. "In the event that we are joined by pilgrims, I will wait until they're done prayer and kindly ask them to take their leave." A request only suitable for a Divine to make.

"These are the foothills of the Orösía Mountain range?"

"Yes, the mountains will rise up far above these, past the Obsydían Marsh."

Lilith gazed into the distant south, curious of what it would feel like to set her eyes upon the impending mountains. Would she ever get the chance to bask in their glorious shadows, or venture into their valleys, or climb to their summits? She prayed she would.

Patting Skydancer's sinewy neck, she observed her surroundings. The long ride had proven strenuous for her mind. For her heart. Her thoughts drifted to Larkin far more often than she'd like. The pain of losing him hurt like an open wound, it still seeped crimson, staining everything in sight.

Her mind often wandered to Julius, and she prayed that his trip to the capital was swift and safe. She often stole glances in the direction of Kenora, as if she could see the rising ivory turrets of the Emperor's castle.

Arduen shot her a knowing look. "Do not worry about our emissaries. Quintus is a well-weathered warrior and Julius has received the highest quality training since he was a child."

Lilith nodded, her anxieties not entirely doused. "I just hope they're all right."

◎ ⑤ ⤳ Ⲙ ◊

THE DAYS PASSED QUICKLY. THE WEATHER PROVED TO BE ON THEIR side. Perhaps a blessing from Constantine Himself, Lilith was almost certain.

One afternoon, Skydancer reared in alarm, his front hooves kicking into the sky. Alarmed, Lilith clenched her legs and grappled for the reins. She snapped her head from side to side, searching for the cause of his panic.

There was no movement.

Arduen dismounted and soothed the gelding, prompting her to do the same. Having gleaned no anxiety in her Master's face, she drew Constance from its scabbard. Would she be able to sense beasts nearby? She reached out with Discernment but found nothing out of the ordinary.

"There are no predators nearby." Arduen eyed her sword.

She shrugged. "I'd like to be prepared."

Arduen dipped his chin in understanding before he ambled away without an explanation. He placed his hand above his brow to shield his eyes from the sun as he gazed back toward the towering Megálos pines.

There, above the trees, close enough to brush their tips, a large eagle flapped its wings. Lilith beamed as the bird approached them. Was it Evös? Slowly and silently, she moved to stand by Arduen's side as the eagle swooped down, landing on his outstretched arm.

Evös screeched a greeting.

Arduen stroked Evös's neck gently with his knuckles.

Lilith reached out, running her fingertips along the soft feathers of the eagle's chest. Evös screeched again and nipped her fingers before she could pull away.

"Ah," Arduen said. "She does not fancy her chest touched."

Lilith mumbled, "Thanks for the reminder," as she sucked her bloody finger.

Evös slowly blinked once in recognition before she untied the scroll that had been fastened to her leg with glittering gold thread. Arduen caught the roll as it fell and raised his arm into the air.

"To the Frourío, Evös," he said. And the eagle took off with one impressively powerful flap of her wings.

Lilith waited patiently as he read the letter. It was from the Emperor, bearing the Imperial wax seal that Arduen broke with little care. She shuffled on her feet anxiously as she watched his expression transition from curiosity to dread. Only when he finally folded the piece of parchment, securing it inside his cloak, did Lilith dare inquire about its contents.

"The Màtia's reconnaissance has determined that Spiro's troops are closing in on the capital."

"And…" she pressed.

"Spiro's forces outnumber the Emperor's Milítia severely. Not only that, but Spiro has manufactured machinery. We do not know what the contraptions can do. There's no time to form alliances and gather reinforcements. If we intend to make it to Kenora before the attack, we need to make haste." He stalked away from her, face drawn and distant.

Arduen mounted his steed and Lilith mutely followed suit. They broke into a quick gallop, eager to reach their destination. She welcomed the silence as they continued on. She assumed they both had become victim to the worries that afflicted their minds.

Arduen's voice broke through the silence, drawing her attention. "Have you given your Dâs Thymó enough consideration?" he called over his shoulder, the echoes of his voice drifting back to her.

Lilith drew Skydancer alongside his mare. "I've been contemplating my deepest fears, hurts, and desires. It feels like a waste to wish that I will always be happy." She sighed, her heart fluttering nervously.

"Why is that?"

"Because we are Divine. We aren't meant to be happy, not in a constant state anyways. I don't believe it's possible for anyone to be in a perpetual state of contentment, regardless of wealth or status. I think happiness is fleeting. Joy is eternal. Being content is practical…" She trailed off, lost in thought as she spoke the words aloud for the first time.

"You are growing wise, my fledgling."

My fledgling. Her heart warmed at his words.

⊙ ⥁ ⟿ ⋔ ♦

THEY RODE AT A STEADY PACE ALONG THE WORN PATH THROUGH the snow, now a mucky trail winding through the fields toward the valley. It looked like the Gods painted it with an Elysium-sized paintbrush. The road was well travelled by devoted acolytes and pilgrims seeking Constantine's presence, but Arduen and Lilith were alone.

Fresh powder began to descend from the gathering clouds as they made their way to the temple. The contents of Lilith's mind drifted to and fro more often than she would have liked.

She remained silent for the majority of their trip knowing Arduen would give her space to consider her Dâs Thymó. One wish for an eternity. She only wanted to make it count, though the pressure was near-suffocating.

Lilith thought about war and what it might look like. She knew how to forge weapons, how to wield them, yet she knew not what a battlefield entailed. They had only a matter of weeks—possibly days—before they stepped onto that field of chaos. The tales she'd heard in her childhood painted a romantic image of handsome, valiant men sacrificing their lives, much to the anguish of lovers that awaited them in the home they would never return to. Lilith wasn't naïve enough to believe that those stories were entirely true. There was always more to every tale. Always truth hidden in the fables.

As they reached the foothills, the sky cleared. The foothills rolled beneath the vast cyan, coated in white, save for several patches of rocks and pines.

"All we have to do now," Arduen said, "is enter the hills through that valley and follow the Aoös River along to the base of the great steps."

"The steps?" she asked, bemused.

"Yes, we will have to climb up to the temple," he clarified. "You know, Lilith, there is symbolism in the climb."

Undaunted, they entered the valley, the trees not nearly as dense as those of the Megálos.

"And what does it symbolize?"

"The ascent to Elysium. It signifies that the temple is the most intimate place to meet with Constantine. It's the highest point in the Realm of Sonös. It's commendable to travel to the location monthly, though many of the local pilgrims make the trek weekly."

They trotted along the Aoös, the water rushing through the artery, ice coating its edges.

"That's beautiful," Lilith mused. "Will it make the ascent any less unbearable?"

"In these temperatures… unlikely." Arduen adopted a comical grin. "Be thankful, this temple is the most accessible, but the steps are not so easily navigated. Many perish along the journey."

Lilith flashed her Master a wide-eyed glare as they rounded the first hill and the temple finally became visible.

"The Temple of Constantine," Arduen announced proudly, his arms outstretched.

There were few words that could do the sight justice. The view aroused in Lilith a deep sense of longing and *belonging*. She ignored Arduen's glance as she followed him along the river to the base of the steps, incapable of tearing her gaze from the temple.

It was a structure of astounding grandeur, constructed entirely of white marble that shimmered in the winter sunlight. The proverbial pillars, thicker than any of the pines in the Megálos, lined the entrance. Five of them. One for each of the Gods, similar to the house of prayer in Utica. The portico of columns supported a pediment whereupon a frieze of Constantine's swirling symbol of Aether was placed.

Lilith steeled herself as she recited her Dâs Thymó in her mind, over and over. It brought as much comfort as it did consternation. Not that she was uncertain, for she'd made up her mind. But as much as the temple imposed a sense of well-being and peace, she was dwarfed in its shadow.

They dismounted and secured their horses to the troughs, the climb being the penultimate task of their journey. Lilith sucked in a deep breath before following Arduen's lead, and placed her foot upon the first of a thousand steps. Her Master stood above her, his hand proffered.

"Better to climb together," he spoke gently, his voice unfaltering. She looped her arm through his, and tightened her grip on his bicep, thankful for his presence.

They climbed in silence, arm in arm, until they finally reached the summit. Nestled upon the flat surface stood the monumental temple, a gargantuan bleached marble structure. Ancient and majestic. Primeval. Lilith gaped in awe, ignoring Arduen's amused cackle.

"Welcome home."

They stepped through the open archway. The inside of the temple was as glorious as the outside, if not more intricate and articulately crafted. The ceiling was a breathtaking rendering of Constantine's constellation in a clear night sky. The dark violet abyss that she could now wield, constituted the outer edges, bordering the aerial masterpiece.

The walls bore an array of ancient engravings that had long since lost their meaning. Sigils carved into the marble bordered the base of all four walls. The floor was constructed of tiles that were placed strategically to form the symbol of Constantine, a swirling eddy similar to the one carved into the door of her bedchamber at the Frourío. Lilith marvelled at the sanctuary. How impregnable it must be to have endured centuries upon centuries.

Arduen allowed her to wander and observe as he made his way to the altar. When she finally composed herself, Lilith traipsed to her Master's side.

"Are you ready?" he asked.

She nodded, dropping to her knees as he had schooled her

on the journey. Arduen stood beside her, a gentle hand on her shoulder, a confidant to his apprentice. Clearing his throat, he stood ramrod straight. Lilith gulped and tore her gaze from her Master's unflinching stare.

"I will first recite the declaration in Modern Tongue, but when we declare your Dâs Thymó formally, I will recite the verse in Elder Tongue, and you will repeat after me. If you are not privy to sharing your one wish, I can step aside, and you may speak in our tongue. The Gods will hear you just as well."

He went silent for a moment. Her pulse throbbed on her neck, so powerful it had to be visible. Cold sweat dripped down the backs of her arms, and she inhaled deeply to calm herself. When he began, her blood had long since run cold.

Arduen said, "I, Lilith Oak, Anointed Divine by the Holy Constantine, God of Aether, and the Holy Kyril, God of Water, stand before thee to declare my Dâs Thymó, that is my right by Anointment, through my service and sacrifice as Your Divine."

Lilith shifted nervously, her attention being summoned to the present.

"Now, please repeat after me." Arduen cleared his throat again, and with his eyes closed, he began, his voice strident. Commanding. He spoke in Elder Tongue, the syllables slithering from his lips, caressing her ears like a cool breeze.

"Von, Lilith Oak, Avidr Divinè se qu Honr Constantine, Tsat un Ether, teq qu Honr Kyril, Tsat un Wàtre, ducc unfel thee sa quelsna va Dâs Thymó, vat uit va síng se Avidrsen, soulè va safice teq saficesu sec Esír Divinè."

A shiver raked through her frame despite the warmth that permeated the temple. The power that composed the ancient words drenched the air with their majesty, and she was suddenly hyperaware of a presence that had settled over them. Lilith repeated each phrase with as much proper pronunciation as she could muster.

When she reached the final line, Arduen made to leave her in solitude, but she reached out for him and caught him by the crook of his arm, fingers digging into hard sinew. He turned to face her, silent as the stone that surrounded them.

Without releasing her hold on him, Lilith spoke in Modern Tongue with as much surety and confidence as she could summon. "I, Lilith Oak, desire above all else that the one's whom I give my heart, and those who have a place in their heart for me, will be spared from bearing witness to my demise."

Arduen's body went suddenly rigid.

Unsure whether the ceremony was complete, Lilith cast him a bemused glance. When she met his gaze, a single tear carved its way down his cheek. She raised a finger to wipe it away, but he grasped her hand and held it to his lips in a warm paternal kiss.

30

ON THE PRECIPICE

Rhéa awoke in a cramped, dank cell; gossamer coating the slick stone walls. There was a stillness in the room. A stale atmosphere the likes of which only the dead could take solace in. The kind of place an Enchantress would wither and die, never to join her sisters in Starlight.

Her head throbbed violently, her vision blurred, but not enough to render her completely disoriented. She lay where the soldiers deposited her, well aware that Obadïa would leave her this way for days before she was summoned into questioning. The chamber was barren, save for the stiff cot she lay upon, and the empty bucket meant for relieving herself.

The Enchantress was aware that she was a prisoner of the Emperor, and the High Enchantress would not rescue her. But if she needed to defend herself, if the soldiers took the interrogation a step too far, she would be able to fend them off with the cot and the bucket as her only weapons. For an Enchantress, any common decor could become lethal.

Visions of her patient's wounds flashed behind her eyelids. Rhéa groaned, unable to shake them. She was smaller than the young man, her body wouldn't be able to take such callous treatment. Not to mention, there was no one to heal her, not in the way that she'd healed her patients, offered them reprieve from the pain.

Rhéa would have to resort to bewitching. Prying her way into the minds of the men who intended to harm her, where she would persuade them otherwise. If she had to, she could coerce the Emperor into freeing her, but he would never expose himself, never allow himself to become vulnerable in her presence.

Rhéa's abdomen convulsed as the putrid air engulfed her. Her stomach threatened to spew its contents, or lack thereof.

The cell door groaned as it opened, and a slight man entered. He wore no uniform, just a fitted black leather suit, and a halo of dark-blond curls framed his gaunt face. Rhéa regarded the man with a blank stare, attempting to intimidate him into submission.

"Master summons you," he said aridly.

The Emperor was going to lead the interrogation. Did he know the truth? But there was no possible way he could have discovered her identity. She was Rhéa DaSylvà, Enchantress of the Obsydían Marsh.

"Obadïa may be your Master," Rhéa intoned, "but he is *not* mine."

The man snickered derisively. "As of today, you have one Master. There is nothing that the precious *Stars* can do about it."

Rhéa openly scowled at him, but she didn't deign to refuse. She stood, dizziness threatening to topple her, and floundered in his wake.

The Enchantress was nearly as tall as the lithe man. It would be so easy to overtake him, bewitching or no. She contemplated several spells to incapacitate him. She even began to utter the phrases in Elder Tongue, but no matter how deep she delved into her entity, no magic responded to the words.

"You can stop that," the man spat, smug amusement adorning his fine features.

"Why?"

"Because Master knows what you are. He needs your powers. But you must earn his trust before he will allow you to access them."

Dread pooled in the pit of her stomach. "Fàrmako," she breathed. Fàrmako was the only drug capable of stifling magic. That was usually the only circumstance the drug was ever used in Augusta. Its strength would be detrimental to her power for days before they would need to administer another dose. Rhéa was surprised Emperor Obadïa could afford the drachmae to import it. He would have had to go through a great deal of trouble shipping it in from Xanthë. All for her? Rhéa coughed up bile.

The man halted before two looming iron doors. One couldn't ignore the spikes that protruded from the flat surface. As intimidating and unwelcoming as it was, the iron doors would never compare to the foreboding city of bones that was the Obsydían Marsh.

The doors swung inward and the man waved her on. "Master will see you now."

Rhéa entered the chamber poised and proper, her posture stoic, the cadence of her footfalls even and rhythmic. She approached an oblong mahogany table and paused before it, her golden eyes settling upon a lone figure—a man. With his back to her, his pale-blond hair fell below his shoulders. It was the only distinguishable physical feature visible to her.

"Hello, Rhéa DaSylvà."

That voice… A tremor raked down her spine at the sound of his rich timbre.

When the man faced her, he appeared prim and sagely, like she would imagine Ophelía's ideal counterpart. A man who knew how to instil fear with consummate ease. And indeed, with that piercing stare and smug grin, he summoned anxiety from deep within the her. A difficult feat.

This was no ordinary man standing before her.

Rhéa held herself firm, refusing to balk at the face of death incarnate. Two immortal souls stood, eyes locked on the other, and the Enchantress wouldn't allow the Gods' scion to break her.

He stepped toward her, his gait as antagonizing as the foul words that slithered from his Divine lips. He halted as close as either of them were willing to get, but he was still close. Too close. The exhales of his breath ruffled her hair.

She prayed for safety from the Guiding Stars. The Star of the North, Andromeda; the Star of the East, Dracoladen; the Star of the West, Cepheus; and the Southern Star, Amalthea. *Grant me strength. Grant me wisdom. Grant me stealth. Grant me resilience.*

The Enchantress dared to probe outward with her mind, attempting to subdue the man, concealing the evidence in her face. He chuckled in response, as if he knew she couldn't summon magic. With a flick of his finger, air burst behind her and a gust of Isidore's Wind coaxed her right into his awaiting embrace.

So he was a man of the Gods *and* the Stars.

Rhéa grappled for sentience as his eyes inspected her. The elegant planes of his cheekbones the only gentle facet of his being. His bare fingers slid along her jaw like the delicate legs of a spider, while his eyes shot daggers. Rhéa's bloodstream became tumultuous in her ears. When she gazed into those pale-blue irises—so pale, they were almost gray—a sensation overtook her entire being; mind, body, and soul.

"You belong to me, young Enchantress." His breath caressed her skin as he spoke.

As he pressed his lips to her bare neck, Rhéa's blood turned to lava. It sluiced through every vein and artery with such undeniable force, scalding her from the inside out. He recognized this instantly. There was no part of him that was innocuous. If she possessed half a mind, she'd sully her fear and slam her knee into his bollocks.

But she didn't.

Because she couldn't.

It was as if she were balancing upon the edge of a precipice, and Spiro had just thrust her from it.

31

OPEN YOUR EYES

A great stone cavern stretched into darkness. Several cloaked figures stood encircled by torches, their long ivory robes stark against the obsidian slate surrounding them.

A raven-haired man knelt before a towering man of breathtaking virility. His hair, white as snow, was a cloud around his head. He was regal. Stoic. Rising taller than his companions, looming over them as if they were his subjects. His creatures. In kind, they seemed to cower under his glare of malcontent, as if they feared his censure.

The kneeling man stretched, proffering his arm for his leader to take hold. He craned his neck, dark locks parting to reveal his face.

Larkin!

The man with the moon-silver mane slowly twisted Larkin's arm. Pale, unmarred flesh now exposed and vulnerable.

Another man, this one crowned with golden curls, winked down at Larkin. Silver flashed, and in one swift motion, he sliced through *the skin of Larkin's palm. Blood oozed from the wound, dripping into a silver goblet.*

"Repeat after me," said the lithe man, his gaunt face bearing a solemn expression, nothing more. No ounce of amicable sympathy. No trace of rue. He spoke in Elder Tongue, and the power that emanated from his lips claimed the atmosphere, rendering the air thicker, the torch fire brighter. The flames began to flicker with each syllable as the man's voice reverberated throughout the cavern.

"Von, Larkin Oak, svidrà se qu nàmm un qu entiqè tass un qu Tsatsès híhes, vat Von quelsna va lyffe teq vuíll sec possïvq un Spiro Rèmes. Von svidrà vat Von tées fadrè Hÿm vunqé teq seëth hínd vreäth uit quelvarr sa Hÿm teq Hÿmm castée."

Larkin repeated every word in Elder Tongue, his pronunciation near-perfect.

An elegant woman swaddled in a floor-length gown stood above Larkin. She placed her hand firmly atop the inky crown of his head, dark hair spilling through her slender fingers like streams of ink. Completely concealed beneath a headdress, her golden irises were the only visible facet of her appearance. She spoke in a bone-chilling tone, each word threatening to snuff out the living flames that surrounded them. The words rushed from her luscious lips like lyrics to an ancient chant.

"Se qu pevër seâte unt Vën, Von cômmé vat Oâthe Vizïe vestöne vínde unt säl entretè sa qu vuíll teq lyffe un, Spiro Rèmes. Vàst qu Oâthe Vizïe pershè tèel Hÿmm Menstöré pershè. Híq Hÿmm hndràs vestöne vat un Hÿmm Menstöré, sa qí Hÿmm vunqé teq zïat qu serritíun metàre vat Hÿm wàndrè."

The blond man tipped back the goblet, urging Larkin to drink. Fresh blood dripped from his palm, running down his forearm and dripping from his elbow.

Larkin emptied the goblet to its last dregs.

"Well done," said the regal man with the pale-gray eyes. "Welcome home, Larkin Oak."

You are my entire universe.

⊙ ҧ ⟿ ⋔ ◌

Lilith woke with a cry of horror. She bolted upright, arms outstretched, reaching for Larkin. To protect him. To save him. But there was nothing but empty air.

Arduen rushed over, gripped her shoulders to steady her, shaking her to lucidity. "It's just a dream," he said, stroking her sweat-damp hair.

Lilith sighed and leaned into him, her breaths shuddering. She was unable to make sense of the vision that had impregnated her dreams. *It was just a dream. Larkin is with the Gods.*

"Are you all right?" he asked.

Lilith could only nod, pressing her head into his shoulder.

"You own your dreams, Lilith." He tucked a stray tendril behind her ear to better see her face, his finger tilting her chin, forcing her to meet his gaze. "They are conceived from your own mind." He tapped her temple gently. "Harness your dreams, my fledgling."

"Sometimes," she choked out, "I beg myself to wake because I know it isn't true. I'm running and I'm putting no distance between me and my fears." She trembled, an image of Larkin, blood dripping down his chin, burned on the back of her eyelids.

Arduen sighed, stroking her spine like her mother used to when she was just a little girl. "You can stop it all," he whispered. "You are the only one with the power to defeat them. Choose to face them or choose to open your eyes."

Lilith pulled away and glanced up at the stars. The night sky was just beginning to turn a deep violet hue. Hours still separated them from dawn.

"You need to rest." Arduen encouraged her to lie down again before he returned to his own bedroll. They'd been travelling for days. Another full day's travel awaited them before they reached the capital.

Lilith couldn't return to slumber as vivid images of her nightmare flashed behind her eyelids, antagonizing and mortifying. *But it was just a dream*, she had to remind herself over and over. Yet she remained restive, her heartbeat the only sound, save for Arduen's mumbles of, "Livë, Judeaus, and Art." She listened intently as his moans transformed into desperate groans.

His family, she thought to herself. *Arduen didn't outlive them. They were murdered.*

ⓞ ⓣ ⟿ ⋔ ⓓ

THEY SET OFF AT DAWN, THE RISING SUN WARMING THEIR BACKS AS they followed the darkness westward into unknown evils. Skydancer, well rested, charged along the path, the hills gently rolling in the direction of the capital. Lilith couldn't wait to arrive, to see the others, to know that they were safe.

Arduen's mind was focused on the upcoming battle. He'd been silent since they left camp, and she could tell that he had troubles on his mind by the way he chewed on his bottom lip.

"Master," she began hesitantly, "I don't mean to be rude, but how did Zurí acquire the scar on her face?"

Arduen didn't hesitate to respond. "Zurí's face was sliced by Spiro. That was his morbid attempt to ensure that she wouldn't find another lover. She vexed him by refusing to accompany him to his base. Zurí refused the Oracle's offer to heal her. She wears that scar as a reminder of sorts, I assume."

"You have never explained to me what it is that Spiro wants," she said. "What has driven him to such lengths, to such betrayal and atrocities?"

Arduen considered her question for a time. "He has a vision of a new governing system for Augusta and eventually the world beyond. A vision that requires all the Divine to form the new government. To depose the Monarchy entirely. For one Divine to rule, and the others to follow. He designed it based upon merit and power, over wealth and name."

"That doesn't seem so terrible," she thought aloud. "But why kill everyone who doesn't agree?"

"That's not exactly how it happened..." he said absent-mindedly. "You see, he got so absorbed in his own ideas, in the belief that he was the most powerful. He certainly was, but he was no match for all of us combined. We were greater then. We had many Master Divine as leaders. Yet Spiro was favored by the Gods. He became sick with *Philautia*—self-love—and turned against us. Anyone who refused to bow, he gifted no mercy. He set off on a quest to raise an army large enough to overthrow the Emperor. None of the Divine agreed with Spiro. So we either rejected him or merely bowed our heads and distanced ourselves."

"I don't see why his vision is considered so evil... if the power is distributed fairly."

"We are Divine, Lilith. We are meant to keep our noses out of political affairs, never to rule. That is what the Gods desire, so it is what we must do. Spiro doesn't wish for the Divine to rule the world. He wishes for himself to rule, and he wants our support. When we did not submit, he realized that living amongst us as he once did would no longer be possible. He lost all trust."

Lilith's eyes shot to the winter sky. "And what about the Gods? He was favored, could They not have predicted he'd become so corrupt?"

"Ah," he said, "that is a question none of us will ever know the answer to."

"What did you do when Spiro turned away?"

"We did all that we could to raise the next generation. Spiro spent the first fifty years of his campaign in isolation. The Empire was prospering. There were no beasts—not yet. Most of us continued on with our lives. We found homes and raised families." *Livë. Judeaus. Art.*

"When Spiro acted," Arduen continued, "he came for us first, destroying whatever happiness we'd found in his absence. Noviciates were losing their Masters. They weren't strong enough when they faced Spiro. Many did not make it. Zurí is one of the few who survived, likely because of Spiro's weakness for her."

"I'm sorry," she said, giving his hand a gentle squeeze of succor.

"It is life, Lilith. You will have to say goodbye to the ones you love someday, too."

"I already have," she said sourly. Now it was his turn to squeeze her hand. They hadn't spoken of Larkin much, but

Arduen was always present, always watching, always acting when she needed him.

Lilith adjusted her legs in her saddle, growing stiff. After some time, she asked, "When we come face to face with Spiro, do you think Zurí will want his killing blow?"

Arduen smirked. "I believe she wants them all."

32

STRONGER TOGETHER

There was much that needed to be done before Spiro's army was upon the capital. A few of the Màtia—the Emperor's eyes—had been issued to collect whatever information they could from the impending beasts. Members of the Agemas—the most skilled warriors— were dispatched in an attempt to slow their enemy's advance. And the Divine did not intend to sit around idly while they waited.

Upon their arrival, Arduen and Lilith were led to their tents where they were able to bathe and rest. Lilith fell asleep within seconds of her head hitting a real pillow.

The following morning, Olga led her to a large pavilion where she was pleased to be reunited with her comrades. Only Ambrose and Felix remained at the Frourío.

It was noon when Lord Malos entered the tent with his blacksmith in tow. Servants followed carrying large sacks that clinked and clanked with every step they took.

Malos spoke with pride, a gleam beset his eyes as he looked to his esteemed blacksmith. "Your armor has been brought to completion just last evening. I oversaw the process myself. These suits are of the finest quality!"

When the servant pulled her armor from the sack, Lilith could see for herself just how fine it was. There wasn't much of it, only the pieces that she needed most. Her hands would be free, though she would have vambraces to protect her forearms and elbows. No mail, as that would hinder her movement, but instead they had woven a thick tunic capable of slowing down any blade or arrow before it penetrated deep enough to kill.

The cuirass was molded to her figure; there was enough space to accommodate her breasts and protect her abdomen from assault. The metal was thin, light enough that it wouldn't slow her down.

Lilith marvelled at the intricate designs gilded into the metal, no doubt sigils of Elder Tongue. Arduen helped her to don the pieces, returning whatever he thought she wouldn't need to the pack. Her greaves were slightly too short for her shins, though she refrained from complaining. The cuisses were snug to her thighs once Arduen tightened the straps to her comfortability. To her pleasure, her armor was tinted a faint green, like oak leaves. In contrast, the carvings were gold.

She beamed at the lord and his blacksmith. "Thank you so much."

The blacksmith clasped his hands together and dipped his head, but it was Lord Malos who responded, "It is our honor."

Arduen's armor was of the darkest metal, mimicking Obsidian Steel, matching Constance. The engravings were a deep violet, representative of Aether.

"How does it feel?" Arduen asked.

Lilith moved about, bending at her knees and elbows. She enjoyed the clinking the metal made with every motion. "Good," she said.

Lord Malos proclaimed, "We cannot have the most important warriors in all the world fighting unarmored!" He surveyed the group as they inspected their suits before he bade them farewell.

Arduen moved to stand in the middle of the pavilion so as to address his cadre. His dark-blond hair was damp from washing, brushing against his broad shoulders. "Reconnaissance has confirmed that the beasts are nearly upon us," he said. "Though they may set up camp, we do not know how long they will wait to attack. We must be ready, and I would like for everyone to try to get a few more hours of sleep. I want you to return to your tents and rest. I will send for you when we are ready."

Signalling for the Divine to form a circle, he clasped his hands. His voice rose above the rest, demanding their immediate attention.

Arduen said, "When you face Spiro today, remember that he is not stronger than us because he can wield many elements. Many of the greatest Divine in history had only ever been blessed with one element. Physical prowess was not the determining factor of their worth, they were great because of the arsenal encompassed within their minds. They were superior to all others in wit and intelligence, on strategizing how we can best cooperate in battle, because we are each a part of one cohesive unit." Her Master paused to make eye contact with each of them. Lilith didn't lift her gaze from her boots. "No, he is not stronger than we are because he fights alone. We stand stronger together."

Then he began to sing in Elder Tongue, verses that Olga, Quin, Julius, Wren, and Zurí fortified with their voices. The tent transformed into a melodious choir. The air became thicker, their bodies warmed despite the winter chill. Their armor appeared to gleam in the dimness of the candlelight, as if embers smoldered beneath.

"Vàst vû fíng vuthé salídr stèle,
Forgée courcí teq víne.
Vàst qu Tsat wadnn unè pâte,
Teq duínn unè vledreè teq tísse.
Vhedn säl uit qínn, teq vû svï vestinn unè pevër,
Vàst Quy cârre zî unsà Elysium funewër."

When the pavilion fell silent, Lilith closed off her mind. This sense of unity might be the only thing sustaining her during this upcoming battle. She wanted to be self-sufficient and competent, but she worried about her own inexperience. Perhaps she was too callow to fight. If so, would Arduen sweep her off the field? Would he make her bunker down with the women and children of Kenora?

When she finally exited the tent to return to her own for the night, the camp was astir with the Emperor's soldiers. The din comprised of shouted demands, the clinking of armor, and the sibilant whispers of whetstones on steel.

A FEW HOURS LATER, ARDUEN PULLED OPEN THE FLAPS TO HER

tent. Lilith heard his footsteps crunching on the frozen grass as he approached. They were tethered so instinctually now that she could recognize the rise and fall of his breathing, the cadence of his footfalls.

His expression was grave as he sat down on the cot beside her. He didn't look at her as he spoke, his baritone hushed. "In the grand timeline of immortality you are but an infant. Do not think it does not pain me to watch you walk into the frays of battle. Do not assume that it does not leave me unsettled." He choked on the last words as they left his lips.

Lilith abhorred the idea of fighting for the very man who so unjustly claimed her brother's life. She detested the Emperor, and for what he'd done to Larkin, she always would find him repugnant. But what drove her now was her love for Arduen, for Julius and the rest of her Divine family. She couldn't let them fight without her. She couldn't stand to wait as one by one they marched off the field, as she counted them, only to realize one was missing and would never return.

No. She wouldn't sit idle.

She would fight.

When she didn't answer, Arduen grasped her hand firmly. "Do not be afraid to walk away, if that is what your gut is telling you. If you are not ready, then that is a reasonable excuse and I can send you with the women and children."

His hold on her hand slackened, and he looked at her slantways, as if allotting her the space to make her own decision.

Lilith trained her gaze to the rug beneath her boots. If she was too afraid to fight, now was the time to admit it.

"There is no shame in it, Lilith," Arduen probed. "It would be a wise and humble choice if you are lacking in confidence.

We cannot afford to lose you or Julius. You are far too precious to risk."

Her eyes flicked to his. Those blue irises were clear, bright as the morning sky, silver-lined and imploring.

"I have confidence so long as I am with you," she said, giving his fingers a slight squeeze for assurance.

He only offered a meek smile in response.

33

INTO THE FRAY

The battle was a living cataclysm unfurling before them. It was a confusing orchestra composed of aggravated shouts, anguished cries, and the clamor of steel on steel. It was a near-deafening tumultuous melody that would eventually make the silence seem thunderous.

The Divine positioned themselves amongst the Agemas, the highest-ranked warriors of the Emperor's Milítia. Lilith was surrounded by helms crested with plumes of Augustan blue horsehair, bare arms corded with muscle and gleaming with Gods' blessed oil.

Lilith forced a semblance of confidence as she settled in amongst the warriors. She ignored how much smaller she was as they towered over her. It helped to remind herself of what Arduen had said, that the most accomplished Divine were great *because of the arsenal encompassed within their minds.* These men had no idea what she was capable of.

Many of the soldiers murmured about the Divine company.

Many more whispered of the impending battle. *"If the Great Divine expects his vile creatures to soak their hands in our blood, then why doesn't he join them?"*

According to Arduen, Spiro rarely accompanied his army into battle. Lilith sent up a silent prayer to Constantine and Kyril that the Great Divine wouldn't decide to remedy that today.

After so many days brooding over the horrors that awaited her on the battlefield, Lilith began to lust for the action. Once she was standing face to face with Spiro's grotesque beasts, she wanted nothing more than to tear them all to shreds. To devour them with Constantine's wrath. She would introduce every last one of Spiro's minions to the woman who could unleash tempests.

The beasts charged first, sweeping into the Emperor's Milítia with swift competence. These monsters had fought before, and though Lilith failed to understand their words, it was clear that they could communicate with one another. They had strategized.

Nausea raked through her as the beasts barrelled through the Emperor's men. Her legs became feeble, only strong enough to support her weight, and her head quickly grew faint.

Flaming projectiles soared overhead, crashing into the Milítia and the city beyond. Arduen tackled Lilith to the blood-drenched earth, his hands cradling her head as his body became a living shelter. The earth rumbled as debris and detritus became airborne. Arduen's breath was ragged in her ear, his heartbeat thumping against her chest, echoing her own. She held fast to him, shudders wracking her entire frame.

When the dust settled, her Master pulled her to her feet as if she weighed no more than a sack of potatoes. "Are you all right?" he asked. When she didn't elicit a response, he pulled her against him. "Of course you're not all right. I should never have let you fight!"

But before Lilith could formulate the words to assure him that she was fine, they were moving again, loping over the fallen, deeper into bedlam.

⊙ ☉ ∽ ൜ ◊

BATTLE RAGED AND LILITH STRUGGLED TO IDENTIFY SPIRO'S MEN from her own. There were many Augustan men who had chosen to support the Great Divine over the Emperor, and those soldiers always caught her off guard.

She released a quivering breath as Constance became a mere sliver of light separating her from her enemies, her reflection gleaming on the blade's smooth surface. She paid it no heed. She was different now. She was not the same woman who had once forged weapons of destruction, weapons meant to sweep life from the earth. Now she possessed the ability to both grant life and death, weaponless.

In the midst of chaos, Lilith became devoid of feeling. All that remained was a burning desire to destroy. She wanted to lay to waste Spiro's entire creation. Every beast that walked upon Augustan soil would come to fear her, like the instinctual fear of the depths of the sea or the blackest of night skies.

Arduen's shout rose over the chaos, his words reverberating inside her helm. "We have been separated from the others."

She dared to shoot him a wary glance, but he only waved her off.

"We'll be fine," he assured, "but we must remain together."

He drove his sword through the back of a beast that was feeding upon one of their soldiers' corpses. The monster's wail was near-deafening, dark blood oozed from the wound. Arduen's eyes lit up as he observed the beast struggling to get back onto its feet.

"I pierced him in just the right place. He will be paralyzed," he explained, shooting her a satisfied grin. "Make sure you pay attention. This is as much a lesson for you as it is a mission."

She nodded anxiously, her heartbeat thrumming in her ears.

Arduen grasped her shoulder and spun her around to face him. "You are doing well. Do not kill the men who fight for Spiro, if that upsets you too much. You have slain many beasts so far, an impressive feat. Keep it up!" He banged his helm against hers.

When Lilith turned back to the destruction, she beheld three monsters feeding on a young Augustan soldier. She roared with outrage, her voice barely loud enough to be heard over the tumult. She dared to glance back at her Master, but he was preoccupied with another enemy.

Lilith took it upon herself to free the man. She set off at a sprint toward the spectacle. Tightening her grip on Constance, she sped her gait as she sliced through the neck of the beast. Its comrades shot her furious glowers, their eyes yellow embers set deep in their grotesque faces, bone structures entirely alien.

"How dare you…" one hissed at her.

The Augustan man wept. Lilith didn't need to lower her gaze from the two beasts to know that his state was dire. He wouldn't survive.

"You little witch!" the other beast spat. "He was my brother!"

The brutes rose to tower over her, their heads rising several feet above her own.

Lilith gulped.

"There doesn't appear to be much meat on you, but we'll enjoy separating your limbs from your torso as you scream for mercy."

"You better scream loud, only the Gods can grant you that." Their vicious laughter echoed into the starlit sky.

To her surprise, an arrogant laugh escaped her lips. "I'd like to see you try when you realize who you're speaking to."

They charged.

Lilith released a blast of Aether, severing the first beast's head from its torso. Its giant body thumped to the ground at her feet.

Casting a malignant grin at its partner, she purred, "Care to join him?"

The beast glared at her. "You will pay!" Then it bellowed a war cry that normally would have made her knees buckle, but there was too much adrenaline coursing through her now.

She did not balk.

The beast pounded its chest before lunging, and Lilith reached out a hand, nearly touching its stomach. Its eyes blew wide as Aether poured into the brute, surging through its massive body. Its skin darkened as Constantine's element slowly spread outward from where she touched, stealing the life from its veins. Lilith watched in awe as the vitality had at last drained from the beast, and she stepped back to allow the cadaver to fall to the ground.

With haste, she rushed to the young soldier. He was still conscious, whimpering as she knelt beside him. "T-thank you…" he stammered, blood leaking from the sides of his lips.

It didn't take long for Lilith to confirm her earlier suspicion. He would not live. He had lost too much blood, and several of his limbs had been extracted. There wasn't enough time to get him to the healers' tent before he faded.

Without saying a word, she placed a trembling hand upon his chest. A moment later, the man's eyes were closed, never to open again. As she rose to stand over him, she sent up a prayer to Elysium for the young man's entrance into the Gods' eternal sanctuary, and for the family he'd left behind.

Drained, she peered down at the young man she had mercifully killed. "I'm sorry," she breathed.

Even in the darkness, she noticed a shadow pass over her, and her eyes shot upward.

Large beasts flew like giant midnight bats. They rose over the battle with their bows, striking at the Emperor's soldiers. The foul monsters flew over the capital's walls, shooting at the Frourà legionnaires stationed atop the battlements.

Lilith hoped the women and children were safely hidden. She prayed that the beasts couldn't sniff them out, but would rather plunder what riches they could find before retreating.

Arduen had told her that Spiro's beasts always fled battle, even when they outnumbered the Emperor's Milítia. Even when the castle might as well be Spiro's. There was something much bigger at work here, that much was blatantly obvious. But whatever it was, even the Oracle remained blinded to it, unguided. The first of Spiro's beasts appeared nearly four decades ago, and they've been amassing ever since.

And Lilith wanted to be the one to find out how and why.

Her eyes surveyed the chaos in search of her own comrades but found none of the Divine amongst the madness. Arduen had become lost in the fray. Or he'd fallen. It wasn't like him to lose sight of her. Dread coursed through her.

She was alone.

More shadows blotted out the sky, drawing her attention. Two men sailed above the carnage, shooting arrows into the wreckage. They had no wings, and they were certainly not beasts. Their laughter filtered through the air, taunting her ears.

Divine.

Aether sluiced through her veins, burning oil melding with her blood. Urgency gripped her, thrusting her into action.

LILITH LEAPT OVER COUNTLESS BODIES IN HER HASTE TO REACH the enemy Divine. They'd halted their assault and veered west, away from the battle. She sprinted after them, not daring to take her eyes off the shadows as they drifted across the night sky, their slim frames blotting out the stars as they moved. The men landed upon a large knoll, illuminated by the moonlight.

Lilith scowled at them both.

Wincing, she ignored her aching limbs as her feet pounded against the blood-soaked earth. She bounded to the top of the knoll, stopping herself as she awaited their notice.

One man turned to her with astute calmness, as if he'd

been aware all along that she was in pursuit. "Lilith Oak," he purred as he nudged his comrade.

"You've been Anointed by Isidore," she stated, projecting her voice.

The man chuckled, exchanging a smug expression with his comrade. "No, sweet innocent, Lilith. I was Anointed by *Spiro*."

That's impossible. She shook her head. "Spiro is Divine. He cannot Anoint mortals."

Only the bottom portion of their faces could be seen from beneath the helms they wore, their sneers the only visible facet of their features. In the corner of her eye, Lilith glimpsed the others rushing toward them. Her camaraderie.

Arduen and Julius led the party. She didn't dare take her eyes off her enemies so as to inspect them for injuries. She counted six of them running toward her.

Running, so they had to be all right.

"What a shame, Constantine could have chosen someone so much more… *fulfilling*," the lithe man trilled, the sentiment dripping with disdain.

Lilith bared her teeth, aware of Arduen's presence now several paces behind her. He was giving her space, likely assessing her character. After all, this was a test of her abilities and capabilities. If she were in grave danger, he would be in front of her.

She lifted her chin indignantly, she could feel Arduen's gaze drilling into the back of her helm. "You are fortunate that I don't allow an abhorrent stranger's opinion to upset me"— she chortled—"for the only people who could hurt me are all dead."

The man's face grew taut as he grinned. "I was hoping you

would say that. If my opinion does not affect you, then I will give you someone who will."

Lilith braced herself for an attack as the taller, broader man strode forth. At the lithe man's behest, his comrade removed his helm. Her heart lurched, became a fist-sized ruby lodged in her throat.

Beneath a thick beard, the vitriolic grin stealing her breath, was her brother.

Larkin.

34

THERE WILL BE A SIXTH GOD

Lilith met her brother's gaze unflinching, though her legs threatened to give out at the sight of him. Grief had finally taken its toll. She'd gone mad. This was only a wraith, an apparition of her last living relative. This was the cruel trick of a mind driven off its rocker.

But that grin. It wasn't one her consciousness could ever simulate.

She bolted toward him, arms outstretched. Larkin reached out for her as well. Her chest was going to explode. Warmth seeped into her limbs as that familiar, lopsided smile spread across his lips.

"Larkin!" she cried as she drew near.

Their hands met and she made to pull him into an embrace, but he overpowered her and threw her to the ground. Larkin released a terrifyingly foreign cackle as her body thudded against the frozen earth, her armor clinking in protest. She gasped, more from the emotional pain than the physical.

Larkin knelt and brought his face level with hers, his amber eyes darker than she remembered. But beneath the beard, this man was undoubtedly her brother.

"How?" she croaked.

"You think Obadïa would admit that his castle had been breached by the enemy? Gods, no! That would sow unrest amongst Kenora's inhabitants, and his courtiers would see it as weakness." Larkin pouted. "No. He claimed to have executed me for murder and arson, but it was Spiro who saved me."

Lilith gawked.

"Join him, Lil." Larkin's eyes softened, resembling the gentle young man she remembered him to be. "Join the Great Divine. Reunite with me."

"But Spiro is responsible for Papa… for Mah." Tears welled unbidden. "How could you serve him?"

Frustration simmered in his features but when he answered her, his tone was pacific. "Father died serving a lazy, covetous miser of an Emperor. And Mama was too weak to carry on." He licked his lips, teeth bared. "Join me, Lil. Let's take back what is ours."

She shook her head fervently, pain detonating inside her chest. *This is not Larkin.* She doubted she had much left, but despite her fatigue, she raised her hand to attack.

But Larkin moved with preternatural celerity.

Faster than she ever thought possible, Lilith was tossed into the air, forced backward nearly twenty feet. She skidded across the ground until firm hands brought her to an abrupt halt. She looked up into her Master's face.

Arduen, eyes wide with ire, raised her up and held her against him. Blood trickled down her brow, her helm lost.

"He is not your brother, Fledgling," Arduen murmured gently into her ear.

Lilith struggled to pull away from him. "Yes, he is!" she cried, unable to accept that Larkin was dead. Destroyed. But the true Larkin would have never hurt her.

She was living a nightmare.

Arduen didn't release her, and she knew how bullish he could be. She wouldn't be able to fight him off.

"He has been compromised by Spiro. We cannot trust him!" His voice was pleading, but his words were stern, his arm constricting tighter around her shoulders, immobilizing her arms.

Larkin grinned maliciously, inclined his head in recognition. "Indeed, my little, guileless sister. My Master is Spiro Rémes, as yours is Arduen Alanís." He drew his scim and inspected it, as if it were the blade that would end an era. "Jude's grandfather."

Both Lilith and Arduen went rigid. *Jude.*

She tightened her grip on Arduen's arm, her mind whirling. The Larkin she knew would never swear fealty to a crude man like Spiro. He would never align with the man responsible for their parents' deaths. No amount of power promised could have persuaded him. This couldn't be her brother. He had never been the brightest ember in the forge, but he wasn't daft enough to follow Spiro.

This is not Larkin.

"How could you?" she spat at him. "How could you serve the man responsible for *ruining our lives*?!"

Larkin's eyes grew dark. With careful clarity, he said, "This man has a vision of a better world, Lilith. He has bestowed that vision upon me, granted me gifts from above to exact his will."

Arduen released her once she'd relaxed in his arms, though he remained by her side. "How is he able to do that? For Spiro is certainly no God. How can he create these monsters?!" He advanced a step, and Lilith fought the urge to reach out and hold him still.

Larkin craned his neck and laughed into the sky, his howls echoing off the lips of his slender comrade. "You underestimate Spiro. He is the greatest Divine to have ever existed. He has walked away from the Gods and sustained his hold on every gift he has ever received from Them. They couldn't withdraw Their might once They bestowed it upon him."

Then his voice grew firm and cold as he said, "There will be a sixth God."

The words sent tremors rumbling through Lilith's body.

"I was surprised to hear that you left because of your Anointment." Larkin grinned indignantly. "And now that I have also been chosen. Well, this just makes things all the more entertaining, doesn't it?"

"Lilith, go back to Olga. Let me handle him." Arduen prompted her to leave, but she couldn't move.

"I can't," she whispered, not daring to remove her eyes from her brother.

Larkin.

Arduen released a frustrated grunt. "Lilith, I want you to leave, now!" His voice boomed, an order from a Master to his noviciate. Fury rippled off him with every breath, but still, she couldn't move. Lilith stood frozen, transfixed by the sight of her brother. Arduen moved to stand in front of her, to become a human shield.

"How sweet," Larkin crooned. "You will have to let her go someday, Arduen. She has much potential. I'm sure my Master is aware of just how promising she truly is. Blessed by Constantine *and* Kyril. The first since the greatest. My, my… how that must just tickle your ego, dear sister." His voice was a tantalizing drawl, and he took another step in their direction.

Arduen bristled.

Her brother spat, "Spiro saved me from the man you are defending." He spoke with rancor, with a chaser of venom. "Now you tell me who is righteous."

Lilith shook her head vehemently. *This can't be happening. This can't be happening.*

Larkin continued, "You were the bumptious girl who refused to become a wife. The girl who refused to act a lady." He tutted and shook his head. "How could the Gods deem a dissenter like you worthy of Divinity? You didn't even love your own fiancé, and now you're running around with his grandfather!"

"You think you can best me, *Sister*?" Larkin cocked his head, his grin mischievous. "Let's test Isidore against Constantine and see just how catastrophic the results can be."

Arduen fired a blast of Aether so suddenly, Lilith had no idea he'd even prepared for it. But Larkin was faster, and he forced it back toward them with Isidore's Wind, but Arduen absorbed it.

The line had been drawn and she knew which side she stood on.

Anger blasted through her body. This man was not her brother and she wouldn't allow him to take Arduen from her.

She lunged past her Master toward her enemy. Raising both hands into the air before her, Lilith released a torrent of Aether. It thundered at her enemies.

The blast streamed past Larkin on either side of his body. He stood unfazed with a fiendish grin. "I'm tired of your games, Lilith. You could be so much more powerful if you joined Spiro. Instead you gallivant around Augusta with this *fool*." He flashed his teeth in Arduen's direction.

Lilith didn't dare turn away from him, lest she find herself at his mercy. "You have no right to insult him. He is honorable, and Spiro is filth!"

Larkin's gaze was virulent, impaling. "You left the virile young Jude for this old fox!" he said with a wry smile, a transparent attempt to antagonize them both.

Arduen said nothing.

"Tsk, tsk… you didn't tell your Master of your engagement to his only grandson?"

Lilith relinquished all sense as she advanced, drawing forth every last ounce of Aether she could muster. Arduen lent his strength to hers. Their blasts melted into each other, surging through the air toward Larkin and his comrade.

Unable to see them through the dark cloud, fear clenched her chest as she watched Arduen advance. Fire danced past him on either side, Quin and Julius lending their elements to the assault.

Lilith didn't move, lest she break focus and risk losing control of Aether, harming her friends, her mentors.

Her family.

A maniacal laugh rose above the tumult, and her heart stopped beating. She peered into the abyss, praying that Arduen was safe. What would she do if something happened to him? No, she wouldn't think about that now. She had to keep her wits about her.

Several figures emerged from of the darkness. Before she could see what they were doing, they released a volley of arrows.

Dread cooled her blood as Larkin's voice carried on the Wind. "I look forward to when next we meet, little sister!"

Stemming her flow of Aether, Lilith failed to shield herself from the barrage as multiple arrows became embedded in her armor. She cried out in torment, the sound abominable. The pain was worse. The arrows' trajectory was reinforced by Isidore's Wind. There was enough force to break through the thin armor she wore, through the protective tunic beneath.

The fall to the earth was even more treacherous. Lilith rolled onto her back to refrain from tampering with the arrow shafts, from shifting them and causing more damage.

Hands clasped either side of her face, and Wren entered her blurry vision shortly thereafter.

"You're going to be all right," he rasped. "Olga is on her way. We will get you to the healers' tent immediately." Though his voice shook, he remained unflappable.

Lilith lost sense of all space and time as he hoisted her up into his arms. She howled at the pain that the motion elicited, knowing that the discomfort was ineluctable if she wanted to survive. Wren only hushed her as he retreated. His steps were rough, and she whimpered as each movement summoned further torment.

It wasn't long before the darkness consumed her, granting a slight reprieve.

35

MY FLEDGLING

Arduen gazed down upon his noviciate with evident regret. His arms were crossed firmly over his chest as if he were loath to touch her, his eyes silver-lined and blood shot. Did he blame himself for what happened to her?

Lilith opened her mouth to comfort him but only a guttural moan escaped. Arduen nearly crumbled at the desperate sound.

She never wanted to cause him such strife. He couldn't shield her from the excruciating pain she was enduring, but he could help her through it. She needed him now more than she ever had before.

As she stared up at the sharp underline of his jaw, it dawned on her then how unfair she had been. She'd wanted to grow closer, to become something more than just Divine and noviciate. Wanted more than mere mentorship. Since the beginning she'd expected him to become like a father to her.

We are your family now, he'd said when they first met.

She'd taken him too literally.

Lilith had been looking to him to take on that role. It was unrealistic, and it wasn't fair to him. But she'd done it anyways, subconsciously. She spoke his name then, and it left her lips with a gasp.

"Don't speak," he said in a tear-thick voice, pressing a kiss to her brow. "Don't speak, my fledgling." Only a father would kiss a brow beaded with sweat and gore.

The need to confess overpowered all other desires. Arduen needed to know how she felt, if only to alleviate her guilt.

Another time, she assured herself. Another time when her thoughts were organized and she could speak coherently. Only then would she profess her impossible expectations to him, in the hopes that he would forgive her.

As the healers began their work, Lilith was pulled from her reverie, finding it easy to forget her quandary. She thrashed on the cot where Wren had deposited her, with the healers scurrying around frantically. Fading in and out of consciousness, she hardly remembered the journey to the tent.

Palaís—the only drug in Augusta that could diminish pain —did not work on the Divine. And because her pain was her own and not a result of Discernment, neither Olga nor Arduen could do anything to shield her from it. There was nothing they could do for her—at least until the arrows were removed.

Blood poured in thick rivulets from each puncture, the sight enough to debilitate. The pain was crippling. It pierced every crevice of her body. Left her paralyzed. The only choice she had was to give in to the yawning abyss of affliction.

Thankfully, she hardly remembered *why* she was even in pain to begin with. It supplanted every other emotion, every other dilemma. Larkin became a foggy memory in the back of her mind. The kind of recollection one wouldn't recognize as true or false. Only a dream.

A nightmare.

Lilith's cries rent the night, her voice audible above the frantic voices of the healers and servants, drowning them out. She began to fade in and out. Her fingers tensed and fell limp at her sides, only to furl again when she came to a moment later.

There were several healers tending to her. They had to cut each arrowhead out of her legs and abdomen where they had pierced her deepest. She'd thought the pain of removing her armor to be the worst. Until they took the scalpel to her skin.

Lilith bellowed, but the pain was necessary, lest she bleed out and die. They needed to work in haste. She prayed for relief that no one could grant her. Arduen consoled her as best he could, seemingly unaware of her nudity. She thrashed against the healers, attempting to push them away, but he held her firm, his free hand stroking her hair, damp with sweat. He whispered Divine words of comfort in her ears as she sobbed —begged—for relief.

Lilith glimpsed Olga standing above her, the Oracle's features riddled with concern and empathy. She knelt beside Arduen and began to join in his verses of Divination. Lilith closed her eyes and gripped her Master's arm tightly, the arm he held across her bare chest, confining her to torment.

For your own good.

When the worst part was finished, Lilith's voice was no more. The healers gently smoothed disinfecting solution over her wounds. It stung worst where the arrowheads had been ripped free when they'd removed her armor. The pain swept through her body in waves. A phantom ghost. Eventually, as if the Gods had deemed her worthy, her body went numb.

Lilith heaved a sigh of relief, still aware of Arduen and Olga at her side, like mother and father.

No. She pushed the thought from her mind.

When Olga set to mending her mangled skin, Lilith became aware of the Oracle's gentle hands in juxtaposition to the healers' crude touch.

As fresh tears poured, Arduen's gripped her chin and turned her to face him. She stared into his eyes, her lids half shut, as he said to her, "You're going to be all right. You're going to walk out of this tent a stronger woman. You will survive this battle and face the next one fearlessly." He cupped her cheek and leaned in to kiss her forehead.

Lilith stifled a sob, raising a weak hand to lay upon his. She'd come to favor her Master's presence, and in this moment, she longed for no one else at her side.

Once Olga finished healing, Lilith could finally sit up to inspect her body. Her skin was caked in coagulated blood. Her blood. Arduen helped her to stand, his eyes noticeably focused on her face. When Olga dismissed him, he refused to leave, his shoulders squared and tensed.

"If you're staying, help," she demanded.

Arduen held Lilith aloft as Olga began to wash her body, the hot cloth abrasive on her fresh skin. But she didn't move as the Oracle worked over her, swathing her body in soap and gently wiping it away, revealing smooth unmarked skin.

A servant girl entered the tent with new clothes for Lilith. Breeches and a fitted tunic, comfortable garments that seemed to caress her aching limbs.

Once dressed, Arduen lifted Lilith into his arms and

carried her to her own tent. He accompanied her inside and helped to ease her onto the cot. The tent was blanketed in shadows and Lilith found the gloom rather disconcerting.

Her Master knelt on the ground beside her cot and gazed upon his noviciate with evident concern. He brushed damp tendrils of hair away from her face.

"I should have never let you fight," he said, more to himself than to her.

"Don't blame yourself," she rasped.

Arduen kissed her brow and said no more as he made to take his leave, but Lilith's voice stopped him dead.

"Please don't go," she pleaded, the request a mere burst of air. "I don't want to be alone, not after…"

He reseated himself, their faces inches apart. "I won't leave you," he said with certainty. "I will never leave you."

Lilith released a choked sob at his words, and he joined her on the cot, pulling her into his arms. She rested her head on his chest and relaxed in the comfort that only this manner of intimacy could provide.

"What do the words mean?"

"Hmm?"

Lilith cleared her throat. "The verses you, Olga and Julius always repeat in times of discomfort," she clarified. "What do they mean?"

Arduen was silent for a moment before his hoarse voice broke the quietude and he recited the verse, *"May we fight with valiant steel, forged courage and might. May the Gods watch our path, and quell our bleeding and strife. When all is done, and we are beyond our power, may They carry us into Elysium forever."*

Then he cleared his throat and his voice became wet with melody.

"Vàst vû fíng vuthé salídr stèle,
Forgée courcí teq víne.
Vàst qu Tsat wadnn unè pâte,
Teq duínn unè vledreè teq tísse.
Vhedn säl uit qínn, teq vû svï vestinn unè pevër,
Vàst Quy cârre zî unsà Elysium funewër."

Lilith shivered from the weight that the words impressed upon her. She was cautious of their power, aware of the Divine presence that had settled over them. Neither Divine nor noviciate said a word as the darkness swallowed them whole and night faded into dawn.

36

SMOKE AND ASH

Gulls sailed over the spoils of battle as the sun brought to light the atrocities that the darkness concealed. The aftermath of war was worse than the battle itself, Lilith thought, as they trudged through the carnage.

Studying her Master's face, Lilith was crestfallen to see that his eyes were also rimmed with shadows, a mirror reflection of her own. She tread carefully. If she displayed any signs of discomfort or fatigue, Arduen would march her straight back to her tent to rest.

They still hadn't spoken of her brother, or the fact that she was engaged to his grandson. Her stomach lurched.

You are my entire universe.

Lilith bowed her head in shame.

They joined the city folk as they sifted through the remains. Lilith followed Arduen's lead, Julius on her heels. Soldiers waded through the wreckage, faces drawn and pale.

It couldn't be possible to become inured to the effects of violence and gore, no matter how many times one experienced it.

Quin approached carrying two young men in his arms; one still alive for the healers to assess, the other stiff and ready to be placed upon the pyre. Averting her gaze, Lilith focused on Julius's finely decorated belt, on the foreign assortment of jewels from Dalegonè.

"Olga and Zurí are speaking with the Emperor and his Epistaís," Quin said to Arduen. "The generals have agreed that we will need reinforcements for the next battle, for certainly there will be another."

"We can only pray that Obadïa listens to his generals," Arduen said on a sigh.

Julius was uncharacteristically silent as he followed them. Lilith had a hunch that he'd been assigned to watch over her. She set about helping in the best way she could: searching for any survivors.

The knoll upon which she'd faced Larkin rose up from the debris. She shuddered. His touch was so foreign, so cruel. The same hands that used to help her into bed when she was a little girl. Lilith turned her back on the sight.

They traipsed through the mud, it clung to their boots sloppily. She grimaced; the muck was tinted a deep red. But averting her gaze did little to assuage her unease. For when she looked up, her eyes met the rising plume of ash, a much less gruesome sight than the blood and viscera that coated the earth, but unnerving all the same.

Flames were the only way to transport souls to the Gods' realm. The bodies disintegrated into ashes, floating toward the sky, toward Elysium. It was as such in both Augusta and Dalegonè, save for a few dissenting souls who preferred everlasting sanctuary beneath Thëo's Earth.

Julius burned the remains of the beasts with Fire, and she with Aether. The ashes spread out over the mud like freshly fallen snow. Her energy drained far quicker than normal, her head faint. Julius told her to stop.

Taking a break, she studied the landscape, searching for any signs of movement among the corpses. Arduen approached on silent feet despite the muck. He inspected her inconspicuously, before nodding to Julius.

The prince took her gently by the arm and said, "You don't have to do this. I'll take you back to your tent."

Lilith didn't bother to protest. She didn't want to be here, though she couldn't imagine getting any sleep either. Julius led her away, placing her hand in the crook of his elbow. They stopped only when they reached her tent, Julius clearly disinclined to enter.

She glanced at him through dark lashes. "Will you stay with me?" He opened his mouth to speak but balked. "At least until I fall asleep..." She severed eye contact, abashed.

Julius grasped her hand, his thumb tracing circles on her skin. "Of course, Lilith."

A PROMISE

The camp was a cluster of tents in a mass of frozen mud. Soldiers lounged everywhere, moaning their lament. Kenora didn't have enough healers to assist them all, and the Enchantresses refused to come to the Emperor's aid.

As Lilith, Olga and Zurí meandered in the direction of the Emperor's pavilion, Lilith opened her mind and listened for any information that could be beneficial to her, to the Divine, but she gleaned nothing. When her body began to ache in ways she'd never before experienced, she reinforced the barriers of her mind yet again. She'd endured enough suffering over the past few days, enough to excuse her from shouldering the burden of the wounded.

The Emperor's pavilion rose above the rest. It was ridiculously large, with a blue-and-gold flag at its peak. Quin and Wren held open the flaps for the women to enter. Lilith stood between Olga and Zurí, listening as intently as her throbbing head would allow. She couldn't help but notice Wren studying her from across the tent. No doubt noting the way she held herself, alert for any signs of weariness. He flashed her a meek smile when their eyes met, and she returned it once she deemed it genuine. She wasn't ready to accept that the dynamic of their relationship had altered since he'd carried her off the battlefield. But she was alive because of him, and for that, she was grateful. Eternally so.

An official trumpet blared. Several of the Emperor's Frourà entered, followed by the Emperor himself, his heir, Orìon, and the Crown Prince's squire, a young boy on the cusp of manhood.

It was time to receive the verdict. Would the Emperor pursue an alliance with the Walabeäns?

Emperor Obadïa stood before them, a scowl born of irreverence adorning his flushed face. His son stood beside him, nearly the same height as his sire but not as fully formed. Orìon was as insolent as his father. His squire took up position beside him, nearly a head shorter than the heir. They wore armor still, as if anticipating another attack.

Lilith bit her lip to conceal her scowl. This was the man who'd claimed to have executed her brother. Why hadn't he protected him? Why didn't he have guards? Perhaps Larkin had started the fire. Perhaps he'd known from the beginning that she was Anointed that night she didn't come home.

No.

Her faith in who Larkin was raised to be disabused those ideas. Larkin was Anointed, like she had been, and then he'd been corrupted by Spiro.

Arduen dipped his chin reverently, greeting the Emperor,

the rest of the Divine following suit. Relief flooded through her that that was as close as they would get to bowing.

As respect for the Gods, the Emperor bowed his head in kind, his heir following his father's lead. The squire only stood in awe of the group. Orìon shot him a warning glare, but the squire did not take notice. The boy stirred only when the Emperor focused his attention on him. He didn't make eye contact with Obadïa, but instead directed an apprehensive glance at Orìon. The heir ignored him, a strange glint in his dark eyes.

"Excuse my squire, it seems he has become quite *disreputable* as of late," was all Orìon said as he snapped his fingers. Instantly, two of the Frourà legionnaires seized the boy by his arms and roughly thrust him out through the flaps of the pavilion.

Lilith gawked at them, at their callous touch. The soldiers drew their scims and followed after the squire. She shot a wary glance at her Master, but Arduen's gaze was planted firmly on the lavish carpet, ostensibly inspecting a stain.

"Please, don't! I'm sorry!" The boy's cries were audible. It wouldn't surprise her if Orìon wanted them to hear the boy's punishment. Judging by the malicious grin that festered his would-be handsome face, Lilith knew it to be true.

As the boy's cries reverberated throughout the pavilion, everyone remained still and silent. The Emperor's face bore a stern expression, nearly unreadable, as the boy's cries became hoarse, and eventually, faint. Only the smacking of flat blades on skin met their ears.

Lilith bit back her protests and focused on withholding the salty tears that stung her eyes. It took everything she had to steel her spine. To avoid meeting Orìon's antagonizing stare.

Gods, have mercy!

The Emperor's voice shattered the painfully awkward silence. "I have come to the realization that a military alliance with the Walabeäns may very well be the only means to mitigate our losses. Unfortunately, this battle has taken a catastrophic toll on my Milítia."

The two soldiers re-entered the pavilion, but the squire did not accompany them. Orìon's lips parted in a wry smile. Lilith wanted to smack it off his face.

"Spiro is creating his beasts much faster than we are creating soldiers," the Emperor continued. "That being said, I have conscripted as many as I can from every city and town in Augusta. Whether those men make it to the capital alive or not, that is the next obstacle."

As if his presence wasn't malignant enough, Orìon set his flinty gaze upon Lilith. Undoing and devouring. She instantly redirected her eyes to the Emperor.

Obadïa retrieved a scroll from one of his guards and proffered it to Arduen. "This decree is my vow and bond, my official order for your visitation. It outlines every detail of the alliance and lists exactly what privileges the Walabeän troops will receive, should they accept."

In one long stride, Arduen closed the space that separated him from the Emperor, retrieving the scroll. He scanned Obadïa as critically as he dared, almost as if he were Discerning for any omitted information. Arduen relented to inquire further and tucked the parchment into the pocket of his cloak.

"I do not care if it is easy," said Obadïa. "I only need you to do it. If there is anyone they will listen to, it will be you. They respect the Gods more than they respect me. This is not only a war for my throne as it is for all of Elysium." He glared at Arduen, daring him to interject.

Silence permeated the room. Arduen remained still and refrained from arguing.

"I will leave it to you then." The Emperor dismissed them with a bow of his head and a noncommittal wave of his hand.

LILITH COULDN'T HAVE BEEN MORE RELIEVED TO LEAVE THE WAR camp behind. The wails that assailed her ears day and night were almost enough to make her echo them. The field, which should have been dusted with snow, was now a space of mud. Runnels of frozen blood ran through the ground where the lifeless bodies of beasts, men, and horses had been. Women waded through the carnage, searching for loved ones that hadn't come home. Lilith didn't need Discernment to know how they felt.

The Divine took the back road out of camp to avoid fanfare. The journey back to the Frourío was unusually quiet. Lilith didn't doubt it was due to her brother's appearance, no less due to his allegiance to Spiro.

How Larkin had become Divine was unknown. How he had become even more powerful than she, that was the real mystery. Lilith could wield two elements and she was still overpowered by him.

But Larkin was alive. She should be revelling at that fact. Even if they were sworn enemies now. The man she'd once relied upon, her only living family remaining, was now her adversary. And the man she faced on the battlefield was not her brother. It was almost as if he'd been possessed.

Lilith wanted to bellow to the Gods to take her instead, forfeit her life for his freedom, but that could never be an option.

Galloping silently behind the others, she couldn't help but notice furtive glances cast her way, evincing their solicitude. She feigned interest in the fallow land that surrounded them for miles in every direction. It was enough to convince them that she would be all right, at least for now.

It was Quin who broke the silence first. "Obadïa is scared. He knows that he doesn't have the forces needed to thwart Spiro." He peered over at Arduen from under his hood. "I don't know how he is producing so many beasts. How is it even possible? He's acquired gifts that only a God should possess."

There will be a sixth God.

A shiver ran down her spine.

"Spiro creates them, and they procreate," said Arduen. "It's a reproductive system that works ten times as fast as ours. To top it off, the beasts reach adulthood within a few years."

"Emperor Obadïa wouldn't resort to conscripting children... would he?" Lilith asked, prepared for the onslaught of incredulous looks she received.

"We won't allow that to happen," Arduen assured.

Olga interjected, "Spiro will take the crown if we cannot persuade the Walabeäns to align with Augusta. It won't take more than another battle to siege the capital."

"The Emperor is afraid," Arduen said. Her Master was a pragmatist; he could read and assess people through mere observation. "Obadïa knows that Spiro has the upper hand. He knows that the Milítia doesn't stand a chance—not after that slaughter. If we hadn't have encountered other Divine, the beasts would have taken the city. Spiro would be Emperor right now."

⟡ ⟡ ⟡ ⟡ ⟡

MANY MILES STILL SEPARATED THE DIVINE FROM THE FROURÍO. IT would be nearly a week before they reached the pines of the Megálos. Rain began to fall, which would freeze once night fell and the temperature dropped. The weather only dampened Lilith's sour mood.

She maintained her distance from the others, as if her foul demeanor could infect them like a virus. She burrowed into herself, allowing her pain and sorrow to swallow her whole. Imagining an inky black eddy, she was satisfied swirling around and around until she was sucked into its depths.

Too ensconced within herself, she hadn't noticed Julius riding alongside her, his gaze locked on her expectantly.

"Soldiers are harsh and strict with their squires," he said. "Especially the squire of a prince. A crown prince, no less." He inched his stallion, Stormbringer, closer to Skydancer. "Though I do not agree with the treatment, we cannot question the Emperor's authority. He has every right to discipline as he deems fit."

Lilith shook her head as if the motion could eject the thoughts that infected her. Would that she could drown out the boy's pleas for mercy. "Surely it's not the same in Dalegonè?"

Julius fell silent, considered her question for some time. "It can be, but we would never punish a squire like that—much less a child. Our disciplinary actions are much more beneficial. Instead of beating and inflicting pain, we prefer to bestow extra responsibilities. Make the boy scrub the floors, clean out the pigsty, clean the dishes, wash the baths in the barracks." He huffed a laugh. "Menial and dirty tasks like that can truly humble a person, and they don't render them as damaged as a walloping like that would."

Lilith peered sidelong at the prince, gallant and regal. He was utter perfection. When he met her gaze, he flashed her that charming smile of his that always turned her insides to liquid. She flushed and averted her gaze instantly, too fast not to be noticeable. She cursed herself inwardly.

"That seems like a court comprised of exceedingly wise nobles," she observed, drawing his attention away from her searing cheeks. "To exact justice with tasks rather than pain and humiliation."

"Yes, my father made many changes when he ascended the throne. He values the mind, believes humans are fragile. He deems that if we are to create a better future, it begins with how we train our youth. How adults mold them, which includes how we reward and punish them. Building honorable character is the most crucial element to forging a brighter future."

Lilith could only dream of visiting the desert-continent of Dalegonè. "I hope I live to see it. Your country, I mean. It sounds lovely."

Julius's smile was estival. "One day, when Spiro's body is returned to the earth and his soul is suffering in Hades, I shall take you to Dalegonè and show you how marvellous the coastal capital is."

"Xanthë?"

"Mhmm."

Lilith never believed anyone when they promised her

things. Like when her mother promised to take her to the sea, or when Larkin promised to wash the dishes when she worked late, or when Jude promised to give her space. But this time, she believed Julius, and his promise was the most difficult to fulfil of them all.

38

THE CURSE OF THE IMMORTAL

The hallways were dark, damp, and ominous. Most evenings, when Spiro left her alone, Rhéa spent her free time exploring, mainly searching for boltholes. There were none. She was desperate to feel the Starlight upon her skin, to refuel her, refill the magic in her veins.

By day she'd tend to whatever cruel demands Spiro set for her, then she would heal the men who were injured in the sparring rings. She possessed no care to witness the brawls in the arena for herself. Spiro acquired—kidnapped—a number of human healers from nearby towns and cities. None of them possessed the ability to outright heal as an Enchantress did, but they could clean, treat and stitch, which lightened her burdens.

It was a wonder any of the men had survived more than their first day in the matches. The fights rendered so many completely useless. Their bones cracked under the might of the beasts; limbs nearly severed.

Rhéa wandered through the labyrinthine shadows, the slick tunnel walls closing in on her with every step. Every corridor was infested by the putrid scent of decay. The place reeked with it. As if to distract from the stench, each hallway was lined with colorful sconces. Each hue indicated a route, but she hadn't quite caught on to their meaning yet.

The dungeons were located on the opposite end, so Rhéa ventured in the direction of light, its glow ever escaping her with every turn. She was doomed to never reach its source, but she followed until she entered into a giant cavern.

Entering the arena, Rhéa was surprised to find it empty. It was nearly impossible to determine whether it was a natural cavern or had been hewn by Spiro, whether by physical labor or magic. Several rows of sconces lined the walls, illuminating the great space. Each ring was spotlighted, but when she glanced up to determine the source of the light, she found only stalactites above, threatening to crash to the floor a hundred feet below.

Tempted to walk into a ring to bask in the Starlight, Rhéa ambled around the entire uppermost level of the concentric rings of seats. The arena was the highest-populated area during the days, but none dared venture there in the evenings.

"Breathtaking, isn't it?"

The Enchantress twirled in the voice's direction.

Spiro leaned against the frame of an open archway, his icy eyes boring into hers. Had she not known him to be so cruel, she would have taken him for a charming gentleman. Even whilst leading his beastly army, sending so many innocent men to their deaths, he concealed his morose nature beneath a gallant façade. He wore a fashionable tunic, black with silver trim, his breeches matching. The outfit boasted of his physique. The one she'd seen more than enough of.

"I crafted it myself," said Spiro, stepping into the light. "My ability to wield Earth has become rather excellent. I needed a place for my men to prove themselves, to be motivated to earn their rank. I cannot bless them with rank based upon nobility or birthright, only dexterity." His hand rose to stroke her cheek, his fingers ice cold, their cool caress sending shivers tumbling through her body.

"Why are you so sullen tonight?" Spiro asked. "The boy survived his first battle and is on his way home. Let's hope he doesn't show up empty-handed, hmm?" He was taunting her.

Rhéa didn't resist as Spiro grasped her wrist. "Where are we going?" she dared ask as he pulled her along behind him.

Spiro tightened his grip until she winced. "So inquisitive," he purred. "You will be coming back to the conference room. My men will be returning to us within the hour and I want you to be there to greet them. You will sit by my side, where you belong."

They passed servants along the way, dropping to their knees at the sight of their Master. They were sickly looking people who were no doubt captured and drugged into submission. Just as she had been. Rhéa would prefer to die than to serve this menace, but her children kept her alive, and her betrothed would never want to see her diminished.

Rhéa glared at the back of Spiro's head as they strolled through the halls, his pale-blond hair almost lucent in the darkness.

They entered the conference room. The same austere chamber Spiro had first used her body like some common harlot. She'd allowed him to because she knew that if she refused him, if she put up a fight, he would've had her killed. He was far more powerful than she. Though as an Enchantress, she was exceedingly stronger than most humans, she was not stronger than every man, especially those Anointed by the Gods. Especially when inebriated.

Especially the Great Divine.

Spiro gestured for Rhéa to take a seat in the chair reserved for her, right next to his. She obeyed and waited passively as Spiro poured her a glass of red wine. Their beverages always came from separate decanters. He'd been drugging her from the moment he'd let her enter his chambers, from the moment he forced her to touch his body.

Rhéa would have killed him if given the chance, but the drug numbed her enough that she couldn't access her powers beyond her healing gifts. Whenever she uttered spells in Elder Tongue, the words possessed no greater spirit, no magical qualities. It left her barren and misplaced. It was as if the Stars had abandoned her. There were few feelings worse than that.

The room was insufferably quiet. An hour alone with him and she'd be at her breaking point. Spiro approached her once she'd taken a few sips of fàrmako-infused wine. Rhéa gulped down another so that she wouldn't have to look at him. He towered over her, his eyes roaming the length of her bodice, lingering.

With a long bone-white finger, Spiro tipped her chalice up, angling it so that its entire contents would have to be ingested. Rhéa's eyes widened as she opened her throat and took the wine down in one burning gulp. She gasped. If she so much as let one drop fall from her lips, she would be punished for it. Pleased, Spiro removed the glass from her grip and returned it to the buffet across the room.

Oh, the mighty Stars!

Rhéa's chest burned, and her head was so faint, she thought she might lose it. She closed her eyes in an attempt to ground herself, to steady her mind, as the vortex threatened to undo her. It was only when the shocking touch of cold skin met her breast that she finally opened her eyes. Spiro was upon her instantly, his lips devouring her own. She didn't push him away, though she did not kiss him in return.

"Hair," he murmured, his breath tickling her velvet skin. "Now."

Every time he planned on being intimate with her, he had her change her hair color to a vibrant red. Even under the suppression of fàrmako, she was capable of simple aesthetic spells. Rhéa assumed the hair was redolent of a long-lost lover.

For that was the curse of the immortal, you were destined to always miss someone.

Rhéa made to stand when Spiro began to unlace his breeches, but he pushed her down into the chair. "Not tonight," he murmured in her ear as he bent over her. "I want to feel your tongue work some *magic*." His fingers traced her jawline, applying slightly too much pressure to be romantic. Spiro growled in anticipation and ran his long spider-like fingers through her crimson hair, his grip callous.

The Enchantress fought against her instincts to gag and recoil. Her wine-stained lips were just beginning to part when a knock on the door interrupted them.

"Who dares disturb me?" Spiro's bellow threatened to loosen shale from the ceiling.

"It is Xavier and Larkin," a voice called back.

Rhéa froze.

Spiro backhanded her across the face, the impact jarring her teeth, her jaw clicking in and out of its socket.

"You do not stop until I tell you to!"

She fought tears as she nodded her understanding.

"Good. Now clean yourself up," he snarled as he laced his breeches. "You look like a whore, and I do not dally with the likes of filth."

Rhéa obliged and corrected her dress, finger-combing her hair, wiping the tears from her cheeks. She winced as her fingers swept over the tender skin.

The two young men entered the room. Xavier, the lithe man who had led her to Spiro when she'd first arrived. The Divine who also trained with her patient.

And her patient, Larkin Oak.

Rhéa kept her gaze trained on Larkin as he claimed his seat across from her. He hadn't removed his eyes from his comrade since he arrived. The Enchantress tried to will him to look at her, but her powers were beyond her reach.

Spiro didn't seat himself in his usual ornate, high-backed chair. Instead, he stood beside Rhéa, his hand resting on her shoulder, the touch undeniably proprietary. Suddenly, Rhéa hoped her patient didn't take notice of her. This would be the first time that she'd been in his presence without her veil, but the young man persisted to be ignorant of her presence. He had eyes for his Master only.

That damned Blood Oath.

"Well, where is she?" Spiro demanded.

"We won the battle," Xavier started, his blond curls darkened by sweat and gore.

"Won? You *retreated* with nothing to show for it!" Spiro's fist collided with the tabletop, the crystals of the chandelier above shook from the impact. Rhéa dropped her gaze and focused instead on the twisted pattern of the wood, its polished surface reflecting the dim light from the sconces.

"But we managed to leave the girl with several arrows protruding from her armor!" Xavier flashed a grin at Larkin.

Rhéa's blood stopped flowing.

"You managed nothing!" Spiro roared. "I didn't want you to *hurt* her, I wanted you to capture her. You could have killed her. And if you had, I would be dealing *twice* the amount of damage to the two of you." His tone was nearly feral.

Rhéa's head spun. Was the girl alive? She wanted to ask but didn't dare.

"I'm sorry, Master," Larkin conceded for his comrade, his attempt to placate Spiro futile.

"You are useless!" Spiro slammed his fist down again. Even with her diluted senses, Rhéa jumped. "We could have taken the capital, but you two *pissants* gave the order to retreat, and you came back empty-handed at that."

The men had gone pale as snow, their wide eyes begging for pardon.

"You disobeyed my orders and you cost me a great deal of bodies. I could be wearing that crown right now, the Divine kneeling at my feet. You should be grovelling after all I've done for the two of you." With a swipe of his hand, Spiro sent the chalices shattering against the wall.

Rhéa's heart broke at the sight of Larkin trembling. He still hadn't looked at her.

Spiro began to pace, his long fingers stroking his chin pensively. "What am I supposed to do with you two? I've invested far too much in training you, preparing you. I cannot fix stupidity, much less tolerate it." His pacing continued for a dreadfully long moment in which all of his subjects kept their faces downcast.

Rhéa watched Larkin intently through thick lashes.

"Ten lashes each," Spiro said finally. "As further punishment, there will be no healing once it is over. My Enchantress has other tasks to tend to tonight."

My Enchantress. Rhéa cringed at what those *tasks* would entail.

Xavier bowed his head in submission and began to remove his tunic. Spiro strode to the buffet where he retrieved the whip from a drawer. Larkin removed his tunic, scars standing out stark on his skin.

"Xavier, you first," Spiro ordered, and Xavier dropped to his knees. He gripped the sides of his chair so tight, his knuckles turned white.

The crack of the whip sounded and every hair on Rhéa's body rose in response. She counted each one, attempting to distract her mind from Xavier's cries of anguish. Larkin's face had gone wan. He remained seated, torso bare, olive skin ashen.

Spiro chuckled menacingly as Xavier cried out. Rhéa's hands were numb as she watched. Blood now pooled beneath the young man, but not enough to be concerned with.

The last lash was always the worst. Several chunks of skin sailed through the air as Xavier collapsed to the floor, moaning and bathing in his own blood.

"You may go," Spiro announced—an order—and stepped back, the whip coiling like a snake at his feet.

Xavier took a moment before rising on trembling legs which no longer seemed capable of holding him upright. Rhéa made to stand and assist but Spiro shot her a warning glare, and she seated herself submissively.

"Hurry up, Xavier!" Spiro barked. "You are truly disappointing me tonight." An undertone of amusement was palpable in his voice.

Xavier scurried from the room, shooting Larkin an encouraging nod before exiting the chamber. Rhéa hoped that he would be waiting outside for her patient.

"Larkin, come here."

He rose to his feet and sauntered over to kneel in the pool of blood before his Master. He held his shoulders back, maintaining an esteemed disposition. He gripped the chair just as Xavier had.

Rhéa's heart shattered, but she withheld her tears. Now was not the time to break.

"Because you were only to follow orders," said Spiro, "you will suffer seven lashes."

Relief flooded Larkin's features as he stared at the back of the chair. The sound of the whip slicing through the air made Rhéa choke on her breath. She shut her eyes as Spiro brought it down upon Larkin's bare skin.

Larkin roared in agony, and Rhéa stifled a cry of her own.

"Rhéa, darling, do not close your eyes," Spiro chided.

Larkin glanced up at her, acknowledgment dawning his features. Their eyes locked, fixated in awe and recognition as Spiro brought down the next lash. A wicked grin beset the Great Divine's features and Larkin's attention was wrenched from her. Rhéa pursed her lips to keep them from quivering.

Three. Larkin did not cry out. Rhéa's heart stilled in her chest at the silence that enveloped the chamber.

Four. He bowed his head in shame as his blood poured from the gaping runnels lining his back.

Five. A gasp, the only sound he'd elicited thus far. Larkin's face contorted in distress. Rhéa desperately wanted to reach for him, to shield him, but she couldn't access her magic.

Six. Larkin's knuckles were white as he gripped the chair. Rhéa watched his ribs expand and contract incrementally, his breathing heavy, erratic, yet he maintained silence.

Seven. The final blow. Larkin didn't fall to the ground as Xavier had. Instead, he took a moment to rise, using the chair to assist him.

A smug smile spread across Spiro's face as he studied the latticework of deep crimson lacerations decorating Larkin's back. Blood leaked from the gashes as he moved, his body trembling visibly. Rhéa's heart swelled with a mixture of pride and relief. He would be all right. Her eyes didn't leave Larkin until he exited the chamber, floundering into the corridor and out of sight.

The Great Divine stood before her now, beckoning for her to stand, the glint in his eyes baleful. Rhéa obliged him. His fingers were tender as they wiped splatters of blood off her skin, but the grin that adorned his face was not. He'd become nefarious. His pale eyes studied hers closely, as if he could sense how she felt watching him dole out punishment. But Spiro said nothing as he leaned into her, his lips grazing her neck, her collarbone. Rhéa merely clamped her eyes shut and surrendered, imagining him to be her own husband.

Spiro growled with ravaging lust as he untied her dress, and the chiffon and silk pooled around her ankles, just like the blood of Larkin Oak.

39

A SKELETON OF A PLAN

The waves thrashed against the shore, their caps white as snow. The early morning sun reflected off the water in tiny, near-blinding flashes, rendering the Northern Galatëa Sea a sparkling landscape extending into eternity. The perfect sight to come home to.

The Divine arrived at the Frourío one evening before dark, exhausted from a full day's ride. Ambrose greeted them with a hot meal set out on the kitchen table. Felix was anxiously awaiting their return. The young noviciate wouldn't cease his relentless pestering for insignificant details of battle.

No one mentioned Larkin. Arduen merely explained that the beasts had retreated suddenly, and the battle was done. She wanted to thank him for that.

Once everyone had satisfied their bellies and excused themselves from the table, Lilith shrugged off Arduen's prompts to head to her own bed. She refused kindly as she wanted a moment alone with Wren. The surly Master seemed to have a similar idea, as he remained seated at the table. Once the kitchen had cleared out, she approached him like she would a slumbering bear.

"I haven't had a chance to thank you."

Wren cast her a meek smile and sipped his tea. "You need not thank me, Lilith. I'd do it for any one of you." His voice was husky, raw.

"I know, but I would have died had you not carried me off so swiftly. I know what it meant for you to do that. I could have—" She cut herself off before she said it. *I could have died in your arms.* She wasn't close enough to him to reveal that she knew about Cordova, but a hint was enough.

"Do you?"

Lilith dropped her gaze, the temperature in the room suddenly rising.

Wren sighed deeply and she sat back in her chair, ready for his onslaught of ire. But the room remained silent, save for the crackling of burning embers in the hearth.

His face hardened, brow furrowed, his eyes lit with energy, potent with emotions she understood all too well. "I will never watch another young Divine suffer and be taken so unfairly, so abominably. You've been blessed twice, Lilith. You are so young and yet the Gods have chosen you. I'm no fool, I know what that means. They can see into your soul. How can I stand by and watch the life bleed out of you?" His hands were balled into fists on the table, his mug cradled between them.

"But they also saw into Spiro's soul," she countered.

"Yes, even the Gods can make mistakes." A statement not many would ever dare voice. "But I choose to believe that They have learned from them. Never again will They bless a

Divine who is not worthy of the power. You are worthy, Lilith, you must be.

"For what it's worth, I do not doubt your capabilities. But at the end of the day, you are young. Everything is new to you and will be for the next century. I want to help ensure that you live to see it." His eyes sparkled with ancient wisdom.

Lilith bit into her lip. The sense that she owed more than she could give hung suspended above her.

When she didn't take her leave, Wren said, "There are few words to describe what happened, how it affected me so. But when her eyes closed for the last time, mine did, too." And that's when Lilith resolved to open them.

Odd it was that two people so vastly divergent could find mutual ground in loss.

"Now off to bed," he snapped, assuming his usual mulish mien. "We all need some rest and recovery."

THE FOLLOWING MORNING, LILITH WAS LEFT WITH NOTHING TO distract herself. Training didn't resume for her and Julius as Arduen and Quin were busy preparing for the mission trip to the Isles of Nysía. She debated going out to fire as many arrows as she could in one day—her current record was 327—but the inclement weather had kept them all confined to the Frourío.

Lilith had spent the previous night lying awake, fearing sleep and her torturous dreamscape. Frequently, she'd slumber, only to wake up screaming, sweat coating her like a second skin. Arduen came running every time, but there was little he could do to assuage her lament. Her Master would coerce her back to sleep, only to come running back an hour later. How could he mitigate her loss? Her brother was a traitor in the worst way. And he'd tried to kill her—or had made it seem like that was his intention.

That was the most difficult part to accept.

Seated on her windowsill, she watched the waves crash onto the beach far below. They appeared so rough, so broken, the caps stark white against the deep blue. That's how she imagined her insides: roiling like the sea.

Lilith wished that Xander had blessed her instead, so that she could unleash His Fire unto the world and blast Spiro's army of beasts in an epic conflagration that rendered this entire war finalized. The ashes would help to fertilize the land, and the Empire would begin anew. Augusta would win. The Gods would be victorious. And Larkin could come home.

A knock on the door startled her.

"Come in," she called.

It was Ambrose, peeking his head inside tentatively, a wary expression beset his features. He had flour caked to his cheeks and it dusted his hair so that he appeared almost elderly. Despite her foul mood, Lilith failed to stifle a snort. As she approached him, she did her best to conceal her semi-permanent moue.

"You're covered in flour," she said on a chuckle.

"Oh… yeah. I'm not surprised. I've made about ten loaves of bread." He smiled, abashed, his dark cheeks flushing under the smudges of ivory powder. "I was sent to retrieve you. Arduen and Olga would like to see you in the study."

Instantly, she recessed back into the all-too-familiar void of darkness.

AS LILITH APPROACHED THE STUDY DOORS, RAISED VOICES MET her ears. Halting outside, she listened to the heated conversation within.

"Absolutely not!" Olga's voice turned shrill. What could have caused Olga to become so upset?

Lilith hesitantly nudged the study door open.

The Oracle rose to her feet suddenly. "Oh, Lilith! Come here, darling." Olga stretched out her arms and embraced her.

Arduen sat at the desk. He didn't rise to greet her, rather he glanced up at her from under his brow. Deep lines were etched into his skin, granting him a wan appearance. It was unlikely that he had slept at all.

"Are you leaving for the Isles?" Lilith asked.

"No, dear," Olga answered in his stead. "Arduen and Quintus will not leave us for a couple of days."

Lilith's breath hitched as the Oracle beckoned for her to sit. Planting herself, she seeded her eyes on Arduen. He didn't glance up from his folded hands.

"We do not know how your brother has become Divine, or how his comrade has, but they have been Anointed by Isidore." Arduen finally met her stare, his irises turning glacial with every word.

Olga claimed a seat beside him and carried on for her Master. "I highly doubt Isidore blessed them before Spiro took them under his wing, as I would have been notified of their Anointment."

Arduen sighed, bracing himself. He didn't seem to be aware of how much his disposition frightened his noviciate. "It would be an abomination had Isidore blessed them after falling into Spiro's clutches. We would never suspect a betrayal from within Elysium. And if Spiro has discovered a means to transmit his Divine gifts unto his acolytes…"

He and Olga exchanged glances, and Lilith knew then that she'd been excluded from a previous conversation.

"What is it?" she breathed, as prepared as she could ever be to hear the truth.

"We believe," Arduen began hesitantly, "that your brother has sworn the Blood Oath to Spiro." Her Master rose to his feet and rounded the desk to stand before her.

Lilith couldn't lift her eyes to meet his as Olga placed a comforting hand over hers. "It is the only possible way he has become Divinely powerful."

A rushing chill sluiced through her body as if icy water had been dumped over her head. Her insides churned. Her chest heaved. The physical indications of resignation. Her mind recalled the dream she had after the declaration of her Dâs Thymó. Surely it was the Blood Oath ceremony. Perhaps the Gods had bestowed those visions unto her.

There was no possible way to redeem her brother. The implications of Larkin's actions, whether he commandeered them or not, were dire. He had never planned on a subterranean afterlife, but there was no way he would be granted entrance into Elysium now.

Arduen pulled her into him as she struggled to stifle a sob. She felt Olga's slender hands stroking her hair in comfort, though Lilith found little of it. This was what utter devastation felt like. She'd survived the death of both parents. Though they had left the earth far sooner than she'd ever anticipated, she always knew she would have to lay them to rest someday. She'd always thought she would have a lifetime with Larkin, that he would be the perfect uncle to her children, the centre-piece of their family.

Now he is gone.

Spiro had taken him away as he had her parents. His beasts butchered her father in battle, drove her mother suicidal. And now Larkin. The Great Divine had claimed her entire family.

Lilith balled her hands into fists. She beseeched the Gods to pardon Larkin's soul. To grant him salvation among Them, where her parents were waiting with open arms. He would be with them at last, far sooner than she'd ever hoped, but he would be with them. The only reward for his suffering.

She racked her brain, rehearsing the skeleton of her plan over and over, steeling herself for what she would have to endure to orchestrate it.

"It has to be me," her voice rasped against Arduen's chest.

He pulled away slightly, brows nudging toward each other as he stared down at her in confusion, his lips parting slightly. "What has to be you?" he asked, pronouncing each word slowly, clearly.

"I have to be the one who frees him," Lilith said defini-tively, so succinct, she felt both Arduen and Olga stiffen at her words. Their faces paled. "I have to be the one who frees him from Spiro. I must do this. I will find a way to free him. There must be a way, and it must be me. It is the only way I can ever live with myself." She shuddered at the thought of it, the image of Larkin's depthless eyes narrowing on her. That was not her brother. And she would find a way to bring him back. She would devise a plan to free him of his bond to Spiro.

"There is no way to break the bond of the Blood Oath, Lilith." Arduen pulled her against him again. Her ire flared at his words, but she quashed it. Arduen wasn't the one who did this to her. He wasn't the one who corrupted her brother. Their enemy was mutual, and they were stronger against him standing together.

Arduen whispered into her hair, "I am so sorry, my fledgling." Though his body, his words, were warm and inviting, Lilith felt cold.

"I will find a way," she said. "Do not try to convince me otherwise."

Olga's features transformed into an expression so grim, doubt assailed her at the sight of it. But this was the only way the direness of the situation could be rendered palatable. It was her only option if she wanted to move on. She had many years ahead of her, years that she didn't plan to mourn her way through. She couldn't give up on Larkin without trying to save him.

Prying herself from Arduen's embrace, Lilith exited the study before her Master could compose himself and object, leaving her elders bewildered.

40

A WOMAN OF AETHER AND WATER

Lilith splashed milk into her tea and watched as light and dark eddied. She became entranced by the liquid as it continued to swirl. Could she fall into it and re-emerge someplace else, someplace quiet? Of course not. No one can escape the prison of their own mind.

Since Arduen and Olga informed her of the Blood Oath, Lilith had spent every free moment sequestered in the study in an attempt to parse out various remedies to the Blood Oath. All were prophetic. None were tried and true.

But hope did not relent.

"Zurí will take charge of your training today," Arduen said, breaking through Lilith's trance.

"Yes, Master," she mumbled distractedly, too invested in mulling over a promising tome to pay him heed.

Nearly an hour passed before Zurí emerged. "Darling." She embraced Lilith in a genuine hug before inspecting her attire. "Run upstairs and don your leather suit. Pack your fur-lined leathers as well. I don't want you freezing to death." Lilith marched upstairs to retrieve her pack.

They set out under a blue sky dotted by flocculent clouds. Zurí had packed a loaf of bread and cheese, gifted by Ambrose. He'd handed them to her with trembling arms, words of praise stumbling from his lips, much to her amusement.

Zurí was a devastatingly beautiful mystery to those who didn't know her before she arrived. Even Julius kept his distance and said very little to her—Lilith wasn't entirely sure why she'd noticed that. She shook the thought of the prince from her head.

Zurí Ságe was an enigma, Lilith thought. All the elder Divines had greeted her with familiar affection, as if nearly fifty years hadn't passed since they'd last seen her. Perhaps half a century wasn't very long for the Divine.

The dry grass, magnificently painted white with frost, crunched beneath their boots as they crossed the field and entered the pines. There was no sense of urgency as they meandered through the trunks until, without warning, Zurí took off at a sprint. Her mellifluous laughter carried on the wind, her fiery locks writhing like flames in her wake.

Lilith caught up in good time and kept pace with her new Master. After running for nearly two hours, Lilith was delighted that her muscles didn't protest. It seemed that her Divine body had replaced the ache with strength and vigor. There was nothing but freedom as the rushing wind whipped through her hair, tearing it free of its plait. Her body sang with ecstasy with every bound and leap, Zurí close beside her.

The pines finally broke to reveal sunlight, the snow melting on the ground below. The sound of a rushing stream met Lilith's ears. Zurí halted at the edge of the tree-line, barely panting as she observed the small clearing, a narrow river carving through its centre.

Lilith took a moment to observe her Master discreetly. The scar that Spiro had carved down her left eye was stark in the natural light. She doubted such a mark could ever diminish the woman's beauty, for even with the scar marring her face, she was stunning. The scar was the only indication that Zurí was more than a beautiful, prim woman; a veneer sheltering the honed warrior within.

Zurí removed her boots, her bare feet crunching on the frosted grass. Her Master nodded once in silent command and Lilith followed her lead, reluctantly tearing her boots off her feet, her socks with them. She suppressed a shiver as her bare feet settled onto the frozen earth.

Without instruction, Zurí stepped into the water. "This is the Anstï River, the northeastern side of it."

Lilith's heart nearly stopped at the mention of the river, the same serpent of water that she and her mother used to bathe in on hunting trips. She stepped toward the river's edge and stared into it, no longer heeding the bite of cold against her skin. Her mother's body had touched this water, and it was almost as if by entering it, Lilith would be closer to her.

"Are you all right?" Zurí asked.

"Yes."

"Then come on in." An order.

Lilith obliged, stepping into the river, her feet slid along the hardened riverbed. Stones dispatched themselves from the bottom as her feet scaled along. The water rose to just below her knees and rushed around her legs southwest. The river would rush and flow until it pooled into Lake Ozeros and then back into the larger Anstï River. Then it wended its way down the western coast of Augusta, until it released into the Western Galatëa Sea. The same expanse of water that separated Julius's country from Augusta.

"All I want you to do is to watch and observe," Zurí said.

A moment later, thin pillars of the clearest liquid geysered out of the river, reaching up into the sky. Lilith gaped at the marvellous display, freezing droplets landing on her skin. "I don't know why I am still amazed every time I see one of you wield your element," she admitted to Zurí, exasperated.

"It was always that way with me too," Zurí said. "I still marvel at what Quin and Arduen can do. Even Wren can do some amazing things when he chooses to display it."

Zurí lifted her arms into the air, twisting her fingers, the pillars of Water moving as she willed them. They spiralled around each other in a languid dance. "If I could choose another element," Zurí continued, "it would be Thëo's Earth."

"Why?"

"Wouldn't you want to shape the world exactly how you desire to see it?" Zurí withdrew her hold and gently lowered the columns back into the river, the Anstï now flowing slightly faster. Lilith braced herself as best she could, though she couldn't conceal her alarm from her Master.

"How do you do it?" Lilith asked. "How do you just *will* it to obey you?"

"The same way you summon Aether."

"But it's not the same. I can summon Aether from within me. Water already *exists*." She paused to consider her thoughts. "It's odd…"

Zurí's brow furrowed as she glanced at her noviciate. "What is?"

"That I can summon Aether. Julius can summon Fire. But I cannot summon Water. I can only control what is existing. Yet it is the one element of those three that is already present in my body."

Zurí laughed, the sound comforting, easing Lilith's mind. "Well, you could summon what is in your muscle tissue but that would kill you. Our bodies cannot exist without Water." Her laughter trilled. "Though it was a good observation. Two points for you!"

"The only two I've ever received," Lilith quipped.

"The only two you'll ever *need*." Her Master mocked her sardonic tone. "Now, there isn't much of a difference between summoning an element and wielding an element. Just stand where you are. Close your eyes if it helps you to access the part of your mind Kyril has altered. Reach for the Water, sense it and control it."

Lilith obeyed her Master's command and closed her eyes. She lowered the barriers around her mind and reached out with Discernment. "I don't understand how to sense it. I open my mind, but I don't feel anything. There's nothing even living in this river."

Zurí's voice rose above the river's tinkling, indicating that she'd distanced herself from Lilith. What did she expect? Lilith felt incapable of summoning another tidal wave. "Spend enough time in this state and you'll feel it. Water is like a living entity. The more it moves, the more it is filled with life, and the mightier it surges within you."

Lilith continued to sense her surroundings, to feel what

was rushing around her legs, caressing her calves. "I still don't sense anything."

"Keep trying. If you don't feel anything in the next hour, anything at all, then we will move downstream where the river is wider and the current is fiercer." Zurí walked back to the edge of the pines and waited. She crossed her arms over her chest, her eyes raking over her noviciate's frame, assessing and analyzing.

Lilith couldn't wait for the vetting to be over. She closed her eyes again and lost herself in the tedium of the task, her consciousness groping desperately at her surroundings. Her mind gripped and relinquished its hold on the Water as it rushed past her. She seethed as it remained elusive.

Falling short once again, Lilith sighed in defeat, much to her chagrin. Zurí displayed no inclination to excuse her from the task. Instead, her Master remained at the edge of the trees, leaning against the bare trunk of a large pine.

Grimacing in frustration, Lilith persisted. The last few days had left her drained. Maybe there just wasn't enough left of her to control and manipulate Kyril's Water. She wanted to blast it right into whatever hole Spiro had dug himself and drown him in her tears. The man who had taken—no, *stolen*—everything from her.

A dam exploded inside of her and Lilith fretted the river would react to it.

It did.

Water rushed through her muscles. Blood sluiced through her veins like quicksilver. The feeling was so unlike Aether. Where Constantine's element surged within, commanding Kyril's element felt almost as though the God was using her body as a tool. The only sound besides the flow of her insides was Zurí's distant cheers of triumph. But when Lilith opened her eyes to share in the celebration, she couldn't see her Master.

The Water tunnelled around her like a vortex. When she looked straight along the river's long, slithering body, she could only see a tunnel of white rushing around her. Lilith raised a trembling hand to touch the Water as it soared past. As her fingertips pressed into its marbled surface, their indentations stretched out for several feet. She laughed breathily in disbelief.

No one else could ever experience such a magnificent view.

The miraculous sight arose such a deep sense of appreciation, Lilith was forced to her knees, her bones jarring against the pebbles that decorated the bare riverbed. As tears spilled down her cheeks, as her heart once again mended within the Water's abyss, she relinquished her hold over its entity. The Water crashed down onto the riverbed, soaking and chilling her down to her marrow.

Silence fell over the dense pines of the Megálos, interrupted only by Lilith's rasping breath as she panted for air. She continued on this way, eyes squeezed shut. When she finally caught her breath, she rose to her feet and straightened her spine. When she opened her eyes, Zurí stood tall beside her noviciate, a satisfied grin spreading her full lips.

"That's it," her Master purred in approval.

Lilith braced her hands on her bruised knees, allowing her chest to rise and fall. "I've always been a woman of flame and steel. These past few days all I've dreamed of, the only thing that could bring me joy, would be to burn Spiro's army to ashes. But Xander did not bless me."

"You are a woman of Aether and Water now, Lilith Oak.

You can consume an entire army with Aether and you can suffocate them with Water. You don't need to be near a large body of Water for this gift to be lethal. Water is the essence of all life. It is the most virulent of all the Divine elements. You have been gifted the ability to both grant life *and* take it."

41

HOPE CANNOT EXIST

Originally, it had been determined that only Arduen and Quin would travel to the Isles of Nysía, but plans changed when Olga complained that Julius would be wasting time lounging about the Frourío. She argued that the prince should accompany them. He was trained to analyze such political matters, after all, and he possessed credible diplomatic skill as heir to a formidable throne. Quin couldn't object.

Lilith was told to remain at the Frourío with Zurí, but Olga pushed Arduen to take her along as well. The Oracle argued that it would be an important lesson for Lilith, that visiting the Isles would be a great experience. But Lilith knew Olga only wanted to distance her from the study, and Arduen couldn't object.

They departed at dawn on horseback, travelling at break-neck speed. For the duration of their ride, Lilith mustered all her energy into keeping her suffering ensconced in a façade of calm acceptance. Any one of her comrades would have dismissed her bitterness as fatigue.

Truth be told, there wasn't much to conceal. She was bereft of emotion. Reservoir emptied out. Hollow. A mere shell of what she once was. It was as if the river had cleansed her soul, eased her pain, and cleared her head. But when would she fill up with life again?

The others conversed as they crossed into the Realm of Elïath. As the towering pines of the Megálos faded into oaks, a dormant longing roused within her soul. Her heart recognized it instantly.

Home.

Arduen could see through her mask, see into her soul, into the swirling abyss of darkness that it had become, but he never acknowledged it. Every time he glanced at her, his heavy eyes appeared gray and vacant. Was he still struggling to accept her desire to save Larkin? He was so opposed to her hope of freeing him, it summoned doubts that haunted her dreams.

"So after a night of wringing the pleasure from her body, he wrung the life from her neck the next morning!" The comment grabbed Lilith's attention.

Confounded, she asked, "Who did?"

"The last Walabeän *Igítís*—the Chief. They rioted against him, of course, and Marlowë led the resistance to victory. The old tyrant's head was on a pike by nightfall and his wife was given a burial fit for a queen." Quin spoke with animation that rarely emanated from him.

"So they love Marlowë?" Julius clarified.

"Oh yes. They *worship* him and he loves his people in return. They live in such peace… it will be difficult for them to accept our offer." Quin nearly muttered the last sentence.

"It is not easy to send your people to war when you know almost all of them personally," Arduen added, his tone sombre.

Lilith avoided her Master's gaze as it swept over her.

⊙ ⏾ ᴖ ᴍ ᖚ

THOUGH WINTER WAS COMING TO AN END, THE AIR WAS CRISP along the northern coast. Droplets of melting snow dribbled down upon them from the canopy of bare branches. Lilith bided her time playing with them, much to Julius's amusement. The prince shook a branch until thousands of sparkling droplets slipped free, and Lilith halted their descent before they landed on him.

"Don't drop them on me," he chided with humor. But Lilith knew that if she did fail, he would likely commend her efforts trying to control it. Giggling, she released the droplets, just when Julius was out of the way.

"Hey!" he exclaimed. "That one got me!" Indeed, several droplets now ran down the back of his cloak, soaking Stormbringer's rump.

Their cackles echoed through the trees. Arduen and Quin often glancing over their shoulders to observe their noviciates' mirth.

Genuine laughter was rare these days, it was nearly shocking to Lilith's ears—especially for her own chest to heave with it. Her abdomen ached, but she welcomed the pain, because that kind of pain signified growth and joy. The pain she'd become accustomed to was far beneath the surface. It was the kind of pain that stifled one's breathing. It was the kind of pain that made someone forget who they were.

"One hour and we will reach town!" Quin called back.

"I hope they have enough rooms," Lilith groused under her breath. "I refuse to sleep in a stall."

Julius chuckled, amused. "We are Divine. The whole inn would clear out for us if we asked them to."

Rolling her eyes, she quipped, "Spoken like a true spoiled-rotten *princeling*."

He scoffed, aghast. "Wouldn't *you* like to know just how spoiled I am?"

"I think it is *you* who would like me to *want* to know just how spoiled you are." She waggled her brows.

Julius craned his neck and barked a laugh, his sable curls glistening in the moonlight. "Yes, I think I would."

As he rode ahead to join his Master, Arduen fell back to ride alongside Lilith. Skydancer nudged his favorite mare's neck with an affectionate chuff.

"How are you enjoying the journey so far?" he inquired sheepishly. That couldn't be why he'd fallen back to speak with her. Maybe he would finally open up about what was on his mind. Maybe he would finally ask her about Jude.

Lilith studied him but could glean nothing of his intentions, so she entertained him. "Well, I felt true excitement when I saw the first oak appear. Haven't seen one of those in a while." Though her tone was washed dry with sarcasm, she meant what she'd said sincerely. Her home was surrounded by thick-limbed oaks. Her family name was Oak. She couldn't help the nostalgia that fogged her mind as she galloped along.

Arduen, having saved her from the flames of her burning

smithy, knew her home well enough. Especially since his extended family resided in Utica. He would know why the oak trees affected her, possibly *how* they affected her.

He said quietly, "Many hundreds of years ago, I was born in a lively town on the western coast. Trade with the western continent was flourishing. Back then it was not called Dale-gonè, but it was ruled by Julius's family still. Life was abundant and we thrived, a little town nestled in the oak trees. The same oak trees, some centuries later, that surround your home."

Lilith caught her breath. "You were born in Utica?"

Arduen inclined his head. "It was Kavala then."

Why he had never told her, she couldn't understand. But the thought that her Master hailed from the same region, the same cluster of buildings, brought her peace.

"Kavala..." Lilith repeated wistfully. "And what of your family?" Instantly, she regretted the question. *Jude.*

Arduen's features grew sullen once again and she berated herself for prying. "When I discovered Aether, there was no one to help me. My own Master was across the country, near the Marsh. I believe the Oracle at the time was also far from him. I was left without guidance for months as my gifts progressed within me."

Lilith recalled the first time Aether had been released from her own body. She hadn't known what had happened, she had no control. She shuddered at the thought, and Arduen reached over and drew the hood of her cloak over her head.

"What happened?"

"I destroyed my home, my parents, and my sister with it. Somehow, I survived, though I was gravely injured. My neighbours didn't know what had happened, so they took pity on me and treated my wounds. Little did they know that they harbored a weapon. That there was a killer in their midst. A killer with a God's blessed abyss roiling beneath his skin.

"When my Master finally arrived, I was so lost and confused, I was ready to end my life. I knew there was no longer a place for me in Elysium, where my family would be. The fear of Hades is what gave me the will to persist."

The distant rush of crashing waves was the only sound as she waited for her Master to continue.

Arduen sighed. "My Master saved me, differently than I saved you. He formed me anew. Gave me reason and purpose."

Hmmm… Lilith thought. *Not so different at all.*

"With every life I save, I remember their faces," he said. "After so many years, I remember their eyes, their smiles. But I can't seem to remember their voices beyond the screams. I see them in the family I made…"

Jude. Lilith could see it. The same dark-blond hair, prominent cheekbones, the defined jawline. How had she never noticed? She shifted in her saddle, turning to her Master, observing him intently. There was indeed sorrow coating his features. His eyes were silver-lined, but no tears slipped free. He had many years to accept what he'd done.

"I'm sorry," she said to him, her voice thick with emotion. "Thank you for telling me."

"It was time for you to know. And I want you to be able to tell me anything as well." His gaze was knowing as it lingered on her. It didn't make her uncomfortable, though she still didn't want to talk. There wasn't much to say.

"You've told me a story, so it's only fair that I tell you one, too." She cleared her throat and organized her thoughts. She could sense Arduen's attention as if it were tangible, as if his hands gripped her shoulders, holding her still until she spoke.

"I used to be afraid of the dark," she said, voice drawn. "So afraid that I would beg my parents to let me keep the candle lit in my bedroom while I slept. Of course, for safety's sake, they wouldn't allow it. I used to keep my shutters open wide to allow for any moon or starlight to enter, to nullify my fears. On the darkest of nights, in the dead of winter, I went without sleep, or I crawled in between my parents and slept with them."

Lilith gulped past the dryness in her constricting throat, emotion spilling into her voice. "Now it is so different…" She swallowed. "The darkness has become my safe place. The only place I can find repose. The only place I can truly hide."

For a long moment, there was nothing but silence as they made their way toward the speckles of light in the distance.

Arduen tilted his head back to breathe in the night air. "Yes," he said finally. "I've learned, not long ago, that without darkness, it is impossible to see the light. Without sorrow, without despair, hope cannot exist."

◎ ⑤ ⇒ ᴍ ♭

GOURNÍA ROSE FROM THE BARREN GRASS TO MEET THEM, THE trees sparse around the town's walls. The town was alive with nighttime activities, and the Divine had no trouble gaining entrance through the front gates. The legionnaires sanctioned there seemed to be familiar with Arduen, to Lilith's surprise.

The white buildings blended into one another as if the

entire town shared a single house, as if they were all family. The rounded roofs were painted emerald green, like Lilith's eyes. She began to wonder if the color had faded from her irises since she returned from battle, like Arduen's had.

The dark thoughts that contaminated her mind were washed away at the sight of several entertainers juggling and dancing. Instruments were strummed while couples madly in love listened nearby, gazing reverently into each other's eyes. Her chest caved in at the sight of them. How long had it been since she'd given Jude any consideration? Indeed, she missed him, but not in the way a lover was supposed to.

When they reached the inn, Lilith was shocked at how many emotions the town had wrung from her in a matter of minutes. The inn's taverna was abuzz with laughter and music, and people ate and drank and danced with each other, unaware of their Divine presence.

The Divine cadre procured a table at the taverna located in the lower level of the inn. Together, they enjoyed their meal in silence. Lilith noticed several young women batting their eyelashes at Julius, who continued to eat, paying no heed to the bustle surrounding them. She glared at the women, and when their eyes met hers, they shied away, much to her satisfaction. But shame forced her eyes to her plate. It was cruel to assume that Julius was hers, for he wasn't, he belonged to no woman. They were friends, nothing more, and Lilith had a fiancé of her own at home. The heat of shame pierced her like a spear to the gut.

There were only two rooms available, and Quin didn't bother to put up a fight as both rooms contained two beds. Quin and Julius would take one while Lilith and Arduen took the other.

As they prepared to turn in, Arduen chided, "Would you like me to leave the candle lit?" A grin split his short beard, the first indication of a lightened burden.

"Snuff it out," Lilith ordered, eyebrows arched for dramatic emphasis.

Arduen chuckled, the skin around his eyes crinkling as he did. The sight made her heart leap with joy. True joy, even if it only lasted a second.

◎ ⺓ ⟿ ⋔ ♦

WHEN THEY FINALLY REACHED THE SHORE, LILITH'S HEART stilled at the sight of the sea. More specifically, the sight of the Isles rising from crashing waves recoiling off the sleek rock-sides. It was magnificent.

There were four islands in total, three connecting to the largest isle in the centre by what appeared to be swinging bridges. All of the land masses rose high out of the Galatëa. Even the shore where they stood was elevated.

Waves crashed into the isles, caressing the rock-sides with long, wispy, white fingers. There was no beach like at the Frourío, only a steep cliff which Arduen had tersely ordered them to stay back from, lest the horses quail.

The clouds had mostly cleared, and the sun began to warm them in intervals, providing shade when concealed behind a large cloud. Lilith was lost in wonder, so utterly mystified, gazing out at the view and the crashing waves below.

Birds erupted from the top of the trees, taking to the sky in waves of flocks.

"Dismount," Arduen barked at them, and she nearly

jumped out of her saddle at his command. "Julius, secure the horses over there."

The prince did as he was told and took Skydancer's reins from her.

Silence.

Lilith didn't dare voice any questions as Arduen and Quin turned to face the trees expectantly. The rustling of leaves and snapping of branches met her ears shortly thereafter, and just as Julius returned, four large wolves emerged. She staggered back in surprise.

Each of the giant wolves bore riders mounted on their backs. The riders were clad in leather and furs, weapons dangling from their belts, makhairas strapped across their backs. Three males and one female. They waved amicably from atop their mounts, and the man who was undoubtedly the leader, dismounted and greeted Arduen.

"Good day for a flight," he said. "I'm Zakk." He touched his hand to his chest.

The four beasts sniffed the Divine curiously. One even attempted to lick Arduen's face, though he raised his hands to block the gigantic tongue. The riders laughed in unison.

"These are harpies." Arduen addressed Lilith and Julius, though she suspected the prince had learned all there was to know about the Walabeäns. "Come," he prodded. "Don't be afraid."

Lilith marched forward, forcing a calm gait. She halted at her Master's side and dipped her chin in greeting to Zakk.

"Nice to meet you, Lilith," he said, grinning when she started at the use of her name. How did he know who she was? "We will fly you over," he said. "Then we will send our best caretakers to transport your horses."

"You fly them over too?" Lilith asked in surprise.

"Of course!" he scoffed. "If we don't, we would be donating them to Spiro's beasts."

She hadn't thought of that, and she was surprised that they hadn't encountered any beasts on their journey. Arduen said it was because they'd been rounded up, likely to prepare for another battle. She didn't get much sleep after that.

"I will take you." Zakk gestured to Arduen, then turned to the other Divine. "Find yourselves a rider and we will help you mount."

Lilith eyed the only female in the group and approached her cautiously, stretching her hand out to the harpy in greeting.

"This is Noala," the rider said. "She is very gentle. This old girl won't harm you."

Lilith let Noala sniff and lick as she pleased. She gazed into the wolf's large silver eyes, and the harpy blinked once in acknowledgment. Content that Noala had accepted her, Lilith approached the saddle where the female rider sat.

"I am Hestîa," she said.

"And I am—"

"Lilith," she interjected. "We know." Hestîa eyed Zakk with a smirk. "Place your foot there," she instructed with command, her accent rolling pleasantly. "Then grip my hand and I'll pull you up."

Lilith did as she was instructed and a moment later, she was seated in the saddle behind the woman. She got comfortable while Hestîa buckled her into the saddle. She watched the girl as she worked, her long pale-blonde braids swaying with every movement—all one hundred of them.

"Ready!" Zakk called to them. "Take off!"

The harpies leapt into the air, massive wings unfurling from their sides—wings that Lilith had failed to notice when they approached on foot. She gripped Hestia's shoulders fiercely as they escalated into the air and the ground fell away behind them.

THE ISLES OF NYSÍA

They landed on the largest island, the heart of the Isles. Noala's landing was smooth, despite the lurch of Lilith's guts. To her surprise, she wasn't comfortable with heights. Unstable as she was, she was thankful to place her feet on solid ground again.

The main isle was inhabited by the *Igítís* and his retinues. It was the centre of business and trade for the Colony. It was also the place where the warriors trained and proved their worth, climbing the ranks. The arena, located in front of the Chief's estate, was a large pit surrounded by concentric rings of spectator seats.

The *Igítís*'s manor was a grand fortress comprised of logs. The estate appeared to be capable of housing a great number of families. As substantial as it was, it was equally quaint, welcoming even. Lilith far preferred it to the Emperor's castle.

They dismounted as a group of Walabeäns marched toward them. Lilith quickly waded to Arduen's side, standing back so as to be close to Julius as well. The prince granted her a nod of approval, a charming smile besetting his sensuous lips. Her stomach lurched again.

"So you are the Emperor's liaison?" one of the men questioned, his accent thick and euphonious.

"Emissaries," Quin corrected.

The man bowed slightly. "The *Igítís* will meet with you. Please follow me." He led them to the great log fortress, stopping before the staircase leading up to the main doors of the manor. As their escort turned to face them, the grand doors swung open and the *Igítís* emerged.

Igítís Marlowë was dressed just as his people: a plated leather suit covered his muscular limbs, clad in thick furs, a large himation draped over the ground in his wake. The only distinguishing facet of his ensemble was a leather band around his full head of long white hair. His irises were of the palest blue, like the sky before it meets the sunset.

Marlowë's people adored him. Lilith could glean that much by the way his presence had torn their unyielding attention from the Divine. They respected him not like a God, but like a father. An affection he earned through a reign of justice and love, and he returned that love to them all.

The *Igítís* halted several feet before them. Lilith kept her chin high as Marlowë inspected each of them, taking their measure in a public display of dominance. She stood tall as the Chief's eyes panned up and down her frame. He was surveying her, but his eyes did not devour her like Emperor Obadïa's had. Marlowë's deep-set eyes beheld a sense of respect and honor.

"Tell me the reason for your sudden visit?" His voice was an arid rumble.

Arduen stepped forward, pulling the Imperial decree from his cloak pocket. Marlowë took the scroll, his face betraying no emotion as his eyes panned each line. When he lifted his gaze from the parchment, it settled on Arduen, his irises froze on him like ice. Lilith wanted to scream at the insufferable silence as they awaited Marlowë's response.

"I have no doubt that my legions could sway the outcome of this war," said Marlowë. "My warriors could slice their blades through every last one of those beasts with ease and emerge with not a scratch upon them. But I will not send my people to war without some advantage, without some element of incentive. The Emperor is offering us nothing but sharing the barracks with his Milítia. That is not enough to render this so-called *alliance* savory." He rolled up the decree but did not return it to Arduen. Lilith acknowledged the gesture—or lack of one—but she didn't know if it was an indication of consideration or an outright refusal.

"I understand, *Igítís*, I do—"

"Do not call me *Igítís*," Marlowë snapped.

Arduen's eyes widened at the harshness in his tone. "My apologies… I only—"

"Call me Marlowë." The Chief's glower transformed into a comical grin. The Walabeän warriors surrounding them began to laugh, not tauntingly, but joyfully, finding humor in their leader's jesting.

"Marlowë," Arduen corrected. "I am not asking on the Emperor's behalf. I am asking on behalf of the Gods, on behalf of those of us who have fought against Spiro for the past century." Arduen then turned to Lilith and Julius. "I'm asking because I cannot bear to see the new vanguard of Divine destroyed by a power-hungry man. I ask because if we do not win this battle now, we may lose our only opportunity. We may lose *them*."

Lilith stiffened at the weight of his words as Marlowë's gaze drifted over her, surveying her up and down until his eyes met hers and rested there again. She relaxed only when she found understanding therein.

"That I can relate to," Marlowë said on a sigh. "The fear of losing the next generation. It is exactly why I struggle to send my warriors to the battlefield." He then gestured to the bevy of warriors surrounding them. They were young, couldn't have been older than their thirties. They were likely betrothed, had children of their own. Those children would miss them if they did not return from war, just as Lilith missed her own father.

"If I send my people to the mainland to fight," Marlowë said, "I expect recompense of some kind. There must be something in this worth fighting for."

"Of course," Arduen conceded, and after a short moment of consideration, his teeth digging into his bottom lip, he said, "Is peace not worth the sacrifice?"

A rumble of murmurs spread through the assembly. Lilith refused to take her eyes off Marlowë. She prayed he felt their force, their need for his assistance.

The *Igítís* grumbled, "My people live in peace *now*."

Arduen heaved a dry chuckle. "They won't be when Spiro takes the throne. He will claim the Isles, his birthplace. He considers this land his by birthright. You will be deposed, surely because your people love you. Seizing the Isles will be his first conquest as Emperor."

"You come to forge an alliance, yet you threaten us?" the Chief's ambassador snarled, his tone accusatory.

"Enough, Adonís."

The ambassador stood down at Marlowë's order.

"I do not threaten. It is not I who poses a threat to your tranquility here." Arduen waved to the people surrounding them. "This alliance will redeem your people's reputation across the Empire."

"Is the Walabeän reputation important to you?" Marlowë inquired sceptically, his head angled shrewdly.

"I may not have been born here amongst you," Arduen admitted. "But my blood is yours. My heart is yours. I have always fought with the Isles in my soul. I am a warrior of the Walabeän Colony, as I am Augustan, as I am Divine." He inclined his head in reverence.

Lilith blinked in astonishment. *Arduen is Walabeän!* The dark-blond hair. The light-blue eyes. She couldn't tear her gaze from her Master.

Marlowë's eyes guttered with fire as his gaze danced over Lilith and Julius once again. "It seems to me," the *Igítís* raised his voice, speaking loud enough for all to hear, "that this matter can only be determined through tradition. The only viable solution would be to decide by combat."

Murmurs echoed again.

"The two fiercest warriors of the Isles versus the next generation of Divine."

ONLY STEEL BREEDS GLORY

The entire Walabeän Colony congregated in the arena. The *Igítís* occupied a modest wooden throne situated upon a low dais. Arduen and Quin were to sit with Marlowë, level with the combat platform. Varying shades of blond encircled the arena like a golden banner. It seemed as though every able bodied Walabeän was present to witness the contest.

Lilith observed from the competitors' dugout. She didn't know who her opponent would be, and she wouldn't find out until minutes before her match commenced.

As Julius and his opponent stepped onto the sparring platform, the Walabeäns in the audience became a yapping pack of wolves. The stands were abuzz with excitement and anticipation.

Despite the bite of the late winter air, the sparring pit was warm. Lilith changed out of her fur-lined leathers and into her plated sparring suit. Arduen had taken her bow and quiver…

and Constance. She'd griped a litany of complaints as he handed her the steel rod she'd be using in place of a traditional blade.

The rules were simple: the first to fall off the platform forfeits. There would be no fatal blows but inflicting minor injuries would be tolerated.

"Ustè stèle vreäqq grínndr!" the Walabeän's shouted as the competition began.

Julius stood opposite his opponent, his smirk arrogant and boastful, his too-calm eyes resting steadily on his enemy. This was a front he no doubt reserved for single combat. A front so convincing that only his fellow Divine could see through it.

Lilith couldn't avert her gaze from the Crown Prince of Dalegonè as he began to circle his opponent, a warrior they called Agónas, the Assiduous. The Walabeän mirrored Julius's every movement with sharp precision. Seconds turned into minutes. The standoff drawn out in order to intimidate the other. Julius was goading Agónas into the offensive, and maybe the warrior knew it, too. Their boots crunched in the dirt, the only sound to be heard upon the isle.

The Walabeän warrior fell prey to Julius's ploy and attacked first, his long white braid slicing through the air like a whip. Agónas's speed was impressive, but the prince was quicker, a result of his superior royal training and his Divine strength.

Julius hacked at his adversary with furious swipes of his rod and Agónas stumbled backward. The Walabeän stopped himself just in time, lest he would have tumbled off the platform, ending the bout quickly. His skidding feet stirred the dirt, dust rising like a cloud around him.

Julius did not provoke him. He didn't charge when his

enemy was at his most vulnerable. He retreated, still sporting that devastatingly arrogant sneer. Poised across the platform, his entire carriage was achingly cavalier.

It was enough to impel Agónas to strike again.

Sparks flickered through the air as steel struck steel. The crowd erupted in a concurrent ode of elation. The combatants' bodies became a blur as dust rose higher, surrounding them like mist.

A steel rod shot out of the cloud and landed at Lilith's feet. She stared down at it, her blood running cold. *That was close.* Grunts could be heard from the platform, and she stood on the tips of her toes in anticipation, struggling to make out the two men through the veil of dust. Who had lost their weapon?

When the second rod soared overhead, a chorus of gasps emanated from the crowd. The dust rose higher as Julius and Agónas battled with their fists, but the pall settled enough for the crowd to glimpse an outline of their twisted bodies wrestling toward the drop off.

In a heap of tangled limbs, the Walabeän warrior plummeted, landing heavily beside the steel rod at Lilith's feet. His face bore an expression of bewilderment as he glared back at the platform, utterly dumbfounded. The cloud of dirt slowly dissipated, revealing Julius standing erect upon the platform, redolent of an elegant Godly statue.

The crowd detonated into a cacophony of laudation. Lilith stared at the prince in awe. Even the *Igítís* stood and clapped his overt approbation. Julius bowed his head in Marlowë's direction before gracefully hopping off the platform and marching to his opponent's side. Agónas, still seated at Lilith's feet, clasped hands with Julius amiably. They exchanged a few polite words before they departed.

One battle down.

One to go.

Gripping her steel rod with newfound determination, Lilith marched to the platform. She was vaguely aware of Arduen's eyes on her as she hoisted herself up, but she didn't meet them. Truth told, her confidence was waning, and she didn't want to glimpse the disappointment on her Master's face when she failed Augusta.

"Nice to see you again, Lilith Oak," a familiar accent trilled to her from across the platform. It was Noala's rider, Hestîa. She wore a similar leather suit to Lilith's, and a fur shawl wrapped tightly around her shoulders. Her blond hair was plaited down her skull in hundreds of tiny braids, which hung from the nape of her neck like ropes. The bright blue of her eyes seemed to smolder as if her brain was alight, burning as her stare devoured her adversary.

"Lilith Oak versus Hestîa Swiftdaughter!" the announcer called.

"Ustè stèle vreäqq grínndr!" The Walabeän's mantra thundered inside Lilith's skull.

Hestîa strode straight to Lilith, steel rod at her side. She stopped at a healthy distance, eyes locked on Lilith's, her shoulders squared with confidence. She was a few inches taller, and her long, lean limbs were corded impressively with muscle. As feminine and regal as she appeared, Lilith wasn't foolish enough to assume she wasn't equally lethal.

Lilith gulped, her throat so parched she bet all the Isles could hear it. She didn't hide her intimidation, her anxiety. Let them think her inferior. Let them assume she was not as well trained as her male counterpart. If Julius could make his opponent tremble under his conceit and hubris, Lilith could manage the opposite. Let them think she'd be an easy win for Hestîa.

She did her best to show her hand tremble as she raised it, steel rod clasped in her palm. She smirked inwardly; she wasn't even holding the hilt properly. A crowd full of warriors would notice this immediately.

Hestîa smiled grimly and breathed, "Let the best *woman* win."

Lilith gulped again, ensuring it was audible—even visible —as she awaited Hestîa's attack. A swell of adrenaline churned in her gut. Her limbs itched with the anticipation of battle. She could do this.

You are Lilith Oak. You are Divine.

"Do you know the meaning of our mantra?"

Lilith shook her head, not daring to lose concentration. Her opponent was a trickster, no doubt. She couldn't allow herself to become the fool.

"It means, *only steel breeds glory,*" Hestîa said. "That's why we fight with these," she said as her rod connected with Lilith's ribcage.

Lilith dropped to one knee. Winded. Hestîa held up both hands, steel rod on display. Lilith seethed.

Then she struck.

Sparks flew as their rods met with a clang. Hestîa flicked her wrist and parried Lilith's blow, a modest attempt at disarming the Walabeän warrior. Hestîa chuckled as she turned to face her, and the latter did her best to feign fright.

"I know you can do better."

"How?"

Hestîa tilted her head. "Rumors reach the Isles, my dear."

Lilith struck again, only this time she repositioned her grip on her rod in an attempt to disarm Hestîa. The warrior deflected her rod and planted her fist in Lilith's gut. The crowd gasped and murmured. Lilith did her best to ignore them as she clenched her abdomen and winced dramatically, dropping to one knee.

"Oh, come on!" Hestîa said between laughs. "I barely touched you."

Lilith snickered and retreated, assuming her best—*worst*—defensive stance. She could only imagine the expression of outrage adorning her Master's face right then.

I'm sorry, Arduen.

Hestîa advanced, swinging her steel rod around and around, her shoulders stretched wide in calm disdain. She gazed down her nose at Lilith, her pale eyes glistening askance.

"You're playing me."

Lilith staggered back as Hestîa took another step toward her. Then she stumbled and fell onto her back.

The crowd erupted into cheers of triumph and gasps. They almost forced Lilith to *try*. But Hestîa didn't take the bait. Instead, she raised her chin, snorted. Then, turning her back on Lilith, she retreated.

Lilith recalled Arduen's lesson: *never take your eyes off your opponent.*

She sprang to her feet and charged. Hestîa spun around instantly, and the clash of steel met their ears yet again.

The crowd erupted as Lilith discarded her façade and truly sparred with Hestîa. The audience was riled. They must have thought their chanting would rattle her nerves, but the tumult only sharpened her focus. It only stoked her appetite for victory.

Lilith withheld nothing. Arduen's instructions echoing inside her head as she cut, parried, blocked, and slashed. The Walabeän warrior deflected every blow with ease, though sweat beaded upon her ivory brow.

Hestîa pivoted suddenly and Lilith fell forward. One moment she was slashing down at Hestîa's steel, the next she was falling to the dirt with formidable force, gasping as Hestîa knocked the rod from her grasp with one flick of her own. Lilith stared after her weapon as it rattled its way across the dirt and off the platform.

She was defenceless.

The crowd cheered and celebrated as if Hestîa had won, but the warrior did not advance to make her killing blow. Instead, she waited by the edge of the platform, expression insouciant, steel rod resting on her shoulder.

Rising to her feet with as much confidence as she could muster, Lilith's glare shot awls at Hestîa.

"Valiant effort," the warrior crooned.

"It's not over yet," Lilith grit out.

"No, it's not!"

Hestîa struck first and Lilith leapt out of the way with lithe grace. The crowd's jeers were doused as they awaited the verdict of their fate—if they didn't already know it.

Lilith proceeded to evade Hestîa's attacks, though she was growing tired quickly. She could see on her opponent's face that she was tiring as well. The Divine only needed to get on her right side, and she would be able to disarm her.

It seemed as though Hestîa knew what she was attempting, and she kept her empty hand guarded. Just when Lilith realized she might have to change her strategy, Hestîa switched hands.

"You didn't think a warrior with the accolade *Swiftdaughter* wouldn't be ambidextrous, did you?" Hestîa tutted. "Foolish girl."

Lilith bared her teeth and advanced, twisting as she did. One second, she had her back to Hestîa, and the next she was braced in her opponent's free arm. Driving her knee up to her abdomen, Lilith kicked the steel rod with brutal force. Hestîa gasped in shock as her hand was forced to release its grip. The rod rolled off the platform to join Lilith's.

Thrusting herself away from her enemy, Lilith purred, "Bet you didn't see that one coming, did you?"

Hestîa only gaped at her in return.

They stood facing one another, feet set wide apart so as not to be thrown off balance. Refusing to tear their gaze from the other, they waited.

The air grew significantly cooler as the sun threatened to plunge below the horizon. Flickers of torchlight danced across Hestîa's skin. Lilith nearly lost her focus observing the patterns. Then she flinched, provoking Hestîa to attack.

Lilith pivoted, barrelling her shoulder into Hestîa's gut. The warrior let out a guttural *oomph,* before toppling under Lilith's weight. Her head singing with the reverberations of the collision, Lilith twisted effectively and planted herself atop her opponent, pinning Hestîa to the ground.

The Walabeän grunted in frustration. She writhed beneath Lilith and wedged her legs between their bodies. Lilith recognized what Hestîa was doing, but couldn't stop her in time, so she pressed all her weight into the warrior. Their muscles trembled in tandem, exertion near, but they remained taut against one another, locked in place. Hestîa growled at Lilith, teeth gritted, and Lilith returned the glower with equal intensity.

Pressed against one another, both women struggled to secure the upper hand. Lilith backed off slightly, but only when she was positioned high enough above her opponent. She had to find a way to get Hestîa to the edge.

Hardening herself, Lilith summersaulted over Hestîa's shoulder and flipped the Walabeän over her head. Hestîa's body smacked against the dirt, dust rising around them. The crowd murmured in shock and awe.

They were treading dangerously close to the precipice now.

Grunting and seething, the two women pushed each other toward the edge. At this moment it was unclear who would emerge the victor. Lilith clenched her jaw as she pushed against Hestîa with all her strength, both women now on their haunches.

Hestîa bellowed as she thrust her body into Lilith. With the sudden force of pressure, Lilith couldn't brace herself. She lurched to the side in a desperate attempt to regain control, sending Hestîa tumbling off the edge. The crowd erupted in a near-deafening uproar before Lilith had even realized she'd won.

Lilith sat on her bottom, amazed at the outcome as Hestîa rose to her feet, her eyes resting just above the platform's lip. From the slight crinkles in their corners, the warrior appeared to be smiling.

The crowd rose to their feet, whistling and hollering. Lilith couldn't help but laugh at her current position, seated in the dirt. She was so unlike the valiant Prince Julius, standing poised like a gilded statue of an ancient hero. No, she remained victorious, on her ass, muscles trembling, covered in dirt, sweat, and debris.

Her Divine counterparts rushed to her side, each of them beaming with joy. Lilith let Arduen lift her to her feet. He was laughing as he clapped her on the shoulder and embraced her with fierce affection. Her heart swelled to see him so jubilant.

"There you have it, folks!" Marlowë's voice rose above the clangor. "It is time to celebrate the alliance."

The crowd exploded again, and Lilith hid her face in the crook of Arduen's neck.

Mission succeeded.

WALABEÄN FINERY

It was tradition, following an official match, that the loser hosts the victor as a guest in their home. So it was that Lilith and Julius accompanied their opponents, joining their families under their roofs. Lilith had the opportunity to walk one of the swinging bridges that tethered the Isles. She'd held onto the thick rope for dear life, much to Hestîa's amusement.

The isle that housed the majority of the population was cluttered by white stone homes carved out of the face of the isle itself. They rose up to the sky in the centre, redolent of a mountain peak. Hestîa explained that the wealthier and more venerable lived higher up whilst those with less to their names lived below. Houses were passed down through generations, rendering construction nearly unnecessary.

The harpies occupied an isle to themselves, where they bred and raised their young, and were trained to fight. The parents taught their young to fly without human interference.

Hestîa explained that they only stepped in once the adolescent harpies were ready to be ridden.

"Blessed Elïath, we stink terribly!" Lilith exclaimed and then laughed until she was hoarse.

Once they reached Hestîa's home, Lilith was beyond thankful to wash the grime from her skin. Releasing a long-suffering sigh, she scrubbed vigorously until her flesh was smarting.

Hestîa laid out clothes for Lilith to wear to the celebration. The garments were made of fine-woven cotton, thin enough that Lilith wondered if she would freeze before the festivities even began. Hestîa had assured her that she would be all right, the fire within the torches and the body heat would provide enough warmth.

Lilith investigated the ensemble. What she'd thought was a long flowing dress was actually a jumpsuit, the legs loose and featherlight, cuffed at her ankles like harem pants—the kind the Emperor's slaves wore. The loose, diaphanous sleeves ended in small cuffs at her wrists, a dainty belt outlined her waist, her décolletage sinfully exposed. Hestîa retrieved a pair of fur-lined slippers, her munificence extending so far as to bend a knee to place them in Lilith's feet.

Once outfitted in Walabeän finery, they sat down on the bed and Hestîa began to paint Lilith's face with foreign cosmetics.

"So… your comrade is very handsome," the warrior said as she began to paint the sensitive skin around her eyes.

Lilith flinched.

"What?" Hestîa gawped.

She shook her head, calming her piqued senses. "Nothing."

Hestîa scowled. "In the confines of my bedroom, no information may leak out to meet unwanted ears. You have my promise." The room was quiet, despite the faint howl of wind outside.

"I was just hoping," Lilith began uncertainly, "that if I do look silly, Julius would be my equal."

Hestîa paused and gripped Lilith's chin with firm fingers. "You could never look silly. You are most regal, and I am only magnifying that with these paints and brushes." She gestured to the makeup in front of her. "You will stop all men dead in their tracks tonight." Lilith flushed at the surety in her tone.

"Julius…" Hestîa said his name as though he were a myste-rious newly discovered creature, then she squealed, and Lilith jolted at the sharp noise. "You are enamoured with him!" Hestîa gasped, her pale blue irises small compared to the growing whites surrounding them. "He is beautiful," she said wistfully. "Even I found myself gazing at him as he stood poised upon the platform. The true victor." She sat back and inspected her handiwork, turning Lilith's face this way and that.

"Agónas has rarely been beaten—at least I have never witnessed anyone overpower him. Agónas was always the centre of my attention. I don't think I would have become as strong or as accomplished as I have without him, without constantly striving to please him…" Her voice trailed off. "Yet he does not look at me the way that Julius looks at you."

Lilith's heart stilled in her chest. "The way he *looks* at me?"

"Yes, I noticed what blazes in his gaze the moment it settles on you. Affection," she mused. "But something more than that, something more like *longing*."

"That can't be true," Lilith countered. "Julius is leaving us soon. He is the—"

"Crown Prince of Dalegonè," Hestîa finished.

"*Yes.*"

The warrior abandoned the makeup and began to brush Lilith's damp hair. "And you do not wish to become his queen?"

Lilith's muscles grew rigid at the mention of the title. "I was never meant to rule. It goes against my nature," she said firmly.

Hestîa spoke without inflection, as if the words bore no weight, "Ah, but you are Divine. You were recreated by the Gods to rule in one way or another. Your vision and order supersede that of any king, queen, or emperor. Might as well embrace it. Might as well be a queen."

⑥ ⑤ ～ ⋈ ⑥

ON THEIR WAY TO THE CELEBRATION, HESTÎA EXPLAINED WHY THE Colony hosted celebratory festivities in the gardens of the *Igîtís*'s manor. Not only was the warmth of the grounds maintained by the torchlight year-round, but also because it was the only larger space that wasn't clustered. The Chief's residence possessed a hall large enough to host a formidable gathering, but the Walabeäns preferred to be outside, regardless of the time of year.

Upon her arrival, a young woman placed a brass circlet atop Lilith's head, its polished metal glinting in the torchlight. A larger crown rested on the pillow next to where hers once was, indicating that Julius had yet to arrive.

Lilith observed the crowd as they sprang into activity. She found it interesting how different the Walabeäns regarded their leader, so at odds with the Emperor. How Obadïa had expected those beneath him to bow and drown him in adulation. With the Colony, it was different. Though Marlowë's people likely adored him more, they did not drop to their knees at the sight of him.

Arduen approached then. The broad width of his shoulders and his long, muscular limbs noticeable under his fitted leather suit. His eyes settled on her, his dark-golden hair tousled by the wind, framing a clean-shaven face.

Lilith shot her Master a wry smile. His Walabeän descent so clearly visible now, as he stood surrounded by his like. Bred to be a warrior before he'd been claimed by the Gods.

"You are nothing short of resplendent, my fledgling," he said to her as he gathered her into a tight embrace. Her heart warmed at his words. He was her family, now and forever.

Though resplendent was not the word she would've used to describe herself, she did feel beautiful. Hestîa had braided Lilith's hair into an intricate plait down her back. Ornate jewelled pins only added to the allure. Her makeup had been simple; her lips were painted a deep berry color, much darker than she would have chosen for herself. The long fur himation she clasped at her collar lent her its warmth—and coverage— though Hestîa had been right: the celebration alone seemed to ward off the brisk bite of the late-winter air.

"Walabeän finery suits you," Quin complimented her, appearing at Arduen's side.

Lilith dipped her chin in thanks as Quin leaned in to give her a congratulatory hug. Unable to stop her eyes as they searched the crowd for any sign of Julius, she found no trace of the prince.

Together, the Divine found their seats among the stone slab tables scattered throughout the garden. The treats set out before them beckoned, though upon second glance, Lilith didn't find that they whetted her appetite in the slightest. But at her Master's behest, she plucked what appeared to be the most harmless off the tray. Lilith coughed at the crunch and chew of it, her stomach threatening to heave its contents.

Arduen chuckled, the skin around his eyes crinkling as he handed her a mug of ale to wash it down. Tears streamed down her rosy cheeks as she tipped back the mug. Lilith chugged until her throat burned, Arduen and Quin howling with mirth all the while.

Once recovered, she inquired, "What is this one?"

Arduen gestured for her to taste it. Lilith chewed on the delicacy ever so slowly, trying with a hint of desperation not to discharge her mouth's contents onto the table.

He grinned. "It's cock's heart, stuffed with a medley of gal-fish organs… and cheese."

Lilith gagged, what remained of the treat becoming lodged in her throat. Her eyes watered as she struggled not to spew the night's libations.

When Julius finally emerged, she sagged with relief. No longer would she be bound to a table littered with detritus disguised as delicacies.

Arduen and Quin stood to greet the prince, looking more like a king with a crown upon his head. He was clad in a leather plated suit, golden embroidery indicating that it wasn't meant for fighting. His long crimson himation flowed on the gentle breeze.

Julius's eyes lit up as they settled on Lilith. "You look…" He seemed to struggle for words, bewilderment coating his usually placid features. Arduen and Quin smirked and took their seats again, granting them privacy.

"I look…?" she prodded, approaching with a confident gait.

"Beautiful," he gasped. "You look otherworldly."

Lilith giggled. "If this is the reaction I get when I wear makeup, I can only wonder what I look like back at the Frourío."

"No." He shook his head, the mound of his throat bobbing once. "You look celestial, always."

She arched a brow. "Like the stars?"

Julius recovered himself and said, "Yes, like a woman born of the stars. A woman who shines despite the darkness."

He took her bare hand and kissed the back of it, hazel eyes fixed on hers. "Care to dance?" he asked.

Lilith observed the dancers closely, their movements exotic and unfamiliar, graceful and sensuous. Suddenly feeling self-conscious, she confessed, "I don't know how to dance."

Julius tugged on her arm. "Just follow my lead." He pulled her to the dancing figures, into his undulating hips, swinging back and forth with the off-kilter melody. Lilith always had a strong aversion to dancing, as though it was unfitting of her character, like she didn't belong to any rhythm or melody.

"Relax," Julius whispered as he twirled her around.

As her body turned, she hadn't realized just how tense she was. Even the liniments that coated her skin didn't help ease the tension in her muscles. Julius's words repeated in her mind, *a woman born of the stars. A woman who shines despite the darkness,* granting her confidence, so Lilith danced with renewed vigor.

Julius didn't allow her to back away as he pulled her into him. She collided with his body, their closeness simmering her insides. Relaxing, she let him move her, his hands resting gently—respectfully—on her hips. He followed the motion of her body, his hips moving in tandem with hers, her backside pressed against him. She felt his chin rest against her crown, and she felt him press a kiss against her hair, his hands running playfully up her sides.

This was a moment she'd dreamed of her entire life, and to think she was truly living it with the Crown Prince of the great western continent. A sea had separated them, and now they shared so much more.

Lilith craned her neck, glancing up into his face, emotion threatening to break her. Had he felt the same all this time?

Julius pulled away, twisting her around simultaneously. Finding the slightest separation unbearable, she pressed her body against his, her eyes level with his throat. This close she could see the gentle throb of his pulse. So alive and virile. When she looked up at him, his eyes were glazed over. He was undeniably the most beautiful man she'd ever seen.

"I meant what I said," he whispered into her ear.

Lilith couldn't think, and she definitely couldn't speak. Catching her breath, she inched closer to him in answer, trying to communicate that she wanted more of him, but she needed him to lead. Julius chuckled dryly and leaned down into her, his lips nearly brushing hers, intent clear as the Galatëa.

You are my entire universe.

"I can't," she breathed, retreating suddenly, mortified. Lilith couldn't deign to continue, not with Jude's face flashing behind her eyelids. Not with his grandfather so close. Not with Julius's lips and hands upon her where Jude's would have been—*should* have been.

"I can't, Julius. I'm so sorry."

The prince bowed his head in reverence. "That's all right, Lilith." If her rejection hurt him, he didn't show it.

She searched the crowd for Hestîa but couldn't find her friend. "I should sit," she said curtly.

Julius led her back to their seats, his hand resting reassuringly against the small of her back. As they walked, he proceeded to converse.

"You know…" he began with a breathy laugh, the kind that told her he was uncertain of what he was about to say. Julius was rarely insecure. "We are lucky that the Walabeän fighting customs are as they are."

"Why is that?" Lilith sighed inwardly. That wasn't what she was expecting him to say.

"In Dalegonè, in order to please the Gods, we fight without our clothes."

Lilith's head snapped to face him instantly. "You fight *nude*?" she nearly yelled. His alluring smile made her stomach lurch like it had when Noala leapt off the cliff.

"Yes, to appreciate the male form. To appreciate the mortal bodies the Gods have created." His arms made a flexing gesture.

"What about the women?"

"They watch."

"But when they fight…" she probed.

Julius returned his hand to her back, the press of his palm eliciting gooseflesh. "Women don't fight in Dalegonè, at least it's not celebrated. Neither is their nudity, that is meant only for their husbands to witness and admire. As such, married women are not to attend such competitions, as it is not deemed appropriate."

"Interesting..." was all she said as they approached the table.

Arduen and Quin were locked in a heated discussion with several of the *Igítís*'s retinues, their expressions haughty and irate, but her Master remained calm as always. Arduen averted his attention from their unpleasant company and greeted Lilith and Julius, his smile a sweet slash of white against his tawny skin.

She hadn't expected the entire population of Nysía to be thrilled by the alliance. Many were not present, many were not pleased by the outcome of the combat trials, and so refused to celebrate.

Marlowë's retinues fixed their leering, unwavering glares on Lilith and Julius, and there was no warmth to be seen within. They were so different from their leader. She ignored their overt impudence.

Quin turned to her and Julius. "The other members of the *Igítís*'s court do not agree with the alliance. They cannot see how joining in the war will be lucrative to the Isles. Many decades of seclusion—reclusion—has rendered them unable to understand just how much of a threat Spiro has become... even to Nysía."

"But the Walabeäns are pious," Julius added.

"Yes, they will follow us if we desire, for we are the Gods' disciples," Arduen confirmed.

"They will follow us," Quin parroted. But the look in his eyes didn't convince Lilith.

45

THE ENEMY WITHIN

After a long day of travel, Lilith and Arduen sat by the campfire while Quin and Julius hunted dinner. They were only a few days away from the Frourío, each of them eager to get a full night's rest in their own beds.

"I didn't realize you were of Walabeän descent," Lilith said, knowing it was unlikely Arduen would elaborate on his upbringing. She studied her Master as he deliberated her statement. His eyes had grown heavy as of late, a storm-washed shade of blue.

Arduen sucked in a sharp breath. "Yes, diluted by my father's strong Augustan heritage, but I consider myself Walabeän nonetheless."

"Have you ever lived there? The Isles of Nysía?" Lilith sat up on her haunches, Skydancer curled up behind her.

"I lived there before I received news of you," he confessed. "That's how I was able to reach you so soon after your Anointment. My past is why I came for you immediately.

There was nothing that could have taken precedence, not when it comes to Aether. The gifts we can summon from within, those are the most dangerous when wielded by the juvenile."

"Thank you." Lilith took his hand in hers, savoring the warmth that emanated off his skin. "I know I didn't seem grateful then, but now that I have been enlightened... I truly am."

"Well, I hadn't expected you to fall into my arms willingly," he replied with a huff of a laugh.

◎ ⓖ ⤳ ⋔ ⚡

THE DAY AFTER THEY RETURNED TO THE FROURÍO, QUIN announced that it was time for his noviciate to graduate.

Lilith's heart plunged.

Olga and Zurí helped her prepare for the celebration, the three Divine women preening in Lilith's bedchamber. Zurí was blazing with energy now that the Frourío was full again, but Lilith struggled to exude the same jubilance. Julius's graduation only heralded his inevitable departure.

The ceremony took place on the beach. Quin dipped his noviciate into the sea as he voiced the Hymn of Divination. Whilst the Divine sang—including Felix—Lilith cursed herself for failing to memorize the verse.

After rising from the sea, Julius made his speech, thanking his Masters for all that they had done for him over the past five years. Following the ceremony, they feasted on potatoes, venison, and quail.

Lilith, having finished her meal, began to make her way to her bedchamber for the evening. Julius, who had been locked in conversation for the duration of the meal, impeded her path.

"Where are you going, my *kyría*?" *My lady.* Shivers ran down her spine at his choice of words.

"I am going for a walk along the beach," she answered, hoping he didn't catch her lie. She wanted more time with him, however it would hurt when he departed.

"May I join you?" he asked.

Lilith tilted her head and examined him dramatically. "Hmm… that depends. Do I have to call you Master?"

He howled with laughter. "Only if you want to," he said, arching a brow.

She scoffed and stepped around him. He settled in beside her, matching her pace with his long legs. Neither spoke until the sand met their boots, crunching under their soles.

"I wanted to talk to you about something," he said, his voice nearly a whisper.

She gazed at him suspiciously. "About?"

"I want you to know that I am here for you, regardless of what your brother does. If you don't want to face him—if you can't *end* it—I will step in. I don't want to see this rip you apart any longer." His tone was pleading, but Julius didn't slow his pace or alter his gait.

Lilith choked. She had formulated a loose plan to save Larkin, and if any of them stepped in to deal with him on her behalf—regardless of their good intentions—it would be folly. She would never forgive them.

Julius visibly grappled for the right words. There weren't any. "I just want you to let me in on the *ploy* you've been concocting inside your pretty little head. I need to know that it's not going to cause you to lose it."

At first, Lilith was angry that he'd failed to understand her need to do this alone. But after a moment of consideration, she quickly realized that he couldn't understand. He had no siblings, and his parents were alive and well.

"Thank you, Julius. I appreciate it, I really do. And I will accept all the support I can get, but…" She paused, bit her lip, carefully selecting her words. "I truly believe that I need to be the one who does this. I need to set my brother free. I won't be able to live with myself if I don't do this for him."

Julius grasped her hand gently, his thumb stroking circles on the back of it. "I understand. Just know that he will kill you without remorse, if that is what Spiro orders." His hand clenched around hers. "I won't let that happen. If I have to step in, I swear to all the Gods, I will. Even if it takes you one hundred years to forgive me. Longer. Your survival is more important."

Lilith only nodded her comprehension. If it came to that, if her plan failed her and she was at Larkin's mercy, she prayed that it wouldn't be Julius who stepped in.

Deliberately changing topic, she asked, "Will you be leaving us?"

"I am the Crown Prince of Dalegonè," he said on a sigh. "The moment will come someday soon, and I will have to go to my people. With them is where I belong."

She ignored the pang in her chest. "Yes, I assumed as much." Her voice was a deceptive croon, faked confidence to conceal the fear that lingered beneath. It flickered to life like a flame at his words. Fear that she may lose another friend, a person she'd come to rely on, to love and need in such an irreplaceable way. Talk of his impending departure only whetted her feelings for the prince, her muddled emotions intensifying.

"Lilith…" He stopped her, his large calloused hand coming to rest on her cheek.

She closed her eyes, unable to meet his gaze, the intensity she found therein. Had he sensed her disappointment? Had he suspected her feelings?

"I don't want to leave you," he said mournfully. "And I won't be going anywhere while Spiro is still a threat to us. Especially when he has your brother under his command. That renders you vulnerable to him, and I will be buried in the ground before I allow Spiro to come anywhere near you."

Lilith gawped at the grave undertone in his words, the aggression that swathed his timbre.

"I don't want to lose anyone else right now…" she whispered, placing her hand on his, still cupping her cheek.

"You won't be losing me any time soon, I promise." He pulled her into his body, and she wrapped her arms around his ribcage, pressing her face into his chest. He kissed her temple, the action more intimate than any mouth-to-mouth touch.

Julius repeated, his breath a gentle caress on her skin, "I promise."

THE BROAD LIMBS OF THE OAKS GROANED IN THE WIND. *THEIR sough an eerie dirge, their trunks denser than Lilith remembered them, rotten with age and decay.*

A cry of terror rent the night as she forced her way through the forest, but fear didn't grip at her mind, her soul. The cry did not belong to her.

The snapping of branches alerted her to shadows in the near distance. Lilith darted after them, Constance in hand.

"Larkin!" she called. "Where are you?"

There was no answer, only the howl of wind and the rustle of leaves.

Lilith dropped to her knees, sobs escaped her chapped lips, her breath visible in the chill night air. "Larkin…" she whimpered.

"I'm right here, dear Sister."

Jerked to attention, she glanced up, but she found the clearing vacant. "Where?" she demanded, her voice hoarse from screaming.

How long had she been searching for him? How long had he been evading her? Did he even want to come home?

"Where are you?" she cried.

"Down here, my silly sister."

Lilith peered down to find Larkin pinned beneath her.

"You found me," he said, a smile of elation spreading across his lips, revealing his teeth. They were different than she remembered, sharpened to points.

"Why?"

"I could ask you the same question," he said smugly, his lips curling back, exposing elongated cuspids.

She watched in horror as her hand came into view. Clasped in it was Constance.

"Do it. I know you have been pining for this moment," he snarled.

Lilith's chest heaved as she gasped for air, the blade of her beloved sword dropping closer and closer to her brother's exposed throat, his skin pale, raw, untouched.

"Now we know who the real enemy is!" Larkin barked as the blade dug deep into his neck. Black blood sprayed from the wound. He didn't flinch, his face betrayed no sign of pain.

No sign of fear.

No sign of death.

Larkin only laughed at her.

Then Lilith felt it, the pleasure in the kill. She stared down at her brother, wide-eyed and disbelieving, as he said, "The enemy is within you."

46

SHE MUST BE THE ONE

Training had taken on a whole new meaning. Gone were the books and the relaxed lessons in the study. It was essential that Lilith learned how to hold her own on a battlefield. Arduen was desperate to ensure that she was equipped should Spiro target her. She'd been doubly blessed, and for that reason alone her Masters bore down on her.

Lilith did everything that had been asked of her. She trained with Arduen in the mornings, exploring more ways to wield Aether, how to use the element effectively while conserving as much of it as possible. He'd said, "It may come down to who becomes depleted first… do not let it be you."

They had trained until she couldn't summon even a flicker of Constantine's abyss. Until her hands burned incessantly and the Oracle dipped them in milk to soothe the burns. Olga didn't heal her wounds as the pain was necessary, and the wounds were self/inflicted. Whatever that meant.

Zurí's lessons were thankfully not as taxing. She would order Lilith to pull the Water from the earth in small areas. When the muddy liquid floated in the air, as high as Zurí commanded, her task was then to return it to the soil.

"Exactly, Lilith. You are doing well. I want you to practice this; it will be the same for siphoning Water from bodies."

Zurí then ordered Lilith to return to her bedchamber to rest before dinner. She'd lectured, "Pray, rest, recover. Do whatever you need to. We have been pushing you to the extreme, and part of getting stronger is recovery."

◎ ᗧ ⟿ ℳ ◊

WEEKS PASSED SINCE THE DIVINE RETURNED FROM THE ISLES OF Nysía and life resumed its usual routine. Arduen, Zurí and Julius consumed most of her time, but Lilith still fought for solitude. She needed to parse through her research on the Blood Oath. Her findings had been paltry, but she refused to relinquish hope. Larkin deserved better than that, after all.

Lilith lounged in bed, nestled under the heavy quilt, contemplating all that had happened that day. Her notes had proven futile. Every text and tome pointed to absurd and ludicrous remedies to the Blood Oath. None of which she would be able to perform on Larkin in battle. And Gods only knew Arduen wouldn't capture Larkin. Her Master would drive his sword through her brother's chest before risking his entry into the Frourío.

There was one tome in the study she hadn't explored. One tome dedicated to the world of magic. An Enchantress's grimoire. Though Lilith did not possess the Mark, if the cure was hidden in those pages, she wanted to know. And so she abandoned her bed and crept into the hall. She would exhaust all possibilities. Larkin would have stopped at nothing to save her.

As she approached the study, she noticed the door was left ajar. Dim candlelight filtered through the crack, and low voices could be heard from within. If she had company, they would likely try to dissuade her from her research. It would be nearly impossible to attempt. It had been difficult enough sneaking away in the middle of the night.

Lilith paused outside the door.

It was Wren, frustration seeping into his voice. "You cannot coddle her, Arduen. I know your fears, believe me, I do. But you cannot allow it to stifle her growth, it will only hinder her when battle comes."

"I know." Her hairs stood on end at the recognition of her Master's voice. "I just can't bear to see her like this. She's lost too much already, at such a tender age." He sounded flustered.

Had Arduen told them that she demanded to be the one to face Larkin when he came for her? Was he going to deny her that right with the intention of protecting her? Lilith leaned against the door.

"She's eighteen, Arduen." *Quin*. He always spoke reason.

"Young enough to be too young. Yet old enough to feel the full brunt of the pain… to truly understand it." Arduen was indeed troubled.

Lilith caught her breath. She wanted to run to him, to explain why she needed to do this. Why he needed to let her.

Wren's voice rose above the others. "But you cannot protect her from this, she has to face it. She has to do this on her own, Arduen, and you must stand back and let her." He was right.

"Since when have you become the man to condone a female to fight? Especially a noviciate." Arduen's tone was scalding, his voice rising, quickening Lilith's pulse.

"Wren's right," Quin murmured. "Lilith must do this. She must be the one who slays the minion. It is her right. I believe that the death will be a mercy, it will be a setting free for both him and her."

She stiffened. *She must be the one who slays the minion.*

Arduen remained silent.

Wren cut in, "You can stand by her during it all. And you can stand with her after, when the reality of the situation settles within her and she is daunted by the task of moving on. That is when you will be needed, only when she is mourning."

Mourning. Her heart plummeted, her mouth suddenly arid and pasty.

"My only regret regarding Cordova was denying her the right to take arms against Spiro," said Wren. "To defend what and who she loved. I favored her mental instruction over the physical and look where she is? I've got no bloody grave to mourn her by. She's gone entirely. Because I failed her. Clever she may have been, but young and callow, too. It was because of her inexperience that she is no longer with us, and her inexperience was a direct result of my overbearing protection."

Wren's gravelly timbre softened. "Do not make the same mistake, Arduen. You will regret it until your Star burns out."

Silence.

"For that is our purpose as their Master." Quin's voice was powerful yet gentle. "We must bear the light that guides them through the dark. We must show them the way that they cannot distinguish on their own. And when it is our turn to ascend the steps into Elysium, it is they who will light the way for us and light our Star in the skies."

"And that Star will continue to guide them, long after we have departed the terrestrial realm," Wren added sombrely.

"This may be the most difficult task I have ever been confronted with," Arduen grumbled, his voice barely audible.

"So be it. I know you love the girl enough to accomplish it."

Lilith leaned in closer, ears to the wood of the door. This conversation wasn't meant for her, but she couldn't resist the lure.

"Aye, Brother. You will face a far greater task of dealing with the consequences if you don't."

"So I am to let her do this?" Arduen's voice rose to a desperate volume. Lilith hoped she could get away before one of them stormed out. "And then what?" he pressed.

"You connect with her," Quin drawled. "You tear down those mighty walls that you've built up over the years and you confide in her all that you've endured, all that you have lost. Find that connection, strengthen that bond, and *never let it go!*"

Lilith gasped.

As much as she prodded Arduen for answers, for details of his past, he had rarely surrendered that part of himself to her. He'd held her when she told him of her parents' deaths, of how it wrecked her completely. But he hadn't given her everything.

Arduen countered, "She is not the scion of Constantine! She can die at any moment. Replaced the next."

Quin shouted, "You cannot protect her from every adversary! She is Divine now, a Divine twice blessed will amass many enemies in their lifetime. Let her acquire a taste of what it's like face them now. She is not your ward, Brother. You cannot stop her."

"She is more than that, Quintus. She is family!" Arduen's voice rose above the others. "We may spend a thousand years together. Longer. I know you don't regard Julius as any less than your own son. How dare you dismiss Lilith like she is *dispensable!*"

She sighed with relief as her Master's words registered in her mind. She considered him family too, as she would for the rest of her life.

"I didn't dismiss her," Quin objected.

Wren aided Quin in placating Arduen. "We are only trying to lighten your burden, ease your mind."

"You cannot. Not until this boy is buried in the ground and Lilith is free, you cannot. Not until Spiro is punished for all that he has taken—"

What had Spiro taken from Arduen? *Livë. Judeaus. Art.*

The room grew silent, and alarm shot through her as the door creaked open and Wren emerged, unnerved.

Lilith's eyes grew wide as his gaze settled on her. He shut the door behind him and ushered her down the stairs, neither Divine uttering a word.

⊙ ☉ ⌇ ⋔ ◊

THE SKY WAS WASHED VERMILLION AS THE SUN SET IN THE WEST. Lilith wondered what the sunset looked like in Utica. She'd returned to her bedchamber, her mind reeling from the conversation she'd overheard—or eavesdropped. Wren hadn't said a word as he led her to her own room, his footsteps rushed. All he'd given her was a knowing look and an encouraging pat on the shoulder.

Lilith trained her mind on the matter of saving Larkin. Her attention now on her plan to save him, she thought back to the battlefield, back to the moment she first saw him since Utica… and the last.

Her brother's warped voice resounded through her skull. *I look forward to when next we meet, little Sister.*

Lilith dropped her head into her hands. *Would that I could, Brother.*

Clasping Constance's scabbard to her belt, she descended the stairs, her fingers making fast work plaiting back her hair. Julius had been outside since dinner ended, working on his swordsmanship—not that there was much room for improvement. But if there was anything that was certain to get her mind out of such a gloomy state, it was sparring with a very sweaty, handsome prince.

Assuming her best defensive stance, Julius attacked first, and she let him. The twang of steel on steel was all that could be heard in the night, save for the odd hoot of an owl. He grimaced as he cut down, then up, then down again. She blocked every blow, though the force of his cuts threatened to wear down her muscles. Light and slow for him was still hard and fast for her.

Lilith receded two steps, putting enough distance between them for Julius to halt. They panted for air, glaring at one another.

"Are you all right?" Julius asked between gasps, his expression softening from warrior to friend.

"You shouldn't be asking your enemy those kinds of questions," she quipped, and before he had enough time to digest her words, she attacked.

Julius reacted instantly, blocking and parrying every blow. She swung her body around, twisting away from him, then sliced back toward him. He evaded every attack as if he could read her mind, as if he knew exactly what she had intended before she even conceived it herself.

He stopped and signalled for her to do so as well. "If you plan on dealing with the matter concerning your brother by yourself, then I insist you allow me to verify that you're prepared."

Lilith straightened, stance abandoned. "You don't think I am prepared?"

"Do not grunt or grit your teeth before you take the offensive, you are giving away your intentions."

"What do you suggest I do?"

He gave a closed-lip grin. "Become more aware of your pretty little face. It's just as much a weapon as the sword in your hand."

Lilith gasped as a smirk lit up the elegant planes of his face. "Yes, Master," she crooned playfully.

They took up position again just as a horn sounded throughout the clearing, its tone deep and rolling. Lilith and Julius locked eyes immediately, and confusion transformed into panic when she beheld the alarm in his.

Julius scanned the surrounding trees at once, sheathing his sword. "The Horn of Cornucopia…" he nearly whispered, his expression one of pure shock. "Come with me, now!"

She obliged and let him take her hand. Together they sprinted for the Frourío, Julius casting frequent glances back at the pines, inspecting the Megálos for any signs of danger. It didn't appear that they had any unwanted visitors. *Yet.*

Hearts racing, they reached the front door. Ambrose swung it open as they approached.

"Thank the Gods," he said breathlessly.

"What's happened?" Julius demanded.

"Olga has received a premonition. A legion of Spiro's beasts are headed this way. They will attempt to lay siege to the Frourío." Ambrose's eyes were lit with rage, but his tone remained calm.

Lilith's blood ran cold, her hand still clasped in Julius's. He noticed and pulled her inside, but the warmth did nothing to soothe her. Spiro was coming for her home, her family, and he would wield her only living kin to do it.

"Listen to me," Julius said, spinning her to face him. Dark locks fell like a curtain over his eyes. Through the curls, she met his gaze.

"We will be fine," he said. "These grounds are warded against unwanted visitors. They cannot touch us here."

Her trembling only intensified as Arduen and the others emerged from the armory beneath the Frourío, her Master's eyes fixated on her.

Julius didn't release her as he whispered into her ear, "I am with you. We will do this together." He relinquished her then and marched up the stairs to prepare.

"Lilith!" It was Zurí who approached her first. "Go and get yourself ready. We have some time, thank Kyril. Plated fighting leathers. Your bow. Full quiver."

"We will need spears," Arduen said to Ambrose. "Bring as many as we have. Glaives as well."

"Our largest shields," Quin added, his voice hoarse.

"Now, Lilith!" Zurí ordered.

Lilith stood frozen, transfixed on the scene before her. Arduen rushed to her side, waving Zurí off, a dismissal from the first Master to the second. Zurí stepped back, arms crossing over her full chest.

"You will be fine," said Arduen. "We are guarded well here. We have time to prepare. I will round up proper weaponry for you, but you need to compose yourself. You have fought before; you will fight again."

Lilith couldn't summon more than an incoherent moan in response. The anxiety was debilitating. How was she going to fight like this? How was she going to save Larkin if she couldn't organize her thoughts?

Arduen nodded once, patting her shoulder, then turned away. He rushed down to the armory, to the cache of weapons stored beneath the Frourío. Lilith watched in petrified horror until Zurí grasped her by the shoulders and shook her violently.

"Go and don your plated suit, *now*!"

Lilith leapt for the stairs, taking two at a time, her breathing ragged. They had time, she reminded herself, yet she couldn't quell the panic that surged within. Her muscles were numb, and she stubbed her toe on several steps, grimacing from the pain that lanced through her legs. Good. So she wasn't *that* numb.

She hastily donned her gear as Zurí instructed; leather plated suit, bow and quiver across her back, Constance at her hip.

Evös sat perched on her windowsill. The eagle squawked at her as she worked. The animal could likely sense her anxiety, the thrumming energy within the entire tower. Lilith patted her feathered head with the tip of her finger—careful to avoid her chest—then she gathered her weapons.

The door moaned as it opened, and Arduen entered. "How are you faring?"

"Fine," she managed.

He grimaced, seating himself on the edge of her bed. He patted the empty space beside him, and Lilith sat, every muscle in her body rigid.

"Lilith," he began, "Know that I will step—"

"No." She cut him off.

In his eyes, realization flared to life. He knew it was too late to deter her. Larkin was hers to deal with.

To pacify the growing unease, Lilith took his hand, her fingers scraping against the worn calluses on his palm.

"When I was a little girl," she said softly, "I'd often pester my parents with questions about Elysium and the Gods. Questions that no mortal could ever answer. I used to ask my father if we get what we deserve when we meet the Gods." She licked at her lips, gulped down air. "I hope he was right when he said we do."

She turned her searing gaze on Arduen. "I hope Spiro pays for every ounce of suffering he's inflicted. I hope he burns in Hades for all that he's taken from us."

47

ISIDORE'S WIND

After nearly an hour of sorting through weaponry, the Divine of the Frourío were prepared for the attack. Arduen shouted the orders, and they were obeyed without question. Her Master was to be Philías with Quin, as they would protect the eastern border of the Frourío grounds. Julius had requested to be Lilith's Philías, which was only acceptable because he was now a Master Divine. Zurí and Olga were Philías, and Felix was with Wren. Being his first battle, this was meant to be a lesson of sorts.

Lilith turned to Arduen. "How will I know where the line of demarcation is?"

Her Master didn't remove his gaze from the trees to the south, where the beasts would emerge at any moment. "The border is where the beasts stop."

They formed a single phalanx in front of the Frourío. The night was strangely quiet, and Lilith chewed on the inside of her cheeks until they bled.

"Stop that," Julius snapped, nudging her.

She flinched at the harshness in his tone, at how vast the prince's mien altered in battle. "Yes, *Master*," she droned sardonically.

For a long while, the Divine of the Frourío stood before the line of trees, the pines towering high above them. The stars had finally appeared in the night sky. The Guiding Stars shone the brightest: Andromeda, Star of the North; Dracoladen, Star of the East; Cepheus, Star of the West; and Amalthea, Star of the South.

Lilith's mother possessed an affinity for the Southern Star. Lynne Oak had prayed and swore by it all her life. Her mother used to gaze up at the golden star, reciting stories of magical beings.

Lilith prayed to Constantine that her mother wasn't watching from Elysium tonight. And she prayed, too, that she would forgive her son, for this was not the man she'd raised.

The moon was full, illuminating the would-be battle-ground. No one spoke as they listened in silence for the telltale signs that the beasts had arrived.

"Shields up!" Arduen ordered.

In unison, the Divine raised the thick sheets of metal, forming one large shield. Lilith wasn't armed with one of her own, so she crept closer to her Philías. Julius stepped to the side to accommodate her, his warmth calming her trembling muscles.

"Are you all right?" he murmured in her ear.

"For now."

No one so much as twitched as the beasts' marching became audible. Spiro's army didn't thrash their way through the Megálos in unified chaos as Lilith had expected, but they marched slowly as one cohesive unit. When they finally reached the border, the beasts screeched as they hit the protective ward, and the monsters stopped dead along the borderline.

Upon their arrival, Lilith reached out with Discernment, feeling the primitive minds of the beasts before her. No sign of Larkin or his comrade. There was nothing human amongst enemy lines.

Blood sluiced through her veins as she observed their enemies. They were vastly outnumbered. If not for the ward that separated them, they would be monster meat.

"We stay within the border!" Arduen bellowed, his eyes lingering on Lilith a moment longer than the rest. "Use your spears. Use your swords. Do not forget to shield yourselves, for they have arrows. If anyone leaves the protection of the ward, there will be consequences."

Dread crept through her then. This seemed like an impossible feat. They could never win. Then Olga began the Hymn of Divination and the rest of the Divine lent their voice to hers —including Lilith.

Spears in hand, the Divine stepped forward once, twice. The beasts snickered, chittering various foreign noises that they couldn't interpret. Were they laughing? Lilith's eyes narrowed with loathing and disgust.

An incomprehensible order sounded through the battalion of beasts and they raised their bows in response.

Lilith jolted but Julius held her firm. "We will be fine," he assured. "You need to stay with me, behind my shield." His breath stirred the stray hairs by her ear. She pressed into him again and watched as her spear wavered in the air before her, and she wondered if the others noticed. Even Felix seemed confident, eager for bloodshed.

Twangs broke the silence as the beasts released a volley of arrows. Lilith glanced up. The shafts could have blotted out the sky, had it been day. She could only hear the arrows slice through the air as she waited for them to bounce off the ward, but the ward didn't halt their descent.

Arduen cried out in warning, and as one, the Divine raised their shields over their heads, their formation nearly impenetrable. Arrows rained down upon them. There was only one cry of pain as the arrows struck the shields and sunk into the ground around them. Lilith glanced over in panic. Felix's calf had been pierced. Studying the faces of her fellow Divine, she recognized true horror spread over them.

"Spiro must have an Enchantress aiding him. Only a very complicated spell could break through these wards." Olga spoke as if someone else—someone *otherworldly*—spoke through her.

"Can they get through?" Lilith asked, trying her best to maintain her composure as Wren ushered his noviciate inside, Ambrose following them with his shield raised. The Oracle wouldn't have the energy to heal Felix now, and there was a possibility that this was going to get messier than they'd anticipated.

"No, otherwise they wouldn't be stopped where they are. Only the most powerful Enchantress could cast a spell to allow our enemies in. But arrows… that's not as complicated." Olga never took her unfaltering gaze off the enemy line.

Arduen's brow furrowed. The front line of beasts already nocking the second volley of arrows. "We have to use our gifts. It may deplete us wholly, but we have no other choice.

We're far too outnumbered." He glanced over at his comrades. His cadre. "You know what to do. Do not leave the protection of the ward!" His order was final as they broke apart, the beasts firing their arrows at last.

Lilith clung to Julius's side like a leech, and he held her firm as the arrows rained down upon them, bouncing off the shield above them. As Julius protected their heads, Lilith used a sheet of Aether to protect their legs.

The prince led her westward, Zurí and Olga close behind. Everyone seemed to sigh with relief as the last of the arrows struck and no one cried out. Lilith nocked an arrow and fired. A second passed following the twang of her bow, and a beast roared.

"We have plenty more where that came from," snickered a beast, sauntering to the border, no more than ten feet away. His olive hide was dry and patchy, scaled like Lilith had imagined a lizard. His eyes were entirely onyx, like a daemon of Hades.

"I will shoot you from here, while my friends shoot from above. You have only one shield, you can do the math," it sneered.

Lilith scowled at the beast, but Julius spoke first, "We are *Divine*, don't you forget!"

The beast's breaths came in heavy pants like… *laughter*—he was laughing at them. "I have yet to see any part of you that is Divine, unless you wish to remove your pants." The wheezing laughter came again, and Lilith realized the beast was female. Her face heated as she took in Julius and the death stare that beset his features at the bawdy jest.

A flash of light blinded her, and Lilith fell to the ground with a shriek. When the darkness returned, the beast was nothing more than ash circling on the breeze. She gaped at what remained of the monster.

"Up," Julius demanded, keeping his eyes locked on the Forest as more monsters approached, staring down upon their fallen comrade, expressions inscrutable. She grappled for her bow and rose to stand beside her Philías.

"I have a lot more where that came from," Julius growled, cinders swirling around him like fireflies. He sent another torrent of Fire at their enemies.

"That's it, Julius," Zurí commended through desperate pants. The beasts that lingered near her only collapsed, hands or paws clutching at their throats, a horrifying death lasting about a minute. Zurí was drowning the beasts with the Galatëa Sea. Drawing tendrils of Water and forcing them down their throats, soaking into their skin, filling their lungs. What an awful way to go.

A savage grin spread across Lilith's face. If battle demanded a sadist of her, then that's what she'd become.

She sprang forth from the prince's side. He opened his mouth to protest but Zurí held up her hand to stop him. "She knows what she's doing," she reprimanded.

Julius only dipped his chin and continued to blast Xander's Fire through the trees, careful not to hit his comrades.

With a shield of Constantine's abyss protecting her, Lilith shot Aether-limned arrows into the army of beasts, the dead piling up along the border to outline the ward.

Suddenly the holy trees of the Megálos turned eerie. Odious. The mutilated bodies of the beasts mounted up, but not one Divine yielded, not one Divine slowed their stabbing and jabbing as the monsters approached. And as the battle waged further, orders from Arduen and Quin became convoluted.

Abandoning her spear and bow, Lilith blasted Aether into the throng of beasts, pushing her body to its limit.

Wren had appeared for a moment, as if to observe her for weakness, and when he found none, he returned to the fore-front. Arduen had likely sent him. Since they'd Discerned no Divine amongst their enemies, she doubted she would see her Master again until the battle's cessation.

Lilith and Julius forged onward, protecting each other when necessary. It wasn't long before she became lost in the chaos, lost in her death dance.

The beasts were running rampant through the trees now, their war cries bone-chilling. They'd broken formation, run out of arrows. Lilith watched them, only looking back when Julius or Zurí cursed. She shook the worry from her mind as more beasts climbed over their fallen brethren. Julius burnt as many bodies as he could, but Lilith began to worry he would deplete himself too soon.

A gust tore through the night, so powerful that it knocked Lilith to the ground, tearing her bow out of her grip. She cried out in pain as her muscles tensed under the impact, and she watched in horror as her bow drifted away.

A Divine is present.

Lilith's heart stilled, and when she looked up, vision blurred, she could see Julius, Zurí and Olga on the ground, too. Another forceful draft rent through the space, clearing the bodies and ashes.

Clearing a path, she realized with horror.

She gazed over at her friends, their faces blanched. She

searched the Frourío grounds for the others. Where was Arduen?

A choked sob escaped her lips as Larkin emerged, halting before the borderline, the beasts clearing the way for him.

The Wind forced Lilith's face into the muck. What had Spiro done to transform her pacific brother into a warrior of such ruthless calibre? The thought frightened her stiff.

Larkin watched her keenly. She was equally aware of his every motion. Of every breath he drew. The path to him lay unimpeded, as if the beasts had been instructed to stay away from her, as if she were *reserved* for him.

A familiar scent drifted on the Wind. *Home.* The family forge, fresh soil and iron, roasted quail, Mah's *fassolatha.* But this scent had been tainted.

When his voice did meet her ears, a shudder rippled through her body. This man was not her brother. If Spiro ordered him to kill her, he would not hesitate. He would not show her mercy.

As havoc was released upon the Megálos, Lilith's limp body slid across the charred ground, against her volition, obliterating any sense of confidence she had.

"Stop!" she screeched.

The forceful Wind ceased instantly, and when she glanced up from the earth to meet her brother's gaze, he only stared at her expectantly.

"I will come out," she conceded.

Larkin arched a brow, his dark hair strewn across his face in the night breeze. "So brave of you," he mused, the arrogance so unlike him. "My beasts will refrain from touching you. So long as you cooperate."

"*Your* beasts?"

"Well… this particular battalion is under my command. So, yes, *my* beasts." He slapped a gloved hand to his armored chest with evident pride.

"Stay here, Lilith. That is an *order!*" Julius roared.

Despite the Wind that fettered him to the ground, Julius managed to rise to his knees. Lilith nearly sobbed at the sight of the Crown Prince kneeling. It aroused in her a primal need to protect, to defend.

"Please, Lil," Julius begged, the sound of her name on his lips almost convincing her to stay. "Don't do this," he pleaded. "He cannot be trusted. He is *not* your brother."

Larkin scoffed and waved his hand, the flick of his wrist sending Julius crashing into the ground with a bone-crunching thud. With his yelp tattooed in her mind, Lilith wanted nothing more than to rush to her Philías's side. But even the most asinine warrior could see that they were all at Larkin's mercy. If they even dared to attack, the recoil could destroy them all.

So Lilith looked Julius square in the eyes and said, "I am the only one he won't kill." She sucked in a deep breath, gathered her bearings. "I will call for you if I need your help."

And with that, she turned away and stepped over the borderline.

48

DO NOT FORSAKE ME

"My sweet Lilith," her brother trilled as she stepped free of the protective ward. "I have been *itching* to see you again."

Lilith didn't elicit a response. She couldn't. Both pain and zeal warred within her. She was aware of Julius and Zurí's watchful gazes planted on her back. But where was Arduen?

Larkin didn't move, he only glared at her with preternatural stillness. He was so close, yet so distant.

"I have come for you," he said.

"I didn't want you to." Her voice was faint, a near-whisper. She knew he could read her lips, just as he had many nights in their childhood, or in the smithy when the roar of the forge and the clang of the hammer drowned out their voices.

"Do you know what it cost me to return to my Master empty-handed?" Larkin glowered at her.

She shook her head. She could only imagine Spiro's cruelty.

"I paid heavily for it, and I can't allow it to happen again. There will be no mercy this time, Sister. You will come home with me." He stomped his foot on the ground, armor clinking with the movement.

She steeled her spine. "I am home."

A dark scowl distorted his features. "*I* am your family. *I* am where your home lies. Do not forsake me, sister. You will come to regret it." A stark threat.

Lilith lifted her chin, staring him down, fists clenched at her sides. "I know you're in there, Larkin." She spoke his name slowly, as if hearing it from her lips could awaken him, wash clean Spiro's bloody grip. "This isn't who you are. You are not Spiro. You are Larkin Oak."

When his face remained impassive, she moaned, "Larkin…"

Julius's voice cut through her like a shard of ice. "Lilith, he swore the Blood Oath. He is gone!"

She winced. *He is gone.*

"I'm right here, sweet Lilith," Larkin said aridly, his voice a lure. "Come with me. You can be with me again. Together we can serve a vision far greater than either of us could ever anticipate. All those stories we were told as children, they are real, and now we are creating new ones."

"Spiro's vision was born of *Philautia*. It is one of self-righteousness and glory for himself. Not for the Gods. You're nothing more than a tool for him." Lilith nearly shouted, her heartbeat thundering in her ears.

Larkin glared at her. "Do not insult my *Master*." Had he come to regard Spiro as a father, as she had Arduen? Panic welled within her. If that was the case, she wouldn't be able to convince him that Spiro was his enemy.

"He is not your Master," she said. "He doesn't care for you. Not in the way a Master should."

Screeches rent the night as Xander's Fire spread over the army of beasts, devouring them whole, avoiding Lilith entirely.

"Oh, no..." Larkin snickered, eyes narrowing on the spectacle behind her.

Lilith whirled. Julius stood outside of the protective ward. He'd killed many of the monsters that surrounded her and Larkin, but one great beast stood before him now, challenging him.

Exhaustion visibly gripped Julius. He was evidently depleted as he swung his sword, over and over, never hitting his mark. The beast was strong and agile, dodging every attack with accuracy. The monster roared and slashed down at the prince, gouging his shoulder with its talon.

Julius bellowed in pain and stumbled, dropping to one knee. Lilith watched in horror as blood spilled from the gash. She cried out for her friend. She couldn't lose him like this, not when it would be her fault.

The beast bared its fangs as Julius fumbled for his fallen sword, his fighting arm hanging limp at his side. Just when his trembling hand wrapped around the hilt of Orphëus, the monster raised its massive arm into the air, preparing for the killing blow.

Lilith screamed at Julius, beseeched him to flee. But he wouldn't listen.

As the beast lowered its mighty talons with fatal speed, Julius hoisted his sword up into the beast's armpit with lethal precision. Its agonizing howl sent shivers raking down Lilith's spine. The beast toppled to the ground, shaking the earth with its weight.

Larkin shook his head and clucked his tongue. "Shame he had to graduate. Spiro could have used him, too."

"What do you mean?" she asked, turning back to him.

"The Blood Oath is not as effective on Master Divine as it is on noviciates." Larkin tilted his head, his eyes inspecting Julius as he struggled to stand. "Let's see how strong he really is, shall we?"

Larkin's laugh was one born of malicious intent. It rumbled in his throat as Isidore's Wind coaxed Julius toward them. His knees ground against the earth, leaving two bloody trails in his wake.

"Larkin, stop!" Lilith screamed, but he ignored her desperate command.

The instinct to protect surged within her, and by the time Julius had nearly reached her, she summoned a shield of Aether to surround him. The prince looked up at her with gratitude. She averted her gaze immediately, his ashen face enough to break her. This was the riskiest thing she'd ever done, and she struggled to keep Aether controlled under the sway of Larkin's power.

Studying her brother, Lilith tapered her gaze on him. He was not Larkin Oak. He was only the physical aspect of him, but her brother was gone. This was a wraith. It was an insult to use his body against his will. Lilith spat on the ground with revulsion.

"Impressive," Larkin lilted. "I would like to see more." He shot a harrowing gust in her direction—in *their* direction.

Lilith—aware of Julius's presence at her side, still on his knees—raised her hands and shielded them from the onslaught. She frowned at Larkin from behind the dark sheet of Aether. If she was going to follow through with her plan to save her brother, she couldn't use Constantine's element. It was too dangerous. These gifts were meant to be used together, not against each other. But she had the advantage: Larkin wanted her alive, he wouldn't kill her.

"We cannot stand like this all night, *Sister*," Larkin drawled. "You will exhaust yourself."

"I only want to talk." Her tone was pleading, convincing enough that Larkin released his assault. The howling Wind quieted, and she relinquished her hold on Aether, though she kept Julius shielded.

"You cannot sway me. I have one Master." Larkin's chin lifted indignantly.

"I don't believe you."

From the corner of her eye, Julius sagged with disappointment. "Lilith…" he groaned, his voice gruff, strained.

"Then let's do this the old way." Larkin gave an insouciant shrug of his broad shoulders, metal spaulders clinking. "Let's spar. Winner dictates the outcome."

Lilith crossed her arms defiantly. "No vague rules. Let's outline the conditions thoroughly."

"Fine."

The battlefield had grown still. Every beast that remained was focused on her and her brother, their fallen brethren smoke and ash at their feet. Zurí stood behind the boundary, silently killing from behind her shield. Lilith could sense the other Divine watching, and she forced the thought of them from her mind as her brother approached.

"If I win," he began, "I take you back with me."

Lilith gulped. She had no idea what to expect of Larkin's

swordsmanship. "And if I win," she countered, willing her voice steady, "you don't go back."

He sniggered arrogantly. "Deal."

They took up position. Lilith ordered Julius to return to Zurí, which he thankfully obeyed, though he could barely walk. She refused to allow herself to glance at him, for if her eyes lingered there too long, she would balk, and her heart would be in fissures.

Larkin stood before her, scimitar clasped in hand. She recognized then, as he revealed his second blade, that she had two problems; Larkin was wielding *two* swords. She cursed herself, not bothering to conceal her regret, and he beamed triumphantly.

For a long moment, neither Oak sibling moved, only muscles twitched under tension. Se had defeated the most dexterous female warrior the Walabeän Colony could offer up. She'd taken down Hestîa Swiftdaughter unarmed. There was no doubt in her mind that she could best Larkin with one sword—with their mother's blade. She only needed to focus, forget all else, and *concentrate*.

"You should be more careful when you make bargains with your superiors," Larkin chided, swinging that second blade tauntingly.

Lilith waited until she heard Julius reach Zurí, then she snarled at her brother, "Get on with it!"

Without hesitation, Larkin pounced, swinging both blades furiously. Lilith parried and blocked, deflecting both blades with Constance, grunting from the speed and force it required of her. His maneuvers were executed with precision and unnatural strength, she couldn't hold out for long.

Pivoting and twisting her body, Lilith caught Larkin off

guard. She wedged Constance under his scim, and with a jerk of her wrist, sent it flying. It clattered away, monsters shifting to make way for it. A cloud of dust wafted toward the sky as it landed.

Not dust—*ashes.*

Larkin grimaced. "You've improved."

Lilith flashed him a bright smile in response. They were equal now.

She anchored her feet again, readying herself for the next blow. Larkin charged with a roar that his beasts echoed, their thunderous bellows near-deafening. Lilith's teeth clattered as their swords met. Her arms barked in pain, but she pushed onward. She would be stiff tomorrow, but she would wake up at the Frourío, she promised herself that much.

"Your Master has convinced you that my fealty to Spiro has *debased* me," Larkin growled. They were inches apart, their swords shaking against each other.

"Spiro is insidious," Lilith protested. "Any contact with him is contaminating."

Larkin's hysterical laughter boomed, and the beasts snickered and hissed at her. She ignored them as her brother struggled against her. He was attempting to hook his foot around her calf in an attempt to trip her. She skipped backward, severing contact, avoiding his sword as it fell. He grinned balefully.

But by the moment she realized her plan wasn't well-coordinated, Lilith had tripped over a root. She winced as someone gasped behind the ward. *Arduen, where are you?*

If Larkin's goal had been to kill her, she would already be marching through the gates of Elysium.

Lilith chanced a glance at her companions. Julius's face had grown pallid. He knelt at Zurí's feet, Olga on the ground beside him.

"I wonder if Spiro will make you prove your worth in the Champion's Ring," Larkin mused as he approached.

She jolted to her feet, eager to put more space between them.

"You cannot retreat, Sister."

Lilith countered, "That wasn't outlined in our agreement."

"Always a delight being your opponent."

"You've never been my opponent."

One second they were standing face to face, swords at their sides, the next they were swinging their blades, steel flashing in the moonlight. In a series of twists and turns, pivots and parries, Lilith and Larkin came to a stalemate. They stood with swords locked, criss-crossed before their faces, noses inches apart.

"Are you ready to come home?" Larkin taunted between clenched teeth.

Lilith gasped as he pushed against her, her muscles trembling from the strain. She had mere minutes until fatigue would render her inferior, and she would have no choice but to surrender.

"I'm doing this for you," she whispered. "As mercy. As freedom." The words erupted as sobs. "I'm doing this for Papa and Mah... for the family that we once were but can never be."

Larkin only stared at her, amber eyes blank, unreadable.

"I promise, one day I will avenge you!"

A confused expression bloomed upon his face as her gift began to take effect.

You are my entire universe.

Jude's words echoed through her mind. This is what it felt like to lose everything.

"If you're still in there, I love you." She backed away a step, lowering Constance to her side.

Larkin's sword fell to the ground with a thud. He dropped to his knees, clutching at his neck, his chest, his eyes wide with panic and disbelief. He paled as his eyes met hers, and the putrid scent of urine permeated the air.

She prayed, despite the Oath binding him, that he glimpsed the agony in her eyes. Increasing her hold on her power, she prayed that she wasn't causing him pain, as she drained more and more from him.

"Lilith," he rasped, reaching a desperate, gauntleted hand out to her.

Dropping Constance, she fell to her knees before him. His outstretched hand dug into the ground now, his eyes blown wide, skin ashen, just beginning to wither. He had only a moment before death would claim him. Her chest collapsed at the sight, but she couldn't look away from him. *Larkin.*

You are my entire universe.

The night was silent. The Forest dark and barren. The beasts had forsaken their commander.

You are my entire universe.

"I love you, Larkin."

Her shoulders shook with each breath-stealing sob as he slumped to the ground, his breaths coming in slow rasps. Only when his heart finally stilled did Lilith allow herself to break.

KIN-SLAYER

Lilith's grief surpassed destructive.

No one rushed to her side as she knelt before Larkin's remains. She was aware of Julius's presence close behind her, and Zurí not far behind him. Even Wren remained near. All of them watchful but allowing her space.

Her hands shook violently as she drew Larkin's painfully dry face into her hands. Her mind vaguely registered that this was the last time she would ever hold him. She forced herself to maintain composure, if only to bring honor to her brother in a way he deserved.

The true Larkin Oak.

How many times had he wiped her tears away? How many times had he corrected her archer's pose, or sparred with her in the field behind the smithy? Those memories seemed so distant. A lifetime ago. Maybe it had been a lifetime, she was so different now. Had he even recognized her?

Every member of the Oak family was buried under an oak

tree, it was tradition. But there were no such trees in Sonös, and she couldn't travel halfway across Augusta to take Larkin home.

When she'd watched his eyes glaze over, when she'd watched his olive skin pale and turn gray, the entire world had shattered around her. Lilith tilted back her head and faced the star-stricken sky. Though she trembled and her lips quivered, she sang the Hymn of Divination over Larkin's corpse with as much clarity as she could muster.

"Vàst vû fíng vuthé salídr stèle, forgée courcí teq víne."

Her voice faltered as she sang, but Lilith's only concern was whether Larkin would be granted entrance into Elysium. She prayed the Gods would show him mercy, as he was only ever a victim. A victim of the true enemy.

"Vàst qu Tsat wadnn unè pâte, teq duínn unè vledreè teq tísse."

Would Constantine or Kyril disapprove to the point of conviction? Would They smite her down before the verse could be finished? Or would They understand and acknowledge her pain, her loss? She was truly alone now.

"Vhedn säl uit qínn, teq vû svï vestinn unè pevër, vàst Quy cârre zî unsà Elysium funewër."

Lilith watched in awe as Larkin's body became incandescent with Elysium's light. His form began to dissipate before her, the glowing particles rising into the crisp air, floating toward the night sky.

Afraid to remove her eyes from her brother—or what was left of him—Lilith observed the stream of stardust as it rose higher and higher until only a shining Star remained. A new Star. One to honor Larkin Oak. His Athánatos Star. For the rest of her immortal days, her brother would be with her.

May we fight with valiant steel,
Forged courage and might.
May the Gods watch our path,
And quell our bleeding and strife.
When all is done, and we are beyond our power,
May They carry us into Elysium forever.

LILITH HAD SO LONG TO ACCEPT LARKIN'S FATE THAT SHE HADN'T expected the blow to be so catastrophic. Her ears rang as she sobbed hysterically. She vaguely heard Olga and Zurí's voices nearby, perhaps in the corridor outside her bedchamber, but she was disinclined to join them. One day rolled into two, and still she confined herself to her bedchamber.

Life was always grim after battle, but there was a definitive difference this time. When she faced her brother on the battle-field before the capital, the others had kept their distance. They had allowed her space to sort through the direness of the situation. This time it seemed everyone wanted a chance to comfort her. This time it was absolute, and there was no other option but to mourn and move on.

Of course there were consequences for disobeying strict orders. She was only a noviciate. Stepping over the protective ward surrounding the Frourío was surpassing any other ill behaviors. Once she'd resumed eating, Lilith wasn't surprised to find herself summoned to the study for discipline.

Arduen led the discussion, the others nodding their agree-ment, their eyes resting unwavering on Lilith.

"I was finally at peace with you confronting La—your brother alone." They'd all been afraid to speak his name, as if doing so would break her, but Lilith stood her ground. "Stepping free of the ward was unacceptable." Arduen's tone was deep and sombre, but his eyes were wicked with rage.

Lilith shifted uncomfortably, exhaustion gnawing at her limbs, her body beseeching her to sleep. For whatever reason, she had taken much longer to recover after this battle.

"Spiro doesn't want me dead," she countered. "Larkin wouldn't have hurt me."

Arduen tugged at his hair in frustration. "He rained arrows down upon you! He did not *care* what became of you, Lilith!"

The other Masters encircled her, their heads shaking in disapproval. Zurí was angry with her. Olga was very disappointed, but her mood was lighter than the others, as if Lilith's survival atoned for her disobedience. Wren was silent, no expression beyond mere sadness and disappointment.

"I will do what I have to do, regardless of my own safety. Is that not what it means to be Divine?" Lilith glanced around the study for approval, but when she looked at the others, they shifted their gaze from hers. Even Julius ignored her.

She swore. "Who I am doesn't matter. I have never fucking mattered! These gifts are not my own. The Gods can choose someone else and raise them to my level. Beyond. What am I worth if I am not risking *everything*?" She glanced at each of them. "Nothing," she finished. "I am *nothing*."

"We have waited over one hundred years for you, Julius, Felix," said Arduen. "That's one hundred years of suffering for mortals who will *never* see the Dark Age come to an end. How many more lives will be spent under the cloak of darkness when you die? We may not be blessed with a Divine as powerful as you. Not in the next hundred years, maybe not ever." He turned to the desk, his back to the room.

Olga stepped toward him but kept her gaze locked on Lilith. "You see, dear, this is about so much more than us. This is about the lives that have been lost, the quality of the lives present, and those to come."

Lilith closed her eyes and shook her head as if to shake off Olga's reasoning. "I did what I had to, and I won't hesitate to do it again."

Julius's voice cut through the silence. "Lilith…" he warned, his tone pleading.

"Enough!" Arduen faced her again, and her head snapped up to attention.

The room went deathly silent. The verdict impending.

"You disobeyed orders," Arduen said, his tone softening. But Lilith could see in the set of his shoulders, he was ready to blow. "The entire population will call you Kin-Slayer."

Lilith rolled her eyes. "And what will be my punishment? I freed my brother from a prison. I gave him the highest honor. Destroying my public image is a small sacrifice to free him from Spiro."

Olga spoke quickly to cut Arduen off, his face emitting a searing glow. "You will continue to train with both of your Masters," she indicated to Zurí. "Additionally, you will assist Ambrose with chores around the Frourío; tending to the horses, cleaning dishes, honing blades."

"Fine," Lilith grumbled, "less time I have to spend with *you*." Her glare narrowed on Arduen. She saw the hurt flash in his eyes, and it hurt her, too. If only he'd been there when she'd faced her brother. If only he had supported her as a Master should have, this rift between them wouldn't be gaping.

"You are dismissed," Arduen hissed, his fist pounding down on the desk in resolution.

"Good night," Olga murmured as Lilith turned her back on them, trudging toward the exit.

Footsteps approached. She recognized Julius's cadence before she heard his voice. "Lilith," he called to her. "Wait."

When he reached her, he cut her off. She did her best to conceal her irritation. Never had she been so desperate to put distance between her and Arduen, not even when he was a stranger trying to steal her away from home.

"Please be forgiving," Julius said in earnest. "I know it's difficult, but they mean well, and you know it."

"Arduen is a coward," she said brusquely. "He wouldn't come to my side when I needed him most. Is that not what a Master is supposed to do? If it came down to life or death, a Master is expected to sacrifice their life for their noviciate, and he failed to even stand *beside* me." Lilith flinched at the venom in her words, but her gaze was unyielding.

Julius placed a reassuring hand on her shoulder, and she wondered if it was to comfort or to placate. "I understand that, but that may be why he wasn't there. He may be afraid to watch you fall. You've seen what it has done to Wren."

Lilith shrugged him off. "But Wren was there. He watched the entire thing, and he was ready to intercept the moment the battle went in Larkin's favor. Arduen wasn't."

Julius opened his mouth to riposte but she placed her fingers over his lips and shook her head. The prince respectfully nodded and closed his mouth.

"Good night, Julius," she whispered.

Everyday Lilith awoke to an empty bedchamber, eyelids slowly parting against a tear-stained pillow. Her aching muscles gave way to sore bones. Every other day, Zurí would force her into the bathtub, and her Master would sit on the stool beside her, talking, venting. Lilith never spoke, but she listened more and more until Zurí's words became coherent, breaking through the torpor that had beset her mind since the battle.

Refusing to join her fellow Divine for dinner, Ambrose would bring meals to her bedchamber, which she picked at. She ate enough to persist, though she found little comfort in it. Ambrose would retrieve the tray, frowning at the amount of food untouched.

Days passed and she hadn't seen Arduen. She was supposed to resume her studies, but he hadn't given her orders to do so. After a fortnight of grieving ceaselessly, Lilith rose from her bed and dressed herself. She needed closure.

The Frourío was silent but it wasn't late enough for the others to be asleep. Lilith ascended the stairs, marching past the many closed doors, her bare feet silent on the wooden floorboards. When she reached the study, door ajar, she pushed it open.

The door creaked as it swayed inward, and Arduen glanced up from his seat at the desk. His face was drawn, the dark circles around his eyes emphasized by the shadows in the room.

Lilith tried to mask the contempt in her expression, but to no avail. Averting her attention, her eyes swept the room for something to read. Something to take her mind off of all that had happened.

Arduen finally relented. "Lilith…" Regret coated his gruff voice.

Pressing her brow into the books' spines, she ground out, "Why weren't you fighting *with* me, Arduen?"

Hold it together. Hold it together. Hold it together.

His emotions were unreadable as he buried his face in his hands. "I'm so sorry," he choked. "I'm so sorry, Lilith." His voice was a hoarse plea. "I never meant to hurt you, but I couldn't watch. I couldn't relive—" he broke off, his shoulders trembling, his breaths coming in small gasps.

Lilith gaped at him, in awe of what he was about to say. "You couldn't relive *what*?"

Arduen lowered his hands, revealing a tear-streaked face, his beard longer than usual. He balled his hands into fists as he brought them down upon the desk, the skin of his knuckles worn away.

"I cannot watch you go, Lilith. I couldn't watch him hurt you. Even if you were the victor of that battle."

"You mean to say that…" She paused, choking on her words, wincing as she spat them out. "You mean to say that you can't be there for me? You can't even *try* to protect me? To fight with me? I needed you and you turned your back on me!"

"I couldn't just stand idle and watch you die!"

"You didn't have to!" she shouted. "You could have helped me. Julius nearly lost his life trying!" Tears slid free from the corners of her eyes, though she tried to stave them off.

There was a sharp edge to his voice. Her muscles tensed, they burned, but it was all drowned out by her rage and pain. "You told me to let you do this," he said. "And I stood back and allowed it. Meanwhile, I defended my home where

I was needed. You had Julius and Zurí, they were there for you."

She waved off his excuses.

"Someone had to fight from either side of the Frourío. I kept watch on your side of the battle. I hadn't seen Larkin arrive."

Lilith retorted, "This is *sacred* land, as you once told me. Those beasts are not of the Gods, they couldn't enter our borders. We were safe from all but their arrows!"

She had never been so angry in her life, never felt so betrayed. At least when Larkin turned against her, it was against his will.

Her eyes searched her Master's face for any sign of penitence. It was there, but it wouldn't be enough. It couldn't be enough.

"You once said to me, *do not let the pain of losing the ones you love render you useless.* Well I hope you're glad to know that it didn't. I faced Larkin. I *killed* my own brother! My only living relative left on this earth. And you weren't there to support me because you're a hypocrite! *You* are the one who let fear render you useless!"

Arduen gaped, dismay writ on his face.

"I thought of you as a father," she sobbed. "But my father never would have left me to handle that on my own."

She stalked from the room, not daring to look back. She could feel Arduen's stare boring into the back of her head, but he didn't chase after her. It wasn't until she shut the door firmly behind her that she allowed herself to break, to melt the steel that had become her bones, to allow her riven heart to shatter.

Lilith braced her hands upon her knees and wept.

50

AUGUSTA WILL BE OURS

Shadows had become the only safe place for Rhéa DaSylvà. Every time she was forced to don the flaming hair, she was reminded of what Spiro had stolen from her. What vestige of joy remained in her life had been washed away by his noxious swell.

A month had passed since Xavier returned from battle, and Larkin had not. Rhéa barely held herself together when Xavier came into Spiro's conference chamber, blood splattered across his pale face. The expression he adorned told her what she so desperately needed to know: Larkin would not be returning.

The Enchantress listened to every detail of the battle. When Xavier admitted to Spiro that their numbers were depleting and he ordered them to flee, Spiro gave him fifteen lashes as punishment. He didn't attempt to capture Lilith when Larkin had weakened her enough to make it possible. Xavier had honored their sibling bargain and fled, knowing the consequences. He'd spared the girl, but Rhéa knew not why.

Spiro dismissed them both, freeing her from another evening of *duties*. Rhéa stormed from the chamber as Xavier nearly crawled across the floor, trailing crimson ribbons behind him. She waited for him in the hall, far away from Spiro's ears. When he finally reached her, she hoisted him up and carried him like a child, his head on her shoulder, his legs wrapped around her hips, her hand slipping in his blood.

Arriving at his bedchamber, she gently laid him down on the unmade bed and began her work.

"I like your hair better like that," was all he had said to her, his voice raw.

Ignoring his comment, the Enchantress began to clean the deep lacerations on his back. There wasn't much skin left. He soon passed out, head buried in his pillow. A good thing, because it would have been excruciating otherwise.

She continued to work in silence, casting spells to heal from within, to prevent potential infection. Part of Spiro's punishment was refusing them to visit a healer, so she was forced to keep the wounds visible, but she could protect them whilst they healed naturally.

When she finished, Rhéa washed the blood from his skin, the splatters on his face and neck melting away under the steaming cloth. Tears streamed down her cheeks all the while, but she never sobbed, never gave herself away. There was still so much work to be done. She prayed to the Amalthea Star to grant her the strength to weather the tempest.

Rhéa turned to leave, taking the evidence with her. She cast a spell that rendered the blood-soaked clothes and bucket invisible, should she run into Spiro or any of his faithful retinue.

"I know who you are," Xavier croaked from behind her.

The Enchantress stilled.

"I'm sorry…"

Rhéa twisted slowly, meeting his gaze with mournful eyes. "Thank you," was all she managed to say, and then she walked away. She didn't let herself break down until she reached the privacy of her own bedchamber.

That had been a month ago, and she'd cried herself to sleep every night since—except the nights Spiro summoned her to his bed. She would lie awake beside him, her eyes scanning the room for an article that could be used as a weapon. All she needed to do was slit his throat and this would all be over. But Spiro took precautions. The Great Divine didn't allow anyone near him who could overpower him—even in his sleep.

When Xavier finally emerged from his bedchamber after a week of convalescence, he was stiff and sore. His wounds scabbed over, sometimes cracking and in need of her attention. He was forced back into training immediately, for the purpose of capturing Lilith at the next battle.

The Enchantress fell to her knees before Xavier, begging him to spare the girl. He only waved her off, such a vague response, and told her that there was someone she needed to meet.

"She was captured by one of the sentries last night, treading a little too close to our doorstep. We believe she has potential to serve beyond a kitchen maid, but I will need you to confirm that." Xavier turned and led her through the hallway to the infirmary.

Rhéa observed the girl from the doorway. She was slight, tenuous even, like she hadn't had a full meal in months. Her chiton dress hung loose from her shoulders, the usual gowns that the maids of the Emperor wore. Her long black hair hung to the small of her back, curling slightly at the ends and along her temples. The girl didn't quail as they approached.

The healing chamber was balmy, the walls moisture licked. Rhéa felt the humidity cling to her skin like liniment. The girl lifted her head as they came to a halt in front of her, sable locks falling away to reveal a familiar tear-stained face.

"Irís," Rhéa whispered in shock.

The girl glanced up knowingly, eyes wide. Releasing a pent sob, she leapt into Rhéa's arms.

Xavier peered at them incredulously. "You know her?"

Rhéa nodded gravely.

"Why are you here, Irís?" Xavier's question wasn't posed gently, earning him a reproachful glare from the Enchantress.

"It's a long story," the girl said between sniffles, pulling away from Rhéa.

"I want to hear it." The Enchantress sat down on one of the chairs strewn throughout the infirmary. She patted the one beside hers, and Irís seated herself obediently.

"But you didn't come here to listen to me gripe, did you?" Irís's eyes flicked between them warily.

"No, but we will listen," Rhéa responded kindly, placing a hand on the girl's delicate shoulder. She looked to Xavier, encouraging him to agree.

He cleared his throat unconvincingly. "Oh, yes… please continue."

A deafening silence stole over the room. The kind of calm that permeated the battlefield before war commenced. Then Irís exhaled, her shoulders sagging in defeat.

"I grew tired of the barracks." She addressed Rhéa only.

What about the barracks? Rhéa didn't dare interrupt her story. She'd inquire after.

"I couldn't take it anymore. I became a personal plaything of the prince and I could do nothing to negate his approaches. When he summoned me, I had no choice but to oblige. Even if it meant forsaking my menial tasks and being punished for it later.

"No one believed me when I said the prince was targeting me. Some of the other girls were jealous that I had been chosen. They treated me with outright derision." Irís sucked in a deep breath, comporting herself as her suffering was laid bare before them, unvarnished.

"The prince's affection was wanton, and I could do nothing to stop him." Her voice shook. Rhéa placed her arm around the girl. Now she fully understood her woes. Xavier stood across from them, his face set in a sour moue.

The Enchantress stroked the top of the girl's hand in an attempt to assuage her lament. The sound that emanated from her throat was guttural as she continued to fight off tears.

When Rhéa spoke to her, she used utmost discretion. "How did you manage to escape?"

"A kitchen maid helped me. She saw the bruises, the scrapes. She had more freedom than I did, so she devised a plan to whisk me away, with the help of a soldier. He was kind, so unlike the others. I hadn't seen him in the barracks before."

Rhéa stilled. "What was the man's name?"

"Achilles."

Rhéa became dizzy but she pulled herself together, ignoring Xavier's bemused glance. Of course Miles would help her.

"He got me as far away from Kenora as he could before he had to return. He gave me enough provisions to make it to

Thassös, but I must have lost direction at some point. The night came when I should have been able to see the city, but there was only darkness. I ran out of food and I couldn't find water… then this *beast* appeared." She shivered. "I just curled up and waited for it to kill me, but it picked me up and brought me here." She shook her head. "I gave up!"

Rhéa pulled the girl into her arms and let Irís sob into her shoulder. The Enchantress looked to Xavier to say something helpful.

The young man dropped to his knees in front of them and said solemnly, "It takes more courage than I can ever comprehend to accept your own death." Irís didn't seem to hear him over her sobs, her shoulders quaking with them. Rhéa nodded her approval to Xavier.

They remained that way for some time, allowing the girl a moment to grieve for herself. Both Rhéa and Xavier did whatever they could to console her, though nothing seemed to mitigate her anguish.

The Enchantress vividly remembered the bruises that decorated Irís's skin. She pulled the mass of dark tresses away from the girl's face and paused, gaping as she gazed down at the star-shaped birthmark etched into the girl's skin behind her ear—exactly where her own Mark was.

Magic. The girl was an Enchantress!

A horn sounded throughout the keep. Xavier's eyes met Rhéa's and dread blossomed there like a midnight flower. Spiro had summoned his people, his beasts.

She helped Irís to her feet and allowed the girl to lean against her as they made their way to the archway that led out into the arena. Rhéa's heart thundered inside her chest. It would be up to her to ensure the girl remained safe. She had promised her long ago to help her escape, and now, by the grace of the Guiding Stars, the girl had come to her. She would not fail her this time. Even if Spiro was worse than the Emperor.

The Great Divine materialized from the shadows on his balcony. The cavern was full of his creations, all of them obnoxiously expressing their adulation to their Master. Their King.

Spiro raised a hand and they quieted, all of them anxiously awaiting his oration.

Rhéa held her breath, Xavier stiff beside her, his eyes planted on his Master. Irís whimpered faintly at her side.

"Our ranks are growing," Spiro announced, hand still raised to maintain the silence of his creatures. "War is coming. It is time for us to take what is *ours*.

"Augusta is ready for change. A new beginning. An end to the so-called Dark Age is upon us. We will lead this generation to greatness. Glory and sovereignty will be ours!" His raised hand balled into a fist and the beasts erupted. They cried out their love for their Master and stomped their feet with excitement.

Spiro stood above them all, a smug grin spreading his lips as his creatures deified him. His pale eyes scanned the crowd until they met Rhéa's. Under his piercing stare, the Enchantress forced her face to depict nothing but neutrality.

After a tense moment, Spiro bellowed, "Augusta will be ours!"

The beasts howled in response.

51

THE PRINCE'S INFERNO

The waves crashed into the sand, the cool liquid kissing Lilith's bare toes. The spring sun had warmed the Megálos, awakening the dormant flora and fauna. Every evening, Lilith would steal time away to witness the setting sun, the cessation of another day of survival.

It had been a month since the battle to defend the Frourío. Over the past week, Lilith had become more present among the Divine in an attempt to create some semblance of who she was before the battle. She'd joined them for meals again, even sitting by the hearth with Julius and Felix. She resumed her training, running every morning at dawn, schooling in the art of commanding Kyril's Water. When Zurí perched herself on the stool to rant to her as she sat in the tub, Lilith finally engaged in the once one-sided conversation.

Lilith hadn't seen much of Arduen, had not so much as glanced in his direction when she heard his voice. Zurí had taken over her training entirely, monitoring her sessions practicing with Aether, pushing her when she learned to control the Galatëa Sea.

When she'd first emerged from the confines of her bedchamber, Zurí had been adamant that she accompanied her wherever she went, but Lilith refused. She merely explained that what she needed most was to return to her normal schedule—minus her lessons with Arduen.

That couldn't last long, she knew. Arduen would have to end his brooding and take up his position as mentor, and Lilith would have no choice but to acquiesce. Thankfully, for the past month, he was granting her space.

Booted feet stopped beside her. Lilith trailed her gaze up the long legs to meet Julius's face. He glanced down at her, a saccharine smile on his lips.

"May I join you?"

Lilith gestured a welcome and he sat down beside her, removed his boots and socks, airing out his feet. She laughed at the size comparison.

"What?" he demanded defensively, nudging her foot with his. "I am tall!"

Lilith snorted and turned to face the sea again, her eyes flicking to the west, trying to picture the Isles of Nysía on the horizon. Silence befell them, the only sound the rushing of the gentle waves and the high trills of the birds. The sun was beginning to set, gilding the sea with its fiery glaze.

"Arduen retrieved you," Julius blurted.

Lilith started, shifting uncomfortably beside him.

He turned pleading eyes on her. "I called your name, but you couldn't hear me. I want you to know that I couldn't come to you. I couldn't have carried you."

"I could never expect that of you," she said. "Not after you battled that beast." The gash that had torn through his shoulder had rendered his arm useless. Of course she hadn't expected him to carry her to safety.

Julius sighed as if he'd been holding onto his breath for too long a moment. "The beast was going to strike at you from behind. I couldn't let that happen."

"Thank you."

"I never took my eyes off you," he confessed, his cheeks rosy in the golden glow of the fading sun.

"When that monster looked down at me, I felt dwarfed. And that's when I realized that I'm not done yet. I am not yet finished learning. I need to stay and continue my training. A free Divine I may be, but I am no Master. I am not prepared to walk the earth, to defend it. I'm not equipped to become a king. I'm not disposed to rule a nation, not yet."

He set his golden eyes on her. "I haven't had a chance to thank you. If it weren't for you, I'd be dead. You saved my life."

"And you saved mine," she said as she placed her hand in his, their fingers entwining in the sand.

Lilith couldn't hold back her contentment that he wasn't leaving. He squeezed her fingers gently, confirmation that the touch was welcome, wanted.

"How's your shoulder?"

Julius twisted to look at it. "There will be a scar, but Olga made sure that I gained the use of it again, that all the nerves are intact. My swordsmanship is coming along, but I am not what I was."

She tried not to imagine how awfully long that night must have been for both Olga and Julius. She had been so utterly spent that she hadn't remembered anything after the battle ended. She was carried away, lost to delirium, faintly aware of Arduen's presence at her side.

"I remember when I first met you," Julius said breathily. "How you were so fragile… so sweet."

She tilted her head and scoffed. "And then you took a bite of the apple and realized just how sour I truly am."

Julius barked a laugh, his chest heaving with mirth. "Everyone can be sour at times. But at your core, Lil," he tapped her abdomen, his touch inciting a shiver, "you're the purest woman I've ever known."

Her lips parted, but no words could ever convey the tide of emotions that washed through her.

"I want you to know," the prince continued, "I will always be here for you. I will watch your back always. Regardless of who your Philías is. I will always fight for you… *with* you."

Lilith struggled to meet his gaze as it lingered on her. The air grew frigid when he finally removed it, as if his presence warmed the earth, and the absence of it summoned winter back again.

"I also want you to know…" His voice began to waver, and Lilith's heart palpitated as she waited for the words he was about to speak, the words she'd dreamed of him uttering for too long. "This is a promise. I am making it because I care about you so deeply, Lilith. This vow means more to me than mere friendship."

"More?" she asked, breathless, wishful.

"*More.*" Julius leaned into her, his hand trailing down her side, resting on her hip. She made a muffled squeal and he chuckled under his breath, his mouth resting an inch away from hers, as if awaiting permission.

Under his touch, her skin became hyperaware of every whisper of the wind, of every breath that escaped his lips and washed over her like a caress of his fingertips. And when those lips leaned in to meet hers for the first time, warmth rushed into her limbs. The heart she'd thought fractured now seemed to beat with renewed intensity. A hurricane unleashed.

The kiss was urgent. A frantic need coursed through her as she arched into him. How else would she convey that she wanted—no, needed—more?

The press of his hand on her hip sent sparks cascading under her skin and she nibbled at his bottom lip, marvelling at the groan it elicited from him. The sound granted Lilith the brazenness to remove his blouse, revealing sculpted muscle sheathed in golden-brown skin.

Julius tore his lips from hers, and ignoring her squeak of protest, averted his attention to her neck, his breath tickling her ear. She released a ragged sigh of pleasure before tugging him down onto the sand, his body fitting atop hers perfectly.

Their clothing became the only barrier between them as they folded into one another. She allowed every part of her body to meld to his, and he embraced her with tenderness, a controlled eagerness. His body grew tense as stone, like this was an act of vile cruelty, like this was forbidden but it couldn't stop him.

When she felt the firm press of him between her legs, the sparks beneath her skin erupted into flames. She muffled a moan against the skin of his neck, revelling in his answering shudder. Julius continued to kiss her neck, her shoulder, his breaths coming in desperate pants. His hands roamed with reckless abandon, down her abdomen, lower, lower.

This was like falling into an open void or losing control of her body in the sea. This was like being born again, forgetting everything that constituted her being before his lips ever grazed hers. He was claiming her soul, redefining her, and she had relinquished all control to him.

Lilith's fingers dug into the rippling muscles of his back. *Don't stop. Don't stop. Lower. Please!* Gods, his touch was torment. The kind of suffering she delighted in.

Just when she mustered the gall to divest him of his breeches, the door to the Frourío sounded.

Someone was coming.

Her hands paused on the laces of his pants and their wide eyes met at once. They were about to be caught in a flagrant act of passion.

Julius jumped to his feet, careful not to hurt her as he pushed up and away. He quickly donned his blouse, smoothed the wrinkles from the fine cotton, his skin flushed to the tips of his ears.

As Lilith stood to stand beside him, they scrubbed their feet in the sand to obscure the outline of their tangled bodies.

"We should go inside," he said.

Lilith could only nod, slightly embarrassed at what had just occurred between them. She didn't speak a word as they casually sauntered to the Frourío, her mind drifting back to that moment in the sand.

This is what it's supposed to feel like, she thought to herself. *This is what the beginning of love is.* Her face seared, the heat creating beads of sweat on her skin. She was thankful for the cool breeze, and the shadows for concealing her flushed complexion from the man who had caused it.

As she lay in bed that evening, after Julius had so sweetly tucked her in and kissed her brow, she finally allowed her body to relax. Yet she reminded herself that Julius was a prince, not just a man of noble birth, but a *crown prince*. He had great responsibilities across the sea, far from here, and he was now a Master Divine. He could leave at a moment's notice, at the beck and call of his sick father, to return home and ascend the throne. Yet she could not forget that moment they had on the beach, the rawness, the intimacy.

As she succumbed to her dreams, the weight of Julius's body remained upon hers, his breath on her skin, Xander's Fire thrumming in her veins.

◎ ⓒ ⤳ ⋔ ◊

THUNDER RATTLED THE CRYSTALLINE WINDOWS OF THE FROURÍO. Strangely, Lilith had always found thunderstorms comforting. Even still, after finding her mortal fate in one, she felt her soul soothed and lulled to sleep by the pitter-patter of the rain on the windows. But tonight, she didn't fall into the dreamscape of her mind. Instead, she came more alive with every roll of thunder.

Lilith emerged from her bedchamber, the staircase empty, the tower quiet and dark. She stepped into the kitchen to find it vacant. Only embers burned in the hearth, illuminating the living section of the large chamber in a ruby glow. The door beckoned to her and she answered its call, forgoing a cloak for warmth.

The night was chill against her skin, her only attire a thin nightgown that fell to mid-thigh, leaving her arms exposed. The full moon was high in the sky, its reflection painting a path for her on the sea. Lilith followed, ignoring the gooseflesh that rose on her limbs.

The water was cold on her feet as she stepped into the sea; she hardly noticed, she had eyes for the moon only.

Splaying her arms, the sea rising to her navel, Lilith closed her eyes and faced the night sky, the firmament speckled with an array of twinkling stars.

First, she thanked Constantine. Second, she thanked Kyril. Then she gave each of the Gods her expression of gratitude.

Larkin's Athánatos Star glistened brightly. It seemed to go out for a second, as if he blinked down at her in recognition.

With her brother's encouragement, she swore to all the Gods that she would avenge all who lost their lives at the hands of Spiro. She beseeched Them to grant her the strength to overcome him, even if They took it away as soon as she succeeded. She vowed to take on every obstacle in succession. One day at a time.

She was Lilith Oak. She was the blessed Divine of the Gods, Constantine and Kyril. The bringer of life and death. Aether and Water. Her sole purpose was to bring an end to the Dark Age. Her sworn purpose was to bring light to the shadows that had devoured the Empire for over a century.

When she finally opened her eyes to the endless expanse of sea before her, those emerald irises smoldered with stark resolve.

You are my entire universe.

At dawn, Lilith sat with Zurí at the kitchen table. The room was empty. Despite the lack of sleep, Lilith was brimming with energy, with a burning desire to train.

Her Master lifted her gaze from her book and drilled Lilith with a destabilizing stare. Zurí sighed, dropping the book. Her voice resounded throughout the room as if the voice of Kyril spoke *through* her.

"Be careful what you wish for," she said. "If there's anything I've learned in my lifetime, it's that the Gods have a sense of humor."

A prescient warning.

But it came too late.

KEEP READING FOR A SNEAK
PREVIEW OF THE LEGEND OF
LILITH, BOOK II: ELYSIUM

CHAPTER I: ELYSIUM

The harrowing winds assaulted the stone walls of the Frourío. Their howls usually lulled Lilith to sleep, but since the battle at the Frourío, torturous night terrors made her restive.

When she did find sleep, it was never peaceful. There had been brief moments of repose when Julius joined her, silently wrapping her in strong arms, though those reprieves were few and far between. Shadows hovered beneath her sunken eyes, her hair hung limp regardless of how she cared for it, and her limbs ached in defiance with every movement.

The others kept their distance, all but Julius and Felix who often invited her to spar. Meals were spent in silence as the inhabitants of the Frourío were somber. The atmosphere was stifling at best, and Lilith often found her belly swarmed by wasps when she made to leave her bedchamber.

After a fitful rest, the sun lured Lilith to the beach. As her toes sunk into the sand, she found her ill temper to be as it had been since she last saw her brother. She cursed the sky and the Gods that ruled it. Glaring at the sun through squinted eyes, she willed the flaming orb to fall back beneath the earth's surface and continue to burn the evils thriving in Hades. Sleep was of the utmost importance, the heaviest need, and it seemed utterly unattainable no matter how long she lay swathed in darkness.

Lilith nocked an arrow and, aiming for the sky, shot straight at the burning ball of fire. She watched with unrelenting rancor, seething inwardly as the arrow reached its summit and began its descent. The vast blue of the Galatëa boiled with her anguish, she could feel it as an extension of her being, palpable as the rush of her pulse. For as an Anointed disciple of Kyril, the sea was now a reflection her emotions.

"You can't shoot the sun, but it was a decent attempt," said a husky voice behind her. Lilith paid it no heed.

Sighing audibly, she turned and strode back to the Frourío. Her shoulder brushed against Arduen's as she passed him, but she made sure to avoid his gaze entirely. Keeping her eyes trained on her boots, the morning dew soaking them, she feigned ignorance to Arduen's eyes boring into her back.

"Will you ever forgive me?" he called after her, tone grievous.

Lilith loved him. She did. But there was no way she could alleviate his pain when he never attempted to assuage her own. She used to stiffen at the sound of his voice. Her limbs used to tingle with anxiety when he spoke directly to her—anxiety or anger, she wasn't entirely sure.

"I'll consider it when you *ask* me," was all she could think to say. As she walked away, focusing to keep the cadence of her steps confident and even, she doubted she would ever truly forgive him.

Her relationship with her Master had not improved since their quarrel after she killed Larkin. The worst day of her life. The worst day she'd spent on this earth and her immortal *fatherly* figure couldn't stand by her side and support her as he should have. He was her Divine Master. It was his responsibility to guide her through such dire situations, and yet he had acted so cowardly. A great chasm had formed between them. So great, it might have been as gaping as the Great Rift of Dodöna was rumored to be. The space between them was certainly as dead and soulless as the depths of the Rift.

In the two months that had passed since the battle at the Frourío, Augusta had been relatively peaceful. The sun reigned longer in the sky. The leaves budded and bloomed within weeks. And the clouds drenched the soil with rain, turning the Forest floor loamy, rendering the grass an emerald fur. It was the kind of weather that could summon joy from even the most miserable of folk, but it did little to abate Lilith's dejection.

After all this time, she hadn't forgotten her promise to the Gods. She hadn't forgotten that night when she waded into the Galatëa's frigid waters and vowed to avenge all the lives Spiro had ripped from the earth. And she had not forgotten the promise she made to herself the morning after: she would not renege on those promises, even if it meant her own doom. Even if one of the wisest women in Augusta had warned her to never beseech the Gods for anything.

It was Lilith's first week trying. The first week she actually felt driven to move on. Every morning she awoke to sprint through the Megálos. The pines blurred into an emerald void as she loped at an inhuman speed. Her Divine strength was not yet fully formed—so Zurí told her—but she was faster than she'd ever been.

Following her run, she would train with Zurí, controlling and contorting Kyril's Water as she pleased. Her control was impeccable, but the amount of Water that she could manipulate seemed to lessen every day.

Discernment had grown nearly impossible. Every time Lilith lowered her mental shields and submerged her consciousness into the waves, she felt nothing. This time of year, the sea should be teeming with life, but Lilith was blind to it.

Ignoring these slight shortcomings, she pushed herself to her physical extremities. Her body was rippling with muscle, fat was scarce. This wasn't the most appealing of physiques, but Lilith cared not for appearances.

Lilith watched her opponent's blade as metallic obsidian flashed before her eyes, the light wrenching her from her reverie. Zurí slashed down at her with a faint grunt and Lilith parried the blow with ease.

They'd been sparring for nearly two hours, her Master not yet displaying signs of fatigue. But Lilith felt like she was going to spill the contents of her lunch on the ground.

Julius and Felix fought on the other side of the field, Quin and Wren bellowing orders. Quin was no longer schooling Julius, as the prince was a Master Divine now. But Julius had expressed that he didn't feel ready to take on the responsibility of becoming a Master, and Quin hadn't waved him out the door.

The prince had taken on Felix's training alongside Wren, and the young Divine had excelled. Though Julius and Lilith were close, he had given her space over the past two months. Since their heated moment on the beach, Lilith had pulled away, save for the nights he crawled beneath her sheets in an attempt to ease her nightmares, his charming smile a slash of white splitting the dark.

A bolt of pain lanced through her right arm and her hand went numb, dropping Constance.

"Pay attention!" Zurí barked.

"I'm sorry, Master." Lilith knelt to retrieve Constance. "I haven't been myself lately."

Zurí lowered her sword to her side. "We are done for today. Go wash up."

Lilith jumped to her feet. "No!" she nearly shouted. "We can get another hour in at least."

Her Master paid her grousing little heed. "You are too distracted. No." She waved Lilith off. "You will go bathe and pray. We can talk after supper about whatever is on your mind."

"I'm fine," Lilith grumbled. "Really..." Foregoing what would have been a heated altercation, Lilith marched to the Frourío.

⊙ � ⊸ ᛖ ⏀

Ambrose had quite enjoyed Lilith's help whilst she served her punishment for stepping over the protective wards during the battle at the Frourío. Now that she was free of those duties, she still preferred to assist their designated knight. After every meal, Lilith joined him at the sink to assist with the washing and drying of the dishes.

Arduen's voice wafted through the air to meet her ears.

Lilith prickled at the sound. "I wish I could say that I believe the worst is over," he said. "We have destroyed many of Spiro's beasts, but of the damage we've dealt him, he's done worse to us. We hope to have many months of peace before he considers attacking again."

Lilith rubbed her aching wrist. These days, she didn't seem to be healing as quickly as she used to.

"Let's make use of the reprieve," Arduen continued with his oration.

"Get stronger and smarter," added Julius, Felix echoing his enthusiasm.

"If we could locate where Spiro is then we may be able to catch him off guard," Wren mused.

Ambrose nodded toward the kitchen table. Lilith knew he wanted her to sit with the others, but then she might have to speak with Arduen. The knight snatched the drying towel away from her and gently pushed her toward the others. She obliged, seating herself in her usual seat, avoiding Arduen's gaze.

"That would be horrendously stupid," Quin snapped. Wren bristled at the comment but withheld his rebuttal.

Arduen drawled, "It would make sense, but we are not strong enough and no other Divine have joined our cause from the other continents. We do not know how strong Spiro's army is now."

"He took a hit after the battle at the Frourío," Olga stated. "The beasts fled because Lilith prevailed over... Spiro's Divine."

"Send reconnaissance." Wren stabbed his fork into the table, ignoring the reproachful glare Olga impaled him with.

Zurí was the first to counter their arguments, on both sides, as though she couldn't stand to agree with any of them. "Neither option is viable. We should focus on our noviciates."

Olga's glance flitted warily from Divine to Divine, her eyes beseeching Arduen to calm the brewing storm. But Arduen did not intervene, or even reprimand, as the men argued. He simply stared into the distance, at the door, in what appeared to be longing. His blue eyes bloodshot as though withdrawing from morphine. His eyes caught Lilith's and he flashed her a belated smile, betraying his own belief in his earlier statement, as well as erasing any comfort or reassurance intended by it.

If there was anyone who truly understood Lilith, she would have always said it was her mother; but she is Divine now, and with that, she had transformed into a whole new person. Regardless of his betrayal, it was truly Arduen who understood the tide and flow of her emotions, try as she might to keep them concealed from him.

Then there was Zurí, Lilith's second Master, the disciple of Kyril, God of Water. The woman was as elegant as she was stern, yet soft-hearted in regard to Lilith. Balanced atop her long neck was a head full of crimson curls that glistened even on a cloudy day, a face of an angel set with scalding turquoise eyes.

Since the battle at the Frourío, Zurí acted complacent amidst the tension between Arduen and Lilith. How she was able to recognize when enough was enough for her noviciate, Lilith hadn't the faintest idea. She had come to consider Zurí as more than her tutor, but a friend.

Lilith ate her meal while the others conversed about the best course of action. She didn't understand why they argued. They had very little choice on the matter. They didn't know where Spiro's base was, half of their force was young and untested. It was a futile prospect to consider approaching the Great Divine, but one she hoped they would overcome despite the odds.

"Lilith…" It was Julius, sinking into the vacant seat beside her. "Would you like to accompany me for a walk along the beach?"

She would, but she knew it would only lead to complications. "I'm sorry, Julius, but I have not been sleeping well and would prefer to rest tonight."

There hadn't been time to sort through her feelings for Julius. She cared so deeply for him, in a way she had never before, but good sense told her not to entertain those emotions. Julius would leave her eventually. He was to become King of Dalegonè. And Lilith was never fit to be a queen.

He frowned. "Are you all right?"

Lilith nodded, flashing him a meek smile, a poor attempt to assuage his worries. Thankfully he relented and returned to the table with the others. With anxiety eddying in her stomach, Lilith marched up the stairs to her bedchamber.

⊙ ⊌ ⤳ ᾙ ◊

LILITH'S TOES CURLED IN FRUSTRATION, HER BODY CONTORTING under the pain of the scalpel. He was slicing her, carving her, so he had said. Perfecting her for her new Master—her only Master.

"Please, Larkin…" she whimpered.

"Shush." He soothed her with a tutting noise, his fingers stroking her cheekbone, a tender brush of his skin against her own, the bloody scalpel still clasped in his hand. "This won't take so long if you lay still. Enjoy the process, sweet Sister."

Lilith nearly vomited as he brought the blade down onto her skin yet again. "Arduen…" she moaned, a plea for her Master. "Please. I didn't mean what I said. I forgive you."

"You don't favor him anymore. Don't you remember? He gave you over to me." His voice slithered from his lips, a sibilant hiss so unlike him.

"No!" Lilith cried. "Arduen wouldn't do that to me."

Larkin said nothing as he continued to work on her. The pain had given way to a numbing sensation wherever he sliced and prodded, morphing her into the perfect Divine. She closed her eyes then and allowed him to work. He'd assured her that this was for the best. He was her only sibling, he knew what she needed most.

"Larkin…" she mumbled as he cut into the sensitive skin of her abdomen.

"Shhhh!" He patted her sweat-damp hair. "Larkin is no longer with us, sweets."

Her eyes flashed open.

That voice.

"You killed him, remember?"

Lilith tried to lift her head, but she couldn't muster the strength. It was all too much for her. It was only when a shadow moved over her, blocking out the light above, did she see to whom the voice belonged.

A man with hair white as snow stared down at her with soulless-blue eyes. "Hello, Lilith. I am your new Master. But you may call me Spiro."

Lilith thrashed on the table, her body smacking against the stone slab, bruising her horribly. She didn't care. She had to get away from the sadist. But with one stroke of his had on her hair, he managed to calm her.

"Dear Lilith, did Arduen not instruct you well enough?"

She cried at the mention of her Master. How could she have been so angry with him? He loved her and she loved him.

Lilith surrendered herself as Spiro's voice caressed her ears. "You must relinquish your freedom for power, or your power for freedom."

⟡ ⟡ ⟡ ⟡ ⟡

"LILITH!"

"Wake up, Lilith!"

"Lilith Oak!" Arduen bellowed through the madness.

Her eyes blew wide at the sound of her name. She couldn't see anyone. She lay on her bed at the Frourío. No stone slab, no Larkin, and no Spiro. But the abyss of Aether swirled around her bed, obscuring the others from view. A mighty fear stole through her then, for Aether was the most unforgiving element to wield, and she could kill them all.

Before Lilith could stem the flow of the great abyss, it melted away before her, revealing Arduen standing at the foot of her bed. He inhaled deep, his fists balled at his sides, a large vein flickered on his strong neck. He'd absorbed what she dispelled in her night terror. He moved to the window to release it, for no one could contain such a force.

Olga and Zurí rushed to her side immediately, the latter bearing a hysterical expression. Lilith couldn't fight the guilt that assaulted her. Night terrors were not uncommon for her, not since she'd first been exposed to battle. But they were growing evermore frequent. It only took one mistake to claim a life, and she couldn't lose another loved one.

"You're all right," Olga murmured, pulling Lilith into a tight embrace. No one could provide comfort the way the Oracle could, but it was another's touch Lilith needed.

The sheets were soaked, and Lilith scowled as she realized that she'd soiled herself. Neither Olga or Zurí seemed to mind or to even notice as they petted her head and soothed her anxiety.

Julius stood in the doorway, his expression drawn, his golden-brown skin unnaturally ashen. He stared at her with silver-lined eyes before Arduen approached and shoed him away, assuring the prince that he would handle this.

But for the first time, Lilith wasn't so sure that he could.

ACKNOWLEDGMENTS

Wow. Is. Me. My first book! I have dreamed of this day since I was a child. I remember being the student in my second grade class who needed extra help to learn to read. I remember being so embarrassed that I couldn't grasp the concept. I couldn't sit still, I didn't enjoy it, and the more difficult it became, the less effort I put in. Of course I got it eventually, I just didn't realize how much I would come to love it!

I was eleven when I fell in love with reading fantasy/fiction, and the summer that I turned twelve, I decided to write my own story. The first rendition of *The Legend of Lilith*. It was much simpler than this book, but the story and the message remain quite the same.

Of course I have a litany of people to thank, so let's get on with that...

First and foremost, to my parents, thank you for pushing me through every obstacle in life. From hockey, to speed skating, to university, to line work, to publishing my first novel.

Thank you for always believing in me, without your affirmation and wisdom, I would not be writing this passage today.

To my brothers, thank you for always pushing me, albeit in a very different way from mom and dad. You guys have shaped me more than you may realize. I was always challenged by you two, always trying to compete with you and therefore always humbled by you. I think we have grown up and turned out quite well. Who should have thunk it, huh?

To Tyler, thank you for supporting me on this journey. Thank you for making dinner when I was too tired or stressed. Thank you for walking the dog when I needed some quiet time to write. Thank you for being the best partner I could have ever dreamed of.

To my dog Azzy, my fur-baby, thank you for lying patiently at my feet, waiting to be taken out for a walk. Thank you for your endless cuddles and emotional support. Thank you for being your fluffy self and providing me with some insight on what it means to be a parent, if only a fur-mom.

To my editor, Iveta. Thank you for pouring every remaining ounce of energy into this book. Without your professional guidance and insight, I would not be as confident in these words as I am. You're a blessing. PS. Gear up for book 2!

To my BETA readers (I'm talking to you, Annette!), thank you for your support, your invaluable honesty, and your willingness to read LOL over and over. Without your feedback, this novel would not be what it is today.

And finally, to my readers! Thank you for purchasing my debut novel! It means the world to me. If you don't mind giving LOL an honest review on either Amazon or Goodreads, (or BOTH, if you're feeling especially munificent), I would appreciate it more than you know! Every review helps me to reach more readers like you. If you have so kindly taken the time to review me, please send an e-mail to hillaryoliver@hotmail.ca to receive exclusive content!

Thank you all from the bottom of my heart!

Hillary Oliver

Hillary Oliver hails from Toronto, Ontario. With a degree in English Literature and History from Trent University, she has dreams of delivering rich historical fiction with a fantastical twist, as well as dark fantasy. When not writing, she is a telecommunications linewoman, an amateur photographer, and a dedicated canine mom.

Follow Hillary on twitter and instagram for news and updates!

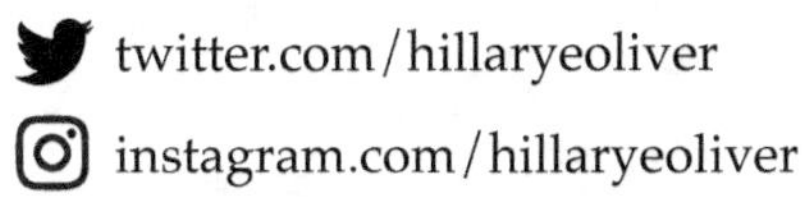

twitter.com/hillaryeoliver

instagram.com/hillaryeoliver